Nephilim Rising

Book Five of the Chosen Chronicles

Sirena Robinson

Supposed Crimes LLC • Matthews, North Carolina

NEPHILIM RISING

PROLOGUE

AMAYA STOOD with her shoulders hunched against the biting wind. Her black hair swirled around her face, and tears dripped down her cheeks and off her chin. Her glove-clad hands were buried in her pockets.

The man next to her flicked his wings and shifted from foot to foot.

"We should go soon. It's not safe to stay here for very long."

Amaya stared stoically ahead. "What do we do now?"

"We keep doing what we've been doing. He died to save us. We have to honor that and keep pressing forward."

She turned her head to the side and stared at him. "Do you think it would be okay if I went to see my parents for a day or two? I'd like to be home."

The man slipped his arm around her shoulders and hugged her close. "I think it would be okay. Do you want me to go with you?"

Amaya nodded slowly. "I do." She took a trembling breath. "I can't believe I've let things get this out of control. I thought we could do it. I thought I knew better than he did, and it ended up getting him killed."

"He knew the score. We all know it. It was a calculated risk, and we knew it could go wrong when we went into it."

"Can we really do this? There's been so much death." She turned to face him, grasping the lapels of his coat in her hands. "I'm just so tired, Deacon."

Deacon sighed deeply and rubbed Amaya's arms briskly, trying to keep her warm. "There's always going to be death, Maya. It's part of life. More a part of our lives than most people, but that's the risk we take with what we were born for."

"I'd have done this even if I had the choice. I grew up with the stories about our parents and how they tried to save the world. I always wanted to be a part of that. I dreamed of the day I would get to pick up a weapon and charge off into battle." She sniffed and dragged her arm under her nose. "I never thought it would end like this."

Deacon took a deep breath and expelled it into a frosty puff. "It hasn't ended. It isn't over until we're all dead, and last time I checked, we were both still breathing. We still have a chance to make this right. We can make his death worth something."

Amaya tipped her head back and blinked away the tears. "What do we do now?"

"We keep fighting. We take a couple days to regroup and figure out a plan, and we keep trying." He reached down and tipped her chin up so she looked directly at him. "We do not give up. Whatever we do, we keep fighting."

"It almost doesn't seem worth it." She gestured to the charred remains of a town at the bottom of the hill on which they stood. "The world is full of places like this. Burned down, empty, dead. You either join Lucifer, or you die. Our parents gave up everything to prevent this from happening, and God gave up on them. Now, we're involved in a war that has actually managed to destroy the entire world."

Deacon surveyed the snowy ground and long-abandoned buildings. "We're making progress. You just have to keep trusting that we can succeed at stopping them. He knew that. He lived and fought for it. We have to do the same, and if we have to die for it, too, well then it's all worth it as far as I'm concerned. You've put your life on the line time and again without even thinking about it. We all have. It could just as easily have been any one of the rest of us who died. It's horrible and sad and hard to deal with, but this isn't the first time we've seen death, and it won't be the last."

Amaya's chin trembled as she struggled not to cry again. "I just wish I'd have had a chance to talk to him first, to tell him everything was okay and I'm not mad at him. I wish—"

Deacon shook his head sternly. "No. No wishing. There's

nothing good that would come of that." He looked around at the quickly darkening sky. "We need to get out of here before it's dark enough for the vamps to come out." He extended his wings fully. "Want to take a ride?"

Amaya smiled and wrapped her arms around him. "With you, always."

Chapter One

January 1st, 2060 – San Diego, California

Ezekiel Mackenzie strode down the dark street with a purpose. All around her, people scrambled to get inside before dark, but Zeke was unafraid. She glanced at her watch and expelled a deep breath.

Her pace quickened as she hurried toward the club. There was a fence around the building with armed guards patrolling. A line stretched halfway around the block, the throng of people vying for admission at the single entrance. Most of those lined up were scantily clad women desperate to find someone who had money to pay for an hour or two of their time.

Zeke gritted her teeth and held up one hand to mask her from the other people in the line. Power rippled through the air as she sent out a stream. She weaved her way through the throng of people to the guards at the gate. Leaning close, she spoke, her voice whisper-soft and her eyes swirling with color.

"Open the gate and let me in."

The demon stepped back and lifted the latch, swinging the gate open and allowing her to pass. She patted him on the shoulder as she walked by, brushing against his arm.

"Good dog."

Bright lights pulsed inside the building. The music was

deafening, and the whole club seemed to vibrate to the beat of it. Waitresses carried trays of glasses, and two bartenders served drinks behind a worn bar.

A writhing mass of bodies gyrated on the dance floor. The smell of booze and sex filled the air, and Zeke struggled not to gag from the strength of it. She sidled up to the bar and held up a hand. One of the men behind it looked at her questioningly.

"Beer. Draft." She held out a coin and watched with little more than mild interest as the man handed back change and poured the drink. She took it and studied the glass, looking for a clean spot to sip from. Finding none, she rubbed the glass on her sleeve and sipped, wincing at the rancid taste.

Zeke glanced down at her watch again, squinting to read the time on the small dial. If the information she'd gotten was right, her target would be arriving within four minutes.

Knowing she had to draw attention, she shrugged out of her leather jacket and slipped the barback another coin to keep it safe. Reasonably satisfied it would be there when she returned, she smoothed her clothes and headed out to the dance floor, her heels clicking on the sticky stone floor.

She wore tight jeans, boots, and a low cut corset-top. Her breasts strained the material and breathing was made slightly painful from the snug fabric covering her body. Zeke had never been comfortable in sexy clothes, but getting the attention of one of the top Cambion still alive required some savvy clothing choices.

She made her way into the gyrating crowd and moved her body to the music, twirling and sliding her hands down her hips. She caught a flash of movement through the crowd and looked up. Moving sleekly, like a predator, was a man who looked as out of place as she felt.

Instead of tight pants and a bare chest, he wore jeans and a beat up leather jacket. The denim was worn white at the seams and hugged his butt and thighs perfectly. Zeke took in a quick glance at his face and smiled. He was gorgeous.

Full lips, green eyes, and dark hair, though she couldn't tell if it was brown or black in the dim light. He met her eyes and cocked one eyebrow, asking a silent question. Zeke considered the invitation briefly before offering a smile.

She would stand out less dancing with someone else and not by herself. When the Cambion came, she'd ditch the human and do her job. Hopefully the two women she'd contacted on her way to the club would have arrived by then.

The man pressed his chest against her back, reaching around her body to hold her hips as they moved in a dance. His breath was warm on her neck, and Zeke wondered briefly if he was a human or demon.

"Neither."

The declaration took her off guard, and she whirled, her hand clenching as she tried to decide whether or not he was a threat. The man yanked her close, continuing the guise of grinding and pressed his mouth to her ears.

"I'm Nephil, the same as you." He glanced from side to side. "I saw you with the guards on the way in and followed. Being here is a great way to get yourself killed."

Zeke laughed and stepped back. "I don't need help. Thanks."

The man grabbed her by the upper arm. "You have no idea what you're getting yourself into here."

She yanked her arm free and headed back toward the bar. "Just leave me alone. I have stuff to do."

"Alexi will smell you as Nephil from a mile away. He's Beelzebub's prized son. If you do this, you're going to be dead."

Anger swelled up in her, and she whirled to face him. "Stay out of my head!"

The man crossed his arms and smirked. "Then don't think so loud, sweetheart."

The doors to the club burst open and a dozen men walked in, dressed all in black. Their eyes were so pale they were nearly white, and they all had the same white-blonde hair—the mark of a Cambion.

Zeke felt fear rise in her chest for the first time since she'd walked in the door. "Shit, shit, fuck. There weren't supposed to be so many." She looked around rapidly for a route of escape. "Sorry, bud, I gotta run."

The man shook his head. "Too late. Take off and he'll see you. They must have sensed the power signature when you mind-fucked the guards at the gate."

Alexi, a tall man with a broad chest and evil smile, lifted one hand and snapped his fingers. The music stopped and the club fell silent. When he spoke, his voice was amplified to fill the whole room.

"I've been notified that there are Nephilim here. Reveal yourselves now, and I will show you mercy."

Zeke looked around quickly, trying to find an exit that wasn't blocked. The man next to her had his arms crossed and was staring at her with a smirk on his face. She glared at him and turned around in a circle once.

"I don't know what you think is so funny, but if you are what you say you are, then you're in as much danger as I am."

He looked down at her with an amused expression. Reaching out, he wrapped his fingers around her wrist and pushed into her mind, slipping past the barriers as if they weren't even there.

"Give it thirty seconds and you'll see why I'm not panicking. You're not the only one here for a reason, sweetheart. Keep your panties untwisted, and I'll get us both out of this."

Zeke battled down a wave of anger at the condescending tone. She had never met or seen this man before, yet he was asking her to trust him implicitly. She cast a furtive look around the room, hoping to see a way out or an ally she had missed. Finding nothing, she sighed deeply.

"If you get me killed, I'm coming back to haunt you. I swear to God, I will."

The man chuckled softly. "Looking forward to it. Ten seconds now."

Zeke counted down the beats in her head. At the count of ten, an explosion rocked the building and the doors flew in. The glass in the windows shattered, spraying the crowd with shards. The man grabbed Zeke around the waist and hauled her behind the bar.

"Do you have weapons?"

She drew a gun. "Just this. I was expecting Alexi to be alone. One shot and I'm out."

"What're your powers? Other than the mind control and making yourself invisible to humans—nice trick, by the way."

Zeke fought an intense inner battle as she debated what to tell him. Sighing, she gave herself over to trusting him for the time being. "Not much. Strong, obviously. I can participate in a mental convo, but not initiate one, and I can teleport very, very short distances. Unfortunately, when I use that, I leave a signature trail that even a baby Cambion could follow, so I try not to do it. I have some telekinesis, too, but it's not very strong." She narrowed her eyes. "What can you do?"

"Telepathy, telecoercion, I can conjure weapons and I can sprout wings if I need to." He looked around at the stampeding crowd as people fought for the exits. "Let's go!" He dragged her to her feet and out into the crowd.

Zeke grunted as she was pulled through the mob and jostled by people. "Go where?"

"Somewhere safe. My team will be waiting a block down. We'll reconvene with them, and then I'll take you back to the base."

"What the hell makes you think I'm going to go with you?" She ran to keep up as they made it out the door. The man leaped over the fences in one jump and waited while Zeke followed. "I don't even know your name."

"Name's Dev. All you had to do was ask." He winked at her and grabbed her wrist again. "You'll come with me because Alexi knew you were coming, which means he knows where you're staying. Odds are good whoever was there with you is already dead, and there are likely several Cambion waiting for you to come home for the sole purpose of killing you. Do you really want to die tonight?"

Knowing what he said was true and hating it, Zeke sighed. "Lead the way, oh protector of mine."

Dev grinned over his shoulder and ran down the street, veering into an alley. He jumped, snagging a fire escape and dragged it down. "Ladies first."

Zeke laughed as she began climbing. "What floor?"

"Roof." He heaved himself up behind her. "Nice view from here, babe."

Finding it impossible to be angry at the teasing tone in his voice, she laughed again. "Why do you have to be so damn likeable?"

Dev chuckled. "It's a curse. I can't help but be charming and likeable." He glanced over his shoulder to make sure they weren't being followed. "What the hell made you think you could take on Alexi by yourself?"

"Because I can. Me and him in a fair fight? I win every time." She hopped off the ladder and onto the roof. "I really hope these very heavily armed people are your friends."

Dev grinned at the tremor of nervousness in her voice. "They're mine." He stepped off behind her and placed a hand against the small of her back. "Let's get out of here."

Zeke shook her head. "Where do you think you're taking me? Don't get me wrong, I appreciate the help, but I still don't know who you are, where you're from or what you want with me. If you think I'm just going with you without knowing anything, you're out of your damn mind."

One of the other men stepped forward and offered her his

gloved hand. "I'm Zane. You're Ezekiel Mackenzie. Your best friends are Amaya Winslow and Lux Windsor. Your parents are Damon and Greer. You're an only child."

Her mouth dropping open, Zeke pulled her hand back. "How the fuck did you know all that about me?"

Zane smiled. "You were set up, Zeke. Your intel was planted. You were being lured in so Alexi could take you out. If we hadn't been notified about the setup, you'd be dead right now. We're the people who just saved your ass." He opened his arms to encompass the five people standing behind him. "You can either take off and risk it out there alone, or you can come back to our base where you'll be safe. You can call Lux and Amaya from there." He studied her. "We're all Nephilim, the same as you. We're all fighting the same fight, and the seven of us are training to kill Lucifer the same way you are."

Zeke felt her stomach drop. Fear rose up in her and her eyes darted around nervously. No one was supposed to know what her mission was. No one was to know what she was capable of.

"How the hell do you know that?"

Dev laughed and nudged her forward, a smile filled with good humor lighting up his face. "You didn't think you were the only one, did you?"

Zeke shook her head as she walked across the room. "Actually, yeah, I kinda did." She surveyed the others on the roof. "Deacon!" She sighed in relief at seeing a familiar face and rushed forward.

Deacon turned to face the group behind him. "Carys, get your mojo pumping. We need a trip for eight back home. Zane, do a sweep and make sure we're not being followed. Everyone else, stand by and get ready to leave." He laid a hand on Zeke's shoulder. "Try not to worry so loudly. You're going to give us headaches." He squeezed reassuringly. "You can call Lux and Amaya when we get there. I'm sure they'll want to come join us after you've seen the setup and talked to Dad."

Dev slung an arm around her shoulders. "Deacon's daddy is Michael. His mama is Lilith, but we don't hold that against him. Half Angel, Half Devil, all jackass."

Deacon flipped the other man off and smiled good naturedly. "The only time I met my mother, she tried to kill me. Needless to say, I'm not very close with her."

Zeke pressed her fingers against her temples. "This is enough to give me a migraine." She shook her head to clear it before responding to Dev. "I know Michael and Deacon. He came every few weeks to check on my parents when I was growing up. He never mentioned any of this."

Deacon looked somber. "We weren't allowed to know about each other until we were old enough to be able to handle the information. As kids, we were all unpredictable and volatile. We didn't know how to use our powers. Letting us know about the others would have put everyone in danger if we got caught." He grinned, then reached out and tugged her hair gently. "No one's going to hurt you here. I promise."

Feeling oddly at ease with the group, Zeke let herself grin. "You wouldn't be able to hurt me, but I appreciate the sentiment."

A pretty blonde dressed in a leather catsuit came from the other side of the roof. "Carys is all charged up and ready to go." She smiled at Zeke. "I'm Elisa. Mother human, father Metatron. Nice to meet you."

Zeke shook the woman's hand and followed them to another woman who stood with her eyes closed. "Is that Carys?"

Dev nodded. "Carys is a little odd, but you'll learn to like her. Her main ability is transporting people anywhere in the world. It takes her a few minutes to charge it up enough to transport this many, but one or two she can do instantly. We use her as a main mode of transportation since there's no limit on the range. She could take us from here to Timbuktu if she wanted to."

Carys opened her eyes and glared at him. "I'm not odd."

"Keep tellin' yourself that." He put his hands on Zeke's shoulders. "It feels a little weird, but it doesn't hurt."

Zeke glared at him over her shoulder. "Seriously, what is it with you people and touching? Haven't you ever heard of personal space?"

Dev chortled and let his hands fall to his sides. "Anti-social tendencies noted. Hands off."

Deacon rolled his eyes as Carys reached out and touched each of them. "Dev can't help but try to charm a pretty girl. Carys and Elisa are immune to him. He can't resist trying his wiles on anyone new and female."

Carys sighed deeply, obviously very used to the antics of the two men. "Here we go. Hold on tight." She clapped her hands together, and they all disappeared with a loud crack.

Zeke felt a sharp tug on her spine and then a jerk that felt like falling. She had time to suck in one breath before she was on her feet again, this time safely on the ground instead of on a roof. She looked around, taking in the large black manor.

"Where the hell are we?"

Deacon opened the doors and strode inside. "This is home. Michael keeps this place. I'm sure you know about Angels and how they can create spaces for themselves. Michael made this for us so we would have a safe place to stay. He taught us how to access it, though Carys is the only one who can get in carrying someone else. We'll teach you, too, if you decide to stay. You were probably at the one he had before Lilith and the other demons found it. That's when Amaya stopped staying here so much. She's been alternating between up here and on Earth ever since."

Zeke hesitantly stepped inside. What had looked dreary and dark from the outside was bright and warm inside. Carys and Elisa headed for the kitchen, arguing animatedly about what to cook for dinner. Deacon shrugged off his Kevlar vest and placed his rifle in a cabinet.

"Dad! We're back!"

Michael, dressed in jeans and a sweater with his wings tucked tight against his body, loped down the stairs. He embraced his son quickly. "It's good to see you home safely." He looked past Deacon to where Zeke stood, her arms crossed over her chest. "Ezekiel."

Zeke grinned and went into his arms willingly. "Uncle Michael." She laid her head against his chest and breathed in deeply, letting her nerves calm down. "I'm glad you're here."

Dev laughed. "She thought we were luring her here to kill her." He hung up his vest and weapon, revealing tightly muscled biceps and tawny golden skin. "Zane had to use his mind reading crap to convince her we're not the bad guys."

Michael smiled softly. "We're not the bad guys."

She laughed. "I figured that out when I saw Deacon." She looked around. "Why haven't you ever brought me here before?"

"Your parents were training you, and they're highly equipped to teach you everything you needed to know. I didn't want to interfere with your family. Instead, I kept track of you, talked with your parents routinely and made sure you were getting everything you needed. Once you, Lux and Amaya were together, I wanted to let the three of you train and bond. You knew Amaya came to me to train when her powers were developing. This group here has been together since they hit puberty and began training to control their powers." Michael smiled at Dev. "That rascal there came to me when he was twelve years old. I've had him for twenty years now."

Dev wrinkled his nose and brushed past Zeke to get to the kitchen. "My mother was an Angel. She died fighting off Abalam when I was little. Michael found me afterward."

Zeke lifted her eyebrows. "I thought all the female Angels abandoned their children as soon as they were born just like the male ones did? I've never heard of one keeping the baby."

Michael looked at Dev fondly. "His mother was different. Gladriel loved her son and left Heaven when she was being forced to abandon him. She chose the same path I did." He cleared his throat. "Back to you. Lux and Amaya are welcome here. They pop in and out routinely as it is, but I'm sure they'd want to come spend some time with you. I understand you don't get to be together much these days. There's a satellite phone in the office you can use. We have Nephilim working to keep human communications online. It's a safe line."

Zeke rubbed her hands over her face. "Is there any way I could get some food first and maybe a shower? I'm filthy."

Michael grinned. "Dev, show her to a room and lend her some clothes until we can get some for her."

"Can't Carys or Elisa fork over the clothes?"

Zeke scoffed. "You're such a man. There's no way in hell I would fit in their clothes. I'm six inches taller and a solid thirty pounds heavier."

Dev shrugged. "Whatever. Just don't forget to give them back." He climbed up two flights of stairs. "The last time I lent out clothes they disappeared, never to be returned." He opened a door and entered. "Come on in."

Zeke stepped into a bedroom and cast a look around at the rumpled bed, piles of clothes on the floor, and dresser drawers hanging half open. She lifted one eyebrow. "I think you need to hire a housekeeper."

Dev grinned as he rifled through drawers. "I'm a guy. Guys are messy." He pulled out a t-shirt and held it to his nose, sniffing. "It smells clean." He threw it to her. "Do you want pants or shorts?"

"Pants."

He opened two more drawers before finding a pair of black sweatpants. He tossed them to her and went into the bathroom, emerging two minutes later with a toothbrush, comb and towel.

"I don't know if the spare room is stocked, so here." He jammed them into her arms. "The empty bedroom is right across the hall. I'll get some blankets and sheets for the bed while you shower."

Zeke balanced the armful of stuff and nodded. "Thanks."

"Don't mention it."

She crossed the hall and nudged the door open with her foot. The bed was a bare mattress on a metal frame, and the closet was full of empty hangers. A box sat on the dresser, stuffed full of photos and knick knacks. Curious, she lifted one flap and looked in, a picture of a blue-eyed woman and Dev staring back up at her.

"She's my sister."

Zeke jumped at the sound of a voice behind her and whirled to see Dev standing at the door, bed clothes in his arms. "I'm sorry. I wasn't trying to snoop."

"It's sitting there in the open. Not like you picked a lock to look. Her name was Denise. We were twins. She was killed nine months ago the last time we went up against Alexi. He cut her head off."

"I'm sorry." She reached out and took the pillows off the top of the pile, placing them on the floor before grabbing the bottom sheet. "She's beautiful."

"Was." Dev efficiently unfolded the other sheet and blanket. "I'll move the stuff out. There's no reason you have to stare at some dead girls' stuff." He made the bed in several snappy movements. "Carys and Elisa are making dinner downstairs. It should be ready by the time you're done in the shower."

Zeke let him get almost all the way to the door. "Dev?"

He turned. "What?"

"What's your real name? Dev sounds like a nickname."

"It's after my last name. My mother, rest her soul, liked old-fashioned names. She named us Dennis and Denise and gave us our father's last name, which was Deveraux. Don't ever call me Dennis."

Zeke tried not to smile. "Noted."

Chapter Two

January 4th, 2060 – The Manor

ZEKE THREW herself at the two women who walked in the door, wrapping her arms around them and jumping up and down. Amaya and Lux held her tightly, their hugs hard. She kissed each on the cheek before pulling back.

"I'm so glad you're both here."

Amaya glared at Zeke. "What the fuck were you thinking going after Alexi on your own? He could have killed you!"

Zeke glared at Amaya. "I could have handled him on his own. It was the six other bastards he brought with him that made the damn thing difficult." She took one of the duffel bags from her. "I'm fine. That's what matters."

Lux tied her hair back from her face and looked at Zeke with bemusement. "We all know you took a stupid risk and that you're lucky you came through it alive." She smiled softly. "Now we need to figure out how the hell we deal with it."

Michael strode in the door behind the women. "There's nothing to be dealt with. We know Amaya is the one prophesied to have the power to defeat Lucifer. I believe Deacon does as well, given that he is half-Angel and half-Devil. That doesn't mean Lux and Zeke aren't very special Nephilim. They just aren't as powerful as Deacon and Amaya. Now that Amaya is fully grown and fully trained, we must begin to form a plan for how to get her close enough to Lucifer to kill him."

Amaya crossed her arms. "That's why I haven't been allowed out in public since I was fourteen years old. Everyone's afraid he'll see me somehow and know what I look like. I want to do something about it."

Michael smiled. "What do your parents think?" He sobered. "What does your father think?"

Amaya's eyes flashed with anger. "My father is Braxton. End of story." She glared at Michael. "Mom and Dad know what I have to do, and they've trained me for it. They also know at this point they can't been seen with me or it increases the risk that I get caught. We check in once a week, but that's it. This is what I was born to do. It's what we all were created for."

Zeke sighed. "I'll take you guys upstairs. We're all sharing a room on the third floor. Michael promised he'll get a couple more beds and such in the next couple days, but until then, we're all bunking in together in a queen-sized." She laughed when both of the other women groaned. "Oh, I know. We'll live though."

Lux looked around the house. "This looks almost exactly like Mom and Dad's house in Scotland." Her eyes betrayed her sadness at not having been home in years.

Zeke slung her arm around Lux. "We'll be fine. I just met the other seven that are here, but they all seem pretty nice. Deacon's a slave driver with the training, but they've got a good regimen and they're all smart." She led the other two up the stairs. "And then there's the fact that they're fun to look at..."

Michael chuckled as Zeke's voice faded when she disappeared around the corner. He looked over his shoulder at Deacon, who stood leaning against the door frame. "Your disapproval is coming through loud and clear, son. Do you think I shouldn't have brought them here?"

Deacon pushed off the wall and approached his father. "It's not that. Amaya has lived here more often than she hasn't for the last decade. Well, until the last few years. It's good to have her back. I don't mind any of them being here. I was just hoping this wasn't going to happen so fast. I don't know if we're ready."

"We're never going to be ready. All we can do is try." He laid his hand on Deacon's shoulder. "We need to have a plan. Those three women are very important to us. I've told you that since you were old enough to understand what we need to do. They all have impressive abilities, and we will need each of them to kill Lucifer."

"I know. I'm sure they know that, too. The question is how do we get close enough to kill him?"

"We're going to need some information. I believe the best way to do that is through Zeke. She has the ability to shield herself and maybe one other from being detected by demons. If we're able to get her into some of the human circles that worship Lucifer, she may be able to get some information we couldn't get otherwise."

"We can't send her alone." Deacon crossed his arms. "They aren't martyrs. We aren't trying to use them to keep us from getting killed. I'll put my life on the line with her. If she goes in, she goes in with backup. More than one."

"It can't be you or Amaya. From this point forward, unless it's absolutely necessary, we have to keep the two of you shielded and safe. You're the only two with a chance of killing Lucifer. We can't jeopardize that."

"Carys might be good to send."

Michael shook his head. "No. We need her here in case you need to be transported and I'm not present. It has to be Dev. With his ability to make humans think what he wants them to, he could be invaluable."

Deacon considered that briefly. "Do we really want to put him in that position? With Denise just dying recently, I'm not sure his head is in the right space, and we need it to be if he's going to be any good to anyone."

"He did fine with the rescue mission, did he not?"

"He did," Deacon admitted readily, running his hands through his hair and shifting his weight from one foot to the other. "I just don't want to endanger either of them if Dev isn't able to keep it together for the entirety of the damn thing. The last thing we need is for Damon and Greer to come and hunt us down."

Michael smiled. "We'll be fine. They'll be fine. Do you want to talk to them about it?"

"Do we even have anything to talk to them about? We know we want them to go, but we don't know what the plan is yet. They could possibly sense Zeke coming a mile away. With her parentage and your genetics in there, she might be pegged as a Nephil the second she enters Los Angeles."

"Which is why we have to be careful not to send her with very many people. Dev could transport them both out if he needed to, and she can shield herself from the demons. As long as we can keep her away from the high ranking Devils or some of Alexi's crew, she won't be detected. I don't believe she's ever been seen, so she shouldn't be at too much risk just being out and about. We've managed to keep everything fairly quiet up until this point. I really think this is our best bet for getting some information. We need to get someone close to the humans who know where Lucifer is and where he is going to be. Someone who will do whatever is asked of them. Carys is not that person. Neither are any of the others. Zeke is. Dev isn't in a good place, you're right about that, but neither is he so overwhelmed with Denise's death that he's unable to see the bigger picture. I actually suspect that some time away might be good for him. He could use a break from seeing her ghost every day."

Deacon shrugged and pushed off the wall. "It's your call, Dad. I don't think it's the best idea, but I'm not going to be the one to get in your way. I value my life too much for that."

Michael returned his son's grin and dragged him close for a hug. "You know I'd never do anything to risk them, son. I love Dev like he's my own. I raised the two of you as brothers."

"I know. Which is why I'm so protective of him. I love him like one, too."

Zeke flopped on the bed and stared up at the ceiling. Lux laid next to her, her head on Zeke's stomach. Amaya perched across the room, sitting backward on the desk chair. She folded her arms on the back of the chair and rested her chin on them.

"Dad said we shouldn't stay here very long. He told me that the more time we spend here, the greater the risk of Lucifer finding us and that we don't want to endanger the others by staying."

Zeke wrinkled her nose. "Your dad has always been a worrier, Amaya. He's the one who never wanted us to be together, so I'm not sure I'm buying it. Michael would have told us if we were a danger to anyone. I think this place he's got here is pretty secure."

Lux lifted up on to her elbows and stared at Amaya. "I agree with Zeke on this one. This in a nonplace. You know as well as we do that you can't find someone else's nonplace without a shit ton of magic or knowing where the door is. My mother's the only one who's ever managed to do it and that was because she knew where the door was and because Beelzebub had used so much energy making Hades that he couldn't guard the door."

Sighing, Amaya spoke. "I know he's a worrier and you both know it, but he can't help it."

Zeke rolled her eyes. "Uncle Brax needs to get drunk and relax a bit. We're fine."

"Your parents also had the advantage of having seen this world once already. It was new for my parents and for Amaya's. There's a bit more of a learning curve for them than for Damon and Greer." She laid back down. "I don't want to talk about that. Let's discuss the absolute man candy that is downstairs." Lux waved her hand, fanning herself. "It's a fucking crying shame that Deacon is practically our brother. I'd totally hit that if we weren't basically related."

Zeke grinned. "You haven't seen anything yet. Just wait until you see the others. There isn't a single man in this place that I would mind seeing naked."

Amaya giggled. "We've met them all, remember? You're the only one who hasn't been here much. Besides, I don't think there's ever been a man who you would mind seeing naked." She stood and stretched. "So let's talk about the elephant in the room. Why the hell did you go after Alexi without calling us?"

Zeke took a deep breath. "Because I had a chance, it was short notice, and I didn't want to pass it up. He's the leader of the Cambion. Cut his head off and we make a dent in them." She laughed bitterly. "It's not like we have Angels fighting for us the same way they get the Devils and demons fighting with them. Ever since Lucifer got loose they've been bowling us over, and for once I wanted to be on the offensive instead of the defensive. I figured if I could kill Beelzebub's pride and joy it would be doubly bad for them. Alexi's the one who calls most of the shots, and he's the most dangerous of the Cambion. If we can kill him, we can send them into disarray, and that's our best chance at hurting them. We have to find a way to end this once and for all. We have to kill Lucifer and for you"—he looked pointedly at Amaya—"to be able to do that, we have to find out where he is and how to get to him, even if that's in a nonplace."

Lux sat up. "You should know better than to do that on your own. We could have been there in next to no time if you'd have let us know what was going on. Goodness knows we want to get to them as much as you do." She climbed to her feet. "We need a plan for ending this whole thing."

Zeke snorted. "The plan is easy. We find Lucifer and we kill him. There's no use in us having the secret weapon that is Amaya if we can't get close enough to use it. We're getting to the point of no return. People are dying every day. People are being possessed, they're being eaten and the ones that aren't dying or possessed are bowing down to Lucifer to try and save their own asses. It's time to stop it." She stood and followed the other two out of the room. "You both know as well as I do that this is going to be a repeat of what our parents went through. Three of us. There has to be three parts to this. We were all created and born for a reason, and we just have to figure out what it is we need to do to kill him."

Lux nodded thoughtfully. "I think you're probably right, but no one here knows what it is we have to do. There's only one person I can think of who might know what God wants from us to defeat them." She sighed. "I don't understand why someone so powerful as God just sits up there in Heaven watching us all scramble to survive when He could just end the whole thing in a split second and it would be done and over with." She turned and looked at Amaya. "We need to talk to Gabriel."

Amaya shook her head. "No. I'm not interested in talking to him. He lied to me my entire life and betrayed my parents to tell me I'm his daughter. I want nothing to do with him."

Zeke hugged Amaya tightly. "I don't blame you, sweetheart. I would say the same thing in your shoes, really I would. But I don't think we get much of a choice right now. We have to find out what we need to do, and we know he's the only one who knows what's going on enough to give us some direction. If I thought Michael knew, I'd say we should ask him, but I think it's clear he doesn't, and Gabriel isn't going to come down here for just anyone. You might be the only person who could summon him and actually get him to listen to you."

Amaya closed her eyes. "I don't want to. I'd give anything not to have to see him. I trusted him, and he lied to me. About who he is and about who I am. He sits up there in Heaven, knowing what we're going through down here, knowing he could help and choosing not to because God gave up. Michael was brave enough to tell God no. Gabriel could have done the same thing."

Lux put her hands on her hips and stared at Amaya. "Call for him. Stop dragging your damn feet, and let's get this done. The sooner he comes down here, the sooner he leaves."

Amaya glared at the redhead. "Seriously. Fuck you, Lux." She tipped her head back and looked up. "Gabriel! I need you!"

The sound of fluttering wings filled the room, and with a blast of white light, Gabriel stood on the landing. He lifted one perfectly shaped eyebrow and inspected the sleeves of his pristine white suit carefully, looking for any blemish. Finding none, he lifted his eyes to the three women and smiled.

"Amaya." He stepped forward to embrace her. "What do you need?"

Amaya pulled back and crossed her arms. "I need you to tell us what we have to do in order to kill Lucifer." She looked between Lux and Zeke. "We're ready. It's time."

CHAPTER THREE

GABRIEL LOOKED between the three women, his eyes sad. "Where are Michael and his son? They're going to need to hear this, too."

Michael appeared at the bottom of the stairs. "I felt your arrival. You have a lot of nerve coming to my house, brother, after abandoning me as you have. What do you want with us?"

Gabriel lifted his brows in amusement. "Amaya is my daughter. I will come whenever she needs me, no matter where she is at the time. Given the choice between Deacon and me, brother, I would be willing to bet my life that you would have made the same choice."

Amaya shoved past Gabriel and went down the stairs. "You chose yourself, Gabriel. Do us both a favor and stop referring to me as your daughter. I'm not."

Hurt flashed across Gabriel's face for a split second before he masked it. Squaring his shoulders, he followed Amaya down the steps. "The girls have summoned me to tell you all what it is that you must do in order to kill Lucifer. Given that you and Deacon have been discussing much the same topic, I think it is fairly apparent the time has come for the instruction."

Michael sighed deeply and flicked his wings in annoyance. "We'll go into my office to talk. Not everyone in this house needs to know what's going on yet."

Gabriel glided down the stairs and past Michael. "For once we agree about something."

Zeke leaned close to Lux. "One of these days, someone is going to get drunk enough to tell us the story there."

Lux giggled. "I'm not holding my breath." She linked her arm with Zeke's. "Let's go find out the many ways we have to risk our lives this time."

Michael waited until the three women, Gabriel, and Deacon were seated before closing the door and perching on the desk. He looked at Gabriel, his eyes flat. "Let me make one thing clear. Angels coming down are being monitored, and I won't have you risking exposure of the Nephilim in this house just because you want to see Amaya. You can go to Earth and then pop in from somewhere else, but never come here from Heaven again. It's too dangerous, and I won't have it."

Gabriel crossed one of his legs over the other. "I find the restrictions acceptable."

Michael sneered. "Good. Tell us what you know so we can get back to our jobs."

"Very well." Gabriel shifted in his seat and folded his hands on top of his knees. "Amaya has asked that I inform you all what steps need to be taken in order to kill Lucifer. As you know, until Amaya was born, the only being with the power to kill him was God. Now, Amaya is that person, though she was never meant to carry the burden alone. I believe Deacon, because he shares the same genetics, will also be a key to destroying Lucifer, and they may need to work together to ensure that Lucifer's death occurs. I'm not sure whether or not you'll find it to be fortunate, but there are no tasks such as there were with the six. Instead, there is but one—kill Lucifer with has three necessary steps. In order to do that, Amaya—and possibly Deacon—will have to embrace the power given by God and channel the wrath of Father himself. Only when they have reached the point that they are pure vessels to control and use God's power will they be able to do so."

Amaya squirmed. "How the fuck do I do that?"

Gabriel narrowed his eyes. "Watch your language, young lady. I'll not abide by any child of mine using such foul words."

Amaya rolled her eyes. "I'll talk however I want to." Annoyed, she repeated her question. "What do I need to do?"

Still irked, Gabriel huffed. "Lux and Ezekiel were born into this world for a purpose. The three of you are linked. The success of one is the success of all, and should one of you fail, all will perish."

Lux leaned forward. "What does that mean?"

"It means that each of you three must prove yourselves worthy of God's power before it will be given to Amaya. Deacon, the same is true of you. Your two closest companions—Dennis and Zane—will be tasked with being your proxies to prove you are worthy of the power necessary to win against Lucifer."

Michael stood. "This is way too complicated and sounds exactly like the tasks that the others had to do. God should not hold one being responsible for the actions of the others."

Gabriel huffed again and sighed. "Would you prefer I put it in terms of tasks? I could do that, I suppose, if it is less offensive to your concept of fairness."

Michael bristled. "I dislike this whole thing, brother. Father could end this easily and yet chooses not to. We are being asked to send our children to war. There is no reason for tasks or linking the three or whatever the bloody hell you want to call it. I just want to know—simply—what it is that has to be done."

"Fine. I'll lay it out for you in a series of tasks so that you can all easily understand what is needed." Annoyed that his initially proffered explanation was neither understood nor appreciated, Gabriel spread his hands to illustrate his point. "First, you must find and destroy Lucifer's sword. Through it runs his connection to Hell and his ability to conjure new demons on Earth without going back there. It will limit his power considerably. Second, you must kill Beelzebub and his progeny. As the second in command to Hell, his death will weaken Lucifer as Lucifer bound himself to Beelzebub when he fished him from the Lake and that bond runs through his children—of which there are eight. Lastly, Amaya and Deacon must find Lucifer and channel the power of God and use it to kill him. To do so will require them to give themselves over to the power of God and merge it with their own powers and the magic that flows through the Earth. The first two do not need to be done consecutively, and they do not need to be done by the same individuals. All that matters is that both are done before Amaya battles Lucifer."

After several seconds of silence, Deacon whistled. "Simple then. Easy as pie, right?"

Michael laid a hand on his son's shoulder. "Easy is not the word I would have picked to describe what Gabriel has just laid out." He leveled a glare at the Archangel. "What is it with you and sets of three tasks?"

Lux was the one who answered. "It's not just three. It's one, two, three, and six. They're very important numbers for magic. Six in a circle, three as one, two as one, each one individually. Woman to man, woman to woman, man to man. It's all about infinity and no beginning or end. It makes total sense. By breaking things down into groupings of threes and having three women and three men—essentially three pairs as well—you increase the natural magic that flows and it helps us win."

Gabriel wrinkled his nose in disgust. "I sincerely doubt God has any interest in human witchcraft."

Lux glared at him. "Funny how God was the one who chose my mother and how He passed her gifts along to me. It seems to me God doesn't have a problem with witchcraft at all."

Michael held up a hand. "That's enough. First things first, and that's apparently finding the sword and destroying it. If the last time we did this is any indication, that task will fall to two of you."

Zeke lifted her hand. "That would be me. Not only am I the one who can be invisible to demons, I'm also the one who can mind-control them. I can get in and out easier than anyone else."

Michael nodded. "We'll send Dev with you. He has the ability to compel humans temporarily, so that will make it even easier still. As long as you can avoid high-level Devils, you should be able to move in, get the information, use it to get the sword and get out without being in too much danger."

Zeke lifted one shoulder in a shrug. "Fine with me, but we need to make sure that Deacon and Amaya are safe until we're done with these two. Obviously Lux and someone will be off trying to find and kill Beelzebub and his children. Since Gabriel said they don't have to be done one after the other, there's no reason we can't be going after the sword and Beelzebub at the same time."

Gabriel considered for a long moment before nodding. "The sheer number of offspring Beelzebub has leads me to believe the second task may take considerably longer than the first. Because of that, it is not only possible, but preferable to do both assignments at the same time or to even begin the second before the first."

Lux smiled tensely. "All the more reason for me to get started." She looked to Michael. "Who is it I'm going to be working with? Did you say Zane?"

Michael nodded, then offered explanation for Zeke and Gabriel, neither of whom knew Zane. "He is a very powerful Nephil. His mother was a witch, the same as Aradia is, and his father is the Angel of Death. Zane inherited the power to kill with nothing more than a touch. So far that ability is hit or miss on Cambion and Nephilim, and we've never managed to get close enough to a Devil for him to try, so I'm not sure whether or not it would work on Beelzebub. I'm going to guess it would not since that would make things too easy, and if I know anything from the last time we did this, it's that God doesn't like to make anything easy for us."

Gabriel stood abruptly. "It is not right of you to disparage the name of God, brother. He is still your creator, and as such, you owe Him a measure of respect."

Michael crossed his arms. "When He starts acting like a Father instead of a petulant child, then I'll give Him respect. Until that time, I'll handle things my own way." He stood and opened the door to the office. "I think it's time you leave, Gabriel. We obviously have some planning to do, and I'm sure you're uncomfortable having been out of Heaven for so long."

Gabriel ran his hand over his slacks and stood. "It's obvious I am no longer welcome." He stroked his hand over Amaya's hair. "Call if you need for anything, my child. I love you."

Amaya stiffened until Gabriel was gone. When he had faded from the room, she shuddered. "I hate it when he does that!" She looked at Michael. "What is with his incessant need to pretend he's my dad?"

Michael's expression was one of sympathy. "There is much about Gabriel you don't understand and that you may not ever understand, but for all he is and all he has done and will do, he does love you and he would do anything within his power to make sure you survive what is upon us."

"I don't like it." Amaya stood up and rubbed her wet palms on her jeans. "I think I'm going to go find something to eat. I'm hungry."

Zeke waited until the others had cleared the room before looking at Michael. "Has God given up on us?" She shook her head. "I know the stories, that the only reason you failed the first time was because God lost faith that our parents could complete the tasks, and when they did, it was His lack of faith that made them lose. I don't want to risk my life and for Lux and Amaya—who I love like sisters—to risk theirs, only to find out at the last second that we've been doomed to fail from the very beginning because God couldn't be bothered to believe in us."

Michael took a deep breath and expelled it slowly. "Child, I wish I could tell you with certainty that we were going to survive this and go on to live long, happy lives, but I can't do that. The truth is I don't know whether or not God has lost faith in us because I lost faith in Him long ago. All I know is that we have to try because we couldn't live with ourselves if we didn't. It's the reason your parents kept fighting—the reason they still fight today—and it is why you, Lux and Amaya will follow in their footsteps." He patted her shoulder reassuringly. "We'll get through this together. Your parents know I would never let anything happen to you that I could prevent. I'll keep you safe, and I'll help you through your tasks as I helped them through theirs. I promise you that."

Zeke closed her eyes and took a deep breath. "Can Dev handle this? I don't know him, but I know his sister died not too long ago, and I don't want to take someone on a mission who's going to be a danger to both of us."

Michael smiled. "Dev will be just fine. I believe he'll enjoy a chance at seeking some revenge for what happened to Denise. I'm sure he'll tell you about what happened to her at some point. I expect the two of you will get along quite well." He waved her out the door. "I'm sure you're hungry, and I have some work to do figuring out where exactly it is that I need to send all of you. The sooner we get this done, the better."

Zeke pulled the clothes from the dryer and folded them carefully. Laying the t-shirt and sweatpants over one arm, she padded from the laundry room and up the back stairs. Her bare feet were quiet on the carpet as she slipped down the hallway toward Dev's door. She reached out and knocked softly, waiting until she heard him approaching.

He opened the door and leaned against the frame, his blonde hair mussed and his eyes heavy lidded. "What's wrong?"

Zeke held out the clothes. "I didn't think you'd be asleep. I brought your clothes back. I washed them." She handed them to him. "Thanks for the loan."

Dev rubbed his hands over his eyes and peered down at her. "You washed them?"

"Yeah." Her voice was incredulous. "What did you think I'd do, bring them back dirty?"

He shrugged and took the garments. "I'm amazed you brought

them back at all. Every fucking time I lend something out it disappears into the ether."

"Well, I like to bring back what I borrow." She shifted, slightly uncomfortable under his gaze. "Thanks again for lending them to me. I appreciate it."

Dev laid the garments on the dresser. "No problem." He studied her closely. "You look tired."

Zeke laughed. "That's an understatement. Michael hasn't gotten any new beds yet, so I'm stuck sharing a queen sized bed with Amaya and Lux. It's tight quarters." She lifted her shoulder helplessly. "It's not a huge deal. Lux and I will be leaving in a couple days, so I don't have much longer to put up with it."

"That sucks." He looked over his shoulder at his rumpled sheets and comforter. "Don't think I'm hitting on you, 'cause I'm not, but I have a queen sized and there's just me. You could stay in here if you wanted and we wouldn't even have to touch."

She lifted her eyebrows. "First your pants, now your bed. If I keep up at this rate, we'll be married by Saturday." When he grinned widely, she giggled. "I'm glad someone gets that I'm joking."

Dev snorted. "It was a bad joke, but I recognized it as such." He folded his arms across his chest. "Yes or no, Mackenzie. I want to go back to sleep."

Zeke looked over her shoulder toward her door and the bed where she knew Lux and Amaya were already sleeping. She nodded. "Sure. Why the hell not?"

"Don't be so enthusiastic about it." He held the door open until she entered the room and then closed it behind her.

"I didn't mean it like that."

"Uh huh." He moved to the closet and withdrew a pillow, tossing it to her. "Here."

Zeke caught the pillow and held it against her chest. "Thanks. Do we need another blanket or can we share the quilt?"

Dev stared at the bed blankly for a long moment before answering. "I can share if you can, but if you're going to hog the covers, tell me now so I can go get another one."

"No one's complained thus far."

He gave her an appraising look and smiled cockily. "I would imagine not."

Ignoring him. Zeke peeled back the blankets and slipped between the sheets. She adjusted the pillow beneath her head and waited until Dev had laid down next to her, the heat of his body strangely inviting.

"This is weird."

Dev sighed and rolled onto his side to face her. "Do you want me to go sleep downstairs on the couch?"

"That's not what I meant."

"Then what did you mean?"

Zeke rolled so they were looking at each other. "I don't think I've ever slept with a guy and not had sex first."

Dev lifted his eyebrows and grinned. "Well if that's the problem, all you had to do was ask."

She giggled. "That's not what I meant. What is it with you and thinking if I bring it up I want to do it?"

"Normally people don't mention sex unless they're thinking about sex." He wiggled his brows. "Now that you've brought it up, I'm thinking about it, too, and I gotta say, the thought's a pretty pleasant one."

Zeke laughed. "You are so weird."

Dev rolled and turned off the light before turning back to her. "Just FYI, I wouldn't complain if you were to come on to me in the middle of the night." He grinned and folded his arm beneath his head. "As a guy, I find the thought of getting woken up by an attractive woman looking to ravish me very appealing."

Zeke laughed and shook her head. "I'm going to sleep. Goodnight, Dev."

Before she could roll over, Dev slid closer, suddenly serious. He curled one arm around her and tugged her close, grateful when he met no resistance from her.

"I just want to see what's there." He leaned in until their mouths were a hairsbreadth apart. "A goodnight kiss never hurt anyone. What do you say?"

Zeke shivered at his proximity and stared at his mouth, debating on whether she wanted the kiss. Oddly comfortable within his arms, she shifted forward slightly to see how his body felt against hers. Deciding she liked the feel and liked the idea, she nodded.

"I say okay."

His mouth was warm and firm, and Zeke smiled as she let him kiss her. A slow burn started deep within her, and she made a small noise against his mouth, parting her lips to let his tongue in.

His flavor burst against her tongue as he kissed her, dark and rich. She slipped her fingers into his silky hair and moved her mouth against his enthusiastically. He tightened one arm around her and aligned her body so she was pressed firmly against him.

Pulling back much more quickly than Zeke wanted him to, Dev grinned at her in the dark before speaking. "Well, that certainly gives us something to mull over, now doesn't it?"

Zeke nodded, her lips swollen and red from his kiss. "I think it most certainly does." She ran her knuckle down the side of his face. "One hell of a goodnight kiss."

He kissed the tip of her nose and rolled over, his back to her. "Goodnight, Zeke."

Zeke woke slowly, warm and comfortable. Her back was pressed against something firm and hot, and she jumped when she saw a hand between her breasts, resting on her chest before remembering she'd spent the night with Dev. Smiling softly, she rolled slightly to look over her shoulder at the man who slept beside her.

He was taller than her by close to half a foot. She was long and athletic where he was tightly muscled. His hair was a dark, golden blond and she knew his eyes were a bright, lively green. There was a scruff across his jaw from not shaving. She lifted one hand to lay across his, and she marveled at how much larger his hand was than hers. His skin was slightly rough and dry, and there were small scars across his knuckles.

Scars intrigued her. Each one told a story. Zeke had many of them herself—four from bullets and seven from being stabbed. Hers was the body of a warrior, and she knew instinctively that Dev's would be much the same. She wondered briefly what scars he had on that magnificent body.

Dev's eyes fluttered open, and he woke slowly, stretching his legs and arching his back. He froze when he felt her pressed against him and blinked several times, looking down. A sleepy smile curled his lips, and he withdrew his arm from around her.

"Sorry. I didn't grope you, did I?"

Zeke laughed. "Not that I remember." She craned her neck to look out the window. "It's not even light outside yet."

Dev snorted. "This is a nonplace, remember? Day and night is completely at the mercy of Michael. He decides how long it's day and how long it's dark."

"How big is the outside?"

He considered that for a moment. "It's not unsubstantial. Why?"

"I'm thinking about taking a run. I've been cooped up in this house for days. It would feel good to loosen up some and stretch out a bit. Is it big enough to take a jog?"

"I think it's probably sufficient for what you need. You probably have a half mile or so running the perimeter of the grounds. As long as you don't mind repetitive scenery, you'll be just fine." He rolled onto his back and laid his hands on his stomach. "Are you the type who likes to run alone or do you want some company?"

Zeke lifted one shoulder in a shrug. "I don't mind company as a rule." She rolled out of the bed and to her feet. "I'm gonna change. Meet me out front in five?"

"Sure."

She opened the door and slipped out into the hall, jumping when she saw Amaya standing in the hallway, leaning against the wall with a smirk on her face. Zeke scowled. "What?"

"How long have you known him? Three days? Four?"

"I didn't sleep with him."

Amaya lifted one eyebrow. "Oh really? Then why are you sneaking out of Dev's room at six in the morning?"

Zeke frowned. "Well, I did sleep with him, I suppose, but I didn't bang him. There was actually legitimately only sleeping, whether you believe me or not." She headed down the hall to the room she shared with Amaya and Lux. "We're going for a run around the grounds. Want to join?"

Amaya made a face. "I hate running. Pass on that one." She followed Zeke. "You really didn't bang him?"

"I really didn't bang him."

"He's awfully pretty."

Zeke giggled. "He is pretty to look at, and I wouldn't mind taking a nice bite out of him, but I'm not sure it's a good idea. I have to work with him and I'm going to have to basically go undercover with him to find this sword. I don't want to muck things up with hormones, so for the moment at least, I think I'm going to keep my clothes on and resist taking his off." She stretched and shucked off her pajamas to exchange them for running shorts and a sweatshirt.

Amaya leaned against the door and smirked. "I know you, Zeke. That isn't going to happen for long."

CHAPTER FOUR

January 10th, 2060

ZEKE STRUGGLED to stay still while the woman pinned the suit on her frame, making humming noises in the back of her throat as she tugged at the fabric to make it fit better. A rack of clothes hung behind the door, and several boxes of shoes sat on the bench.

"If you want to blend in, child, you have to look the part. You're supposed to come from old money, not be dressed in ratty jeans and sweatshirts."

Zeke scoffed. "I'm not from old money, though. I'm the child of two soldiers. I'm more comfortable in fatigues than anything else."

The woman glared up at her. "You can't let them know that. Regardless of your upbringing and powers, they will be able to smell a fraud a mile away. You must be polished and sophisticated if you want to accomplish your task."

Michael crossed one leg over the other and studied Zeke closely. "Margaret is right. Your powers can shield your nature, but they cannot make the others believe you. You're going to have to put on the performance of a lifetime if we're going to figure out where the sword is and how to get it. You have to get close to the humans who are close to Lucifer. One step at a time, and this is the obvious first one."

"I don't need a lecture. I know what I have to do and I'll do it."

She shifted uncomfortably. "No one said I had to like it."

"Liking it would be preferable if you can manage." Michael smiled. "I know it's a lot to ask, but if you were comfortable in the clothes and with the role, it would go a long way toward ensuring our success." He stood and inspected the silk fabric being made into a skirt and blazer. "Margaret, she's going to need an eveningwear wardrobe as well. There will likely be cocktail parties and balls she'll need to attend. Church-appropriate clothing is also a good idea. Regardless of what's in your heart, you will have to act the part of a devout Satan worshipper. You may be asked to prove your dedication to him, and you must go into this willing to do whatever it takes. God knows your heart, and I will not allow you to be punished for anything you might need to do."

Zeke cocked one eyebrow. "Did you have this talk with Dev, too, or just me? Because I can handle this. I'm not a kid, and this isn't my first rodeo. I've been fighting this since I was old enough to fight. I'll do what has to be done."

"Dev will get the same lecture. You're both very dear to me, and I would be remiss in my role as your guide if I did not advise you as to what might be asked of you during the course of your mission." He laid a hand on her shoulder and rubbed gently. "I have utmost confidence you'll succeed."

Zeke covered his hand with hers. "I know. Did Gage get our identities and a house and everything arranged? Finding a place to live in Los Angeles is next to impossible."

"Nothing is impossible for Gage. He's lived almost fifteen hundred years and knows how to make a fortune better than any other I have ever had the displeasure to meet. He's secured an appropriate house for you and Dev and is having it stocked with everything you might need. Rest assured you will be well cared for."

She jerked when the sharp point of a pin dug into her flesh. "Are we almost done? Surely you know every inch of my whole body by now and could make this stuff in your sleep." Shifting to avoid another prick, Zeke frowned down at the seamstress. "I'm sorry. I don't mean to be bitchy, but I've been standing here a while."

Margaret chuckled. "I need a model for each piece, child. Hold still and this will all be over soon."

Biting her tongue to keep from saying anything she would regret, Zeke turned her attention back to Michael. "Please tell me Dev had to go through this."

Margaret laughed again. "Men are much easier, my dear. I only had to measure him."

Michael bit his cheek to keep from smiling. "Dev and Deacon are taking Lux to gather any magical supplies you'll need for the next few weeks."

Zeke sighed and closed her eyes. "So not fair."

"Life rarely is, my darling girl." Michael sat back down. "How are your parents?"

"Fine last time I talked to them. We only talk once a week. It's been almost a year since I saw them. They move around a lot, training Nephilim and Warriors wherever they're needed. I know Brax and Gage call them if they need help every once in a while. They're ready for this to be over as much as I am."

"It's a miracle they've managed to survive this long. I'm very proud of how they have done."

"They lived this world once before, remember? If anyone knows how to survive, it's Mom and Dad. This is what they've known since they were born." Zeke shook her head. "It's so weird thinking that Dad was born a couple years ago and Mom would be born this year."

"Time is fickle and hard to understand. It took centuries before I grasped the complexities. It's not easy to comprehend that something may exist in one time and not in another but then be introduced there by someone tampering with time. Time is fluid for Angels and some other creatures and totally tangential for humans. I'd advise against questioning it too intensively. The likely outcome is that you will develop an ache in your head."

Zeke laughed. "A headache, Michael. I swear, most of the time you do just fine but sometimes you talk like an Angel instead of a person."

"I have made quite the effort to pick up the slang and vernacular you humans use. It's not easy. I must know every language that has ever or will ever be spoken. Learning the local trends with speech and idioms makes a large task even harder."

Shifting topics, she put her hands on her hips. "Did you tell me Zane's dad is the Angel of Death?"

Michael nodded. "I did. Because of that, Zane can kill a person with nothing more than a touch."

"Can he control it?"

The Angel looked pained. "He has some difficulties in controlling his abilities. Zane prefers not to touch people or to be touched because of some unfortunate missteps with his control."

"He's killed people accidentally?"

"Unfortunately, yes. The ability to give life or bring death is the hardest to control. Zane has done an admirable job, and he take steps to make sure everyone remains safe from his particular talents. I think he and Lux will get along well. He, too, has a not insignificant measure of magic that should complement hers well. I don't imagine there is a better pair to find Beelzebub's offspring and kill them."

"The odds aren't bad Dev and I might run into a couple on our mission. Is there a way to know which are Beelzebub's and which aren't?"

"His are the most powerful and will be easy to spot. I don't believe a single one of them will hesitate to announce their parentage at every given opportunity. You'll find that from most of the offspring of the high ranking Devils. If you do happen to come into contact with one of the Cambion we need to kill, don't hesitate to eradicate it. If that cannot be done without compromising your mission, just make sure to notify me or Gabriel as soon as possible so we can arrange for Lux and Zane to step in." He stood and stretched his wings. "As much as I wish I could stay here for your entire appointment and talk, I do need to check in with the others and check with Gage to make sure everything is on track for you to move into your new home this weekend. I'll return for you in two or three hours. Call for me if you need something."

Zeke opened her mouth to speak, but Michael had already disappeared. She looked down at the seamstress and sighed. "Is this really going to take another two or three hours?"

Margaret patted her hip sympathetically. "At least. Okay, girlie, get this off and we'll start on some of the dresses. Those should move a bit faster."

Zeke stripped off the suit and huffed deeply. "Thrill, thrill."

Amaya paced as Zeke packed her suitcases. Lux, her bag already packed, sat on the bed. Amaya sighed deeply and glared at them both.

"I don't like the idea of the two of you taking off and working on this and me just staying here all safe and cozy while you're trying to save the world."

Zeke snorted. "You're the chosen one, Maya, not us. All we're doing is setting the stage for you to be able to do what you need to do. Your job is likely going to be more dangerous than ours. Enjoy the break, do some training and work on developing your abilities. The more time you have to prepare while we're laying the groundwork the better off we'll all be."

Lux nodded. "I'm with Zeke on this one, babe. You're the one we need to keep safe. Without you, we could work on this until we're old and gray and wouldn't get anywhere. The only way we do what we need to is if you're here safe and waiting until it's your turn."

Amaya barely resisted the urge to stomp her foot. She raked her hands through her hair and tugged on it sharply. "If you need anything at all, you call for me. Both of you. Anytime at all. I don't care about the danger. I don't care about the risks of being seen. The two of you are as much my family as Mom and Dad and the kids are, and I'd rather die than let anything happen to you."

Zeke zipped up her bag and wrapped her arms around Amaya in a tight hug. "I love you, too. But we'd both rather die than see you fail. I know you understand deep down that this is the right thing to do, no matter how much it sucks. So you're going to stay here, and you're going to train and get ready, and if Lux or I, or both of us, have to die to make sure you succeed, then that's the risk we take and it's one we're taking with our eyes wide open."

Lux smiled sadly. "As much as I love to argue with Zeke, she's right. We have to do this, and you have to let us without interfering. If they find out where you are and what you can do, they'll come after you before we're ready for them to. We know they're looking for you—they have been since you were born, and we're super lucky you've stayed hidden for so long. We can handle this. I promise. We've been preparing for it just as long as you have." She looked down at her watch. "I gotta get going. Michael is taking Zane and me home to my parents for a couple days. Dad has been working on where these Cambion are and helping develop a plan, so we're going to work with him for a day or two before we get started." She hugged both women. "Let's still check in once a week. I need to know you're both safe, okay?"

Amaya nodded. "I'll be the relay. Both of you can call me, that way there's no risk of you two getting found out by calling each other. It's safer that way."

Zeke grinned. "Look who's finally learning!" She picked up one of Lux's bags. "I'll help you down the steps."

Before either woman could take a step toward the door, a knock sounded. Amaya reached out and turned the doorknob, pulling it open to reveal Dev. He looked between the three of them and smiled.

"I always feel like I'm walking in just as I'm the butt of some joke with the three of you. It's like some secret, girls only club."

Amaya laughed and waved him in. "This time the fears are unfounded. Lux is getting ready to leave. What's up?"

Dev stuffed his hands in his pockets. "I was actually just checking to see when Zeke would be ready." He grinned lopsidedly at Zeke before looking back at Amaya. "I feel like you're the gatekeeper, keeping people away from the other two. It's a very unpleasant sensation."

Amaya grinned. "I'm the oldest. It makes me protective of them." She patted his arm. "I'll help Lux downstairs. You figure out when you're leaving, and I'll be back in a couple minutes."

Dev didn't speak until the other two women had left the room. "I feel like she's very scary when she wants to be."

Zeke lifted one eyebrow. "You're scared of Amaya? She's half your size."

"Just because I'm big doesn't mean she isn't scary. That is a woman who could kick my ass if she wanted to. I know what powers Deacon has, and she's supposed to be just like him. It's scary shit. I didn't get to know her very well when she was here before, but she always intimidated me."

"We're pretty badass, too." She turned to continue stuffing clothing into her bag. "Are you packed and ready to go?"

He nodded. "I've been ready for hours. I just wasn't sure how long you needed or if you'd talked to Michael about a timeline. I've learned pretty quickly not to rush a woman. Carys made sure we all got that lesson early on."

Zeke zipped up the bag and sat down on the bed. "Has anyone ever told you that you're strange?"

Dev cocked his eyebrows at her. "What do you mean by strange?"

"I don't mean it in a bad way. I mean that you're weird. You've got this odd mix of boyish charm, manwhore tendencies, and smoothness going on that's hard for me to deal with. I don't quite know what to expect from you or if you're serious or not."

He crossed his arms and stared at her intently. "I really want to be offended by that statement, but I'm pretty sure it's a lopsided compliment, so I won't be." He shook his head slowly. "You'll know when I'm serious. We live in a serious world, and I've found the only way to be even marginally happy in it is to make light of things you can. I like to joke and to have fun, but I don't let it get in the way of what needs doing. I like women and make no apologies for that. I don't like an empty bed, but I have one more often than not because I don't like being with someone just for the sake of sex. As far as being smooth and charming, well, that's just my natural state of being." He grinned at her. "I can't help it."

Zeke shook her head and retrieved her coat from the closet. "I'm sure you could if you wanted to." She pulled on the coat and buttoned it slowly. "I think we should have some ground rules before we go. I know we're masquerading as a couple, so I fully accept there's going to be physical contact on a fairly routine basis. I don't want us to get caught up in that and make mistakes, so I think we need to have separate rooms and I think there needs to be a no touching rule when we're alone."

Dev wiggled his eyebrows. "Afraid you won't be able to stop touching me if we keep it up when we're alone?"

She nodded. "Frankly, yes. I think the other night proved there's some chemistry, and it would be all too easy to let ourselves get wrapped up. All that would end up doing is making us weaker and more likely to get sloppy. Because I don't want to do that, I think it makes the most sense for us to agree right now we will not have sex with one another. I know you're a guy, and by your own admission you like women, so I won't mind if you find an outlet for any stray horniness so long as it's done discreetly and if I need to do the same, then I will. Is that something we can agree on?"

"I feel like we're in the seventeenth century and working out the terms of an arranged marriage." He sighed deeply and shook his head. "I'm not some grope-monster, Zeke. I can deal without sex for weeks—months if I have to. I'm not going to touch you if you don't want to be touched, and I certainly don't need your permission for a one night stand. I'm not going to do anything to jeopardize either one of us or the mission, and I think if we, as two consenting adults, make a choice to explore anything, then we should be mature enough to do so without risking our job. I know I can." He grinned. "The one statement with some merit is that there was some chemistry the other night. That's something we'll either deal with, or we won't, but it'll be because we want to, not because of some artificial rules you're imposing on things."

Zeke shrugged. "You know where I stand on it. Whether or not you agree doesn't really matter." She wrapped a scarf around her neck and picked up her bags. "Let's get going. We've got a lot to get done."

CHAPTER FIVE

January 11th, 2060 – Los Angeles, California

ZEKE RAN her hands over the thighs of her slacks nervously as she looked around the house Gage had secured for her and Dev. Her heeled boots clicked on the polished wood floors, and all around her chrome and granite gleamed in the soft lamplight.

"In almost every other part of the world, people are running for the sewers and subway tunnels trying to stay safe for the night, but here, everyone sits around sipping wine and watching television." She glared at the set anchored to the wall. "Don't these people know television shows haven't been filmed since I was two?"

Dev glanced up from the fireplace where he was building a fire. "They don't care. You know as well as I do when societies started falling there were some very adaptable humans who took advantage of the opportunities they had. Instead of running and hiding, they joined with Lucifer. Now the rest of us get to struggle to eat, and these fucking people get to live like nothing has changed since before the Choosing."

Zeke ran her hands through her hair, scowling when her fingers tangled in the curls. "At least they'll burn in Hell someday. We can take some comfort in knowing they'll get what's coming to them."

"That'll only happen if we win. If Lucifer wins, these people will be in Heaven and we'll be the ones burning."

"We won't let him win." She stalked into the kitchen and opened the fridge, groaning at the array of fresh vegetables and meats. "Jesus fucking Christ, this had to have cost more than most people make in a year."

"Gage has a lot of money, even now. So does Braxton, and you know they're using it to fund this." Dev climbed to his feet and brushed dirt from the wood off on his pants. "Don't think about it too much. We need to at least look like we're comfortable with this even if we're really not. We can't let people know this is the first time in years we've seen stuff like this." He pulled out an apple and took a bite. "Michael does pretty good making sure we have what we need, but when we're out on missions, it's rare we get anything not in a can. A lot of people do worse."

Zeke uncorked a bottle of wine and poured a glass before curling up on the couch and staring into the fire. "My parents have told me stories about how it was before they went back in time. We're about twenty-five years give or take from when they got pulled back. Most cities were underground. More than there are now, and the ones topside were either ruled by demons and vampires or they were practically ghost towns. We're not far off from the time they left. People were starving to death, food was hard to find, and it was dangerous to be on the surface during the day, let alone at night."

Dev sat next to her. "It's that dangerous now. Their reality is here. The only people up top are demons, vampires, and the humans who work for them. There are a few places like this, where humans worship Lucifer and get rewarded for it, but even here there's a price. From what I know, most humans have to work for the demons, feed the vampires, or do something to make themselves useful. Other than that, unless you're a hooker or a drug dealer, most people live underground or in hiding." He stretched his arm across the back of the couch. "You know there's no telling what we might be asked to do here."

"I know." Her voice was small and soft. "We'll have to do it, no matter what it is."

"Yeah, I know that, too." He sighed deeply. "No use being morose about it now. I'm going to make some dinner. Are you hungry?"

Zeke nodded. "I could eat." She stood. "I'm going to go unpack and change out of these fancy clothes. I should at least be able to wear my own pajamas without offending anyone. I'll make sure your room is set up while I'm up there."

"Thanks."

She ascended the stairs slowly, the sound of her heels on each step echoing through the house. Annoyed, she stopped at the top and pulled off the boots, holding them in one hand as she padded down the hall in her socks.

The master bedroom contained a king sized bed piled high with brightly colored pillows, a dresser, armoire, and a sitting area. It was the largest bedroom Zeke had ever seen. The closet contained all of the shoes and clothes Michael had had made, and the bathroom held both a shower and a bathtub.

Whistling softly, she ran her hand over the marble countertop and idly toyed with the various bottles of lotions and soaps on the sink. Shaking her head in amazement at the luxury of everything, she stripped off her clothes and stepped into the shower, smiling when the water turned warm almost immediately.

Efficiently, she scrubbed her body and hair. Stepping out, she snagged two towels from the rack. Humming under her breath as she wrapped them around herself she walked into the bedroom, she hefted her duffel bag onto the bed and unzipped it, already looking forward to burrowing into a sweatshirt and yoga pants.

Instead of the pajamas she had packed, she found silk slips, satin pajama sets and lacy lingerie. Surprised, she emptied the bag out onto the bed, pawing through it, hoping against hope she would find anything inside that was hers.

"Dev!"

Zeke stood with her hands on her hips, listening to Dev's footsteps on the stairs as he ran up them. He swung into the room and skidded to a stop when he saw her in the towel.

"What's wrong?"

"Did you do this?" She pointed to the piles of clothing, leveling an accusatory glare at him.

Dev lifted his eyebrows. "Why the hell would I pack girly nightclothes? I certainly don't wear nighties." He crossed his arms over his chest. "I'm going to guess your pajamas have gone missing?"

"Brilliant deduction, Sherlock. What was your first clue?" She scowled at the piles. "I have nothing to wear to bed. I am not a lingerie type of girl, and I'll be damned before I prance around this house in a nightie with all these fucking neighbors so close you could spit on them."

He sighed and ran his hands through his hair. "Why do I have a feeling this conversation is going to result in you borrowing my clothes again?" He glared at her. "I hate lending out my clothes."

Zeke fought against grinning unsuccessfully. "I brought them back last time."

Grinning, he rolled his eyes. "Yeah, smelling all flowery and girl-like." He sighed again and left the room to retrieve sweatpants and a t-shirt from his duffel bag. He returned with the garments draped over one arm and handed them to her reluctantly. "This is all you get. You're just going to have to wash them frequently, because I'm not lending any more out."

"What is your obsession with not letting people borrow your stuff?"

Dev smiled sadly. "After our mother died, Denise and I were on our own for a few years. We were six when she died, and twelve when Michael found us. For those few years, we didn't have much. No food, clothes, nothing. I got pretty protective of the stuff I did have. I obviously still have issues with it."

She patted the clothes with one hand. "Well, we live together. You can come visit them anytime I'm not wearing them."

Dev grinned despite himself. "That would be weird." He reached out and wiped his thumb across her forehead. "You missed some soap."

Zeke clenched the clothes against her chest and took a half-step back to put some distance between them. "Thanks." She gestured toward the bathroom. "I'm going to get dressed now. I'll see you downstairs."

"Dinner's almost ready. Don't take too long."

Zeke ducked into the bathroom and closed the door, leaning heavily against it. Her heart pounded in her chest and a knot had formed in her stomach. She pressed her hands against it, trying to calm her nerves.

She was no stranger to chemistry. Typically, she enjoyed the feeling of sparks igniting between her and another person. Logically, she knew she had no business allowing anything to start between her and Dev. The kiss had been a nice distraction and a hint at something hot, but she was unwilling to risk their mission for a fling.

Zeke knew from experience that emotions and hormones got in the way. Shaking her head to clear the unwanted thoughts, she stepped into Dev's pants and yanked them up, tying the drawstrings to hold them to her hips. His shirt came down to the middle of her thighs and enveloped her in fabric.

She allowed herself five seconds to revel in the memory of how he had felt pressed against her the night they'd shared his bed. Zeke had never been a small woman, standing five feet ten inches and with a solid build. Men typically weren't much taller or larger, and it had been nice to be pressed against someone so much taller.

Scowling when her five allotted seconds bled into thirty, she yanked open the door and stalked down the stairs, turning at the bottom of the steps and swinging into the kitchen. Dev was at the stove, flipping hamburgers onto buns. He grinned over his shoulder when she walked in and nodded toward the island.

"I figured we could eat in here. I know you had wine earlier, but I think beer goes better with burgers, so I opened a couple. Don't worry if you don't want it. I'll drink it." He winked at her. "You look pretty damn good in my clothes, Mackenzie. I suppose if I have to share, it's only right that the borrower look as good as you do in them."

Zeke laughed and sat down, picking up the bottle to take a long drink. "I like beer. I got it a hell of a lot more than I got wine." She sniffed the air appreciatively. "Good to know you know your way around a kitchen." She laughed as he sat a plate in front of her. "I could burn water."

Dev sighed deeply. "Great. Now I have to do all the cooking too." He shook his head. "Please tell me you have some talents that will make living with you palatable?

"It's your lucky day. I am absolutely amazing at washing dishes, and my laundry skills are unrivalled."

He grinned at her over the island. "I like you. In a totally platonic, 'you're an awesome chick' kinda way."

"Don't call me a chick." She returned the grin. "I like you, too." She picked up the burger and took a bite, chewing slowly. "This is amazing."

"Told you I was a good cook."

Dev stiffened and turned, his hand clenching next to his side. Zeke recognized the movement as one that would conjure a weapon and dropped her sandwich back onto her plate, standing up and moving next to him.

"What is it?"

"Someone is coming up the sidewalk."

Zeke swore. "Can you sense what it is?"

"Not yet. I have to be able to see them before I can do that." He slowly unclenched his hand, forcing himself not to conjure a gun. "We have to be friendly. Do you want to run upstairs and change back in to the fancy clothes while I stall?"

"Do you think I should?"

"Couldn't hurt."

The doorbell rang. Zeke shook her head. "Too late now." She ran her hands through her hair and looked down at herself. "I don't even have a fucking bra on."

Dev scowled. "Thanks for the visual."

He strode through the house toward the front door. Before he got to it, he felt Zeke throw up her defensive field, blocking whomever was one the stoop from sensing they were Nephilim. He turned the deadbolt and opened the door, finding two men standing on the front step. One was obviously human, and the other had the white blonde hair and pale blue eyes so distinctive of a Cambion.

"Can I help you?"

The Cambion stepped forward and extended his hand. "We got word someone new had bought a home here. It's standard practice to meet the new residents and make sure they fit in. I'm sure you're familiar with the rules."

Dev leaned against the door frame. "I am. I also know the rules we received when we paid for the house said we have seventy-two hours to move in before we have to introduce ourselves. By my watch, we've been here about three."

"I'm not a part of the official housing committee. The work I do is more...quiet." The Cambion smiled. "I'm sure you understand we need to make sure no threats move in, and even three days is too long to allow a threat to remain here."

Zeke entered the room from the kitchen, and Dev noticed she'd managed to change into dark jeans, boots, and a sweater. "Honey, who's at the door?"

Dev stepped to the side to let the two men into the foyer. "They haven't introduced themselves yet, love."

The human laughed nervously. "I'm Greg Thompson, and this is Rafael. He's one of the Cambion leaders in our little community. He serves as the head of the church and acts almost as a Mayor around here. He's the one who approved your application to move in."

Zeke smiled as she held out her hand to each man in turn. "Such a pleasure to meet you both. Come on in. I can put on a pot of coffee or offer a glass of wine. You'll have to excuse the clutter. We've only just started moving in, and with hosting the meet and greet on Saturday, it's making for a very hectic couple days."

Rafael raked his eyes over Zeke, allowing them to linger long enough she had to resist the urge to shift from foot to foot uncomfortably. "Wine would be lovely, Mrs. Deveraux, thank you."

"Oh, please, call me Zeke. I'm much too young to be Mrs. anyone." She strode into the kitchen and returned with a tray holding four glasses, a corkscrew, a bottle of wine and a plate of cookies. "Have a seat, won't you? The furniture came with the house, so I can't promise it isn't dusty, but it looks comfortable enough."

The two men sat on the couch while Dev deftly uncorked the wine and poured glasses. Rafael sipped appraisingly and leaned forward on the couch, placing his glass on the coffee table.

"What brings you to Los Angeles?"

Dev recited their practiced story. "My wife and I lived in Hartford for the last few years since we got married. When the church there fell in a Nephilim attack, we fled with everyone else. We laid low for a few months, waiting for things to settle, and then began looking for a new home. There aren't a lot of places that could support the type of lifestyle we grew accustomed to, so L.A. was at the top of the list. Finding this house was the icing on the cake."

Zeke smiled brightly. "Finding any full house still in usable condition is so hard to do. When Dev told me about this place, I knew we had to come here. The fact that it's one of the largest churches in the world was a huge bonus for us. We've so missed being a part of worship."

Rafael clapped his hands once. "I think you'll both be happy here. We have a strong community support system. I understand from your application that you earn a living training humans to fight. Is that right?"

Dev nodded. "We owned a gym back in Hartford. It's something we'd love to start doing here if it's needed. Otherwise, I'm sure there are things we can do to be useful. My wife is an expert in martial arts, while I do pretty well with weaponry."

"Have you any experience with manufacturing?"

Zeke laid her hand on Dev's leg. "Don't let him tell you no. It was always a hobby, but he's a very good sword-smith. He has a way with steel that is just a thing of beauty." She smiled up at him. "He tries to be modest."

Rafael frowned. "There's no room for modesty here. I need to know the skills you have so I can make use of them. We're fighting a war, and there's only room for people who can be useful to me. Weaponry and training soldiers are both very nice skills I can make use of." He took another sip of wine. "You seem to have been able to do well for yourselves. A house like this didn't come cheap."

Dev squeezed Zeke's fingers. "As you just said, we have skills that are useful, and we aren't afraid to make use of them. My weapons don't come cheap, and Zeke commands quite the pretty penny for her training. We made a very nice living taking on private clients. There's still money in this world to be had, especially in the cities where the churches have settled. I expect it will be much the same here."

Rafael lifted one eyebrow. "What makes you think I was offering to pay you for your skills?"

Dev sat up straight and met the Cambion's gaze unwaveringly. "Because that's the only way you get them. This is your town, and we accept the Cambion run the show. That being said, I don't want you to think you own us because you don't. We have enough money to survive pretty damn well anywhere we go. We settled here because we want to be a part of a church and a community and because we serve the same master. I don't need you. If you need what I have to offer, then you'll pay for it, the same as everyone else. If you aren't interested, well, that's on you, not me."

Zeke shifted nervously as she felt the Cambion scanning them. She amped up her dampening to cover the scent of Nephilim and sent out a wave of compulsion, knowing it would fool the human and hoping it had some effect on Rafael. After fifteen tense seconds, Rafael grinned.

"I think you'll fit in just fine here, Mr. Deveraux." He drained his glass of wine and stood up. "We'll see you at church tomorrow night, and I'm looking forward to the dinner Saturday night. I'm sure your lovely wife is an excellent hostess."

Zeke smiled tightly and stood. "Thank you for stopping by. I'll see you out."

Rafael and Greg followed Zeke as she led them back to the front door. She held it open as they stepped outside. Before she could close it, Rafael reached out and ran his fingers through her hair, stroking them down over her cheek and resting his hand on her shoulder.

"I'm looking forward to getting to know you, Zeke. One of our biggest duties is to ensure the fight continues until the last Nephil is eradicated and the last Angel's wings ripped from their backs. In order to do that, I'm sure you know certain sacrifices have to be made by human women." He leaned forward until his nose touched her collarbone and inhaled deeply, taking in the scent of shampoo and soap. "I think I might keep you for myself."

Zeke pulled back. "I don't worship you. I'll respect you as the head of the church and the leader around here, but you don't have a right to my body just because you like what you see." She stepped away from him, putting the entry between them. "In the same way my husband doesn't work for free, I don't bed a Cambion just because he's a Cambion. I'm a married woman, and I take that seriously. I'd request you be more respectful of that. Have a nice night."

Before the shocked man could answer, she slammed the door and turned the lock, leaning against it heavily. She sensed the Cambion on the other side for several moments before she heard him retreat down the sidewalk. Only when she heard the car engine start and the sound of tires crunching the leaves on the street did she relax.

Dev appeared in the foyer. "Are you okay? You took an awfully long time to walk them out."

Zeke shuddered. "That's because our Mayor decided he had to feel me up before he left for the night. He apparently thinks he's entitled to fuck any woman in Los Angeles on top of all his other privileges."

"Did he hurt you?" Dev grabbed her arm and pulled her into the light so he could look at her, his gaze showing how concerned he was. "What did he do?"

"I'm fine. He made a pass, and I deflected it. I doubt he'll do it again." She sighed when Dev ran his hands up her arms as if looking for broken bones, amused by his concern. "Seriously, I'm okay. He sniffed me, creeped me out touching my face and basically said it was my duty to let him impregnate me with the next generation of Cambion filth." She pulled her arms free and grasped his hands in hers, stopping his inspection of her for injuries. "Dev, I'm okay. I promise."

"If he touches you again, I'll kill him. No one has the right to do that to any woman."

Zeke looked up at him, her witty retort sliding back down her throat when she saw how serious he was. She lifted her hand and placed it against his cheek. "He didn't do anything. I think he expected me to swoon and fall at his feet full of gratitude that he would find me attractive enough to fuck." She smiled when Dev's hand covered hers. "Thank you, though."

"I should have walked them out. If I had, you wouldn't have had to be groped. I'm sorry."

"You don't have anything to apologize for." She looked up at him, his head only two inches above hers in her boots. "You really are one of the good guys, aren't you?"

He chuckled and took a step back. "I try to be." He looked at her for a long moment. "We'd better go finish dinner before I do something you don't want me to do."

Zeke let him get almost to the kitchen before speaking. "Dev."

He turned. "Everything okay?"

"It's not that I don't want you to." She lifted her shoulder in a shrug. "I do. I want to. I just don't know if it's a good idea given that we have to live together and pretend to be married. I don't want what we actually feel to get mixed up with what we're pretending to feel."

Dev lifted one shoulder. "I can't make you. I wouldn't even try. If you gave me the go-ahead, I'd have you naked and under me in thirty seconds flat. I want you. I make no bones about it, and I won't apologize, but I also respect you, and you told me no, so it's no until and unless you tell me otherwise." He grinned at her. "If you ever decide to change the no to a yes, all bets are off, babe, and you aren't going to know what hit you."

Zeke shivered from the knot of desire that formed deep in her stomach. She hesitated for a beat before speaking. "What if I change the no to a maybe?"

Dev laughed. "Then we talk about what maybe means while we finish our dinner." He held out his hand to her and waited until she slipped hers into his. "You seem to really like rules, so I'll let you set them, but I'm warning you, Zeke, don't give me an opening unless you're prepared for me to take it."

CHAPTER SIX

January 12th, 2060 – Los Angeles

ZEKE TWISTED her hair on top of her head, pinning it up and letting tendrils float down to brush against her neck. The dress she wore was blood red. It draped across the front of her body, tying around her neck with thin straps and the back swooped down to just above the rise of her butt. Annoyed with the amount of skin showing, she scowled at her reflection in the mirror. The heels she wore already pinched her feet, and she knew she'd be limping home by the end of the church services.

Dev rapped lightly on the door and poked his head in. He wore all black, from his tie to his shoes, and his hair was tousled around his face, hanging just a bit too long. A scruff that would look unkempt on most men looked sharp on him. He grinned at her in the mirror and shook his head in appreciation.

"That is one hell of a dress."

"You can barely call it a dress. It's hardly fit to wear out in public." She slicked lipstick across her mouth. "Are you ready to go?"

"I've been ready for an hour. It's you that's taking forever to put crap on your face."

Zeke snorted. "You think I do this on a daily basis? It took me three tries to get it on right." She walked across the room and picked up a thick coat. "You might have to carry me home. These heels already hurt."

Dev followed her down the stairs. "Then why do you wear them?"

"Because they're the ones the stupid stylist marked that go with this dress." She pulled on her coat and tied the belt tight. "I've never been to one of these churches before. All I know is it's typically bloody and often results in an orgy, which I'm going to refuse to participate in."

He laughed. "I don't think it's going to be as dramatic as all this. You're probably right with the blood. I know there are a lot of rituals, and some sacrifices go on. I've heard stories of public rapes, murder, all sorts of things, but from what I know, most of the humans opt out of participating in that stuff. It's mostly for the demons and the Cambion." He laid a hand on her back and led her to the car. "The good thing is that this is only once a month, so with any luck, this is the only time we'll have to go through this."

Zeke slid into the car and waited until Dev was behind the wheel. He started the engine and pulled away from the curb, easing out into the narrow streets. She reached over and laid her hand on his arm.

"I don't know how much power I'll have there. We might have to participate in whatever it is they have going on tonight. I wish I could tell you I'll be able to compel them all, but that just goes for the humans."

"I can handle the humans on my own. We're in the same boat there. Our powers work on humans and most demons, but they're basically ineffective on Cambion. It's the drawback of being Nephilim."

"Lux has it easier there. She's a Nephil, but she's also a witch, and her witch powers translate to Cambion."

"I'm just grateful it works both ways, to tell you the truth. Their abilities don't work on us, so we're left to hack at each other with swords and guns." He squeezed her fingers and turned his attention back to the road. "Might as well relax a bit. It's a forty-five minute drive to the chapel."

"I'll relax on the drive home. We're about to try and pull off pretending to be Satan-worshippers. All the while I have to shield us from everyone in the room finding out we're part Angel."

Dev's lips quirked in a ghost of a smile. "When you put it like that, I think we should have had a couple drinks before we left the house."

"Fuck that. We'd need a couple bottles to calm my nerves right now." She laughed. "I'll be glad when this is over."

The building being used as a church was an old Catholic chapel in an upscale neighborhood. It was surrounded by burned out, abandoned buildings, and the air smelled of blood and gunpowder. Cars lined the parking lot and people milled about, all dressed up in gowns and suits. Some of the women wore coats over naked bodies.

Inside, the pews had been removed in favor of long, low pillows. The walls, carpet and draperies were all dark red. At the front of the building was a deep wooden altar and a tall cross that went from floor to ceiling. On it was a rendering of Jesus, which had been dressed in leather and painted to resemble a clown.

Rafael was greeting people at the door, passing out goblets of wine. He wore nothing but a pair of leather pants. As Zeke walked by, he smiled at her hungrily and reached out to hug her tightly. Zeke stiffened when his arms went around her and forced herself to smile as he released her.

"We'll do your welcome ritual tonight. We're all so pleased you're here with us." He shook Dev's hand. "Nice to see you again. The service will start in about fifteen minutes. Feel free to mingle until then."

Dev helped Zeke take her coat off and hung it up on the rack. He smoothly tucked her hand into the crook of his elbow and led her into the sanctuary. She ramped up her power and extended her shield to make sure no one would be able to sense what they were, grateful that unless she was injured, keeping the shield intact was a natural instinct.

There were pedestals in each corner of the room, and on each pedestal was one woman, laid out completely naked and writhing as they touched themselves. Several naked women weaved through the room, carrying platters with canapés and flutes of champagne.

Zeke leaned up so her lips were pressed against Dev's ear. "This is fucking creepy."

He patted her arm reassuringly. "I don't think we've seen anything yet."

They were forced to mingle with the crowd of humans, shaking hands and exchanging pleasantries. There were several demons and a handful of Cambion in the church, though Zeke didn't think any of them were more powerful than Rafael, and even he was nowhere near the power of Alexi.

After a few minutes of small talk, Rafael glided through the crowd and climbed onto the altar, standing atop it and raising his voice so he was heard over the din.

"Welcome to our monthly worship service. This is a bigger turnout than normal, which is nice to see. Before we get started with the ceremony, there are a few announcements I'm sure you're all going to want to hear." He grinned widely and rubbed his hands together in a way that made the hair on the back of Zeke's neck rise.

She looked to Dev. "This isn't going to be good."

Rafael continued to speak. "As you all know, we're engaged in a war with the Nephilim and the Angels. It's a war that's stretched for millennia outside the view of humans and for decades here on Earth. Your God—Lucifer—wants to end that war so Earth can be a peaceful, loving place once more with him as your benevolent God. I know that's what we all want." He paused as a cheer went up from the gathered crowd. "That's what I thought." He held up his hands to quiet the group. "The unfortunate reality of war is that it requires a lot of sacrifices. Though you all have a lot of money, that's a purely human invention, and we do not require it. We don't buy what we need. We take it. Instead, we need bodies, blood, and weapons, and those things become harder and harder to find as this war goes longer."

Zeke shifted from foot to foot, a nervous knot in her stomach. Her nails bit into Dev's arm, and she looked around the room, noting the added presence of more Cambion. She tugged on his arm sharply and leaned up to whisper in his ear again.

"They've got this place surrounded. Something is about to happen here."

Dev nodded. "I know. I'm going to guess he's about to ask for volunteers."

Rafael cleared his throat. "I need everyone's complete attention for this. Lucifer is leading a siege against the Nephilim and against God. When he wins, all those who served him will be richly rewarded and all those who fought against him will be severely punished. Greater still is the reward for those who sacrifice themselves for the cause. Tonight, in churches across the world, my brethren are going to their congregations and asking the members to present fifteen vessels per church and for every remaining member to give a donation of blood, both for spell work and to feed the noble vampires who fight for us. Those waging this war require bodies to house their spirits and blood to live, and as Lucifer's followers, it is your duty to meet the needs of those fighting. I now ask you produce fifteen able-bodied men and women to house demon spirits."

The crowd again cheered, and many people raised their hands. Rafael's face lit up when he saw how many volunteered, and he gestured to the Cambion on the edges of the room. They moved forward into the crowd and selected fifteen people, pulling them out of the congregation and to the front of the room. Rafael jumped down from the altar and went to each of them, touching their heads and murmuring to each in turn before raising his voice so everyone could hear.

"Your brothers and sisters will leave at dawn to join the ranks of our demonic warriors. Tonight, to celebrate their sacrifice and willingness to serve, we shall have a special ceremony. Remember, before you leave tonight, everyone is required to give a donation of blood." He held up his hand and gestured to someone out of sight.

Two demons came through the back, a young girl sandwiched between them. Zeke felt her heart clench in her chest. The girl was no more than twenty and wore a red cloak. Her feet were bare, and Zeke knew from the way the edges of the cloak fell away that she was bare beneath it.

The demons pulled the woman up onto the altar. Rafael reached out and pulled the strings on the cloak, untying it and sending it falling to the floor. The girl looked out over the crowd with an expression of pride on her face. Rafael drew a slim dagger from his belt and held it up. Light glinted off the blade.

"Beatrice here has been chosen to be a sacrifice unto our Lord. By the spilling of her blood, we will worship tonight. Beatrice, do you willingly offer yourself as tribute to Lucifer, our Lord and Savior?"

The girl jutted her chin forward. "I do."

Zeke took a step forward, the expression on her face clearly telling Dev her intent was to stop the sacrifice from happening. He grabbed her arm and pulled her back, anchoring her to his side with one arm. He stooped to press his mouth to her ear then changed his mind and pressed into her brain, his voice filling her head.

"Don't you dare. If we interfere, we expose ourselves. They'll expect we'll have seen this happen a dozen times. You know they do human sacrifices when they're taking volunteers for possession."

"She's just a kid." Zeke fought the urge to kick Dev in order to get free. "She doesn't know any better."

"That's not for us to judge. We can't get involved in this. Our mission is more important than her life. I know you don't like it, but it is. We knew we'd have to do hard things, and this is just the first of them. You need to watch this, and you need to look like it makes you happy."

Rafael spoke again. "Beatrice, having given your life in willing tribute to Lucifer, I hereby bless you. Your reward in Hell will be great." He reached out and touched her forehead. "Go in peace, daughter."

Rafael grabbed the girl's hair and used it to yank her head back, exposing her throat. He slashed once with the dagger, ripping into her skin and opening up the slender column of her throat.

Blood poured out, thick and dark. One of the other Cambion held out a goblet, filling it with the dark red liquid. Six more goblets were filled in rapid succession, then placed on the altar. Blood ran down the girl's body, pooling on the floor and slowly dripping down the steps. A cheer went up from the crowd as the body was carried to a platform and laid upon it. Rafael held up his hands to quiet them.

"To finish the celebration, we are going to welcome our newcomers. They will each perform the ceremony of dedication. We're privileged to have three new couples joining our ranks. Would the Deverauxs, Christians, and Harrisons please make your way to the front of the church?"

Dev gripped Zeke's arm firmly in one hand and led her through the crowd, weaving his way to the front. Two other couples, one a young couple likely in their early twenties and the other likely in their mid-forties, also came forward. They stood shoulder to shoulder in front of the altar, the slowly thickening blood from Beatrice' death under their feet.

Rafael handed each of them one of the goblets. "Take the goblet and see in it the blood of a virgin. Pure and clean, she gave her life to bless this service. We will honor that sacrifice tonight. Each of you, disrobe to the waist."

Dev took both cups and placed them on the altar. He quickly unbuttoned his shirt and stripped it off, draping it over the railing. Zeke slowly turned to allow him to untie the straps to her dress. She folded her arms across her breasts when the garment dropped to her hips, looking uncomfortable.

Rafael leered at her, obviously enjoying the sight of her bare skin. "Each of you will place on the other the symbols declaring yourself to be the son or daughter of Lucifer." He spread his arms wide. "You may begin."

Dev pressed into Zeke's mind. "Try not to wince when we do this. Drawing the sign of Satan on a Nephil will burn like hell."

"I know. I can handle pain."

Zeke picked up one of the cups and dipped her fingers into the warm liquid. She drew her fingers across the broad planes of Dev's chest, drawing the symbols indicative of Satanic worship. She felt his skin heat under her fingers, and she saw pain in his eyes.

When she was done, she had to fight not to close her eyes in meager defense against the pain and humiliation of being marked with the symbol of the one being she had been created to fight against.

Dev picked up the cup and wet his fingers in blood, quickly drawing the symbols across her chest. Her skin burned from the contact, and pain speared through her. It took all of her power and concentration not to allow tears to well in her eyes so great was the burning. As the burning increased, so did the focus required to keep their shield intact.

Rafael watched carefully as all six people marked themselves. Once the symbols were completely drawn, he reached out and took the goblets from Dev and Zeke, holding them up for everyone to see.

"I hereby anoint you with the blood of the innocent, given in reverence to our Lord, Lucifer. Welcome to our church."

He tipped the cups and spilled blood onto their heads. It ran down their faces and backs, tinging their skin and mingling with the blood smeared across their chests from the symbols. Zeke bit her tongue to keep from gagging as it ran into her mouth. She had to blink rapidly to keep it out of her eyes. Dev stood stoically, neither moving nor reacting to the ritual.

Rafael repeated the motions twice more with the other two couples, who eagerly accepted it. One woman even lapped at the blood, drinking it as it ran down her face. Zeke nearly retched.

Rafael laid his hand on each of their heads for a moment before addressing the entire congregation. "Lucifer bless each of you. Tonight's worship is complete. Feel free to stay and mingle for as long as you like. We'll reconvene next month."

As soon as Rafael dismissed them, Zeke laid her hands over her breasts, shielding them from view. Dev tied the straps back around her neck and took her arm in his, leading her through the crowd. Several times they were stopped as people waylaid them to introduce themselves and talk. Zeke forced herself to be polite, smiling and exchanging pleasantries with the myriad of people.

The Cambion had set up blood donation centers in the foyer. They were stopped on their way out the door and guided to seats. The collection process was relatively painless, involving a needle and twenty minutes of waiting for the blood to collect in the bags. There was a crowd gathered waiting to donate, and several more people stopped them to chat. After ten more excruciatingly tense minutes, they made it to the coat rack. She gratefully wrapped herself in her coat and eagerly followed Dev out the door and into the parking lot. Neither of them spoke until they were securely locked in the car.

"That was fucking disgusting."

Dev barked a laugh and started the engine. "I concur." He looked sideways at her. "Are you okay?"

"My chest hurts, I need a bath, and I'm still pissed we couldn't help that girl, but yeah, I'm okay." She looked over at him, meeting his gaze. "What about you?"

"Feeling about the same." He put the car into gear. "Let's get home, hmm? We both need showers and some clean clothes. I think a few drinks are probably warranted, too. This has been one hell of a night, but I think it went pretty well. I don't think anyone suspects what we are. You did an awesome job keeping the shield up for the whole time."

"Practice makes perfect. I'm used to keeping it up all the time. It's what allows me to go out in public." She sighed deeply and leaned her head back against the seat. "Thank you for stopping me. I almost did something very stupid."

"I know." He patted her leg. "That's what I'm here for."

CHAPTER SEVEN

January 17th, 2060 – Los Angeles

ZEKE STOOD in the dining room, watching as the workers moved all the furniture into the basement and replaced it with chairs and long buffet tables. Four men worked in the kitchen, preparing trays of appetizers and desserts. All around the room, buckets of ice chilled bottles of champagne and white wine. Every available surface was covered with crystal wine glasses and flutes.

Dev loped down the stairs, dressed in a sleek black suit with a silver tie. His hair was slicked back from his face, and he was completely clean shaven for the first time since before meeting Zeke. She studied him with an appraising eye as he approached and blushed when he wiggled his eyebrows suggestively.

"I look damn good in a suit if I do say so myself."

Zeke rolled her eyes. "You clean up pretty good." She looked around the room, taking stock of the flurry of activity. "I need to go get ready. Can you handle this from here?" She gestured to her hair, which was held up with pink rollers. "They called me down an hour ago when I had just gotten these in. If I don't get them out soon, I'll look like a poodle."

"Is there anything in particular I need to do?"

"Make sure they don't break anything." She started up the stairs and turned halfway up. "If any guests start arriving before I get back down, make sure the waiters bring out wine and food. If we get them drunk, they won't notice the hostess is missing."

Dev held two fingers to his forehead in a mock salute. "Yes, ma'am."

Zeke wrinkled her nose and dashed up the stairs. She carefully shut the door to her room and locked it to ensure no wandering wait staff stumbled in. Muttering under her breath about needing to have the party in the first place, she hastily unwound her curlers. Carefully, she twisted the curls into a messy up-do, allowing several tendrils to frame her face.

Scowling at the makeup on the counter, she applied it quickly, rubbing foundation into her cheeks, lining her eyes with black liner and applying both blush and mascara. Satisfied, she slicked a coat of gloss onto her mouth and stripped off her clothes, walking to her closet in nothing other than a pair of underwear.

She perused the contents of the closet with a wary gaze, completely unsure as to what her guests would arrive wearing. Shrugging, she crammed her hand into the closet and yanked out the first thing she touched.

The garment was forest green and covered her from neck to toes in a sheath. It fastened around her neck with a jeweled collar and bared her entire back. There was a thin band of elastic that held the back to her body.

Giving herself a critical look in the mirror, Zeke smiled tensely and stepped into her heels. Wincing as they pinched her feet, she stooped to tug at the leather, hoping to make a bit more room. Giving up on making the shoes comfortable, she spritzed perfume on her neck and wrists and left the room, pulling the door shut behind her.

She heard the bustle of people downstairs before she reached the steps. As she came to the top, she saw several guests mingling in the foyer, all holding glasses of wine or champagne as waiters moved through the crowd smoothly. Dev stood at the bottom of the steps, talking to two other men about guns.

He turned and grinned when he caught sight of Zeke. He watched her descend the stairs with a glint of appreciation in his eyes. Zeke met them with her own—rich, liquid brown locking onto bright green. She stepped down onto the next step and a shallow squeal escaped her lips when she tripped on the hem of her dress and toppled.

Dev took three steps in one hop and grabbed her around the waist, righting her and helping her down the last few stairs. He brushed loose hair from her face and smiled down at her, his gaze swimming with good humor.

"Be more careful. Next time I might not be standing near enough to catch you."

She glared up at him. "I'll keep that in mind." She tucked her hand into the crook of his arm. "How many people are here?"

"About a dozen. All human." His voice was little more than a whisper, and he nodded at a man in greeting as he passed by. "You look phenomenal in that dress, by the way. You have the most delectable set of shoulders I've ever seen in my entire life." He leaned in closer. "How are you hiding your protection tattoos?"

She looked up at him, blinking in surprise. "I don't have any. Nephilim can't be possessed." She cocked her head. "Do you have them?"

He shook his head. "A lot of the others do. It makes them feel better. I guess I just assumed. I meant to ask the night we went to church, but it slipped my mind with everything else going on." He sighed as the doorbell rang. "How long do we have to entertain these assholes?"

Zeke giggled and let him guide her toward the door to answer it. "As long as they want to stay, I suppose. This is part of the job, so we'll do it. No matter how badly the shoes hurt."

By nine, her feet were cramping. She greeted her guests, nibbled on appetizers and allowed several of her neighbors to awkwardly dance with her. By eleven, there were a dozen Cambion in the house, and keeping her shields up to cover both herself and Dev was taking a toll on her. There was a sharp pain behind her eyes, and she could feel her energy beginning to wane.

Seeming to know something was wrong, Dev smoothly appeared next to her and slipped his arm around her waist. She jumped slightly and offered a slight smile to the women she had been talking to.

"Excuse me for a minute. I'm sorry." She let Dev lead her away from the crowd and into the pantry. Lifting her eyebrows as he shut the door, she folded her arms. "What's going on?"

"I can feel the shield slipping. I don't think anyone else has noticed, but I can tell. What can I do?"

Zeke rubbed her temples. "Stay closer to me. The closer you are, the easier it is to keep it strong. There have been people here since early this morning, and I've had to cover the whole house for going on twelve hours. It's taking a lot out of me."

"I can do that. How close? Ten feet? Five?"

Zeke closed her eyes and picked one foot up off the ground to give it some relief from the pain of the heels. "Five would be good."

Zeke cocked her head, her ears picking up a slight noise outside the door. She opened her mouth to speak, but Dev cut her off, pressing one finger against her lips, his eyes darting toward the door as he tried to detect who was approaching.

"I'm sorry in advance, but you're gonna need to play along here or we're both going to be in trouble."

Before Zeke could answer, he hauled her against him and clamped his mouth over hers. His arms crushed her body to his, and his tongue swept into her mouth. Her words slid back down her throat, and she sagged against him, the erotic onslaught of his mouth shutting down every logical thought in her brain as she struggled to maintain focus on her shield.

Of their own accord, her arms wrapped around his neck, and she pressed herself against him. Before the kiss could go any further, the door flew open, revealing Rafael on the other side. Dev and Zeke sprang apart, Zeke's mouth swollen and red and Dev wearing a sheen of her lip gloss. Rafael lifted one eyebrow and smirked.

"So this is where you ran off to. Some of the guests are leaving. It would be nice if the hosts were there to see them off."

Dev wiped his mouth and grinned. "Dude, if your wife was wearing a dress like that, you wouldn't be able to keep your hands off of her, either."

Rafael's lips twitched into a smile. "You've got me there. You have a lovely wife." He clapped Dev on the back, grinning. "I'll see off the guests until you straighten yourselves up. Next time, maybe sate the desires before or after the guests."

Zeke nodded sheepishly. "Sorry."

"No need to apologize." He reached out and ran his knuckles down her cheek. "If you were mine, I'd have had you on the floor instead of merely slipping away for a kiss."

Dev didn't speak until the door was shut and he'd heard Rafael's footsteps retreat back down the hall. "I'm going to rip his head off with my bare hands." He gently wiped a smudge of gloss from her face. "No one has a right to talk to a woman that way."

Zeke's heart fluttered in her chest. "Thanks for the rescue." She leaned up and brushed a kiss over his lips before opening the door. "Let's go get these guests gone."

He followed her from the pantry and back in through the living room. Together, they stood by the door as people trickled out. Finally, after another hour, everyone was gone aside from the wait staff.

Zeke slammed the door, and turned the lock and the deadbolt before hopping on each foot in turn to take her shoes off. She dropped the heels on the floor and stood on one foot to rub the other, moaning softly as her cramping muscles released. Dev shrugged off his suit jacket and loosened his tie.

"Are your feet hurting that badly?"

She glared at him. "You have no fucking idea." She glanced around at the half dozen people carting around trays of dirty dishes. "How long will the clean-up take?"

"An hour or so, I'd imagine." He unbuttoned the top two buttons of his shirt. "I can finish up down here if you want to go change out of the dress."

"It'll go quicker if I stay and help."

Together, they worked with the waiters collect all of the glasses and empty bottles of wine. Left-over food was placed into bowls and stored in the fridge, and the extra wine was stored in the pantry. By the time the last waiter was out the door, it was past three a.m.

Zeke walked into the living room and looked around the empty space. "Please tell me the people who removed all our furniture are coming to put it back."

Dev laughed. "They'll be here around noon." He held out his hand to her. "Come here."

Zeke lifted her eyebrows. "Why?"

He snapped his fingers and soft music filled the room. "Doesn't seem fair that the only person here tonight who didn't get to dance with you is your pretend husband." He grinned when she placed her hand into his. "Besides, I have to work on changing the no to a maybe, and I can't do that if you won't ever let me do anything romantic."

She couldn't help the smile that curved her lips. Letting him guide her into his arms, she brought one arm up to rest on his shoulder. "You're determined. I'll give you that."

Dev placed one hand on her waist and swayed slowly. He twirled her out from him and brought her back, holding her close. Gently, he lifted her arm and laid it around his neck. When she laid her head against his chest, he stroked his hand over her hair. Slowly, their movements became less and less until they were standing in the middle of the room, neither moving.

Dev hummed softly, his voice rich and deep, enjoying the feel of the silky strands under his fingers. Her fingers tightened in the fabric of his shirt, and she breathed deeply, letting his scent fill her head.

Zeke didn't speak for several moments. When she did, her voice was soft and shook slightly. "We haven't known each other very long." She rubbed her cheek against his shirt. "The reality is we don't know how long we're going to be here, and once this is done, the odds are good we're going to go different ways. Normally, I wouldn't have a problem with that." She ran her hand across his shoulder to the back of his neck. "I'm attracted to you. It's a struggle for me not to start ripping clothes off when we're here like this because the want is there."

Dev growled low in his throat. "You aren't really helping my resolve to let you call the shots here, darlin'."

She laughed softly. "That's not my intent. My point is I don't want to go that way because I'm afraid you could end up being important, and when people become important in this world, they become a weakness. I don't want you to be something someone could use against me. I don't want to be something that can be used against you."

"Not letting people be important makes for an awfully lonely life. It's not one I want." He cupped her face in one hand and tipped her head back so he was looking down at her. "I'm not asking you to marry me or something. I'm asking you to take the damn padlock off and open the door."

Zeke again rested her head on his chest, her heart pounding in her chest. "Do you want me to be honest with you?"

"I always want you to be honest, even if it's not what I want to hear."

"I want to kiss you. I want to get my hands and mouth on every inch of you, and I don't want to stop until we're both satisfied. That's what I want. I feel like this is dangerous, like it could endanger both our lives, and honestly, I feel like you're trying to work me around to seeing it your way without trying to see it mine." She sighed deeply.

"I'm sorry I kissed you earlier, but it was the only thing I could think of. If we're going to do anything, I want it to be because you want to not because you feel I'm pushing you."

"This isn't about earlier. It was necessary, and it took the heat off of why we were in there."

Dev stepped back, releasing her and retreating to stand against the wall, studying her intently. "I never want you to feel pressured, so if I'm doing that, I'm sorry. I'll try to do better with letting you set the boundaries. I'm not used to things being this hard, I don't quite understand why they have to be, and I'm struggling because I am so attracted to you. I don't mean to be pushy." He grinned lopsidedly. "I never want you to think I'm the same as Rafael. I'm sorry if I did anything to cause you to think that way."

"You're not. Rafael is creepy and gross, and when I'm around him, I get the feeling he would act on what he wants. I know you well enough to know you wouldn't, but I need you to let me take the lead here." She threw up her hands in frustration and paced in front of him. "I'm sorry it's not what you're used to, but it's what I need. I don't know how to handle you."

Dev sighed. "You don't have to handle me. I'm a straightforward guy. There aren't any tricks with me. What you see is what you get. No secrets, no traps, nothing. I don't play games. I want you. If you want to go slow, I can do slow. If you want to go fast, well, I'm a strong guy, and I can carry you up those stairs pretty damn fast. If you don't want to at all, then tell me and I'll back off completely, but if you do, I am asking you not to be scared of me. I'll be gentle with you." He strode across the room to stand in front of her, reached out to tuck her hair behind her ears and grinned down at her. "Do you want this?"

"If it were simple, yes, I want it. That's not the problem." She pressed her face against his chest. "It's not you." She sighed and pulled back. "I was with someone once. Someone important to me, and he got killed trying to protect me. I promised myself I would never put anyone else in that position. You could be important to me, too, if I let you, and it scares me."

"I can handle myself." He smiled when she tightened her grip on his arm and willingly moved back into his arms. "Let's go slow. We'll see how it goes."

Zeke tipped her head back to look up at him. "I'll give you the maybe, but I need some time to work my head around this. I want you. Badly. All the talk about hands and mouth and carrying me upstairs is hot as hell, and there's not a thing in the world I want more than to say yes to every bit of it, but I need a little time to figure out what I can give you. Can you do me that?"

"Take all the time you need. If we go to bed together, I want your eyes wide open and all cards on the table."

Zeke studied him intently. "I have this internal struggle between what I want to do and what I should do."

"Then take some time and figure it out." He stepped back, his hands up. "I'll be here when you do."

She nodded slightly and turned toward the stairs, stepping up onto the first one. Halfway up, she glanced back over her shoulder and saw Dev still standing at the bottom, watching her walk away. His bowtie was loose around his neck, and he'd unbuttoned the top two buttons on his shirt. Her stomach knotted with nervousness and desire as she studied him, her throat tight. In an effort to alleviate the itchiness in her palms, she rubbed them across her thighs.

"Fuck it. One kiss never hurt anything."

She lifted the skirt on her dress slightly and loped back down the stairs, striding purposefully over to Dev and wrapping her arms around his neck, pressing her body firmly against his.

"Tonight, what I want wins. I want you to kiss me, and I want you to make it count."

Dev's mouth was firm and warm when he captured hers. He nibbled at her lips gently, teasing her with the tip of his tongue before sliding it between her lips and sinking into her mouth. His flavor, spicy and rich, flooded her as she opened her mouth to deepen the embrace.

He cupped her face in one hand and the other slid from her shoulder to her hip, kneading the flesh there gently. When she groaned and her eyes drifted closed, Dev pulled her closer, pressing her harder against his body.

Her hands came up and slipped into his hair, sliding through the strands and gripping firmly. She returned his kiss eagerly, her mouth hot and hungry on his. Lowering her arms from his neck, she gripped his hands, moving them from her waist to her ass.

With a groan, Dev slid his hand down slightly farther and gripped her thigh, pulling her leg up. Zeke braced her hands on his shoulders and lifted the other foot off the ground, locking both her legs around his waist. He stooped slightly and wrapped one arm around her bottom to balance her, taking four steps to press her against the wall, pinning her to it so his hands were free.

She reached behind her neck and unclasped the collar to her

dress, tugging the fabric down to expose her breasts. Grabbing his hands in her own, she lifted them, placing them on her flesh, goosebumps rising on her skin from the cool air on her naked form.

"Touch me. I want you to." Her voice was raspy and deep when she spoke, and she pressed his hands to her more firmly, accentuating her demand.

Dev dipped his head to lay his lips against her neck, the salty tang of her skin erupting on his tongue as he tasted her. Zeke's head fell back, and she arched her body, pressing herself against him. Her hips jerked against his, and they both groaned when his hardness pressed firmly against her. She removed her hands from on top of his and twined her fingers through his hair, tugging sharply and directing him toward her breasts

Dev lifted one of her breasts in his hand and dipped his head to suck the tip into his mouth. Her hand rested on the side of his face. He rubbed his tongue over her nipple, sucking deeply and nipping lightly with his teeth. Zeke groaned loudly and moved her hips against his, rubbing herself on him, driving them both wild. Zeke's hands dropped to his shoulders, and she clasped his shirt, wrapping her fingers in the fabric and closing her eyes, enjoying the onslaught of emotions rolling through her.

Breathing heavily, Dev yanked back and pressed his face to her neck, his hands on the wall to keep himself from continuing to touch her. Zeke groaned in protest at the loss of his touch, and her head fell forward onto his shoulder. Panting, he placed her on her feet and took a step back, straightening her dress to cover her chest.

"If we don't stop, we aren't going to be able to." He stroked his hand down her cheek. "I can't keep touching you, Zeke, or we're going to do something you might regret later."

Zeke nodded, her skin still flushed. "I'm glad one of us was thinking straight." She clutched the top of her dress to her throat. "I'm going to go up to bed. I think being in separate rooms right now is the best way to be good."

Dev nodded. "Yeah. You're probably right." He stood still until she was past him and halfway up the stairs. "Goodnight."

She paused at the top and looked back down at him. "Night."

Chapter Eight

January 23rd, 2060 – Los Angeles

Zeke knew the moment she opened her eyes that something bad was going to happen. She lay in the dark for several minutes trying to put her finger on what precisely the bade thing was before tossing back the blankets and rolling out of bed. The sky outside was still dim, with only hints of light beginning to peak over the horizon. She scowled at the sky as she dressed.

The house was still as she made her way down the hall and steps. Walking into the kitchen, she paused to push the button on the coffee pot. Before she could take another step, the sound of wings fluttering filled the room and a blast of white light blinded her.

Gabriel stood in the room, pristine in his white suit and a look of concern on his face. Zeke whirled to face him, a mixture of fear and anger in her expression.

"What the hell are you doing here? You know this whole fucking city is Cambion central. Someone could have sensed you popping in and you could have just blown our cover!" She jabbed her finger into his shoulder. "Are you trying to get us both killed?"

"I was not sensed. I am much too powerful to be found out by a mere Cambion, and there are no high ranking Devils within range. I am not stupid, child. I have a situation I wish to speak to you and your partner about. Would you please wake Dev?" Gabriel dismissed her concern with a flick of his wings and stared at her blankly, clearly expecting immediate obedience.

Zeke tossed up her hands in frustration. "Sure. Whatever. I love to be bossed around by Archangels. Totally making my day here, Gabriel." She stomped up the stairs and pushed Dev's door open. "Wake up. Gabriel is here."

Dev sat up blinking. "What? Did he pop in?"

"No. He escaped from the dungeon Amaya's keeping him chained in." When he blinked at her in sleepy confusion, she sighed and continued. "Yes he damn well popped in."

Trying to wake up, Dev scrambled from bed, yanking on clothes over his boxers. "Fucking hell, is he trying to blow our cover?"

"That's what I asked, but he swears he was careful and there's something super important going on he needs to talk to us about."

He brushed past her and took the stairs rapidly, turning into the kitchen and facing Gabriel. "What the fuck is so important that you felt it was okay to risk our lives and any chance we have at getting the sword?"

Gabriel cocked one eyebrow. "As I informed Ezekiel, I was not sensed as I came in, so both your anger and your worry are unfounded." He gestured to the kitchen table. "Please, have a seat. There is a matter I wish to discuss with you." He waited until they were both seated before continuing. "From what I know, you have both been doing an admirable job. Your determination to complete the ceremony during the abomination they refer to as church was noticed. You have both put yourselves in considerable danger, and that will be rewarded for you both. However, the time has come for me to request your assistance with another matter. One separate from the task you are currently working on."

Zeke crossed her arms. "We can't do two things, Gabe. We either work on the sword or we do something else."

Gabriel shook his head. "I don't believe that is true. Do you have any responsibilities here at the moment?"

Dev shook his head. "Not really. I conjured a few swords for them this week, and there are a dozen more coming up, but no one needs to know they only take two seconds to make. Zeke is going to start teaching a martial arts class next week. Mostly, we've just been going to the fucking parties someone is having almost every night of the week." He scowled. "You'd think the people here missed the memo that we're in the middle of a war and everywhere else in the world, to be human is to be either dead or hunted. They act like everything in the world is fine."

Gabriel joined them at the table with a cup of coffee in his hand. "To them, it is. Most of them were born after the six failed to re-chain Lucifer. Those who remember the few years all humans were hunted before these factions began to form are the ones typically the most likely to join these cults. They impress those beliefs upon their children, and the culture is advanced. They are willing to put up with almost anything in order to maintain their way of life. It's completely reprehensible, and I assure you no matter what Lucifer and the Cambion are promising them, they will burn in Hell for all of eternity."

Zeke cleared her throat. "That's all fine and dandy, but it doesn't tell us why you're here, and it doesn't tell us what you want us to do."

"Your parents have dropped out of my detection. Wherever they are, they are warded against Angels. Michael has kept an eye on them for the last three decades, and he is very concerned about their sudden absence. The Angel of Death informs us they are still alive, and there is no indication they have been captured, so we are left with the conclusion there is some reason they do not wish to be found. I suspect if there is anyone who can find them, it will be their daughter."

"How long have they been gone?"

"Three days. We only decided to come here and involve you when we could not find them through the usual means. We would have gone to Aradia, but we did not want to risk exposing their hiding place at the moment. She and Gage have found themselves in some hot water due to the mission Lux and Zane are on, and I thought it best to allow them to lie low for the time being."

Dev straightened. "What's going on with Lux and Zane? Are they okay?"

"They are fine. They are completing their mission as they must, and I will not reveal anything other than that. The less you know, the safer you will be, and I will not be the one to endanger either of you. I may not be directly involved in what is going on, but I do not wish to endure the wrath of either Alaria or Michael."

Zeke chuckled. "What do you want me to do? Find them and make sure they're okay? Or is there some particular reason I need to find them for you?"

Gabriel shifted uncomfortably. "I do not wish to be disingenuous with you. I believe Alexi is after your parents and they are in danger. Lucifer knows the children of the six are the key to his destruction, and he also knows you are all adults now. I believe he is scared of what the three of you can do. Amaya can kill him and he knows that. He is also aware the two of you are nearly as powerful as she is and that the three of you work closely together. By finding your parents and either capturing or killing them, he is ensuring you are distracted or angry. Both of those things help ensure you are not focused on our task as you should be. If you find them first and convince them to seek safety with the Angels, then you will all be much safer."

Dev tapped his fingers against the table as he considered the situation. "It could be a trap. If they're caught and the Devils are holding them, they could be using the wards to try and lure you in. I don't know if we can risk it."

Zeke glared at him. "They're my parents." She looked at Gabriel, determination in her eyes. "Of course I'll find them. What do you want me to do when I locate them?"

"Tell them they are in danger and we can help. They can be transferred to Michael's home and stay there until things are a little bit more easily handled."

"And if they say no?"

Gabriel looked pained. "Then at least I will know they are alive and can reassure my brother as to the same." He smiled at Zeke. "I do not intend to force them to remain in our protection. They have managed for nearly three decades without it, and I don't see a reason that will cease now. They are obviously capable of protecting themselves. However, Michael is exceedingly worried, and I wish to abate that worry in any way I can."

Dev sighed deeply. "In the twenty years I've known you, not once have you ever done anything that benefitted someone else. What's in this for you?"

Gabriel's gaze darkened with anger. "I don't appreciate your presumption that you have some insight into why I do things, Nephil. Until you sit at the feet of God and are tasked with carrying out His orders, you have nothing to question." He stood abruptly. "Find them or don't. I'll shed no tears if they die. These people turned their back on me and closed me out. You should be grateful I'm even willing to continue working with your group at all."

Zeke blinked rapidly as Gabriel disappeared from the room with a crack. She slid her gaze over to Dev. "What the hell was that about?"

When Dev started to tell her about Alaria and Gabriel, Zeke looked annoyed. "I know the story. He's still not over all that shit? It's been almost thirty years."

"Which is nothing when you live forever." He rose to pour coffee and drop pieces of bread in the toaster. "Do you have any idea where they might be?"

She smiled grimly. "They're my parents. They raised me. Do you really think they would ever go so deep I wouldn't be able to find them if I needed them?" She stood and stretched. "They have a few hidey holes they could be in. We're going to have to get there, though, which is what's going to take the most time unless we can get someone to flash us."

Dev handed her a cup of coffee. "I'll see if I can get ahold of Carys. Make me a list of the places we need to check."

"Is it safe for her to come in here?"

"She won't be. We'll have to get out of range before she can flash in, but once we are, it'll make things a hell of a lot easier."

"She can't go check them without me there. Mom and Dad would not appreciate that at all."

"I'm not going to send her to look for them without you. From what I know of Damon and Greer, they'd likely shoot her, and that would just piss her off." He handed her a plate with two slices of toast. "We have to let Rafael know we're going, and we'll need to make sure there's nothing left here that could hurt us."

Zeke took a bite and chewed slowly. "Do you have a forge and such all set up?"

"In the backyard. Molds, tools, the pit. It's all set up."

"The basement is set up for classes, so we should be okay." She yawned. "Can you take care of smoothing things over with Rafael? I really don't feel like dealing with him right now to tell you the truth."

"I'll handle it. I think he likes me." Dev reached around her to open the refrigerator and pulled out a glass bottle of milk. "How long do you think we'll need to be gone?"

"Just tell him we're taking a long weekend to go visit some friends or something. Ask him to keep an eye on the house. It'll reassure him we're not hiding anything and make him less suspicious."

"Good idea." He drained his glass of milk and placed the empty cup in the sink. "We should probably leave soon. I'll make sure everything is good out back while you pack a small bag to make it convincing, and we'll leave in a few hours. I'll tell him we're going to be back Monday night."

"Works for me. I'll start getting things ready." She picked up the second piece of toast. "How are you going to keep him from realizing what you are if I'm not with you?"

Dev grinned. "I can manage for five minutes with the man. Unless he's suspicious, he isn't going to be scanning me. I have powers of telecoercion. I can make humans think what I want them to think. It's not really effective on some Cambion because of the Devil in them, but I'd be willing to bet Rafael is half-demon, which means I can influence him. I'll be all right. It's just if I'm with a lot of them or with one for an extended period of time that I get into trouble. That's why they sent me with you. I'm the only one who stands a chance at not being detected when you're not around to shield me."

Zeke shrugged. "Your funeral if you're wrong."

Rafael looked surprised when Dev entered the front doors of the church. He stood and rounded the desk, offering a hand. "Dev, what a pleasant surprise. Did we have an appointment?"

Dev shook his head and clasped Rafael's hand briefly. "No, we didn't. I stopped by your office, and they told me you'd come out here to work on some things. May I sit?"

Rafael gestured to the chair. "Please." He returned to his seat and folded his hands on the desk. "What can I help you with?"

Dev laughed and crossed his legs. "Zeke has it in her head that we need some time for just the two of us. A friend from back home has a cabin up in Washington he uses to hunt. I was thinking I'd take her there for the weekend."

The Cambion leaned back, considering. "You have a lot of orders for swords. Do you think it's smart to leave with all of those pending?"

"I'm ahead of schedule on them. Four are ready now. They're in my workshop at the house, and I have the molds made for the others. I guaranteed them by next Friday, and I should easily be able to meet the deadline even with a couple days away. Zeke isn't due to start teaching her first class until Wednesday, and we'd be back Monday night. It's okay if you're not comfortable with us leaving. That's why I came to you before I mentioned the cabin to Zeke. Once that woman gets something in her head she's like a dog with a bone."

Rafael laughed and relaxed slightly. "Aren't they all?" He shrugged. "I don't see it being a problem if you're sure it won't interfere with your work. This isn't a prison camp. You technically don't need my permission to leave and go somewhere."

"I know, but we're new here yet, and the last thing I want to do is cause any problems. We've had a rough bit lately with what we went through in Hartford. There hasn't been any time to relax at all, and even though we've enjoyed it here immensely, the schedule can be grueling, and believe it or not, Zeke doesn't enjoy parties too much."

"She masks it well. She was a lovely hostess when you had your get-together. I was quite impressed."

Dev fished his keys out of his pocket. "I wanted to ask a favor while I'm here, too. I don't imagine there's much problem with crime around here, but again, we're still new, and we don't know people very well." He laid a key on the table. "I'd be much obliged if you'd keep an eye on our house while we're away."

Rafael's eyes lit up, and he slid the key across the desk. "I'd be happy to, though I don't promise your plants will still be alive when you return."

"No plants and no pets." Dev stood. "There's no alarm, and the key works both the front and the back door. My work space is in the back yard, so pay careful attention to it. I'm bringing in the swords I have completed to the basement, so they'll be down there."

"Is there a way to reach you if something happens?"

Dev laughed. "There haven't been phones in years, dude. I'm not psychic. If something happens, I trust you to deal with it until I get back." He lifted one eyebrow. "If you can't trust your town leader, who can you trust?"

Rafael grinned and stood. "Very true. I'll take care of everything. Have a safe trip, and we'll see you back here Monday night." He gestured toward the door. "I'll walk you out. When you get home, just swing by my place to grab the key."

"Will do." Dev wiggled his brows. "It'll be nice to have a couple nights with nothing to do other than my wife."

The Cambion barked a laugh and slapped Dev on the back. "You're a lucky man. Zeke is lovely."

"She certainly is. I never have been able to figure out why she ended up with a guy like me." Dev unlocked the car door and opened it. "Thanks for this. I owe you one."

Rafael smiled. "Be careful owing me favors. I always collect on them."

"I wouldn't expect anything else."

Chapter Nine

January 24th, 2060 – Washington

Carys and Elisa were waiting for them when Dev pulled the car into the dark driveway. Zeke sprang from the vehicle the moment it stopped moving and slung her backpack over her shoulder. Both women went straight to Dev, embracing him tightly. Carys looked over at Zeke, emotion shining in her eyes.

"Thank you for taking care of him so far."

Zeke inclined her head slightly. "It's been a mutual undertaking." She offered Elisa a smile. "I didn't expect to see you here."

Elisa shrugged. "The way we heard it, we could be flashing into an ambush if Dev's suspicions are right that this is a trap. I figured you could use the extra muscle." She jerked her head toward the house. "We brought artillery. Come on in and make your selections."

"I don't think it's a trap. I know my parents better than that. If they were in trouble, they'd have reached out to me. With my Hunter and Healer blood, I share a psychic link with them. I don't think it's possible for them to get too far away to contact me."

Carys scowled. "Then why aren't you trying to get ahold of them them that way?"

"My link is just incoming. I can participate in conversation after it's initiated, but I don't have the ability to push into someone else's brain. I can't reach out to them without them coming to me first."

Elisa pushed past them into the house. "Well, that blows." She swept open her arms. "Let's pick guns and get this show on the road. If it's not a trap, we'll flash back to the nonplace as soon as we find Damon and Greer. Dev can call me again when you're ready to come back here."

Dev picked up a rifle and tested the weight in his hands. "One of you needs to keep an eye on this place to make sure we didn't get followed. I don't think we did, but I can't be sure. If some of the Cambion show up, run fast, get safe and flash to get us. We'll handle it from there. There's plenty of hiking trails around, so we can explain why we weren't in the house pretty easily."

Zeke strapped a serrated buck knife to her thigh and expertly donned a shoulder holster, tucking two pistols into it. She chose the sniper rifle and fastened a utility belt heavily loaded with ammunition around her hips.

Carys rolled her shoulders and ramped up her power, preparing to flash them. "Give me a location, Zeke."

Zeke considered for a long moment. "Let's try Gage's estate in Scotland."

Carys nodded and closed her eyes. "Everyone hold on."

She clapped her hands together, and with a crack, they all disappeared. Zeke grunted as her spine jerked and she stumbled a step as they reappeared in Scotland. Snow covered the ground up to her calves, and the air was thirty degrees colder than it had been in Washington.

Gage's estate was dark. Most of the windows had been broken out, and the door hung from one hinge. Zeke squared her shoulders and strode toward the house.

"Don't let the outside fool you. Aradia put up a spell that makes it look like this, but the inside is still fine. We didn't use it much, but it's a good place to hide for a few nights if you're in trouble. It's safe enough."

She lifted her hand to the door and whispered beneath her breath. All four felt the drop of wards, and they entered the house slowly.

Dust covered the furniture, but everything was preserved and undamaged. The kitchen was stocked with nonperishable food and cases of water. Blankets, coats, and firewood were piled in the living room next to the fireplace. Dev turned on a flashlight and gestured to the three women.

"Carys, you take the basement. Elisa, look around on this level. I'll take the top floor and Zeke, you check the second."

Zeke nodded and started up the stairs. "There's an attic, too."

Dev followed her. "I'll check it."

Zeke went straight to the room her parents had shared when they had lived there. Clothes still hung in the closet, and the bed was unmade, as if waiting for Damon and Greer to climb back in. It appeared as if no one had entered the manor since the night they'd had to flee after Lucifer broke out.

Each time she'd come to the estate growing up, they had stayed in the basement. The doors, walls and floors were warded, making it next to impossible for anything to get in that wasn't supposed to be there.

She'd very rarely been allowed to wander upstairs because of the increased risk of being seen by anyone watching. As an adult, once she'd left home and begun training with Lux and Amaya, Alaria and Braxton had brought them to Scotland more often to take advantage of the grounds for training. The last time she'd been there had been nearly five years earlier.

From the look of the place, no one had been there since then. She checked each room on the second floor meticulously, looking in all the hidden places before dejectedly returning to the foyer. Elisa and Carys were already there, voices hushed tones as they talked in the kitchen.

Dev appeared several seconds later, shaking his head. "Nothing. Anyone see any sign of life here?"

Elisa pushed off the island and walked over, her boots clicking on the floor. "It doesn't look like anyone has been here in years."

Carys joined them, her eyes conveying her sympathy. "It's just the first place. How many other possibilities are there?"

"Four I think are likely. If they aren't in any of these, then I can start moving to the less likely, but we get worried if they aren't at any of these five. That means they're trying not to be found by anyone. These first few are places their friends know they would go."

"What's the next stop?"

"There's a safe spot in Las Vegas. The penthouse of where Gage's casino used to be is completely disguised. You can't even see the building without knowing the spell to uncloak it. We won't be able to flash into it, and the only access is through a hatch on the roof. It's probably the most secure of the places they would go."

Elisa wrinkled her nose. "How would they get in there, then?"

"Every time I've been there, they've used the building next door, which is abandoned and burned out. There's one usable staircase inside we used to get to the roof. From there, they used a grappling hook to lock on to the wall and shimmied over it."

Dev snorted. "That's too much work. When we get there, I'll fly us in. If it's one floor, there's no use in four people going up to something that sounds like a fucking fortress."

Carys closed her eyes and let power ripple through her. "Since I don't have a clear picture of this place because I've never been there, you'll have to forgive me if we land a little off, but I'll get us close."

She reached out and touched each of them before slapping her hands together. Three seconds later, they were standing atop a pile of rubble. Frost covered the ground, though there were no trees and no grass.

Dev whistled softly as he looked around at the burned out buildings. "I've never been to Vegas."

Carys giggled and picked her way down. "I hear it's not like it used to be."

Elisa sighed deeply. "Smartass." She held her rifle loosely as she surveyed their surroundings. "Which way do we go?"

Zeke turned her head from side to side. "You got damn close, Carys. We need to go about three blocks west."

Dev shook his head. "Forget that." He pointed to a building across the remnants of what had been a street. "You two crouch in there and stay out of sight. Flash out if anything comes at you. I'll fly us in to that hatch, and we'll check it out. I'll keep in contact via psychic link if anything happens."

He stripped off his coat, followed by the Kevlar vest, and finally his thermal shirt. Bare-chested, Dev closed his eyes and concentrated on feeling the wings that he kept hidden most of the time. Deacon's wings were always present in the form of tattoos running down either side of his spine, but Dev's were buried deeper.

Slowly, the skin on his spine shifted and opened, the tips of his wings poking out. The feathers were silver, and he thrust them out, swallowing a yelp at the jolt of pain as they tore free from his body. Carys and Elisa had seen his wings before, but Zeke was staring at him slack-jawed.

Hesitantly, she lifted her hand and stroked her fingertips over the feathers, jerking her hand back as if she's expected them to cut her. Laughing, she touched again, marveling at the soft, silky feel of the feathers.

"You really do have wings. You told me that, but I didn't believe you." She pulled her hand back. "I always thought these things were weapons."

Dev laughed. "They are. One feather feels soft, but when I use them to whack people, they cut like knives." He flicked his wings. "It's fucking cold out here, Zeke, so let's get this on the road and figure out if your parents are here."

"How do we do this?"

Dev pulled her into his arms. "Just hold on." He tucked his shirt between them and wrapped one arm around her waist.

With four powerful flaps, Dev propelled them high into the air. Zeke struggled not to squeal as her feet left the ground and they soared through the air. She managed to keep her eyes open to look for the marker that would tell her where exactly the building was.

On the roof of a still-standing skyscraper a yellow star was painted. At first glance, it looked like nothing other than graffiti, since the building was covered in various shapes and words, but Zeke had seen that many times before.

Closing her eyes, she whispered the familiar words of an uncloaking spell. The air shimmered and a building appeared. The walls had been damaged, most of the windows were missing and there was graffiti all over the walls. Dev swore under his breath.

"Mother fucker, I'd have flown right into it if you hadn't done that right then."

"No. We'd have flown through it. Aradia is very powerful, and Lux is even more so. She strengthened all of these a couple years ago and improved them." She pointed. "Do you see the hatch on the roof?"

"Yeah, I've got it." He fluttered his wings to lower them until their feet were solidly on the roof. Measuring the circumference of the door, he grumbled as he retracted his wings and dragged on his shirt. "Apparently they weren't anticipating someone with wings needing to get in there."

"Actually I think it was specifically made so no one with wings could get in. It's warded against everything supernatural except for Michael."

"Then why can we get in? We're supernatural."

"We're also human, and I know the passwords. I have no clue if you could get in without me." She spun the combination lock on the door and jerked it open, sticking her hand into her pocket for a penlight.

Slowly, the light clenched between her teeth, they descended into the penthouse. Glass littered the floor, and most of the furniture had been turned up and split open. The appliances in the kitchen were missing and most of the cabinets had been yanked down, smashed to pieces on the floor.

"From what I know, when everything started getting bad, Aradia started putting up protection spells and cloaking spells on all the places she thought they might need to go and hide. By the time they got here, it had been ransacked and looted. She still put up the spells because it can still be used as a hiding place. I was only here once growing up, but the others use it from time to time."

Dev nodded toward the stairs. "I'll check up there."

Zeke frowned. "They're not here. This place hasn't been opened up in years."

"It's just the second place. I'm sure we'll find them at one of the others. Are you doing these in any particular order?"

"I thought Gage's estate was the most likely. This place and the next two were about even odds and the fifth is starting the stretch. The next place I want to go is the apartment in New York where they holed up before Gabriel took them back in time. I've never been inside it, but Mom and Dad make sure it's still there and stocked with the stuff they found so nothing will mess with the timeline. If they just needed a break for a day or two, they might go there, especially since it's nowhere near the time they'll actually go in it."

"Where are the other two places?"

"The house where I grew up in Alaska. It's in the middle of nowhere, and we never had any problems. We sometimes spent months at a time there. It's where Lux, Amaya, and I trained sometimes, too. The last is New York and the tunnels. They'd take a risk running into themselves—even though they're babies right now—but it's someplace they'd feel comfortable and where they would know their way around. From there, it's the less safe hiding spots. The places you go for a couple hours of sleep or to patch up some holes before you take off again."

"Let's assume for a minute they're just feeling uneasy and aren't in a lot of danger. Or that they needed to get away from something and lay low for a while. Where's the place where they could stay for the most time and feel comfortable?"

Zeke ran her hands through her hair. "Home. They'd have gone home."

"Then let's take you home. I think that's going to be our best bet, babe." He gestured to the ladder leading up to the hatch onto the roof.

Zeke climbed out first, waiting at the top while Dev maneuvered his shoulders through the narrow hole and climbed out onto the roof. He glared at the hatch as he fastened the lock.

"That thing was not made to accommodate men my size."

Zeke glanced back at him—the broad shoulders and chest, muscled arms and wide, slightly rough hands. "That's because there aren't many men your size out there." She shrugged. "I kinda like it, though. I'm not a small person, and you don't make me feel like some monstrosity." She chuckled as he pulled off his shirt and extended his wings. "One of these days I will break you of your obsession with protecting your clothes."

Dev grinned and wrapped his arms around her to glide them down to the streets below. "You'd be the same way if you'd gone so long not having them. I always tried to make sure Denise had what she needed, even if it meant I didn't."

"How did your sister die?"

Pain flashed across Dev's face before his gaze hardened. "I don't like to talk about it."

He flapped his wings to lift them off the roof, flying vertically for several feet before changing direction, landing outside the building where Elisa and Carys were hiding. The other two women came out from the entry way, Carys tossing Dev his vest and coat as she strode toward them. He donned them quickly before motioning to Zeke.

"Describe where we're going to her so she has an idea. I don't want to end up in the middle of nowhere."

Carys wrinkled her nose. "You two are cold as ice. Did something happen up there I should know about?"

Dev shook his head. "I'm going to do a sweep to make sure no one's seen us. Get ready to go."

Zeke shrugged helplessly. "I asked about his sister."

Elisa groaned. "Why? Why would you do that?"

Carys glared at her. "Oh, hush. She doesn't know not to ask. You can't blame someone for asking when no one told her not to." She turned to Zeke. "Denise fell in love with a Cambion. He fooled us all, Michael and Deacon included. Dev and Mason were very good friends for a couple years. They went on raids together, Mason had holiday dinners with us. There was even talk that Denise and he were going to get engaged. We were all thrilled. Then, one night, about nine or ten months ago, we were raided. A hundred Cambion warriors blasted their way in." Carys paused and looked pointedly at Zeke. "With Mason leading them. He'd been playing us all along. He killed Denise in the living room. Cut her fucking head off. Dev went crazy. He butchered the Cambion faster than any of us could help him. Mason was one of the few who managed to get away. He was a fucking coward, and Dev hasn't ever recovered from what happened. He's never said a word about it since."

Zeke laid her head in her hands. "I wish I'd have known. I never would have asked if I had."

"You can't help what you don't know, baby girl." Carys slung her arm around Zeke and squeezed. "He'll be back soon. Why don't you tell me where it is we're going to?"

Elisa grinned at the two women and winked at Carys. "Should I be jealous?"

Zeke laughed, surprising herself. "Not of me. Apparently I'm into tall, winged, and broody here lately." She leaned her head on Carys' shoulder. "With all this attitude, he'd better at least be good in bed."

Carys stroked her hand over Zeke's hair. "I'm sure Dev has a very nice penis and knows how to use it adequately. If he doesn't, I can recommend some very good toys you might like." She glanced at Elisa. "I like this one. I think we should be friends."

Elisa rolled her eyes. "Always bringing home strays. I don't know why I put up with you." She sighed deeply. "Enough kidding around, ladies. We need to have a place to go before Mr. Tall, Winged, and Broody gets back or he'll know we've been discussing him instead of doing our jobs."

Dev came out of one of the buildings shaking his head. "I knew that when I walked away." He glared at each of them. "You two, especially, forget I know you just as well as you know each other."

Zeke tried not to grin. "We're working now." She turned to Carys. "Do you have a way to look inside my brain and let me show you a picture of our house? That might be easier than trying to explain it to you. The only way in is either to hike for a few days or to flash."

"How would your parents have gotten there?"

"Mom knows enough magic to manage it. Aradia taught her

some simple spells to help out with stuff, and she has some magic since she's a Healer. She could transport them both in. She did it to us all the time when I was growing up."

Carys nodded and placed her hands on Zeke's head, forging a physical link even as she opened herself for a psychic one. "Yes, I can look into you. It's just like a psychic conversation. Just open your mind and paint me a picture of the house, the surroundings, everything you can remember. The more exact it is the less likely we are to end up somewhere in India."

Zeke nodded and concentrated on creating the picture of the house she'd lived the majority of her childhood. The roughhewn wood exterior and the large porch. The walls were raw wood, and the windows were small and dark to keep people from looking in. She vividly remembered the trees surrounding the cabin and the creek fifty yards away where she'd played as a kid.

Carys let go of Zeke's head and reached out to touch each of them. "I've got it. Hold on."

She clapped her hands together and jerked them all through space. One moment they were in Las Vegas, and within the span of a heartbeat, they stood in Alaska, outside the place Zeke always referred to as home.

She knew immediately that was where her parents were. There was a path through the snow leading from two snowmobiles to the porch. She could barely make out a fire flickering through the window.

"They're here." Relief clogging her throat, Zeke dashed up the steps and rapped on the door, bouncing anxiously as she waited for one of her parents to open it.

She heard footsteps approaching and the telltale sound of the slide on a gun. She gestured to the other three to stay back. Damon opened the door a crack, pistol in one hand. As soon as he saw her, he yanked open the door and dragged her in for a hug.

"What the hell are you doing here?"

Zeke pulled back. "I'm happy to see you, too. Where's Mom?"

Greer appeared at the door, a robe over her pajamas. "I'm right here. Zeke? Oh, baby, is everything okay?" She reached out to touch Zeke's face, her eyes moving past her daughter to the others. "Who are your friends?"

"Gabriel came to me and told me that you two dropped off the grid. He was worried you were in trouble and asked me to find you and check on you. This is Dev, Carys, and Elisa. They work with

Michael."

Carys waved. "I'm just transport, and she's just backup, so we're not staying. Nice to meet you."

Before anyone could speak, Carys flashed out with Elisa, leaving Dev alone with Zeke and her parents. He shifted from foot to foot nervously before working up the courage to approach Zeke's father and offer his hand.

"It's a pleasure, Mr. Mackenzie. I'm Dev. I'm one of the Nephilim who work with Michael." He smiled at Greer. "Mrs. Mackenzie."

Damon looked at Zeke. "He's okay?"

Zeke grinned. "More than. We're working an undercover mission together right now. We're trying to find Lucifer's sword so we can destroy it. It's time, Dad. Amaya and Deacon are training together now, and Lux is training with Zane to go out hunting down Beelzebub's offspring."

Greer sighed deeply. "Come on in, both of you." She slid an arm around Zeke. "I knew it would happen, but I'd always hoped we'd find a way to end it first so you wouldn't have to."

Zeke hugged her mother. "We're going to be fine. All of us. We have help, and we're well-trained. You two made sure of that." She dropped onto the couch and pulled off her shoes before tucking her legs underneath her. "Why are you two here? Last I knew you were working with some of the new Warriors down in Mexico."

Damon sat in the reclining chair. "We were. There was a Cambion attack, and most of the Warriors were killed. We were lucky enough we weren't on site when it happened, and it was over by the time we got back. One of the kids was still alive, and he told us they were there looking for us—and for you, Zeke. Lucifer knows the time is getting close, and he's not content to just sit and hope you pop up and they can kill you. They're actively looking for you now. We didn't want to put you in any danger, so we dropped off the grid and came up here for a while to regroup and figure out a plan. Aradia and Gage are supposed to be here next week. Brax and Alaria went to Michael's to help train Deacon and Amaya."

Dev perched on the couch and folded his hands together. "Why didn't you tell anyone you were leaving? Gabriel made it sound like they thought you were dead or something."

Greer snorted. "He's melodramatic, that one. I know you might not get it, but since Zeke has been an adult and fully come into her powers, it's often safest for her if we don't stay in close contact.

Most of the time there's a rule that we don't talk unless someone's in trouble. We try to see each other as often as we can, but we took great pains to hide her identity while she was growing up. If not getting to see our daughter as much as we would like is the price we pay to ensure she's safe, then it's one we pay gladly." She glared at Zeke. "Don't you think one of us would have reached out if we were in trouble?"

Zeke returned the glare. "No, I don't. I think you'd get yourselves killed trying to make sure I didn't risk myself. I can handle it, and I can help you. This is what I was born for."

Damon raked his hands through his hair. "We're not having this fight again. As long as we're alive, you are our priority. That will never change, and I will never apologize for it. You may have been born for this, but you were also born our baby, and that trumps some Heavenly mission to me." He turned his attention to Dev. "Are you hungry?"

Recognizing that Damon wasn't truly asking a question, Dev nodded. "I could eat, sir."

"Good. Get your coat. You can help me grill." He stood and stopped to kiss Zeke on the top of the head. "You girls get the guest rooms made up." He stroked his hand over Greer's hair. "Maybe we can play Scrabble after dinner."

Greer smiled softly and shook her head. "I'll see if we have it."

Zeke shifted to lean her head against her mother's shoulder, enjoying the feel of being home. She didn't speak until she heard the door leading onto the back deck closed. "Mama?"

"What, baby?"

"I think I like him."

Greer smiled and snuggled in with her daughter. "I know, baby. I know."

CHAPTER TEN

January 25th, 2060 – Alaska

DEV LAY on his back, staring at the ceiling and listening to the silence. The moon was barely visible through his window and cast the dimmest of lights across the floor. He knew he and Zeke needed to leave the next morning to go back to LA, but found he was reluctant to go.

It had been years since he'd had the pleasure of seeing what a real family looked like. To watch Zeke with her mother and father made grief knot in his chest at what he had never been able to experience. Even though they all three made him feel welcome and included, it was a stark reminder of what he was missing.

The sound of a floor board creaking broke through his thoughts, and he sat up, his hand automatically going to the pistol on the nightstand. When the door opened and Zeke poked her head in, he relaxed.

"Unless your goal is for your father to gut me in the morning, tonight is not the night to be sneaking into my bed."

Zeke chuckled and closed the door, turning the lock and crossing the room to stand next to the bed. "I'm not here for sex. Even I'm not that depraved." She folded her arms. "Is there room for me?"

Dev looked from side to side, judging the width of the narrow twin mattress. "I think it might hold us both if you don't mind being close." He scooted over so that his back was pressed against the wall. "Though climbing into bed with me makes my fear that you're trying to have me killed seem much more likely."

Rolling her eyes, Zeke sat on the edge of the bed. "I'm not trying to have you killed. My father knows I've had sex, and I'm sure he's figured out I'm not having it with you." She slipped between the sheets and rolled onto her side to face him. "We have to leave in the morning."

"I know." He looked over at her. "You didn't come in here to tell me that, Zeke. What's going on?"

Zeke scowled. "Can't you pretend that maybe I just wanted to cuddle for a while?"

Dev laughed and propped himself up on one elbow. "I could, but then we'd both know it's a lie. What's wrong?"

"I talked to my mom about you."

Dev paled. "Oh, God. Do I need to run now? Is she going to stab me in my sleep?"

Zeke giggled and rolled onto her back. "You should have been an actor instead of a Nephil." She reached up and laid her fingertips against his face. "She thinks I need to be honest with you about why I don't like being in relationships."

"I think that's pretty sound advice, but this isn't a conversation we need to have here." He picked up her hand and kissed her knuckles. "You'll tell me when you're ready to tell me. It's not like we're getting married or something. We're feeling our way along. There aren't any rules we have to obey."

"I know, but once we get back, we're going to be sucked back into the things we have to do." She took a deep breath. "It's not some huge sob story. I'm not going to get all weepy and cry, especially since Carys and Elisa told me about what happened to your sister."

Dev smiled when she laid her head on his shoulder. "Don't tell me you have a sister who fell in love with a Cambion, too?"

She shook her head. "No. When I was nineteen, I fell in love with a human. Head over heels in love. He was training to be a Warrior because his family had been killed by demons when he was a kid and he'd been raised by a Warrior family. Mom and Dad were against the relationship. They liked Jeremy just fine, but they knew the risk of a human being involved with a Nephilim. They were smarter than me and knew he wouldn't be safe as long as I was around. He and I were together for five years. We were talking marriage and babies and I was dreaming of a life without this. Then, we got a tip about some Cambion going to be at an old church in Denmark. Something about some human sacrifice. I led a team in. It was supposed to be easy."

Sensing where the story was going, Dev frowned. "It wasn't easy, was it?"

She laughed. "Intuitive. No, it wasn't. Turns out the info was wrong, as info I get is apparently wont to be. We burst in on a church meeting. The place was crawling with demons and Cambion. I was the only one who made it out alive. After that, I swore I would never put myself in a position where someone I cared about could be used against me or be a weakness. I tried to save Jeremy, but he wasn't well-trained and he wasn't very strong, and because I tried to save someone who couldn't be saved, I let other people die that I could have helped. Because I loved him, I was willing to risk their lives to save his. I can't do that again. I won't."

Dev looked over at her. "To be honest, I expected you to tell me some love story about how you lost someone and you swore to him on his last breath that you would never be with anyone else. Instead, what I get is that you're afraid your emotions will get the better of you and other people will pay the price."

Zeke lifted her shoulders. "Love is a weakness in this world. It always has been, and it always will be." She laid her hand on his chest, feeling his heart beating beneath her fingers. "I never wanted to take the chance again until you. I know we haven't known each other very long, but I know myself well enough to know you could be very important to me. I don't want to risk the lives of anyone else because of my feelings."

"You won't. It's okay to feel things. You have to care about people if we're going to make it through this. Being in love with someone romantically isn't the only way people get close to you. I haven't seen you with them much, but I'd be willing to bet you'd risk your life and those of a hell of a lot of people if you thought Lux and Amaya were in danger. Or if your parents were. Everyone loves someone else. The weakness comes when the people we love aren't strong enough to survive in this world. I'm not weak, and neither are you. I do what's necessary. I always have, and I always will. Nothing about me is going to change if we get involved with one another."

"I'm scared. I don't know if there's anything you can say that's going to change it." She looked up to meet his gaze. "I guess what I came in here to tell you is that I appreciate you being so patient and I'm working my way around to it. I know I gave you the maybe a few days ago, but you're still not pushing me for more than I'm ready to give, and I want you to know I want more too."

Dev yanked the blanket up over her. "We don't have to keep having these talks. I'm not some caveman who doesn't understand subtlety. I get it, babe. We're good. You don't have to defend yourself to me." He ran his fingers through her hair. "Are you staying here for the night or going back to your room?"

Zeke laughed. "As much as I'd like to stay and cuddle, my dad wouldn't be happy to see me sneaking out of here in the morning. He might know I've had sex, but he doesn't need to see the evidence of it." She climbed out of the bed and leaned over to brush a kiss over his mouth. "Thanks for the talk." She squeezed his hand. "You're a good guy."

He grinned up at her. "I know. I'm just glad you're finally figuring it out." Smirking, he continued. "Though I don't know in what world you call that little peck a decent goodnight kiss."

Rolling her eyes, Zeke closed the door behind herself and went back to her room.

Greer hugged Zeke tightly, tears shining in her eyes. "Check in when you can. Stay safe." She squeezed her daughter's shoulders firmly. "Don't take any unnecessary risks."

Damon shook Dev's hand. "I won't give you a lecture since I'm sure Michael has that covered, but don't do anything to get her hurt."

Dev nodded solemnly. "Yes, sir. We'll be just fine." He smiled at Greer. "It was nice to meet you, ma'am. Thank you for letting me stay in your home."

Zeke frowned. "Don't be so formal. They're my parents."

"Exactly." He glanced back to where Carys was waiting for them. "We should get going. We need to get back to L.A. tonight if we don't want to be missed."

"I know." She hugged her father, squeezing him as hard as she could, enjoying the safety and warmth she felt in his arms. "You two stay safe. Keep Michael in the loop so I don't get sent out to track you down each time you decide to lie low. I didn't like the feeling of wondering if you were safe."

Greer wrapped her arm around Damon's waist and waited until

the three had disappeared before speaking. "Do you think she knows?"

Damon shook his head, his eyes dark and solemn. "I don't think so. She'd have said something if she did."

"I'm glad they came up here." She took in a deep, shaking breath. "It was hard not to let her in on things, but I don't want her in any more danger than she's already in." Greer laid her head on her husband's chest. "What are we going to do, Damon?"

"We're going to stay here until they come for us. We've led them away from everyone else, and we'll cleanse their flash signatures so no one will know they were ever here. Do we know much about the man who came here with Zeke?"

She shook her head. "No. Only that he's one of Michael's, which is enough for me. Michael trusted him enough to send him undercover with our baby, so he must be good at what he does." A single tear slipped down her cheek and dripped off her chin. "I hope he can take this from her. I don't want her to have to do this. Damn Gabriel and him telling us what was going to happen, but we can't let her get caught."

Damon tightened his arms around her. "We knew something like this might happen, baby. We'll face it the same way we do everything else. I'm glad we got a chance to spend a little time with her this weekend. I hope it'll make it easier once this is over. For better or for worse, once we failed, our only job was to keep Zeke alive and raise her to finish what we started. This is the last step in doing that."

"Tell me it's all worth it." Greer's voice shook and her grip tightened. "Tell me we'll be okay and Zeke and the girls will succeed and this will all be worth it."

"The girls will do what they're supposed to. This will all be worth it." Damon kissed the top of her head. "Let's get to work. We don't know how long we have before the Cambion come, and we don't want there to be any sign of Zeke here when they do."

She nodded slowly and took another deep breath, holding it until the urge to cry subsided. "I don't care about us. I just hate that our little girl is going to have to go through this."

Damon paused at the door and looked back. "Zeke isn't a little girl anymore, Greer. She's doing what she was born for. We did our job. Now it's time for her to do hers."

Chapter Eleven

January 31st, 2060 – Los Angeles

"We have to come up with a plan to find this sword. We've been here for weeks already, and I feel like we've lost more ground than we've gained." Zeke paced the kitchen, a glass of wine in her hand and her gaze pinned on Dev, who sat nursing a beer.

"No, we're gaining trust, which is more important than information at this stage. We know Rafael is the key to this sect. We also know from the research Michael did that the sword is likely somewhere in LA because it's one of the largest groups in the world. They only bring it out when they're offering sacrifices to Lucifer himself, and believe me, we don't want to be here for one of those." He took a swig of beer and swished it around his mouth before swallowing. "We have to get close to Rafael and be able to get access to his files."

"How are we supposed to do that?"

"I haven't figured that part out yet." He sighed deeply and ran his hand through his hair. "Burglary will likely be involved, but if not, then we're going to have to figure out a way to get close enough to him that he confides in one of us."

Zeke scowled. "I prefer burglary. But I don't think it's here. I know Michael's contacts say it is, but I don't agree with their conclusion. It doesn't make sense at all. Why would Lucifer leave the one thing that anchors his power with a bunch of Cambion and humans?"

"It's a religious relic for them. They would guard it above all else, and the Cambion and demons know the significance. It's going to be guarded better than Fort Knox."

She looked at him drolly. "Fort Knox doesn't exist anymore. It actually wasn't that well-guarded." She took a swig of the wine. "Seriously, think about it. If you were Lucifer, would you trust a bunch of humans with one of the only things that could really hurt you?"

"I certainly wouldn't have it with me, either, though. If he had it with him, then we could go after him without needing the sword first. I know it's a risk, but I think it makes more sense to leave it with people who would die protecting it and who most Angels are unwilling to kill. Humans are great fodder in this war. God won't let Angels mow them down, so the Devils take advantage of that."

Zeke slid onto a stool and stared at Dev across the island. "Something bad is going to happen."

Confused by the abrupt change of subject, he blinked several times. "What? Since when are you psychic?"

"I'm not, but you know Nephilim and their intuition. I've had a feeling something bad is going to happen ever since the morning Gabriel showed up here. I can't shake it, and the longer I have it, the more sure I am that it's going to be something really, horribly bad."

"Do you get these feelings often?"

"No, which is what makes me concerned. I'm not typically a worrier, but I cannot shake this. Something bad is going to happen, and it's going to be big."

Dev reached out and covered her hand with his own. "Don't borrow trouble. We scanned the house when we got back. They didn't plant anything here. I've already spoken with Rafael, and he seemed fine. You've taught your first class, which went great, and I've got a dozen more orders for swords for Cambion. We're fine. All we need to focus on is finding the sword and getting out of here in one piece."

"I know, but I'm telling you I can't shake this feeling, and I've never been wrong before." She reached for the bottle of wine and refilled the glass. "Have you checked in with Zane or Deacon lately?"

"No, but that's not unusual. We don't normally keep in touch unless something is wrong. Don't you check in with Amaya every week?"

"She says everything is fine. Lux and Zane are still training with Gage and Aradia and Amaya and Deacon are working with her parents and Michael. All seems good. They're expecting to head out to hunt down Beelzebub's offspring within the next few weeks."

"Then trust her that everything is fine. She'd tell you if it wasn't." Dev reached out and snagged an apple from the bowl in the middle of the island. "You need to calm down. Believe me, it'll find us just fine without us going looking for it first." He stood and walked to the door. "I'm going up to bed. You've got three classes tomorrow, so I'd suggest you think about doing the same thing. I have a long day out in my 'shop'" he made quotation motions with his fingers "tomorrow, so you'll be on your own."

Zeke gestured to her glass of wine. "I'm just going to finish this, and then I'll be up."

Dev nodded and started up the stairs. He'd made it to the landing when he froze, turning. Zeke saw him tense and rose, automatically extending her shield to make sure he was covered. He retreated back down the stairs and nodded toward the door.

"Rafael is here."

Zeke looked down at her jeans and sweater. "Should I go change?"

"I don't think we have time."

A knock sounded at the door, and Dev strode across the living room, pressing his eye to the peephole more for show than necessity before unbolting the lock and opening the door. "Rafael. Is everything okay? We were just getting ready to go to bed."

Rafael brushed past Dev and into the room. "I'm sorry to come so late, but a situation has arisen I want to discuss with you both." He gestured to the couch. "Please, let's sit."

Zeke looked over her shoulder toward the kitchen. "Do you want some coffee or a glass of wine?"

"Not this time. I don't have time to make small talk, so I'm going to get to the point. I need to know how serious the two of you are about being a part of this place."

Dev and Zeke exchanged a nervous look before Dev answered. "We're very serious. Have we done something to make you question that?"

The Cambion shook his head. "Far from it. When you asked me to look after this place, I realized you were trusting me with everything about yourselves, and that sort of trust should be rewarded. We have a special opportunity tonight, and I want to offer it to the two of you as a way to prove your loyalty to Lucifer and to the church. If you succeed, then you'll be a part of the Council. It will make you privy to the goings on here. The way we plan attacks, how we use the weapons you make, why you have to teach the classes. It's a privilege very few humans get."

"Why us?" The question was out before Zeke could stop it.

Rafael turned to her, his eyes alight. "Because I see something special in the two of you. You're young and strong, and there's something about you that's different from most humans. I don't know what it is, precisely, but I know I want to take advantage of it. I don't want to let either of you go. Besides, proving your loyalty to the group is common. You were going to have to do something either way. You know that. What I'm offering you is something most Cambion, and even a lot of demons, have dreamed of for years."

Dev's heart clenched in his chest, a bolt of apprehension rocketing through his body. "What is it?"

"I can't tell you. You have to decide, without knowing the task, whether or not you will do whatever is asked of you."

They exchanged a long look. Zeke nodded slightly, and Dev turned back to Rafael. "We're in."

Rafael clapped his hands and stood. "Fantastic. Get your shoes and coats. I'll drive you over in my car."

Hurriedly, they did as told and followed the Cambion to his car, sliding into the backseat as Rafael took the wheel. He drove quickly through the streets, taking roads Dev had never been on and driving away from their neighborhood. After twenty minutes, the car rolled to a stop outside of what looked like it had once been a police station.

"We use this as a holding facility for hostiles we capture. It's warded against Angels so there's no way we can be interrupted by them. Fucking Nephilim can still get in because they're half human, but we'd smell them coming a mile away." Rafael held the door and let Dev and Zeke go in first. "This is far enough away from the rest of the group that what goes on here isn't heard. People don't generally like to see the ugly side of war." He looked between them. "I hope neither of you have weak stomachs."

Zeke shook her head. "We've both fought before. Blood doesn't bother us."

Rafael drew to a stop and looked at them both seriously. "Battle is one thing. Have you ever taken a life in cold blood?"

Dev nodded. "I have."

"Zeke?"

She shook her head slowly. "No."

Rafael looked at her solemnly. "Well, that's about to change. Follow me." He started up a flight of stairs. "Last night we got a tip from some demons that they'd seen some of the most hunted humans out there. A team picked them up a couple hours later, and we brought them here. Alexi wanted us to try and extract some information about the location of some of the Nephilim out of them. Unfortunately, they either don't know, or they're too strong for us to break. We've been unable to possess them, unable to penetrate their minds, and unable to extract any information. At this point, we've determined the risk of holding them here outweighs the benefit of any information we might get from extended torture. Typically, if Abalam can't crack you in the first few hours, he isn't going to be able to. Hypothetically, we could continue with these two forever since one of them is a Healer, but the longer we wait to kill them, the higher the probability Michael will lead troops in on us. Even the best wards won't hold against an all-out attack for very long." He drew to a stop. "So, I decided to use this as a way to let the two of you earn my trust. I want you to kill them. Fast, slow, take your pick. One in each room."

Zeke heard only buzzing inside her own ears. She blindly stumbled into the room when Rafael opened the door and shoved her into it, pressing a gun into her hand. Afraid to look and afraid not to at the same time, she clenched her free hand into a fist and rested her forehead against the door. Knowing her survival depended upon putting on a show, she forced herself to turn around.

The room was dimly lit, the only light coming from one bare bulb in the center of the room. There was a table and two chairs directly under the light. Beneath the table was a drain in the floor that was crusted with dried blood. Sitting in one of the chairs, his wrists bound behind himself and a gag around his mouth, was Damon.

Zeke's knees went weak, and she collapsed into the chair, the gun hitting the floor. Tears rose in her eyes, and her breath caught in her chest. Her entire body began to shake, and she felt hot and cold at the same time. Black spots swarmed her vision, and the whole room began a slow, sick spin.

"Ezekiel! Listen to me!"

Damon's voice sounded in Zeke's head, strong and firm. She tried to focus on it as she fought to wade through her panic. She blinked, barely seeing, and rocked back and forth, her arms wrapped around her body. Her tongue felt thick and foreign in her mouth, and she wondered briefly if she was even capable of speech.

Taking a deep breath, she forced herself to focus enough to attach to the link Damon had opened with her. "Daddy."

"It's okay, baby. It's fine. Calm down. You need to breathe and you have to keep your shield up to cover you and Dev. I'm going to get you through this. Do they know about you?"

She shook her head. "No, I don't think so. After this they might. They brought us here to let us prove our loyalty to them. They want me to kill you. Oh God! Dev! Mom!"

"Mom is in the next room. If you're in here with me, that means Dev is in with Mom. Baby, look at me. You need to clear your head. Now is not the time for you to get emotional." Damon met her gaze, his eyes flat and hard. "We taught you there might come a day when you would have to sacrifice someone for the mission. We raised you to know the most important thing you will ever do is help kill Lucifer. We taught you to be willing to die for that. Do you remember?"

Zeke nodded slowly, her heart racing in her chest and her palms sweaty. "I remember. Daddy, no. Please, no." Her voice was weak and thin inside their heads as she begged.

"No one life is worth failing. Not yours, not mine, not your mother's. You sacrifice one to save ten. Ten to save a hundred. A hundred to save a thousand. My fight is over, Zeke. Yours has just begun."

"They want me to kill you! How are you so calm?"

Damon struggled against the gag but was unable to dislodge it. "I knew the second they got their hands on me that I was dead. The only thing that's changed is now I have the chance to say goodbye to you. You will do this because they will kill us both if you don't. Either you kill me, or they kill us both."

"Dev won't kill Mom! He won't! He can't!"

Damon shook his head solemnly. "That's where you're wrong. He'll do it because it has to be done. The same as you are going to bend down, pick up that gun, and shoot me in the head. You will do it because it is necessary."

His voice was hard and firm inside her head. Zeke rocked from side to side, tears streaming down her face. They dripped off her chin and nose, splattering the table. Her fingernails dug rivets into her own arms, and she shivered though the room was warm.

"There has to be another way. We'll find another way to get the sword. Dev can flash us out. All we have to do is get to him. We'll find another way to do it."

"If that were to happen, then they would know who and what you are. I have not spent the last thirty years hiding you for this to ruin it. Baby, listen to me. I wish more than anything that I could hold you and tell you it's okay, but I can't. You have to listen to me here. I don't want to die. Your mother doesn't want to die. But there is no way she or I are leaving this place alive. You can. Either one of us would blow our own brains out to save you. Don't make me watch you die, Ezekiel. Let me die knowing my baby is safe."

Zeke shook her head and squeezed her eyes shut, holding her breath until her lungs burned. She felt another pressure on her mind and let Dev in. His voice was warm and comforting.

"Zeke, honey, talk to me."

"I can't do this! I won't! You can't do it either!"

"Sweetheart, listen to me. I've been talking with Greer. She wants you to know she loves you and she's okay. They severed the link between your parents, and she's too weak to project through the walls and wards. Is there anything you want me to tell her?"

"Mama." Zeke's voice was little more than a whimper. Her head filled with memories of sitting in her mother's lap, of long talks late at night over hot chocolate, and then later, wine. Memories of long training sessions and lessons on everything from first aid to riflery. She could almost feel her mother's arms around her, could almost smell the familiar scent of shampoo and soap.

Dev's voice was gentle and insistent. "You have to shake out of this. If we don't get through this, they'll kill us all. It's a test. They must suspect who you are, and this is a way to prove ourselves to them. There is no way all four of us come out of here. You know that. Baby, I'd do it for you if I could, but I can't. You have to do this or we're going to die."

"They're my parents!"

"I know. I know it's hard, and I know you don't want to, but you have to do this. Greer says to tell you to remember what she taught you. You are stronger than this and you will go on and succeed where she failed. She says not to let this define you. You have to be strong, and you have to survive this. She says the thing she's the most proud of in her life is being your mother and she knows you're going to do what's right. She wants you to know she'll always be looking over you and you're never going to be alone. That she raised you right and she's taught you everything you need to know and now is the time to turn off your emotions and do what has to be done."

Zeke let the words flow over her, calming her slightly. She forced her eyes to open and met her father's. Dev's voice continued in her head.

"She wants you to tell Damon she loves him and that the best decision of her life was telling him yes. She has no regrets about anything in their life together, and she's at peace with this because she knows they'll be together in Heaven."

Zeke reached out to her father. "Daddy."

Damon's response was instant. "I'm still here, darlin'."

Tearfully, Zeke repeated her mother's message.

His voice was calm and level in her head. "If you can, tell her I love her too and I only wish I'd gone after her earlier."

Zeke relayed the message to Dev, who turned to Greer, his eyes showing his sadness as he passed the words on to her.

Greer smiled around the gag and lifted her eyes toward the ceiling, tears shining in them. Her face was swollen and bruised, and there were red rings around her eyes from where she'd been crying. Her blonde hair was matted with dirt and blood. She took several deep breaths, her lips moving slightly in a silent prayer as she made peace with what was happening.

"We don't have much time, Dev. You need to do this. Will you do one thing for me?"

"Anything."

"Take care of Zeke. I know she's prickly and she's been difficult to deal with, but she's got a soft heart and she loves with all of it. Don't let this define her. Whatever you do, you cannot let her let this define her life. She is so much more than this one moment. Love her for us. Hold her when she cries. Fight with her when she needs it. Don't let her walk on you because she will, given the chance. But whatever you do, love her. Remind her we love her and that what she's doing is more important than I am. Never let her doubt herself, and never let her be alone. Can you promise me?"

Dev nodded, and when he spoke inside Greer's head, his voice was strong and full. "I promise all of that. I won't let you down. I won't let Zeke down." He glanced down at his hand and the gun in it. "How do you want to do this? Do you want me to count or something?"

Greer's voice was bitter. "I never imagined someone would ask me how I wanted to die." She took a deep breath and closed her eyes. "One shot to the head. Point blank range. I don't want to risk you missing or it going through so I have to bleed to death instead. Don't count, just do it."

He crossed the room to stand behind her, his hand resting on her shoulder. He frowned when he felt her shake under his hand, and wished he could do anything to offer comfort. Knowing he couldn't, he spoke one last time, his voice strong in her head.

"Go with God, Greer. You've fought enough. It's time to rest."

Before he could second-guess himself, he lifted the gun, pressed it to Greer's temple, and pulled the trigger.

Zeke jumped when she heard the gunshot. Her heart skipped a beat in her chest, and she blinked back tears, unable to stop them from trailing down her cheeks. Damon closed his eyes, and she saw his whole body tense. An animalistic wail of grief tore from his chest, and he threw himself against the binds. Zeke wrapped her arms around her knees and cried harder.

Damon's voice was ragged and raw in her head. "Get up. Pick up the gun and finish this. If you don't, you're going to get Dev and yourself killed."

"Daddy, no. Please don't make me do this. I can't. Mom—"

"Mom would want you to finish this. Baby, you're our whole world. If I could get loose, I'd end it myself. I'd take this from you if I could, but I can't. I'm begging you, Zeke. Pick up the gun and do what you have to do. Don't make me watch you die. I'm dead either way."

Of their own accord, Zeke's feet moved. She slowly stood and bent to pick the gun up off the floor. Her hands shook as she stared down at it. For twenty years, she'd been trained in how to handle weapons. Never in those twenty years had a gun ever looked or felt so foreign in her hands.

Never had she really thought about what a gun could do. She had always used one with ruthless efficiency. It was a tool, used to accomplish a goal. She'd witnessed the destructive power of guns and bullets first hand. She had felt them rip through her own flesh. She knew the searing pain and the bolt of fear that accompanied each shot. She had ended countless lives—human, Cambion, vampire, demon—all of them without a second thought. Never, until she had opened the door and faced her father, had she ever hesitated to pull the trigger.

The metal was cold and dead in her hand. She looked up at Damon, who stared at her with fire in his eyes. She knew—had always known—her parents would willingly give their lives to protect her. She knew she would unfalteringly do the same for them. She had never imagined a situation in which the only way she could live would be to end their lives.

"Daddy."

"I need you to listen closely here. You make the bastards pay. You walk out of here, you go home, and you figure out how to make them pay. Do not stop until they're dead at your feet. You live. You fight. Whatever you do, you survive. You're a warrior. You keep fighting until you win." He paused, his voice softening. "Don't forget to live, either. If you stop living, if you stop hoping, then you've let them win already. They can't take hope from you. They can't take away love. Let yourself live and love, baby girl. Win or lose, you promise me you'll have a life. Not an existence, but a life. You find a way to be happy."

Zeke nodded, unable to speak for the tears choking her. She took three reluctant steps forward, the gun held against her body. Damon spoke again, his voice calm and soothing as he led her through the motions necessary.

"Hold the gun like I taught you when you were little. Remember that? You were seven, and we used a little .22 pistol out behind the house shooting bottles off the fence. Square your shoulders. Good girl. Click off the safety. I love you, Ezekiel. It was an honor and a privilege to be your father." Damon looked up at her, his eyes showing her both sadness and love. "Do it fast. Put the barrel against my head. Right between my eyes."

Helpless, Zeke followed her father's instructions. Her hands shook as she lifted the gun, and she bent to kiss Damon's head, pressing her face against his and sobbing. Choking, unable to breathe, she straightened and squared her shoulders.

Her thumb clicked off the safety, and she met her father's eyes for the last time. With a gut-wrenching scream, she pulled the trigger.

The sound of the shot filled the room, over powering the sound of her scream. The gun hit the floor with a clang, and Zeke fell to her knees. The echo of the gunshot faded, and she was left with nothing but all-encompassing silence.

CHAPTER TWELVE

"SHE'S NEVER had to do anything like that before. Of course she's upset!" Dev glared at Rafael, panic twisting in his gut both at the state Zeke was in and the absence of her shield. "Let me get her and take her home."

Rafael stood firmly in front of the door, blocking Dev's entrance. "I'm disappointed. I expected you both to meet the challenge. Instead, she's falling to pieces. Are you sure she's been in battle before?"

Dev raked his hands through his hair and snapped his response, hoping he sounded frustrated and annoyed instead of terrified. "Yes, I'm damn well sure. There's a huge difference between killing someone trying to kill you and killing some man strapped to a chair. We have no idea who they were or what they've done. For all she knows, she just executed some father of three from Minnesota. Humans aren't like Cambion. She can't control her emotions when asked to do something like this. You should be grateful she did it."

Appearing bored, Rafael looked over his shoulder to coolly survey the room Zeke was in. "I was very pleased with your efficiency. Actually, both of you did the task within twenty minutes, which is fine. I didn't expect it to be easy, and I anticipated some emotions. I just didn't imagine there would be tears. It's making me reconsider whether or not your wife is right for what we have going on here."

Dev scowled. "Right now I don't give a fuck what you think. Get out of my way and let me go to my wife. I know this mission is your first priority, but she's mine."

He shoved Rafael out of the way and wrenched open the door. Zeke sat on the floor, her gun at her feet and her arms wrapped around her knees. Her eyes were wide and empty, and she rocked slightly from side to side, staring blankly ahead. He grabbed her under the arms and pulled her to her feet, lifting her in his arms and cradling her against his chest.

Rafael stood by the door, taking in the scene. He crossed his arms and sighed. "I'll have one of my men take you home. I need to oversee the cleanup here." He met Dev's eyes. "Get her under control. The first Council meeting is one week from tonight at my house. I'll see you both there."

Dev nodded sharply. "We'll be there."

Rafael jerked his head to one of the other Cambion. "Take them home. Cancel her classes tomorrow. We'll give her a day to recover." Rolling his eyes, he addressed Dev again. "This is a pathetic response. If she doesn't improve significantly, and quickly, there will be changes made to your positions here."

Dev followed the Cambion, Zeke held tightly in his arms, desperately praying no one used their abilities to scan for his or Zeke's. She was stiff against him, her eyes open and unfocused. Her skin was clammy and cold, and her breath was shallow. The Cambion led them to a car and waited while Dev settled Zeke in the backseat. He drove them back to their house silently, not saying a word as he maneuvered through the streets. By the time the car pulled to a stop outside the house, Zeke was sobbing silently.

He carried her inside, stopped to lock the door, and went straight upstairs to her room. Without a word, he sat her on the bed and left her long enough to get her pajamas out of the dresser. Gently, he stripped off all her clothes and helped her into the sweatpants and t-shirt he'd lent her on their first night in the house.

He tugged the ponytail holder from her hair and ran her brush through the silky locks until they were free of tangles. Drawing back the covers, he slipped her prone body between the sheets and covered her up, perching on the bed next to her.

"I wish there was something I could say to make it better. I wish like hell I could, but there are no words. I'm damn sorry this happened tonight, and I'm even sorrier you had to be a part of it.

I'd have given anything to have been able to take that away from you."

Zeke blinked. "That's what my dad said, too. Everyone wanted to take it away from me, but no one could. They're dead. I don't even know what they're going to do with the bodies. I don't get to bury them."

"I'll get ahold of Michael and get him to find the bodies for you. I'll make sure you can bury them, baby."

"It doesn't feel real. This is a dream. I'm going to wake up in the morning and call my mother and tell her about this nightmare I had."

Dev felt his heart break. "No, it's not a dream. Do you want me to call anyone?"

"There's no one who can come. If they do, they'll die, too. There's no one."

He stroked his hand over her hair. "You're only alone if you want to be. I'm here. Amaya and Lux would come. Their parents would come."

"They're just as wanted as my parents were. They'd be killed if they came in here. I won't be responsible for any more death."

"You weren't responsible for this. The only ones responsible for this are the Cambion and the Devils. This is war. We'll kill them for what they did tonight. We won't stop until we kill them all."

Zeke stared past him at the wall. "My parents are dead. I shot my father in the face. You don't get to come back from that." She blinked back tears and looked up at him. "I'm going to Hell for what I did tonight."

"If that's true, then we'll be there together." He reached over and turned off the light next to the bed. "You should try to get some sleep. Do you want me to get you something to help you?"

Zeke started to shake her head then changed her mind. "Knock me out. Make it go away."

Ten minutes later, Dev paced the living room floor, torn between anger and worry. He glanced at the stairs leading up to Zeke then back at the satellite phone on the coffee table. Swearing under his breath, he snatched up the phone and dialed. Deacon answered on the third ring.

"What's wrong?"

"Greer and Damon are dead."

Deacon swore. "Fuck. How?"

"They were captured by Cambion and brought to LA. I think

they suspected Zeke and used this as a test. They came and got us a couple hours ago and took us to where they were holding them. Zeke had to kill her father. I took out Greer."

"Jesus fucking Christ. She killed her own father?"

Dev frowned. "She didn't have a choice. It was kill them or we all died. I need Michael to find the bodies and get them. She at least deserves a chance to bury them. It might be nice if Lux and Amaya could come see her for a day."

"I don't think that's possible. There's no way to shield so many people for long. If you can get outside the city limits, I can send Carys to flash you out. Failing that, we could try to get Michael or Gabriel to come in and get you. Is it safe for you to be away for any amount of time?"

"We'll be fine for a day. I think she needs to see them." Frowning, he continued. "At this point, I'm not entirely sure they bought what we were selling, so I'm on high alert, but if Zeke is going to get through this, she needs her family."

"When?"

"She's asleep now, so first thing in the morning would be good."

Deacon sighed deeply. "I'll see what I can do. Hang tight and don't do anything stupid."

Dev nodded. "I won't. See you soon, bro."

The men hung up with no further goodbyes. Dev put the phone back in his bag and went to the kitchen for a bottle of scotch. He thought about getting a glass before deciding to just drink out of the bottle.

He was sitting in the den, staring into the fireplace when Zeke came down the stairs, a quilt wrapped around her shoulders. Without a word, she took the bottle from his hands and drank deeply, placing it on the floor and sliding into his lap.

"The pills didn't work. I can't sleep."

Dev tucked the blanket around them both and cradled her against his chest. "I can give you more."

"No." She shook her head. "I want to feel it. I need to feel it so when I have the chance to rip Rafael's heart out of his chest, I'll be able to appreciate it fully."

Dev ran his hand over her hair. "I'll make sure you get the chance. I promise. Whatever revenge you want, I'll make it my goal to give it to you."

Zeke stared into the fire and settled her head against Dev's shoulder. "It feels surreal. There's a part of me that doesn't believe this actually happened. I try to process it and my brain refuses to believe it. I looked into my father's eyes, and I shot him in the face to save my own ass. What kind of a person does that make me?" She blinked back tears and wiped her nose on the sleeve of her shirt. "How can you look at me after what I did? How will anyone ever be able to forgive me?"

He sighed deeply, his chest rumbling against her ear. "Baby, you weren't the only one there. I did the exact same thing you did. We didn't have a choice, and deep down, you know that. If we hadn't passed the test, we'd be dead on the floor of that building right alongside your parents. They knew they were going to die no matter what you did. There was no escaping. You're not evil. You're not a bad person. You're a woman who was put in a position I wouldn't wish on my worst enemy. You made the only choice there was to make. You chose to fight. You chose to survive. You chose to honor your parents and do what they asked of you. You did what a lot of people couldn't do and put the good of the world ahead of the good of the people you loved. I know it doesn't feel like it, but you did the right thing."

"There's nothing right about what we did." She turned her face into his neck and pressed her nose against his skin. "I should hate you."

Dev looked down at her, sadness in his eyes. "I don't feel good about it, but I know it was necessary. I will always do what has to be done, no matter who it hurts. We're fighting a war, babe, and saving the world has to come first."

"Apparently I agree with you. That's what I've always been taught. I never thought I was capable of being the person who makes the hard decisions. I never wanted to be that person, but apparently I am."

"It's who we were born to be." He tucked her hair behind her ears. "Is there anything I can do to make you feel better? I hate you're so sad."

Zeke smiled sadly. "I think I just need to be upset for a while. I'm going to cry, and I'm going to grieve. I can't ignore what happened, and right now I can't even process it. It's going to take a while."

"Take all the time you need. I'm here, and I'm not going anywhere."

She sat up, twisting so one of her knees was on either side of him. Her eyes bored into him, intense and bright. Slowly, she lifted her hands and let her fingertips trail over his face, tracing the line of his jaw, the curve of his lips, the deep worry lines between his eyebrows.

His hair was a deep golden blond, and she wondered briefly how she had ever mistaken it for being dark the first night they'd met. His eyes were the brightest green she'd ever seen, and they were locked onto her brown ones, his gaze hot and intense.

He still wore the button down shirt and jeans he'd had on when they'd been taken from the house. Slowly, her hands shaking, she lowered them to the first button on his shirt, working it from the hole and exposing an inch of dusky skin.

"I've been shot four times. Once in the shoulder, twice in the gut and once in the thigh. I've been stabbed seven times. I have three scars from those on my ribs, two in my back, one on my stomach and one right between my breasts. That one went right into my heart. If my mom hadn't been there with me, I'd have been dead within seconds." She stared down at him, her fingers still working the buttons on his shirt. "The first night we stayed together, I noticed the scars on your knuckles, and it made me wonder what other ones you have."

Dev sat still as she spread open his shirt. His chest was tightly muscled with a light dusting of hair across his skin and a darker trail leading down over his abdomen and disappearing into his jeans. There were two puckered scars just above the line of denim and a pink slash across one of his shoulders.

"Apparently you've been in more fights than I have, or you just have worse luck. I've only been shot twice, and knifed half a dozen times."

"Scars tell stories. Each one of mine brings back a memory. I look at them and I remember how my mother healed most of them. It was harder for her to heal a Nephil than a human so she could never take the scars away. I don't know if I'd have wanted her to even if she could've. They're a part of me." She lifted her hands and stared at them. "I can put my hands on someone and heal them just like my mother could. She passed her gift to me. I can smell a vampire a mile away. I got that from my father. I'm supposed to be some super human Angelic warrior who's going to help save the world. I can mind control demons. I can shield Nephilim from being detected. I have more strength than most demons. I can charge out onto a battlefield without a thought and hack my way through an army. I'm supposed to be the one who can save people.

Tonight I killed them." She took a deep, shuddering breath. "I'm a little afraid I killed a part of me, too."

Dev took her hands and folded them between his. "I know it doesn't feel like it, but there will come a time when you're at peace with what happened tonight."

Zeke leaned back and stared at him, her eyes moving slowly over the planes of his face. Her gaze settled on his eyes. Never breaking contact, she gripped the hem of her shirt and lifted it over her head. Her breasts were encased in light blue lace. They strained against the confines of the fabric, rising up into creamy white swells adorned with dark pink tips barely peeking through the lace.

Dev swallowed. "Don't do this, Zeke. Not tonight. I don't ever want to feel guilty about doing something with you, and I would. I'd feel like I was taking advantage."

"It's not taking advantage. I'm sober. I'm clear headed. I'm an adult. You're not trying to seduce me. I want to forget about the pain for a little while. I want you." She took his hands in her own and placed one on each of her breasts. "I want you to touch me. I want this." She leaned down so her lips were less than an inch from his ear. "You once told me if I told you yes, you'd have me naked and under you in thirty seconds flat." She straightened and met his gaze again. "I never understood how people have sex when people die. Now I know why. It's to make themselves feel alive. I feel dead inside, and I want to stop. I want you to make me feel something, anything. I don't feel anything from the pills and I'm not drunk.

Dev closed his eyes and tried to force himself to remove his hands from her body. He jumped when he felt her lips against his throat, warm and firm. Her tongue darted out to taste his skin, and he groaned softly. When she wiggled her hips slightly, he tried to shift so his burgeoning erection wasn't pressing against her.

"Baby, this is a bad idea. Not tonight. I don't want you to ever regret doing this with me, and I think you would."

Zeke straightened and stared down at him, her eyes hot and bright. "I will not regret it. We've been spinning circles around this for weeks." She twisted her arms behind her back and released the snaps on her bra, tugging it away from her flesh to expose herself to his view. "Do you have condoms?"

"Yeah, but—"

"No buts." She silenced him with a searing kiss. "Where are they?"

"In my nightstand drawer."

Zeke pictured the piece of furniture in her mind, using what little telekinesis she had to yank the box of condoms from the drawer and down the stairs. The box hit the wall and spilled onto the floor, silver packets littering the carpet. Dev shifted uncomfortably.

"Neat trick."

"I told you I had a bit of telekinetic ability. Apparently it's good for helping me get laid more efficiently." She grinned and stood up, bending to unbuckle his belt.

She yanked the leather from the loops and cast it aside. His pants and boxers soon followed as she ripped them down his legs and threw them. His penis was engorged and hard, and Zeke lifted her eyebrows and smiled at him.

"You're going to enjoy this, too."

Dev tangled his hands in her hair and brought her in for a kiss. "I don't just want sex with you. I don't want to be what you use to make yourself feel better. I want all of you. I want you to want all of me. If this is only about forgetting, I don't want to do this with you. If you really want to give this a chance, then I'm all in, but I won't be a dalliance or a distraction. You keep telling me I could be important to you. You're already important to me, and I won't do anything to cheapen that. So if we do this, you need to know it's not just yes to sex. It's yes to a relationship. It's yes to sleeping together at night. It's yes to being together. I'm not interested in scratching an itch."

Zeke stared into his eyes. "I know what it means." She ran her hands down his chest and across his thighs until she cupped him in her hands. "Now shut up and enjoy this. We both need something else to concentrate on."

He groaned as she ran her hands down the length of him. Her fingers were long and narrow, and her nails were square and short. She stroked him gently, rubbing the tip of his penis with her thumb. Kneeling in front of him, she dipped her head and engulfed him in her mouth.

Dev jumped and groaned as she enveloped him in wet heat. Her tongue—soft and hot—darted around the head, rubbing his tender skin as she lightly sucked. His hands gripped her hair, and he slid down in the chair several inches, jutting his hips up. She licked him gently from base to tip, sucking the tip and running her hands up and down his length.

He closed his eyes and let himself float away on the pleasure of her mouth. His dick twitched when she sucked harder, and he moaned softly, thoroughly enjoying the feel of her. One of her hands wrapped around his base, pumping up and down as she laved attention on the tip.

Slowly, he caught her wrists in his hands and tugged her up, standing and pulling her to her feet. He slipped his hands inside the sweatpants and lowered them down her legs, leaving her completely bare. Turning so her back was to the chair, he adjusted her so that her knees pressed against the cushion.

"Sit."

Zeke did as she was told, dropping to the chair and staring up at him. Dev bent and gripped her hips in his hands, pulling her forward until her knees were bent and her bottom was barely on the cushion. He spread her legs gently, planting her feet where he wanted them and leaving her open to his gaze.

He knelt and pressed a kiss to her neck, sliding his mouth down over her chest to the gentle swell of her breast. Her nipple was pebble hard as he dragged his tongue across it, and he smiled as he tasted her skin. He sucked gently on the nub, pulling it into his mouth and massaging it with his tongue as one of his hands possessed her other breast, kneading the soft flesh and rubbing her nipple between two of his fingers.

Zeke's chest flushed with color, and her hips lifted slightly. He continued to lick and suck at her breasts until she was panting from want. Slowly, he released her breasts and continued his journey downward.

His mouth was hot and wet, and he pressed open-mouthed kisses to her stomach. He nipped her hip sharply, soothing the sting with his tongue before continuing down her leg. Rubbing his face on her thigh, he breathed in her musky scent before running his hands down her calf to the delicate bones of her ankle and foot.

Dev nudged her thighs farther apart with his face, brushing gentle kisses over her. Slowly, he licked her, lapping his tongue over her swollen, sensitive flesh. Her fingers dug into the arms of the chair, and she lifted her hips, pressing herself against him, a ragged groan tearing itself from her as he moved his mouth against her.

Zeke closed her eyes and gave herself over to Dev's ministrations. Desire rose in her, wave after wave of it crashing down on her, driving her up the crest of orgasm. She rode it willingly, trying to force herself over the edge. As if he read her mind, Dev withdrew her orgasm expertly, changing the speed at which he used his tongue to bring her pleasure.

Panting, she jerked her hips and pressed herself feverishly toward him, begging for more. Dev pulled back from her, wiping his mouth and grinning up at her.

"Damn you're easy to get on edge."

Zeke glared at him. "Not normally." She groaned in protest when he pulled her to her feet and into his arms.

"Just for me then. I'm okay with that." He ran his hands down her back and over the curve of her ass. "Since this is the first time and you're the one seducing me here, I'll let you pick the position."

Zeke grinned and shoved him down into the chair. She stood in front of him, the firelight dancing over her naked body as she waited for him to slide forward enough so she could straddle him. She bent and picked up one of the condoms, ripping the packet open and rolling the latex shield over his penis.

Slowly, she planted one knee on either side of his thighs and lowered herself onto him, using one hand to steady his penis as she sank onto it. She was wet and snug, and he was long and thick. Each inch she took in filled her until she was undulating her muscles around him and actively trying not to start riding him.

When she was finally completely filled by him, they both groaned deeply. Zeke braced her hands on the back of the chair and rolled her hips against his, gasping as a bolt of pleasure rocketed through her. Unable to wait, she thrust her hips against his, sliding back and forth in his lap, driving him in and out of her.

Dev gripped her hips tightly, urging her to move faster and harder. They careened toward climax together, neither fully in control of the frenzy with which they moved. Their bodies collided over and over again, chests crushed together as Zeke rode him.

With a ragged cry, she flew over the edge and came apart, her body clenching tightly. Dev followed her, his hips surging up and his muscles going rigid as he came. She collapsed into his arms, trembling from the shockwaves that went through her and covered in a fine sheen of sweat from the exertion of their lovemaking.

He held her tightly, his hands running up and down her back gently. She pressed her face into his neck as she tried to catch her breath. Slowly, she managed to sit up and look down at him.

"Why did we wait this long to do that?"

Dev chuckled and pulled her back down for a kiss. "Because you needed the time to be sure you wanted to." He tucked her hair behind her ears. "You're sleeping in my room tonight, Zeke. And every night from now on out."

She nodded. "Okay." She slowly stood and reached for her clothes, dragging them on over her naked body. "Can we light the fireplace up there?"

"Sure." He pulled off the condom and tossed it into the trashcan before stepping into his boxers. "Are you okay?"

Zeke shook her head. "No, but I'm better than I was." She took his hand between both of hers. "Let's go to bed."

CHAPTER THIRTEEN

February 1st, 2060 – Los Angeles

THE DOORBELL jerked Zeke from deep slumber. She sat up, blinking against the dim light spilling through the curtains. Dev stirred next to her, opening his eyes when she slipped from the bed and pulled his shirt on.

"Someone's here. I'll get rid of them and be back." She buttoned the shirt and left the room, jogging down the stairs and turning toward the door.

She undid the chain and turned the deadbolt without looking to see who was on the other side. When she pulled the door open and found Rafael, anger and grief rose up within her, threatening to overcome her. She took several deep breaths to calm herself and smiled at him.

"What can I help you with?"

Rafael lifted his eyebrows and stared at her, raking his gaze over her mussed hair, Dev's shirt and her long, bare legs. "Did I come at a bad time?"

Remembering she'd forgotten to take her watch off the night before, she glanced at it. "It's six in the morning. You woke me up."

"My apologies." He leaned against the frame. "I wanted to make sure you're okay. You were very upset last night."

"I don't particularly enjoy being asked to murder a man in cold blood. Yes, I was upset."

Rafael moved fast, grabbing Zeke by the throat and slamming her against the wall. He shoved himself against her, leaning in close until his lips were pressed against her ear and she could feel the moisture of his breath on her skin.

"You are here because I allow you to be." He squeezed her throat tighter. "You were given an opportunity most people here would have killed to be given. Instead of being grateful, you sobbed on the ground like a fucking pussy. Instead of doing what I would have done to anyone else, I allowed Dev to bring you home and even came to check on you. It would do you well to remember I'm in charge and you are at my beck and call. As far as I'm concerned, you should be on your knees thanking me for giving you the opportunity I did."

Zeke fought the urge to use any of her powers to defend herself against him. She stared up at Rafael defiantly. "And how would you have me thanking you?"

Rafael grinned and used his free hand to squeeze her breast roughly, enjoying the look of defiance and anger that sprang into her eyes. "You turned me down once before, and I didn't appreciate that. You get to stay as long as I allow you to stay. You and your husband both have talents we can use, but your behavior was completely unacceptable last night. You're going to need to make up for it."

Vitriol dripped from her words when she spoke. "What did you have in mind for that? By sucking your dick or with my legs spread wide?"

When he didn't answer, she jutted her chin up and wrenched her head loose. When Rafael slid his hand beneath her shirt and palmed her bare skin, she bit down hard on her tongue to keep from yelling. She took a deep breath and forced herself to calm down.

"I'm not your whore."

"Not yet. You will be." He rubbed her, forcing her legs apart and squeezing. "If you want to stay here, you are going to do exactly what I tell you to do, exactly when I tell you to do it." He ripped her shirt apart and trailed his fingers over her breasts, scraping his thumbnail over her nipple. "You are going to fuck me whenever I want you, or I will make sure you and your husband get kicked out of this place."

"Get your fucking hands off my wife."

Dev's voice was low and hard. He stood on the landing of the stairs, a pistol in his hands and the barrel leveled at Rafael. He descended slowly, never taking his eyes off of the Cambion.

"I said to get your hands off of my wife. If you make me repeat myself again, I'll shoot you."

Rafael held up his hands and stepped back. "If I wanted to kill you, you'd both be dead. Surely you're smart enough to know the powers my kind have. I could toss you across this house with nothing other than my mind."

Dev grinned. "I'm smarter than you think I am, Rafael. I know the only reason you're here is because you have very little to offer Lucifer. If you were powerful, you'd be out there fighting the Nephilim and Angels instead of here going to parties. I'd be willing to bet you can't toss me across this house. I'm perfectly willing to find out, but are you really willing to see whether or not I can hit you with a fucking bullet first?" He gestured to Zeke without taking the gun off Rafael. "Get over here." He waited until she was behind him. "If you ever come to my house and disrespect my wife again, I will kill you. Lucifer be damned, your rules be damned. I will put a bullet in your brain. She is not your whore, and you will never put your hands on her again. Do I make myself clear?"

Rafael brushed his hands over his sleeves. "Your time here from this point forward will not be pleasant." He glared at Dev. "I had hoped you would be one of the people I could trust. It would seem I'm wrong."

Dev didn't move until the door slammed shut. He glanced at Zeke, who was clutching the sides of his shirt over herself. He went to her and laid his hands at her shoulders, checking for injuries. "Are you okay? Did he hurt you?" When she shook her head, his focus returned to the more pressing task. "Pack your stuff. We're leaving. Now."

Zeke shook her head. "We can't leave. If we do, we lose any chance we have at getting the sword."

"This is done, Zeke. It's over. We're getting the fuck out of here and going home. We'll find another way."

"No!" Zeke collapsed to the stairs, tears welling in her eyes and streaming down her face. "My parents are dead! Dead! We killed them for this goddammed mission, and I am not seeing that be for nothing! I'll fuck him if I have to! I'll get on my knees and do whatever I have to do to make sure we get it because I am NOT failing!"

Dev sat next to her, reaching out and taking her hands in his. "Listen to me. Your parents didn't die for nothing, and we haven't failed. We have to take a different approach is all. They died so we could live. If we stay here and get ourselves killed, that is what isn't going to honor them. We have to do what is going to keep us alive to keep fighting." He pulled her close and pressed a kiss to her temple. "Go pack your things. We have to get you somewhere safe. We'll regroup, go over what we know, and figure out a new plan. This one didn't work, baby. We'll figure something else out, I promise."

Zeke covered her face with her hands and sobbed, her whole body shaking. She fell forward into his arms, barely able to breathe. She choked and sobbed, burying her head in his chest, tears leaking through her fingers and soaking into his shirt.

"We can finish this. We can. I'll just go over there and apologize to him. I'll do whatever I have to so he forgives me, and I'll make sure we can stay. We were so close with getting on the council. We need to stay and finish it."

Dev stroked his hands over her back, rubbing gently. "Baby, it's over. There's no finishing it. If I hadn't done what I did this morning, he wouldn't have stopped. There is nothing worth you having to let yourself be pawed at."

"If it was worth my parents dying, then me having to let him rut on top of me is a small price to pay. I'd have gladly done it to save them."

His voice soft, Dev spoke. "I know you would do anything to make this work, but there's nothing else we can do here. We need to get out of here before Rafael sends more Cambion over here to eliminate us as a problem. If he does, we'll be forced to reveal what we are and that'll make it damn near impossible for us. I'm amazed he's so stupid he hasn't realized things after last night. He isn't going to let this go. He's going to send people. We have to leave now, before they get here." He hugged her tightly. "Come on. We need to get things packed up and get out of here. We'll get out of the city and flash out." He pulled her to her feet and half-carried her up the rest of the stairs.

Zeke stumbled into her room and haphazardly pulled things from her drawers, stuffing them into two duffel bags. She yanked on the first clothes she came to—jeans and a sweatshirt—and stuffed her feet into her boots without socks on. She was walking to Dev's room when a flash of light filled the hallway and Michael appeared.

"Do not worry. I took precautions to shield my arrival from being detected." He reached for Zeke and drew her into a hug. "Deacon told me of your parents. I've retrieved their bodies for you. We'll have a proper burial for them, child."

Dev came out of his room. "We need a lift out of here. We have to leave now."

"What's happened? Have you been found out?"

"The stupid fucking Cambion came here this morning. He was trying to force Zeke to have sex with him in order for us to stay. I may have threatened to shoot him. He left, but I don't think he's going to stay gone for long. We're going to have to find another way to get to the sword."

Michael sighed deeply. "Do you have all of your things gathered? Don't leave anything behind that could be used to figure out who you both are." He looked between them. "You've both done an admirable job here, and there is nothing to be ashamed of. We knew this was a longshot. We'll go back to the house, take a couple days for you to rest and to grieve, and then we'll reassess the situation and develop a new plan."

Dev gestured to the bags. "We've got all we need. Let's get out of here before we have a fucking army of Cambion to deal with."

Michael reached out and touched them both before snapping his fingers. Within the span of a heartbeat, they were standing in the living room of Michael's house. Amaya raced down the stairs and threw herself at Zeke, wrapping Zeke in a hug. Zeke managed to keep her composure for several seconds before dissolving into tears. Her knees went weak, and she collapsed against her friend. Amaya gathered Zeke close and ushered her from the room, murmuring nonsense words of comfort as she did so.

Deacon entered the room and went to Dev, embracing him briefly. "I'm glad to see you home. What happened?"

Dev looked at him darkly. "Rafael attacked Zeke this morning. I had to stop him, there was a scuffle and we had to leave." He nodded toward the office. "Let's go in here."

Deacon followed Dev into the office and dropped into a chair. "That's going to make it harder to get the sword, you know that, right?" Pausing, he studied Dev. "How is Zeke? I can't imagine what she must be feeling right now."

"Neither can I. She's trying to hold it together, but there isn't much she can do other than grieve right now. I don't care about having to leave. We were on thin ice after last night anyway. With what happened this morning, there was next to no chance they would have ever trusted either of us enough to let us close. It was going to be over no matter what. Even if she'd gone down there and begged him to bed her, I doubt it would've worked. He'd have done it because he's wanted her since the first moment he laid eyes on her, but he'd have tried to kill her when he was done."

"I'm not saying you did the wrong thing. I'd have made the same call. All I'm saying is this puts us in a bit of a predicament since we now have to figure out how the fuck we get to that damned sword and destroy it."

"We'll figure something out. If we knew exactly where it was, we could go steal it. I'd much prefer that to another undercover mission. We really should have thought this whole thing through better."

"It seemed like it would work. It was a solid plan." Deacon leaned back in his chair and crossed one leg over the other. "We need to figure out how they found Damon and Greer. This is all too much to be coincidental. They go dark just a few days before they end up being captured. There has to be some relation between the two things. Especially since they somehow got from Alaska to Los Angeles and were captured and brought to where you and Zeke were. There's something else going on here, and we need to figure out what it is."

Dev rubbed his hands over his face. "I agree with you. I hadn't put things together yet, but hearing you lay it out, it's obviously not just coincidence. Do you have any idea what it could have been?"

Deacon shook his head. "Not a clue. If you're right and they suspected Zeke, then things make a bit more sense. It still raises the question of how they found Damon and Greer and how they came to suspect Zeke in the first place, but it at least makes a little more sense that way."

"How exactly do you propose we figure all of that out?"

"I think we need to call Gage in. Dad is good at this stuff, but his ties with Heaven have been cut off for decades. Gage has always been better at tracking down answers, and he has more contacts than just about anyone else has ever had, even now."

"We should tell Michael before we make the call. We don't want to step on his toes, but we need the help."

"Agreed." Deacon stood. "I'll take care of Dad. I'm sure you want to check on Zeke. Amaya's with her, and they'll probably be inseparable, but I know you care for her."

"We need to make funeral arrangements for Damon and Greer. She wants to bury them."

"We'll take care of it. We should be able to make the estate in Scotland safe enough to use for a few days. I'll send Carys and Elisa to check it out and make the necessary preparations. It's like hiding in plain sight. I doubt anyone would think to look for us in the place they used before. It's almost too obvious."

Dev nodded slowly. "Are Alaria and Braxton still here?"

"They've been coming in to train with me and Amaya, but they aren't here right this second. They have their other kids to keep an eye on. Finley is getting ready to have a baby any second now, and the other two—Eden and Donovan—are off fighting. Eden's been a Warrior for a few years, but Donovan just finished up his training. They were going to go check on them and be back the first of the week."

"Do they know about Damon and Greer?"

"No. None of the others do. We need to tell Aradia and Gage, too. They'll all want to be at the funeral. They've been friends for thirty years."

"Who's going to tell them?"

Deacon sighed. "I don't fucking know. Probably Dad. I don't think it should come from one of us. It should come from someone they know."

"I think we should offer to let Zeke be the one." Dev stood. "She might want to, and I'm not going to be the one to take that away from her."

"I'll talk to Dad and ask him not to tell anyone until Zeke makes up her mind. But it's going to have to be soon. We can't sit on this for long."

"I'll talk to her." Dev left the room and went back to the living room.

Amaya and Zeke were on the couch, Zeke's head in the Amaya's lap. Her eyes were dry but ringed with red, and a wad of tissue was crushed in one of her hands. They both looked up when Dev sat on the coffee table in front of them.

"Zeke, baby, I need to talk to you about some things."

Zeke forced herself to sit up, curling against Amaya, who wrapped her arms around her. "Okay. What is it?"

Dev reached out and ran his fingers down her face. "Before we get into this, is there anything you need? We could put it off a few hours if you want some sleep or can't focus right now."

Zeke shook her head. "I just want to get it over with. What is it we need to talk about?"

"Michael got your parents' bodies. We need to figure out the funeral arrangements." He took her hands. "Deacon and I were talking about it, and we think it's safe enough to go to Gage's estate in Scotland. That's where your parents lived for years, and I think it would be fitting for them to be buried there."

"That's a good idea." Amaya rubbed Zeke's arms briskly. "Greer and Damon would like that."

Zeke nodded. "Okay." She took a trembling breath. "I think that's okay. Is that all?"

"We need to tell Gage, Aradia, Alaria, and Braxton. Michael can take care of it if you want, or I can. Deacon would, too, but I want to know what you want, and that's what we'll do."

Zeke closed her eyes tightly. She was quiet for several minutes. By the time she spoke again, Amaya and Dev were looking at one another worriedly. "I should be the one to do it." She opened her eyes. "They're my parents. I should be the one. It's not right to ask anyone else to do it."

Amaya hugged Zeke close. "I'll go with you. Mom and Dad went to see Finley. Donovan and Eden are going home from fighting to be with her since she's so close to having the baby."

"Is Aradia going to deliver it?"

"She's the only one we know who can, so I assume so. I don't think they're there, though. Last I knew they were in Canada with Lux and Zane, training them."

"Check with Lux and find out where they are." Zeke looked at Dev. "Will Carys take me?"

"I think Michael would prefer to take you."

She nodded. "That's fine." She climbed to her feet. "I'm going to go shower while you figure out where everyone is. I need to wash off the stench of Cambion." She looked at Dev, her eyes sad and dark. "Will you go with me? I don't want to do it alone.""

"Of course I will."

Chapter Fourteen

February 1st, 2060 – Yukon, Canada

Lux Windsor slipped down the stairs at her parents' home quietly. She could hear her mother in the kitchen and knew her father wouldn't be far. She entered the kitchen and found Zane and Gage playing chess at the table while her mother peeled potatoes at the stove. Gage looked up when she entered the room.

"Hey. Everything okay?"

Lux shook her head. "Amaya just contacted me. Zeke and Michael will be here any second. They need Mom to lower the protections so they can flash in."

Aradia turned. "What's going on?"

"I don't know. Amaya wouldn't say. All she told me is that it's bad and Zeke needs to come here."

Gage spoke from the table. "Lower the protections. Let them in."

Aradia reached within herself to the power swirling inside. She felt for the wards stopping Angels from transporting inside the house and lowered them. Within seconds, there was a flash of light and three people—Zeke, Michael, and Dev—stood in the kitchen.

Gage stood and crossed his arms. "What's going on?"

Zeke's lower lip trembled. "Uncle Gage." She rushed forward and threw her arms around him. Gage caught her and held her tightly, cradling her.

"What is it, baby girl? What's wrong?"

Aradia dried her hand on a dishtowel and crossed the room, stroking her hands down Zeke's back. "Sweetheart, talk to us. What's happening?"

"Mom and Dad are dead!"

Aradia froze. Tears sprang into her eyes, and she sank into a chair. "No. I would have known. What happened?"

Michael cleared his throat and glanced at Zeke and Dev with sympathy in his eyes. "Damon and Greer were captured by Cambion and taken to Los Angeles. Zeke and Dev were forced to kill them. If they had not, they would have also been killed."

Gage tightened his grip on Zeke. "You're safe here. We'll take care of everything." He looked at Aradia. "Can you get Braxton and Alaria here? They need to know what's happened."

Aradia nodded. "I can. They're with Finley. I'm supposed to be there next week to help deliver the baby. It won't be a problem to get ahold of them."

Dev spoke for the first time. "We have the bodies. We'd like to give them a proper funeral. Deacon and I discussed it this morning, and we think it should be safe enough to do it in Scotland. We'd like your permission, of course, since it's your home, but I think Damon and Greer would want to be there."

Gage nodded. "Of course. I'll take care of everything." He hugged Zeke tightly. "Don't worry about a thing. I'm going to handle it all." He looked at Michael. "Can you get someone to stay with Finley and make sure she's protected while we're handling this?"

"I'll make sure she's safe. Do you need me to transport you to Scotland?"

"That would be good. Take Zeke and Dev back to your house and then the rest of us on to Scotland. We'll take care of getting the house ready and preparing graves. We can do the funeral tomorrow." Gage looked down at Zeke. "Do you want to bury them? Or do a Warrior's funeral?"

Zeke pulled back from Gage and rubbed her hands over her face. "I want to bury them. I don't think I could stand to watch them burn."

Aradia hugged Zeke tightly. "Your parents were so proud of you, Ezekiel. They won't ever truly be gone as long as you're still here and still fighting." She looked to Michael. "Take them home. I'll tell Braxton and Alaria." She shook her head when Zeke started to object. "No. You've had to do enough. We'll take care of things. Go home, rest, and grieve. There will be plenty to do after the funeral, but for now, let Gage and me take care of things."

Zeke stood in the middle of her room, completely unsure what to do with herself. Amaya had gone with Lux to Scotland to help ready the estate. Most of the others were out for various reasons. Michael and Dev were the only two people still in the house.

She ran her hands through her hair helplessly. No matter what she did, her mind wouldn't turn off. Everything she looked at made her think of her parents. Every time she thought of them, she wanted to cry. Guilt, grief, and anger battled within her and she was as unsure what she felt as she was what to do. Jumbled in amongst the memories of her parents and their death was the remembrance of Rafael's hands on her body, his bruising grip on her skin and the feel of him pressed against her.

She briefly considered taking another shower to again attempt to scrub away the memories, then considered going downstairs to find something to eat. Scowling when neither option was appealing, she settled on unpacking her duffel bags.

Most of the fancy clothes got tossed into a pile in the corner. She would never again have need of pantsuits and cocktail dresses. She sifted through the pajamas she'd never worn—scraps of silk and lace—and stared down at them, her mind racing.

Desperate to do anything other than continue to mope and sulk, she ran her hands over the fabric and looked over her shoulder at the door. Dev was somewhere in the house. She remembered their coupling the night before and was torn between feeling guilty and glad when a ball of desire formed in her stomach.

She stripped off her clothes and pulled on the negligee, smoothing a layer of red lace over her curves. She tucked her breasts into the cups, smiling at the way her flesh filled the fabric. The hemline barely covered her butt and the lace offered only minimal coverage.

She grabbed her robe and pulled it on, knotting the belt around her waist. Mind made up, she left the room and went on a search for Dev.

Zeke checked his room first, poking her head in and walking into the bathroom but finding both empty. Frowning, she went downstairs and checked the office, living room and finally the kitchen, where she found him nursing a beer and leaning against the counter.

"Where's Michael?"

Dev looked up and smiled when he saw her. "He went to help out in Scotland. Gage has decided it's completely uninhabitable and wants to do a lot of work before you get there tomorrow. I think it's his way of grieving, but it's not for me to argue." He held up the beer. "Want one?"

"No, thanks, though." She glanced around. "Are we alone for the night?"

"As far as I know."

Zeke tugged the ponytail holder loose from her hair and let her waves tumble down around her shoulders. "Can I ask you something?"

Dev grinned. "I'm an open book. What's up?"

"Do you have any regrets about last night?"

The smile faded and his gaze darkened. "Of course I do. I would have given anything to not have to see you go through what you have. Zeke, baby, I will always regret that there was no way to save them. Always."

Moved by his concern for her, Zeke's eyes glistened with tears as shook her head. "I'm not talking about that. I'm talking about us last night in the chair. Do you regret us being together?"

"Not for a second. I regret the timing and everything else, but I could never regret being with you." He brushed his knuckles across her cheek. "Do you? Did I do something to make you regret it?"

"No." She fiddled with the tie on her belt. "I don't want you to think I'm using you because I'm not. I wanted you before what happened, and I'll want you after everything is all said and done. You helped me get a little peace from things last night. I was able to breathe and not hurt, and that's something I haven't been able to do since it happened." She untied the belt and let her robe fall open, revealing the lingerie. "I want to do it again. I want you to take me upstairs to your room or to the couch or, hell, right here on the kitchen floor, and I want you inside me."

Dev blinked. "Without sounding too much like a jerk, are you sure? I don't want you to do anything you don't want to do."

Zeke smiled softly. "I want to. I'm sure about it." She chuckled when he retreated across the room, pressing his back against the counter and holding the bottle in front of himself. "Every time I close my eyes, I see my dad's face. Then it bleeds into Rafael's. I can still feel his hands all over me. I want to erase the feeling of that with the sensation of your hands. I want to feel you touching me. I need to take some of the power back. I need this, and you."

Dev sat his bottle down with a smack and crossed the room, placing his hands on her hips. When she rose onto her tiptoes, wrapping her arms around his neck, he stooped, lifting her in his arms and cradling her against his chest.

"Where the hell did you get this?" He ran his hand over the lace of her nightie. "And can I buy you more?"

"It was in the stuff the stylist sent when we went to L.A." She grinned when he started up the stairs. "I can walk ya know."

"If I put you down, you might change your mind, and if you change your mind, my dick is going to explode. I'd really hate to have that happen, but if you do change your mind, just say so. I'll risk the explosion." He paused to take a breath before climbing the rest of the steps. "You should wear one of these every single night."

"I'll keep that in mind." Zeke laughed as Dev pinned her against the wall in order to turn the knob to open his door. He carried her through and kicked the door closed behind him. "You have to put me down eventually."

Dev carried her to the bed and deposited her on it, leaving long enough to lock the door and retrieve the condoms from his duffel bag. Zeke rose to her knees and slid her robe off her shoulders. She reached out and grabbed his belt loops, dragging him toward her.

"You make me feel better."

He stood still while Zeke stripped off his shirt. Her hands were cool on his chest, and she ran her palms over his skin. She pressed her mouth to his neck, flicking her tongue against his skin and scraping her teeth over his collarbone.

Her hands efficiently worked his belt loose and slid the button on his jeans from the hole. The sound of the zipper hissing as she lowered it echoed through the room, sounding much louder than it really was in the absolute silence.

She pushed his pants and boxers down, reaching down to cup him in her hands, her fingers smoothing over the heavy length in her hands. Wrapping her hands around him, she rained kisses on his chest as she rubbed his swollen erection in her hands. Dev reached around her and gripped her ass, yanking her forward. He ran his hands up her arms and gripped her shoulders.

He brought her forward slowly, fastening his mouth on hers and kissing her deeply. His tongue brushed hers gently, and he used his teeth to nibble at her lips. One of his hands wound in her hair, holding her head still while the other glided down her body to cover one of her breasts. He tweaked her nipple through the lace, teasing it until it was a hard pebble he rolled between his fingers.

When he released her mouth, her head lolled back and her eyes closed. Dev slid onto the bed on his knees in front of her and laid his hands on her hips. He dipped his head slowly and caught one nipple in his lips, sucking on it through the lace of her negligee. She squirmed, her hips jumping against his. Slowly, he leaned her back until she was lying flat on the bed.

He gently tugged the cups of her nightgown down to reveal her areolas. He pressed an open-mouthed kiss to the rise of one breast, drawing his finger down it to rub her nipple gently. When she groaned and arched her back toward him, he dipped his head and sucked the tip into his mouth, rubbing it with his tongue.

Zeke closed her eyes and groaned, bolts of pleasure rocketing through her from the feel of his mouth on her skin. She tangled her hands in his hair, tugging sharply and holding him to her. He used one hand to part her legs and stroked his thumb across the entrance to her body, finding her wet and hot. He flicked his fingers against her and chuckled deep in his throat when she gasped and writhed on the bed.

"Don't make me wait. I want you now."

Dev lifted his head, releasing her nipple and stared down at her, his eyes burning into hers. "In a hurry?"

"Yes." She hooked her legs around her hips, using them to drag him forward. The velvety tip of his penis brushed against her, and they both groaned. "I want you now, and I don't want to wait. We can have foreplay later."

Dev reached for a condom and ripped the packet open with his teeth, using one hand to unroll it on himself. He leaned down and pressed his mouth to hers in a deep, seeking kiss. Pulling her harder against himself, he stroked into her in one smooth thrust, anchoring their bodies together.

Zeke lifted her legs to wrap around his waist, her thighs hugging him tightly. Dev gripped one of her thighs in his hand and used his other arm to brace himself, holding himself above her. He drove into her with heavy, slow thrusts that made her pant and writhe beneath him. Her breasts were crushed to his chest, the lace of her negligee rubbing against them, teasing her sensitive flesh.

Dim light from the lamp across the room spilled across Dev's face, and his brow was covered in a thin sheen of sweat. Zeke gripped his shoulders, her nails biting into his skin. With each thrust of his hips, her cries became breathier, and she began moving with him, arching her hips to meet his strokes. Her body clenched around him, wet and tight, and she felt an orgasm building within her.

Reaching for it, she sank her teeth into her bottom lip and concentrated on the delicious feeling of Dev sliding in and out of her. He was long and thick and stretched her body, giving her friction and contact where she needed it.

"Faster. Dev, please."

He smiled down at her and increased the speed of his thrusts. His fingers gripped her thigh tighter, and he drove into her faster. She cried out and dug her nails into his arms harder as her body tensed around him. He pumped his hips against her, thrusting hard, watching as she exploded into orgasm.

She clenched around him, her muscles tightening and releasing as she rode the wave of climax. Her toes curled, and her back arched. He buried his face in her neck and groaned as he followed her over the edge.

Dev collapsed on top of her, rolling until they both lay on their sides and holding her against him. They lay silently for several minutes, both catching their breath. He rolled to the side and disposed of the condom before returning to the bed and curling up with Zeke.

"We should do that more often."

Zeke giggled and sighed in contentment when he wrapped his arms around her. "We will. What is it you've been telling me? This isn't just sex. It's a relationship. That means we get to sleep with each other as often as we want."

"Do you need anything? Something to eat or drink maybe?"

She shook her head. "I'm fine right here." She laid her head on his chest and smiled when his heart beat beneath her ear. "Thanks for everything. I know you had your doubts about doing this now, but I needed it. I need you."

Dev stroked his hand over her hair. "I never want you to regret this. I never want you to doubt we did the right thing here."

"I don't doubt it." She sighed deeply and rolled onto her back. "I never doubted you. I never doubted what I feel for you or that we could be something really good. You're a genuinely good guy. You're kind and sweet and hot as hell and you're tough and strong. It was about me being scared to feel, and it was being scared to let someone close enough that Lucifer could use them against me." She smiled grimly. "If this has taught me anything, it's that I'm surrounded by people who can be used against me. My parents, Lux and Amaya, Michael, Gage and Aradia, Alaria and Braxton. I love them all. They could all be used against me. And I'm not going to give them up. The more I fought against it, the more I came to realize you were becoming important no matter how much I tried not to."

He turned his head and looked at her intently. "I'm glad you decided to take the chance." He kissed her forehead. "Tomorrow is going to be tough on you."

"Today was tough on me. Tomorrow won't be any different, or the day after that. It's going to take time for me to be able to heal, but I will. It will get duller. I don't really want it to, but I know it will." She sighed and stared up at the ceiling. "It's hard for me to really realize they're gone. I keep thinking I'm going to wake up or walk around the corner and they'll be there, just like they always have been. Every time I close my eyes I can see my dad's face the moment before I pulled that trigger. He was looking straight at me, knowing what I was going to do, and he wasn't mad at me for it. He wanted me to do it, and when I pulled the trigger, I swear he looked relieved."

"He was." Dev spoke softly. "He was relieved you were doing it because he knew that meant you would live, and that was the most important thing to him. It was the most important thing to both of them." He sat up and reached for his clothes. "I think I'm going to get something to eat. Will you come down with me?"

Zeke looked down at herself. "I should probably go put on some real clothes first."

He stood and went to the dresser, chucking a pair of pants and a shirt at her. "Here. Wear that."

She stared at the clothes with a look of shock on her face. "You're lending me more of your clothes?"

He grinned and pulled on his own pants. "You've achieved lover status. I believe that entitles you to the items in my dresser. I could be wrong, but I don't think I am."

"I'm not going to complain." She pulled on the clothes and smoothed her hair.

"I didn't think you would." He opened the door. "Come on. There's plenty of time to be sad tomorrow."

CHAPTER FIFTEEN

February 2nd, 2060 – Scotland

GAGE'S ESTATE was much the same as it had always been—a huge house with a sprawling yard. Once, it had been home to Zeke's parents. They had shared it with the other four, and within those walls, they had all learned to love and to fight. They had become a family. Once, they had come together to lay Braxton's family to rest. In the thirty years since, many more had fallen, but none so close to the rest that they were buried at home. Damon and Greer were different.

Two holes were dug in the backyard, overlooking the forest. Gage had managed to bring in two coffins, and they were suspended above the graves, waiting to be lowered.

Zeke ignored the sight of the graves, instead walking into the house. The windows had been replaced with shiny new panes of glass. The electric was on, running off generators. The kitchen was the center of the house, teeming with activity. Aradia manned the stove, cooking for the crowd of people. The others sat around talking. Some eyes were teary, others were dry.

When Braxton saw Zeke, he stood and crossed the room, taking her into his arms and hugging her tightly. The conversations died down within seconds, everyone turning to look at Zeke.

Braxton's voice was low and ragged. "You did the right thing,

Zeke. We all know that. There's a lot going on we have to figure out, but I never want you to doubt you did the right thing." He let her go. "Michael filled me in on what happened, and I agree with Deacon that there's more to this than meets the eye. There's no way your parents would go dark without bringing us in. They had to know something was going down."

Zeke took a shaky breath and fought off the urge to cry. "How can we figure out what was going on?"

A voice sounded from the other room. "I believe I may have the answers you seek."

Amaya scowled. "Gabriel. What the fuck are you doing here?"

Alaria glared at her daughter. "Be polite, Amaya." She put her hands on her hips. "I'm surprised to see you here, Gabe."

Gabriel looked uncomfortable as he entered the room. "I have something to tell you all."

Braxton sighed. "This is never good news. In thirty years he has never brought good news, not even once." He looked at Gabriel. "Please tell me this is the first time you're actually going to bring me good news."

Gabriel shifted from foot to foot. "I wish I could tell you that, Braxton, but I cannot. In truth, what I have to tell you here today will not require any action from anyone. I am merely here to answer a few questions you have regarding the death of Damon and Greer."

Zeke crossed her arms and leaned against the counter. "You know what happened?"

Gabriel nodded. "I think it would be best if I tell you what I know, and then I can answer questions." He sighed deeply. "A week after Zeke and Dev went to Los Angeles, Rafael contacted the Cambion leadership left alive from the town in Connecticut where they were supposed to be. The other Cambion informed him he did not know you. Rafael became suspicious and began looking into you." He closed his eyes for a moment and took a breath. "I wish I could have changed things, but by the time I discovered what was going on it was too late. They figured out who you are, Zeke.

"Rafael was convinced you could be swayed. It would be a huge coup for him to bring one of the children of the six to the side of Satan, and he had no idea who Dev was. He wanted to believe you were really on their side or that he was wrong. Alexi was going to issue the order for you to be killed, but Rafael wanted to keep you for himself. He asked to be given time to prove you were loyal to them."

Zeke closed her eyes and shook her head, tears stinging her eyelids. "Please tell me you didn't do what I think you did."

Gabriel looked at her sadly. "I did what was necessary, the same as you did. Alexi determined the only way you could prove your loyalty was to kill those closest to you. If you were willing to do that, then he would be willing to give you a chance. When I discovered what the order was, I went to Damon and Greer and told them what was going on. I gave them the choice. They immediately agreed to it."

Zeke was crying then. "No. No, no, no. They couldn't. No."

Gabriel shifted from foot to foot uncomfortably. "When I came to you to ask you to find Damon and Greer, I already knew where they were. They wanted a chance to say goodbye to you and see you one last time. When you left, they knew the Cambion were coming for them. I helped plant the information so Rafael discovered where they were. They knew what was going to happen. They were in that room that night because they chose to be. You didn't kill them—they sacrificed themselves for you because they love you and because they wanted you to live."

Zeke shook her head. "No! You didn't! Tell me you didn't! Please God, tell me you didn't ask my parents to die!"

"I did not. I presented them with information, and they made their choice."

Dev's eyes were dark with fury. "You could have told us! We'd have left and found a new way! We had to leave anyway because of Rafael. If you, for once, had been honest about what you knew instead of playing us, then they might still be alive!"

"Your absence from Los Angeles is an unfortunate twist I did not anticipate." Gabriel glared at Michael. "Had I been the one looking after you, I would have encouraged you to do whatever was necessary to ensure you could stay and continue with the mission. However, that was not done, and now we are forced to deal with the situation that has been created."

Amaya went to Zeke and wrapped her arms around the other woman. "You would have asked her to be his whore?"

Gabriel closed his eyes and took a deep breath. "None of you seem to understand. The whole world is at stake. If you fail, there are no more chances. No children waiting to be born to pick up the fight. This is it. One chance. So yes, if it were up to me, I would have insisted Zeke offer herself up to Rafael if that would have made a difference."

Amaya shook her head. "If we win this by being as bad as they are, it isn't really winning." She glared at her father. "I think you've proven the mission is more important to you than the people who have to carry it out. That's why we look to Michael for help. He understands we have to preserve who we are in order to win. If we become the Cambion's whores, if we do all the things they do, even for the right reasons, we're no better than they are. I won't be a part of that. We'll win this, but we'll win it the right way. We don't kill people. We kill Cambion, demons, and Devils. Monsters. We don't kill human beings. We don't ask them to die when there are other choices. There are lines that can't be crossed, Gabriel. Lines we can't come back from if we do cross them. How can you ask us to?"

"I have never asked anyone to do anything that was not necessary. The things I do must be done." Gabriel crossed his arms and glowered at them all. "Eventually you will understand we are fighting a war. There are casualties in battles." He turned to Michael. "You're the Angel of War. You should be teaching them better than this."

Michael stared at his brother, sadness in his eyes. "We are fighting, brother. You sit in Heaven with the rest of the Host and wait while I lead the troops down here on Earth. You're not fighting. The Angels are not fighting. God is not fighting. You have no right to come here and interfere when you deem it necessary and then disappear back behind the Gates where you face no consequences from the actions you set in motion." He looked over at Zeke and Dev. "You asked the children to make an impossible choice and made Damon and Greer believe they had none. You should have come to us and told us what you knew. If you had, they would likely still be alive."

Gabriel chuckled. "One day you will all realize the only thing that matters is that Lucifer is defeated. How we do so or who dies in the process does not matter at all. Some of the people in this room will likely not make it to the end of this. That is the risk you take every day. Every time you walk outside, you risk your life. You will have to do bad things—unconscionable things—and failing to do so will ensure Lucifer wins."

Before anyone could speak, Gabriel disappeared. Zeke sniffled and wiped her hand across her eyes, leaning her head on Amaya. Alaria broke the silence from her position next to the sink.

"I don't even recognize him anymore." She looked at her daughter. "Gabriel was once one of the best men I know. He was gentle and kind and always did what was right." She turned her head to face Braxton. "I wish he still was."

Michael pushed off the island. "He changed when God asked him to impregnate you, Alaria. That was his breaking point. The point at which he had to choose the people he cared for or the God he served, and he chose God. Unfortunately, he believes that choice requires him to continue down that path indefinitely." He sighed. "Gabriel believes he must give God exactly what He asks for. I believe in giving Him what He needs."

Dev shook his head, a look of disgust on his face. "I don't care why. He's a fucking Angel. He's supposed to save people, not kill them."

Zeke wiped her face with her hands and straightened. "I don't care. None of this matters right now. I just want to bury them." She smiled when Lux came to stand on her other side. "I don't want to talk about it anymore. I'm here to bury them, and that's what we need to do. Nothing else. We can deal with all the other shit tomorrow."

"Then that's exactly what we'll do." Aradia stood and walked toward the door. "Is there anything you want for this, Zeke?"

She shook her head. "No. I just want to get it over with."

Together, the group walked out onto the lawn toward the caskets. Michael used his powers to gently place the caskets in the ground, lowering them slowly into the holes. He waited for several minutes before speaking.

"Damon and Greer were extraordinary people. I remember during the tasks, when Greer charged into Hell to find Laelia with no thought for herself. Her only goal was to complete the task. When I had to go after her, she fought alongside me. She never hid behind me or asked me to do more than she. Instead, she stood back to back with me, battling our way through a legion of demons."

Michael stopped speaking for a moment as he stared at the graves, his eyes moist with tears. He took a deep, shuddering breath before continuing.

"Zeke, your father was one of the bravest men I have ever known. During that same task, he took in the spirit of Laelia, knowing doing so might cost him his life. He did it anyway because there was no other choice. I fought alongside him many times, and I grieve for the lost opportunities to do so again.

"When you were born, they made a decision to focus on you

instead of others. It was a decision I supported. They raised you better than almost anyone else could have, and you turned into a remarkable woman with a good heart, a strong spine, and an unshakeable character. It was my honor to help guide your parents, and it is my continuing honor to guide you. I know no one can ever replace them, but I hope you never doubt those of us left love you as we love our own children."

Zeke went into Michael's arms, burying her face against his chest and wrapping her arms around him. Aradia and Alaria were openly crying as they watched the scene unfold. Alaria wiped her hands over her eyes and looked steadily at Zeke.

"Greer saved my life. I won't delve into the circumstances, but I got stabbed. I was dying. I would have been dead in seconds if she hadn't been there. She poured everything she had into healing. When she laid her hands on someone, she had no care for herself or any drain she would feel. I watched her nearly kill herself trying to save people." Alaria choked back a sob. "I had never had friends before. Greer and Damon were two of my very first ones. I never spent much time alone with your dad, but I spent plenty of time with them both. No matter what I needed, they were always there. I know you're hurting, and I know there's nothing any of us can say to make that better. I wouldn't even know where to start, but you're not alone. You never will be as long as any of the people here are still breathing."

Gage smiled. "The thing I remember most about Damon and Greer is the first little bit after they got here. They were so desperately in love with each other and so very determined not to admit it, not even to themselves. The first couple days, Greer was unconscious. Damon and I had our differences. He couldn't believe a vampire would be someone he could trust. Eventually, though, he became my brother. They were my family. We lived here together for more than two years. We fought like family, and we loved like family. When we were in Atlantis, they stayed in the city and ran the whole battle. They could fight viciously, and I wouldn't have wanted to face either of them in a battle. There has never existed a better shot than your mother. You were blessed with parents who loved you voraciously and who willingly sacrificed themselves to save you. I can only second what Alaria said. We are a family. All of us. I know without a doubt if it were me who had died, I could have trusted your parents or Brax and Alaria with my child. We take care of our own, and we'll take care of you, no matter what it is you need. As long as there is life left in any of us, we will keep fighting to make sure they did not die needlessly."

Zeke lifted her head from Michael's chest and looked at the group with red-ringed eyes. She took a trembling breath. "I think I forgot how much they meant to other people. All I've thought about is how I feel, having to do what I did and live through what I did. It's hard for me to look past what I feel and see that all of you knew them at least as well as I did." She looked skyward as she tried to fight back a fresh wave of tears. "Mom always told me Lux, Amaya, and I were like sisters, even though we didn't meet until we were teenagers. It never occurred to me that we're as close as we are because Mom had two sisters, too. And two brothers." She flicked her gaze between Gage, Alaria, Braxton, and Aradia. "I'm sorry I'm being so selfish."

Braxton glared at her. "You're not being selfish. Selfish was my hiding out for months after Griffin died. Selfish was Gabriel going behind our backs again and doing what he thought was best for him. You are not selfish. The night we had a funeral for my parents, I mauled Alaria and mouthed off to Gabriel. You are not being selfish. You're grieving, and you can do that however you need to for as long as you need." He paused to take several breaths. "We've been lucky so far. We've all seen a lot of death, but this is the first time it's been one of us. Damon and Greer have good company in Heaven. My parents, my sister, her husband, Griffin."

Alaria interjected. "Lex and Calder."

Aradia smiled. "My mother and father."

Zeke managed a watery smile. "The families they left." She sniffled. "I know they never admitted it, but I think a part of them, especially Mom, missed the world they left. They were never more comfortable than when they were preparing for battle. They were soldiers to the last." She tipped her head back and stared up at the sky, the brisk wind drying the tears on her cheeks. "They always told me I would be asked to do horrible things. They raised me to believe there is no sacrifice too great for the cause. I believe that with all my heart. I would gladly give my life for this. I know we all would." She wiped her face with her palms and sighed deeply. "It's a whole different level of pain to be asked to kill one of your own."

Michael hugged Zeke close and stroked his hand down her hair. "I know it's cold comfort, child, but I can promise you your parents are safely ensconced in Heaven. They know peace, and they are together."

Zeke smiled. "It's not cold comfort. Knowing that helps." She squared her shoulders and looked around at the group. "What's the plan?" When no one spoke, she glared at them. "I'm not stupid. I know you've put your heads together to figure out what we need to do now. Dev and I didn't get the sword. We need it. Amaya and Deacon can't go after it because they can't be seen until the end when we go after Lucifer. Lux and Zane can't go get it because they're busy with Beelzebub and his spawn. None of your others are powerful enough. That means I'm the only one who can do it." She looked at the others. "No offense, but Aradia is the only one who has any business going out into this anymore, and she's got a ton of other shit on her plate keeping everyone safe. Just because they died doesn't mean I don't still have a job to do."

Gage smiled grimly. "You always were very practical. I wish I was disappointed with that." He stared at her. "I want you to take the time you need to deal with this. The last thing we need is you falling to pieces in the middle of something. I need time to locate the sword as it is. You can stay here or with Michael at the nonplace, but I'll be working on finding everything you need."

Zeke nodded definitively. "Good. I'll be ready when you are."

CHAPTER SIXTEEN

March 1st, 2060 – Scotland

ZEKE WOKE slowly. Light streamed through the curtains and spilled over the bed. She blinked to clear her eyes and snuggled further down into the blankets. One look across the room was enough to verify what her body already knew. The fire had gone out.

Shivering, she wiggled closer to Dev, placing her chilled feet on one of his calves and pressing her nose to his throat. He came awake with a jerk, his eyes snapping open.

"What the hell? You're a fucking popsicle."

Zeke giggled and burrowed closer. "The fire went out."

Dev scowled. "So I see." He threw back the blankets and left the bed to retrieve several pieces of wood from the pile by the door. "I really wish we still had electricity. We get that stuff when Lux and Aradia are here or at the nonplace because they have the power to run shit off." He struck a match and bent to light a fire. "The rest of us get to freeze."

Zeke held the blankets up. "Come get back in bed. We'll wait until it's warm before we venture out."

"As much as I'd love that, I need to go start a fire downstairs to warm it up so we don't freeze once we do get up." He grinned at her. "I'll be back in a minute."

Zeke wrapped the blanket around herself. "Suit yourself. I'm staying here where it's warm."

Dev shook his head and loped down the stairs to the living room. He tossed logs into the massive wood stove and squirted lighter fluid on them. Striking a match, he tossed it onto the wood and watched as flames erupted.

There was one generator they used to run the refrigerator to ensure they had food, and they cooked on the wood stove. He plugged the coffee maker into the generator to perk a pot and checked to make sure the generator had enough gas.

Five minutes later, carrying two mugs of coffee, he climbed the stairs and turned back into the bedroom he and Zeke shared. She was still in the bed, buried under the blankets with only her eyes peeking out. When she spotted the coffee, one hand snaked out toward the steaming cup.

Dev grinned and handed the mug over before slipping back beneath the blankets. Zeke drank deeply, draining half her cup before plunking it down on the nightstand. She wiggled under his arm and laid her head on his chest.

"I've been thinking and I'm wondering if we shouldn't drag the mattress downstairs. We might stay warmer that way, and then we only have to worry about one fireplace."

"That works if we're the only ones here, but if some of the others are here we need to use the bedrooms." He finished his coffee and slid further down in the bed, wrapping his arms around Zeke and pulling her tight against himself. "I'm not about to sleep in a room with other people where I can't just roll on top of you whenever I want."

Zeke shivered and turned her head to look back at him, rolling her eyes. "Sometimes I don't know why I put up with you." She grinned and pressed a kiss to his jaw. "But since it's pretty much true, I can't say too much."

Dev nuzzled her neck with his nose. "You make it hard to get out of bed and do anything productive. It's much more appealing to stay right here and hold you all day."

"I know, but we need to get some training in today. Gage could have info for us any day now, and we need to be ready to run with it when he does."

"We will." He ran his hand down her arm and over her hip. "Babe, we're doing everything we can. It's safest for everyone if you and I stay out of sight until we have something to act on. We know

Rafael is probably looking for us, and the last thing we want is to bring anything to anyone else."

Zeke sat up and cocked her head to the side when the light streaming through the curtains rapidly faded. Without a word, she threw the blankets back and slid out of bed, going to the window and pulling back the curtains.

"It's dark outside."

Dev joined her at the window. "I don't see anything."

"Neither do I." She went to the dresser and yanked on jeans and a long-sleeved shirt. She hopped on one foot to pull on a sock and boot before switching feet and repeating the action.

Dev dressed efficiently and pulled a case out from under the bed, tapping in the code and opening it to reveal an assortment of guns. He tucked a pistol into his waistband and an extra clip in each pocket. With practiced movements, Zeke assembled and loaded a rifle and slung it over her shoulder.

"Can you get a sense for who's out there?"

Dev nodded tensely. "Trouble. I'm getting a few signatures. Some vampires, which is why it's dark, a witch to keep the clouds thick enough to let them be out, and a dozen Cambion. None of them feel high level to me."

"Is one of them Rafael?"

"I'd be willing to put money on it." He looked at her darkly. "If it is them, then we know for a fact they knew who you are. The only people they could use against me are protected by Michael, and there's no way this little twit could go up against them."

Zeke led him down the stairs and into Gage's office. She opened a cabinet and drew out two Kevlar vests. "I know you know, but I feel better saying it. Don't worry about me out there. I can handle anything they've brought." She looked at him, worry plainly evident in her eyes. "Don't do anything stupid."

Dev stooped to kiss her quickly. "This isn't my first rodeo, darlin'. I'll be fine." He shifted from foot to foot. "I'm going to have to invest in a Kevlar with wing holes. If I need to take off it's going to fucking hurt." He pressed his back against the wall at the side of the door. "If it gets to be too much, we'll yell for Michael or Gabriel, but let's try and deal with this on our own. I really don't want to expose anyone else if we can help it."

Zeke nodded and raked her hair back from her face, securing it in a ponytail. "Agreed." She glanced at him. "Sword?"

Dev grinned and clenched his fist, conjuring a short sword and leather sheath. He helped her secure it to her hip and nodded to the door. "Ready?"

She jerked open the door, and they strode out onto the lawn together. Rafael stood in the driveway, flanked by two demons. Behind him were several Cambion, clutching a combination of swords and guns. Farther back, Zeke made out seven vampires prowling, and the witch was in the woods just out of sight.

"Did you really think I'd let you just leave?"

Zeke shrugged. "I can't say I gave much thought to you at all. We weren't your prisoners."

Rafael sneered. "I can't allow two Nephilim to live. Surely you knew I would be coming."

Dev snorted. "I didn't think you had the balls, actually. If I have a sense of you, you aren't even full Cambion. Second generation. I'd bet one of your grandparents was a demon. Decent level since you have some okay powers, but it's nothing impressive." He looked around at the others. "Just like I can tell there are only three of you who have anything other than minor demonic powers."

Zeke chuckled. "That's the problem with Nephilim and Cambion. We can only be as powerful as the creature that produced us. Archangels and Devils make the most powerful offspring. That's why they bred like rabbits for so many years. Want to know who made me?"

Rafael sighed. "I don't doubt you're both strong and well-trained, but we all know how this is going to go. If you lay down your weapons and come willingly, I'll promise you a painless death. Otherwise, you're going to get hacked to pieces right here."

Zeke and Dev exchanged a look. After a long moment, Zeke spoke. "You take the vamps. I've got these guys."

Rafael laughed. "You're outnumbered twelve to one. Don't be stupid."

She crossed her arms. "Don't you know anything about what I can do?"

"I know you have a shield, which is how you fooled us into allowing you into the community. Beyond that, I don't know, and I truly don't care."

Zeke sent out a wave of power toward the two demons. She focused on them, using her abilities to find their free will and cast a net over it, anchoring them to her. She smiled when she felt the tug that told her she had them.

"I want you both to hop on one foot."

Rafael shrieked angrily when both demons did as Zeke told them. "What the fuck are you doing? Kill her! Kill them both!"

Dev drew his sword to face the vampires coming at him, leaving Zeke to handle the Cambion. She sent out another wave of power to the demons.

"Kill one another." She stood her ground as the Cambion rushed her, using her telekinesis to throw some of them back, and her ability to control them to ensnare others, leaving them helpless to do anything other than obey.

Rafael pulled out a gun and leveled it at her. "You might have some nice tricks, but I doubt you can outrun a bullet."

Zeke smiled and used her abilities on him, overtaking his free will and laying hers on top. "Aim that gun at yourself."

Rafael struggled against the command, trying to fight her, but was unable to do it. His hand turned, the barrel of the gun swinging until it was aimed directly at his face. He tried to back up, but his feet were rooted to the ground.

"What are you doing? You can't do this. If I don't get back to Los Angeles, Alexi will come for you. I know you're not stupid enough to want to deal with him."

Zeke shrugged. "The more the merrier." She looked at the Cambion standing around, most stuck and unable to move. The only two she hadn't been able to compel had already fled. "Your reinforcements took off. Seems they don't want to die." She looked over her shoulder. "Dev is almost done slaughtering your vampires. It seems to me you grossly underestimated us."

Rafael jerked as he tried to break free. Around him, the other Cambion looked terrified as they waited to see what Zeke was going to do to them.

"I want you to tell me what Alexi knows. For every question I ask, if you lie to me or you refuse to answer, one of your Cambion dies. If you still aren't cooperating by the end of them, I'll start making you shoot off pieces of yourself. Then I'll heal you so we can keep going until you decide you want to cooperate." She stared at him, her gaze hard. "Don't doubt me, Rafael. I don't make idle threats."

"Go to Hell."

Zeke looked at one of the Cambion disinterestedly. "He doesn't think I'll do it. He thinks I'm too human and too weak. He's remembering how I fell apart when he made me put a bullet in my father's brain." She tapped her fingers against her mouth. "I'd be willing to bet most people would have a big problem with being forced to kill one of their parents."

Rafael sneered. "Your first mistake is in thinking I care about them. They're disposable, the same as you are. No one will miss you once I've killed you."

"How are you going to kill me when you can't move without my permission?" She cocked one eyebrow and chuckled. "Your only chance of getting out of here alive is if you do what I tell you to do and answer my questions with the truth. Dev will know if you're lying, won't you, Dev?"

Dev brushed dust from his pants and nodded. "I sure will." He crossed his arms. "I know you think you brought a lot of reinforcements, but you should have known better than to wage war against Nephilim with only low ranking Cambion. You brought them here to basically commit suicide." He looked around the yard. "Even those vamps were barely vampires. What was the point of this? To give us some exercise?"

Zeke sheathed her sword and put her hands on her hips. "It's almost enough to make me sad. You bring all these weaklings here thinking you're going to take in two Nephilim and be heroes for a while, and instead you've bitten off way more than you can chew and none of you are going to survive." She sighed deeply. "Of course, if you want to change your mind and start talking, you stand a chance at getting them out of here in one piece."

Rafael sighed in resignation. "You know this isn't going to end well for the two of you. There's nowhere you can go Lucifer won't have you tracked down. Our God is here with us, fighting alongside us, making sure we have everything we need while yours is hidden behind the Gates with his army, refusing to let them help fight. It's only a matter of time before we wipe you all out."

Zeke snorted. "I know nothing of the sort." She shifted her gaze to one of the other Cambion. "If he doesn't tell me where Lucifer's sword is in thirty seconds, I want you to shoot yourself in the knee."

Rafael laughed. "You can't make him do that."

Dev sighed. "Don't test her, dude. It won't end well for you. Where's the sword?"

"Twenty seconds."

"Fuck you, bitch." The Cambion holding the gun snarled the insult even as his finger eased back the hammer without his permission.

Rafael began to look nervous. "I don't know where it is. They hide it."

"Ten seconds." Zeke closed her eyes as she counted down the seconds. At the end, the gunshot echoed through the air followed by a scream as the man rolled on the ground clutching his bleeding leg and sobbing. She sighed again. "I can make them all do that and worse. I can make them do it to each other and to you. Don't make me prove it to you. The more I make them do, the more I'm going to want to kill them, and I don't think you really want that, now do you?"

"We all know we're not all going to leave here alive. It's either us or you, because if you let us live, then we all know there will be a fucking army descending on you here within hours."

Zeke looked at Dev and lifted one of her shoulders in a careless shrug. "He's right. They would sic their big brothers on us." She drew her sword. "I suppose we're going to have to kill them after all."

Dev nodded slowly. "You're probably right. The only choice we have is how we kill them. Do we do it fast and painless or slow and painful?"

"I don't know. I mean, Rafael is the ring leader here. The others probably didn't know what they were getting into. They thought this was going to be an easy mission and they'd get to spill some Nephilim blood. Unfortunately for them, Rafael was wrong and they're going to die for his mistake." She looked at Rafael. "Tell me, or I'll make you shoot your own dick off. What happens if you come back without us?"

Rafael closed his eyes and looked pained. "You want the truth? Fine. Here's the truth. Alexi knew what you were before you left. It's why he went after your parents. I thought you were really loyal. I wanted to believe it, well, because I wanted to fuck you. He agreed to give you a chance to prove yourself. You passed the test, but when you both disappeared, it was my ass in a sling. I have to find you and kill you, or Alexi kills me."

Dev considered that for a moment. "That reads like the truth."

Zeke narrowed her eyes at Rafael. "I'm not going to let you live. I want to take you apart piece by piece and then put you together again just so I can take you back apart, over and over until you know the pain I have felt over what you made me do." She took a deep breath to steady herself. "However, if you tell us everything you know, I will keep a lid on my more psychopathic tendencies and promise to make it quick."

Rafael hesitated only a moment. "What do you want to know?"

"How did Alexi find out about me?"

"I don't know all the details. He was at the church ceremony, in the back. He'd come in to collect the volunteers. He saw you and thought he recognized you from some nightclub a couple months ago where some Nephilim escaped from him. It was enough to make him suspicious. From there, I don't know."

"Does he know where we are?"

"No. When you ran away, he gave me orders to find you. If I didn't, he would kill me. Bring you back dead and I get to take back over in Los Angeles. I didn't want to tell him I'd located you until I had you in custody."

Dev rocked back on his heels. "How did you find us?"

Rafael smirked. "You're not as clever as you think you are. There are very few places you could be lying completely low. Everyone knows about Gage's estate. I didn't actually think you'd be so fucking brazen as to hide in plain sight, but here you are."

"What were the other places on the list?" Zeke rubbed her palms on her thighs to warm up her hands.

"Las Vegas, your parents' house in Alaska, New York down in the tunnels—I thought you might want to be with your parents even if they had no clue who you are. If you weren't at any of those places, we'd have put the word out worldwide. You'd have shown up in some city or been seen by someone on my side eventually."

Zeke's head snapped up. "You know my parents were brought back in time?"

"Everyone knows that. Everyone has always known. Lucifer issued orders that no one messes with the timeline because he doesn't want to risk a different outcome to the last task. No one's going to kill them. Nothing is going to change." Rafael snorted. "Do you really think we would risk messing this up? Besides, there's a theory that they couldn't be killed before Gabriel takes them anyway. God wants you to be born, and for that to happen, everything in the timeline has to stay the same. I certainly didn't want to be the one to get deep fried just for touching one of them. No thank you."

"You're awfully chatty." Zeke crossed her arms and stared at him. "You understand you're going to die, right?"

"Just because I'm going to die doesn't mean I want it to be painful." Rafael closed his eyes for a moment. "I'd really rather just get this over with."

"We have a couple more questions." Dev looked amongst the Cambion before continuing. "We need to know where Lucifer's sword is being held and who is in charge of it."

Rafael laughed, the sound slightly desperate. "Do you really think they would tell me?" He took a deep breath. "Truth is we had it in LA a couple years ago. As far as I know, the damn thing gets shifted around between the communities. It's only transported by Devils, and it's guarded by the churches. Lucifer believes the humans who worship him are the most likely to be willing to die to protect it and the Angels are the least likely to go after people, so he uses them. It only ever stays in one place for a few months at a time. All I know is that it went to Miami from Los Angeles. After that, I have no idea."

Zeke tugged on her hair in frustration. "Which Devils transported it?"

"Never Beelzebub. Lucifer doesn't want the two things that are his biggest weaknesses together ever. Other than that, I don't know."

"How long until Alexi misses you?"

"I don't know. Maybe tomorrow, maybe a month. He's fighting a fucking war. He might not surface again for a year. Or Beelzebub could be sitting on my couch right now. We don't exactly schedule appointments."

"What other places were on your list?"

"Other than the ones I named? A couple hideouts we know you used on raids on Cambion. There's one in Paris and one in Ecuador, plus some Warrior complex in Panama that is used as a hiding spot from time to time."

Zeke nodded. "I'm done. Anything else, Dev?"

Dev shook his head. "I don't think so." He glanced at the others. "Want me to take care of them?"

"Nah. They can do it." She sent out a wave of power. "I want you all to pick up your weapons." She waited while they drew guns. "Put the barrel in your mouth and pull the trigger."

Dev winced as twelve Cambion moved in unison to kill themselves. Zeke's eyes were flat and hard as she watched the bodies crumple to the ground. She turned to Rafael.

"I promised you painless, and I won't go back on my word, regardless of how much I'd like to. I'd love to rip your head off your shoulders with my hands. I could occupy myself for days making you scream." She blinked back angry tears. "You're a wretched piece of filth who deserves every bit of pain I could give you." She took a step back. "But I made a promise. If I didn't want to be the one to end you so fucking much I'd let Dev have you since he didn't promise and I have no doubt he would be as ruthless as me."

Dev chuckled. "I'd love to take it from you if you'd let me. There's nothing I'd like more than to kill him."

Zeke drew her sword and stared down at the blade. She stared at Rafael, who was silent, though she detected a slight tremor in his hands. Smiling because she knew he was scared, she tipped her head back and stared up at the sky, feeling the warmth of the sun on her skin.

"I wish you weren't a threat to me. I've never killed anyone who wasn't trying to kill me, but I would like to sneak up on you in your bed and kill you just because I want to and not because I have to." She looked at the blade of her sword again then shifted her gaze to the gun Dev held. "I don't know if I want to cut his head off or shoot him."

Dev lifted one shoulder. "If it were me, I'd be hard pressed not to use my bare hands."

Rafael sighed deeply. "For the love of Lucifer, get it the fuck over with. It's like death by auditory assault."

Zeke shook her head. "You don't deserve the time I'm spending thinking about this. I want to do this the right way so it gives me a little peace knowing I took out the person who killed my parents." She looked at Dev sadly. "Instead, I'm just incredibly tired of all the killing. I have this fire in my gut that wants me to take from him what he took from me, but I know if I do that, I'm no better than he is." She closed her eyes and took Dev's gun from his hand. "Lucifer rejoices in bloodshed. My God is pained by it. That's why we'll win and you won't." She drew back the trigger and leveled the barrel. "I'd tell you to go with God, but we'd both know it's a lie. Instead, I'll tell you you're lucky I'm feeling merciful today."

The sound of a shot echoed through the grounds, and Rafael's head exploded as the projectile rocketed through his skull and into his brain. The body collapsed to the ground, and the grey mist that was the essence of a Cambion floated through the air for several moments before dissipating.

Dev wrapped one arm around Zeke's shoulders and pulled her close to his side. "We need to pack up and get out of here."

She nodded. "I know." She laid her face against his chest for a moment. "We need to lie low until Gage comes up with the info we need." She straightened and cast a look around the lawn. "Let's get out of here. I know where we can go that no one will ever find us."

Together, they hurried back into the house and ascended the stairs to the room they shared. Quickly, they crammed clothing into duffel bags and gathered weapons. Zeke efficiently broke down two rifles and stowed them in a bag with extra clips, pistols, and boxes of ammo. They were nearly done when a wave of power washed over the house, alerting both to Cambion signatures as they arrived outside the house.

Dev darted to the window and pressed himself against the wall to peer out the curtains. "The two who got away sure didn't waste time alerting their bosses. Not Alexi and his crew, but not too far down the rungs. They sent in some of the big boys. Our powers aren't going to work on them. Devil offspring."

Zeke swore. "Okay. We can't flash out or they'll be able to track the signatures." She zipped up the duffel bag and slung it over her shoulder. "You're going to have to trust me. I know how to get out of here, but I need you to follow my lead."

Dev nodded. "Lead the way. Just tell me what you need me to do. Their powers won't work on us, but I don't want to get into a shootout with a bunch of Cambion." He held a pistol in his hand and crept behind her down the hall as she led him to the back stairs.

"I need to get to the weapons cabinets in Gage's office. There are explosives in there. We don't have much time before they'll be in the house, but it will take a couple minutes for them to get through Aradia's protections. I'm going to bring the whole fucking house down on top of them."

He stopped abruptly on the steps. "That means bringing it down on us, too."

Zeke grinned at him over her shoulder. "Hardly. There's a tunnel underneath the house. It runs all the way to the airport in Glasgow and dumps out into an underground hangar with Gage's private plane in it. I don't know if that's still there, but it'll be far enough away from here so we can figure things out."

She jerked open the cabinet and stuffed a dozen charges and a remote into a small bag. She tucked a hatchet into her belt and snapped a buck knife onto one of the loops. Dev emptied the cabinet of grenades and ammunition before turning to Zeke.

"I'm stronger and bigger. Let me take the charges and put them where they need to be."

Zeke glared at him. "I know where the load bearing walls are. I've been taught precisely where these need to go. You haven't. I'll be much faster at it than you would be." She handed him the duffel bag. "Here's what you need to do. Go to the basement, all the way to the back. In the left corner, there's a bedroom. Move the bed. Behind it, you'll find the seam for a door. Open the door up. Wait for me there. Once I get these going, we have fifteen seconds before they discharge, so I don't have much time. There're a couple boxes at the entrance to the tunnel with flashlights. You'll want to have one of them in your hand or else we'll be fumbling around in the dark."

They both cringed when they heard something collide with the front door. Dev swore. "They're going to be through that fucking door any time."

Zeke smiled tightly. "Then we'd better get moving." She shoved him toward the basement stairs. "I'll be there in two minutes."

"Be careful."

"I always am."

Zeke moved through the main floor quietly. She crouched each time she heard a crash against the door and scowled when she heard the wood splinter and the sound of footsteps in the entry. Two immediately went up the stairs and two headed into the kitchen.

Working her way through the floor, she pressed the explosives to the walls as quietly as possible. Upstairs, she heard the systematic taking apart of each room as the Cambion searched for her and Dev.

As soon as the final charge was placed, the lights on them turned from red to green, signaling the countdown. She bolted for the basement steps, no longer caring if she was seen. She heard a shout as she disappeared into the lower level, and ducked her head to move faster. She used her powers to slam and lock the door behind her and raced into the bedroom.

Dev had the tunnel open and was waiting for her. As soon as she stepped inside, he slammed the door closed and slid the bar across the door into place, locking it from the inside. In less time than it took to take a breath, the explosion rocked the house.

Debris fell from the walls, pummeling them both. Dev grabbed Zeke and forced her onto the ground, pinning her between the ground and his body, his arms wrapped around her head to shield her from everything. Because she couldn't see, Zeke flung out her telekinetic abilities wildly, trying to deter chunks of stone and concrete from falling on them.

After twenty terrifying seconds, the ground stilled under them and the debris ceased to fall. The air was thick with dust, and both coughed as they rolled to their feet. Dev clicked on the flashlight he'd stuffed in his pocket and surveyed their position. Waiting until the ringing in his ears had subsided slightly to speak, he raised his voice to a yell, hoping Zeke would be able to hear him.

"It looks like the tunnel is clear for at least a while. I don't know how far into it the tremors could have reached, so we'll have to keep our fingers crossed it'll be passable."

Zeke nodded and scraped her hair off her face, re-securing it with an elastic band. When she spoke, her voice was slightly lower than his was and he struggled to hear her through the ringing that still reverberated through his head.

"There should have been some bottled water and MREs in the box where you got the flashlight."

"There are." He knelt and uncovered the box. "I think the MREs are still good, but a few of the bottles busted. There are batteries for the flashlights, too."

"Good. If we walk fast, we should make it to the airport today. Once we're back aboveground, I'll try to get ahold of Lux so she can let everyone know we're okay."

Dev quickly emptied their duffel bag of everything except one change of clothes for each of them to make room for water and food. Satisfied that his ears were near normal, he spoke at a normal level. "If we get there and there's no plane, what's the plan?"

"I haven't figured that out yet." She took the flashlight he held out and slid it into her pocket. "We could call for Michael to come get us. We'd be far enough away by then that the signature wouldn't be too terribly suspicious." She shouldered the bag with the weapons. "Besides, even if the damn thing is there, I don't know if it'll start, if there'll be enough fuel to get us across the fucking Atlantic Ocean, or if there's even a place to land it where we're going. It's a safe place that might present us with some options, so we'll see what we find when we get there. It's not like we can go back out there. It would take longer to blast our way out through a hundred tons of rubble than to go to the end of the tunnel and climb out there."

"I'm not arguing with going, babe, just trying to get a feel for the whole plan instead of only the next step." He grinned at her as they started to walk. "Want to tell me where we're going to end up?"

"Colorado. Braxton's sister and her husband owned a cabin there before they died. It's where Braxton took my great-grandmother when they were hiding from Alaria. It hasn't been used for anything since. It's one of the places that has always been in reserve, but one we never wanted used unless it was necessary. I can't think of any place safer I know the location of."

"I have a couple hidey holes we could go to if we needed. Nothing as lavish as I'm sure the cabin is, but they'd be safe enough to spend a night or two." He held out a hand to help her climb over a pile of debris. "Regardless of where we end up, Glasgow here we come."

CHAPTER SEVENTEEN

March 2, 2060 – Glasgow, Scotland

"HOW THE hell are we supposed to get out of this tunnel and into the airport?" Dev put his hands on his hips and surveyed the end of the tunnel and the stone wall that blocked them from making any further progress.

Zeke snorted softly and stretched her arms up, fumbling at the ceiling of the tunnel. "There's a hatch here. It's pretty crude. My dad helped Gage put it in about ten years ago when things got really bad and the airport completely shut down. Before, this was just a few miles long and popped out in the middle of the woods just to be an escape if needed." She found the rope with her fingertips and pulled on it, tugging down the hatch and opening a hole in the roof.

Dev drew his gun with one smooth motion and peered up into it. He judged the distance between the ground the airport floor with his eyes. "I don't hear anything right there. If you can give me a small boost, I can easily lift you out." He turned to her. "If you can't, I can just use my wings."

She looked at him drolly. "I can lift you just fine." She knelt and cupped her hands to give him a step. "Let's get this done."

Dev stepped into her linked hands and sprang through the hatch. He dropped to his knees, his gun in his hand and used the flashlight to cast a look around. Seeing nothing that looked like a threat, he lay on his belly and extended his arms into the tunnel. Zeke handed up the two bags and her flashlight before jumping to catch his hands in hers and using his leverage to climb out.

She drew her pistol from her waistband and took her flashlight back from him. She secured the hatch and slung one of the bags over her shoulder before stepping closer to Dev to speak.

"There's a bank of administrative offices toward the back of the airport and upstairs above the terminals. It's too dark outside for us to risk going out there and puttering around without knowing what's around and what we're doing."

"I agree." He shined the light around the space, his gaze flitting from area to area. "Being out with this much open space makes me a little uneasy. Let's get moving."

"I'd like to stop in the food court and see if we can scrounge something better-tasting than MREs. With any luck there's some bottles of water or cans of soft drinks and some junk food. I'd much prefer chips and cookies to reconstituted eggs."

"Let's get there first and then I'll go back and look. I don't sense anything specific, but I'm not comfortable coming into someplace in the middle of the night with no clue what, or who, is around us. For me, the first thing has to be getting into a safer room we can ward and protect."

Zeke nodded. "Follow me."

She led Dev through the airport, keeping her head below the windows to make sure they weren't seen and using only one light, which she covered with her fingers to barely show their way. Several times they froze as one of them heard a noise. After twenty minutes of creeping, Zeke crouched next to a door and dug through one of the duffel bags for a lock pick kit.

"You be ready to fire when this swings open. I'm pretty vulnerable down here with tools in my hands instead of guns."

Dev chuckled. "Don't worry about that, sweetheart. I'm not gonna let a damn thing happen to you."

Zeke tried to ignore the warmth that washed over her at his words. Instead of focusing on it, she scowled at the lock and adjusted the angle of the tools. "What is with you and the endearments, anyway? It's always darlin' this and sweetheart that."

He glanced down at the top of her head, surprise lighting his eyes. "If you don't like it, you should have said something. It's just habit."

"It's not that I don't like it. I don't really care either way." She held a slim metal rod in her teeth and mumbled around it. "I'd just like to know I'm the only one you're calling sweetheart."

He snorted. "When do I have time to go romancing other women, hmm?" He glanced over his shoulder to make sure nothing was coming up on them from behind. "Between training and chopping firewood and taking you to bed every chance I get I haven't exactly been out trolling clubs."

Zeke sighed and twisted the pick, smiling when she heard the snick of it giving. "Not the point." She jumped back as the door swung open.

Dev stepped in front of her to block her from anything that might have been in the room. Finding it empty, he held out a hand and pulled her to her feet. Waiting for her to draw her weapon, they slowly advanced into the offices. Together, they swept the bank. When it was fully cleared, Dev holstered his weapon.

"What is the point?"

She shook her head and dropped the bags onto the floor. "There should be some sleeping mats and blankets in one of these closets. They used to keep them here for people who had to sleep in the airport if their flights got delayed or canceled."

Dev reached out and snagged her hand, drawing her to him. "It can wait one damn minute. We're obviously alone in here. What are you trying to ask me?"

"I'm not trying to ask you anything." Zeke sighed miserably. "It was stupid. I don't mind the 'babe' and 'sweetheart' thing. I just don't like the idea of being one of many."

Dev laughed. "So, what? You think I call you that because I have so many women lined up I can't keep their names straight?" He glared at her when he saw a flash of guilt in her eyes. "That's insulting to both of us."

She tipped her head back and stared at the ceiling. "I don't think that, not really." She huffed and met his gaze. "I'm good at casual sex. I can hop into bed, hop back out and be on my way without a backward glance. If that makes you think I'm a whore, well, so be it. It's all I've allowed myself. If my one try at it was any indication, I do pretty well with relationships, too, when I'm not getting people killed because of them."

Dev crossed his arms and stared at her. "I am so not following where you're taking this."

Uncomfortable, Zeke shifted from foot to foot and rubbed her palms against her thighs. "This isn't either of those things. I don't know what it is or what the rules are, and that hasn't bothered me, or I didn't think it did, until five minutes ago. I don't know why I chose this particular moment to get bothered, but there you have it. Nothing about us, or this, or anything makes sense to me. I don't know why we're together, how together we are, or why it seems to be working when you are the farthest thing from my type. You alternate between being sweet and making crude jokes. Sometimes I think you're a thirteen year old boy and other times you're the best man I've ever met and there has to be something wrong with my head because I like you more because of your quirks."

Dev grinned. "I'm suddenly less insulted." He reached out and stroked a hand over her hair, running the silky strands that had escaped her ponytail through his fingers. "I know you haven't known me long, but I'd hoped you'd have figured out by now I'm a pretty simple guy. I don't like complicated. More than one woman at a time, even if that's okay by the rules, is by its very nature complicated." He looked at her more seriously. "You've never struck me as the insecure type."

Bristling, she glared. "I'm not insecure. I don't like not knowing the expectations. That's what gives this the potential to get messy."

Holding up his hands, he backtracked. "Insecure was the wrong term. You're right. We haven't talked about the rules and not being okay with that doesn't make you insecure. So, rules. I only put my hands on one woman at a time. While you're in my bed, or I'm in yours, no one else is and I'm in no one else's." He gripped her shoulders lightly, rubbing her flesh with his hands to ease the tension in her muscles. "Since we're discussing it, I'll say I'd like the same of you."

Zeke wrapped her fingers around his wrists. "I don't want anyone else."

Realization dawned in Dev's eyes, and he drew her close, tucking her head under his chin. "You let me get important."

Zeke turned her face into his shoulder. "Don't rub it in."

He pressed a kiss to her temple. "You're important to me, too." He chuckled softly. "I suppose this means I get to tell people that you're my girlfriend."

Zeke scoffed indignantly but gave in to the smile that turned up her lips. "We aren't teenagers. I don't need titles and definitions. Just guidelines."

"Okay. Here are the guidelines for me. We're exclusive. If either of us wants to change in the future, we'll talk about it. You're important to me. I'm apparently important to you. We'll continue to be important to one another, likely becoming more and more important at which point we mutually agree that we will spend the rest of our likely short lives being important to one another. Does that summarize it pretty accurately for you, or did I miss something?"

Zeke giggled and rubbed her cheek on his shirt. "Works for me." She looked up at him, meeting his eyes with her own. "Is that going to be enough for you?"

Dev grinned down into her face. "As long as I've got you, it's enough. We'll figure out the rest as we go." He kissed her gently. "I'll work you around to my way of thinking sooner or later."

She narrowed her eyes. "What's your way of thinking?"

He laughed and set her away from him before bending to scoop up his flashlight. "Oh, you know. Marriage. Babies. That sort of thing." He emptied one of the duffels out onto the floor. "I'm going to go see if I can find you some soda and junk food."

Zeke was still gaping at him when he closed the door. She stood for ten more seconds trying to let what he had said process. Marriage? Babies? The man was certifiably insane.

Convinced she needed to have his head examined, Zeke began breaking down the temporary walls that had once formed cubicles and using them to cover all the windows. At least with the windows secured they could use the flashlight without worry of being seen.

As she worked, she mulled over her conversation with Dev. He was important to her. She liked spending time with him—they were friends. They had a lot in common, and the sex was hot. It was enough. And if there was a little flutter in her gut that told her there was more to it, well, then that was fine, too. She could deal with it. Caring about him hadn't snuck up on her. She'd known it was coming.

What had snuck up on her was the tiniest of aches she felt when he had mentioned children. Bringing a child into a world ruled by Satan was stupid. It was dangerous. Two powerful Nephilim having a child was even worse. It would be born a target.

Just like she had been.

Zeke cast the thought aside almost as soon as it popped into her head. Yes, she had been born a target. Her parents hadn't had a choice but to conceive her. They'd still thought they could win. They'd have never made the choice to have children after they failed. That was why she had never had any siblings.

She tried not to think of Amaya and her younger siblings. Ignored the fact that Alaria and Braxton had managed to protect four children from the Cambion and Devils. It was different. The other children were all human. Amaya was the only Nephil.

Annoyed with herself for dwelling on what should have been a dismissed thought, she stomped to the closet and yanked it open, rifling through the contents until she found the rolled up rubber pads and a pile of blankets.

Armed with work, she laid the padding in one corner of the room, choosing the one that gave them a clear view of the windows and the only door. After finding a roll of duct tape in one of the desks, she ripped off pieces and taped the pads together to make one larger one they could both fit on. Satisfied, she spread out two of the blankets on the cushion, rolled two more into makeshift pillows, and stacked the rest next to the pallet for them to use when they slept.

Dev came back into the room and looked around approvingly. "Good idea, covering the windows." He closed the door and turned the lock. Together, they moved a desk in front of the door.

"Did you see anything out there?"

"Not a thing. I think we're the only living creatures in this place. I didn't want to look outside and risk alerting any vampires nearby that we're here. It's best just to hunker down until morning. We'll eat, log a few hours of sleep, then figure out a plan first thing in the morning."

She eyed the bag hopefully. "Did you find anything?"

He unzipped it and handed it to her. "Some licorice, potato chips, and packs of cookies. There was a drink machine gutted down there, and I chased up a couple stray cans of root beer and cola."

Zeke closed her eyes and sighed in pleasure. "Junk food!" She grabbed a pack of Twizzlers and ripped into them. "It's so rare you find anything like this." She bit into the candy with gusto. "It's so yummy."

He dropped onto the mat she'd prepared and took his boots off. "I think we're safe enough in here. We've been through nearly every damn inch of this place, and it's as quiet as a tomb."

She sat next to him and followed his actions of removing her boots. She took it one step further and tugged off her socks, folding them neatly inside each shoe. "Gage always said it was pretty safe. Aradia warded all the safe spots they have so the odds of something being in here were lower to begin with." She tore off another chunk of licorice. "We'll regroup in the morning. Figure out what's here we might make use of and whether or not we need to signal for a lift from the troops."

"If we have to get Carys and Elisa involved, I'll only want them to take us within a hundred miles or so. We can hoof it the rest of the way to avoid leaving a flash signature for the Cambion to follow right to us."

Dev looked at the MREs and debated eating one before sighing and tearing into one of the bags of potato chips. They crunched in companionable silence for several minutes, decimating the supply of junk food. They shared one bottle of root beer and each had a bottle of water.

They settled onto the mat, arguing good-naturedly over blankets before settling in and turning off the flashlight. Had it not been for the array of weapons placed within easy reach around them, it would have been possible to pretend they were just going to bed.

Still, they settled in together, with Zeke tucking her head against Dev's shoulder and laying one of her arms at his waist. He ran his hand through her hair absently, enjoying the feel of her pressed against him.

Dev was almost asleep when Zeke's voice slipped though the haze of exhaustion. "Do you think we'll ever finish this?"

He shifted to look down at her, barely able to discern her face in the dark. "Yes. I think we'll get through it, Deacon and Amaya will do their part and we'll all live long, happy lives once it's done. You're right with what you said before. We'll win because we're retaining our humanity. We're living and loving and fighting. We're defining the fight, not letting it define us. That's going to make a difference in the end."

"Sometimes it feels like we can't ever get ahead of it. Like no matter what we do or how many we kill, there will always be more."

"We're outnumbered. We always have been, and for us, especially, we know we're being chased by a lot of fucking demons and Cambion. It's not this bad for everyone. I haven't been in this with you for very long. I can tell you from experience that for the most part, it feels like we're at least holding our own."

"I've never felt like that. My entire life has been running, fighting, and struggling. I've been hidden since I was born, trained to take over this fight, and shoved into it when I was still a kid. My parents didn't have a choice. We don't have a choice. We just have to keep fighting. I'm so sick of the bloodshed and the killing. Most of the time, I don't even think about it. It's like I'm desensitized to taking life."

Sitting up, he looked down at her, squinting to make out her face in the dark, his expression serious and his gaze showing concern. "Zeke, baby, it's kill or be killed. If you didn't, they would. Do you think I dwell on the person behind every shot I take? This is war. We have to be desensitized to it. If we aren't, then we're the ones who die." He tugged her closer and hugged her tightly. "It's normal, I would think, for you to be having these feelings after what happened with your parents. I know it's hard for you."

Zeke shook her head. "It is, and it does make me think about it more than I had before. I won't deny that. I know it has a lot to do with what I feel, but not all. I just want to be done."

"We all do. We're in the home stretch. I think that's why

everything is getting to such a fever pitch. The other side knows as well as we do that it's time. Deacon and Amaya are going to go after Lucifer, and they're going to kill him. Once they do, it's just cleaning up the rest of the mess."

"I'm ready to be done. I'm sick of fighting. I hate waking up each day and knowing the odds are good I'll see someone die. Eventually it's going to be me who dies, or you, or someone else I care about. We can't keep getting this lucky."

"It's not luck. It's training and knowing what to do and when to do it. We're going to be fine." Dev sighed deeply and shifted to kiss her lightly. "Stop worrying about it and get some sleep. We've got more than enough to worry about tomorrow without borrowing trouble that can wait for another time and place. We're safe for now, we're together, we're not hungry or cold, so I'd call that a pretty good ending to the day."

CHAPTER EIGHTEEN

March 5th, 2060 – Colorado, United States

DEV TUCKED his gloved hands in his pockets as he and Zeke trekked through the woods. She was a half dozen steps ahead of him, her shoulders hunched against the biting wind. Snow swirled around them in a surprising late-winter storm.

"How much farther?"

Zeke glanced over her shoulder. "Couple hundred yards. The woods should start thinning up ahead and the cabin'll be tucked into the clearing. I think there's a road leading to it, but the odds are it's long washed away." She smiled sheepishly. "I've never actually been here before, so I'm following directions my parents gave me and I can feel the wards Aradia put on the place. They're getting stronger."

Dev glared at her. "So you have no clue whether or not this place is even still habitable?"

"Not really. It's a risk but one I think is worth taking. No one has been here since before the Choosing, and even then, Braxton and Griffin left it on their own, not because they were found. As far as I know, no one has been here since years before I was born except when Aradia warded it and that was even twenty-five years ago."

"I just hope it's still there. If we come up to a smoldering pile of rubble, I'm going to be supremely pissed off."

"If it were a smoldering pile of rubble, the wards wouldn't still be there." Zeke sighed deeply and trudged onward, snow gathering in her hair as she walked.

After ten more minutes scrambling up the hill, slipping and sliding in the soft earth made slick by snow, they emerged into a clearing and saw the cabin for the first time. Two stories of rough-hewn wood covered with moss and vines, it faded into the trees so it was barely visible from any distance. Weeds had overtaken the yard, and the stone path leading from the primitive dirt road to the door was badly cracked. Dev drew his weapon as they approached the house and motioned to Zeke before they stepped up onto the porch, signaling to her they would check the perimeter before entering the house.

Finding nothing other than deer prints and snow, Zeke swiftly worked the lock on the back door and popped it open. They entered cautiously, moving together to clear each and every room before reconvening in the kitchen.

"Well, it's still standing, and I think you're right. It doesn't look like anyone's been in here for years." Dev ran his finger through the dust on the counter. "If the dust is any indication."

Zeke dropped her pack onto the floor and looked around. "There are still clothes on the floor in the bedroom. There're magazines on the couch and wineglasses in the sink. It's like they just went out for a walk."

Dev studied her face. "Does it bother you?"

"Griffin's my great-grandmother. Her son was my mom's father. I've been to the Choosing place and seen where she died, but this is the first time I've gotten to see where she lived. From what Braxton has told me, they were happy here, at least for a time."

Dev looked around, taking in the ground level. "There's a fireplace here. One of the fancy two-sided ones so it'll heat the living room and kitchen. There's plenty of wood left. I'll get a fire built. Do you want to look through those drawers and see if you can find some lighter fluid to make it go a little quicker?"

Zeke nodded and began rifling through the drawers in the kitchen. Three produced nothing, but in the fourth she found a tin of lighter fluid. Triumphantly, she tossed it to Dev and involuntarily let out a muffled squeal of pleasure when firelight filled the room.

"The sun is going down fast. There's a pile of wood in the back. I'm going to bring enough in to get us through the night. Will you see if you can scrounge up some food and see about the generator in the basement?"

Zeke nodded and shucked off her coat and gloves. "Coming right up. Even without the generator, there's a little woodstove with a burner in the corner there. I can light it and use it to cook on."

Dev offered a grin as he stepped back out into the snow. "Provided there's any food left, of course."

Zeke laughed and descended the steps into the basement, flashlight in one hand and her gun tucked into her waistband. She shined the light around the basement, taking stock of the remnants of lives long ended.

Boxes of clothes and old toys littered the basement amongst old exercise equipment and an artificial Christmas tree. Tucked in one corner was a furnace and behind it, a massive generator. It was one of the fancy, whole house ones, Zeke noted with appreciation. Curiously, she shined her light on the machine and inspected the gears.

Excited about what she thought she saw, she checked the cables and laughed when she found the generator was hooked into several large batteries. Solar power. She found the switches to turn on the generator and smiled when the machine roared to life.

The gas tank was easy to locate, and she quickly found the stores of gas cans. Doing math in her head, she calculated there was nearly two hundred gallons of fuel. That, along with the solar power derived from the panels that had to be somewhere near the house, they would have enough power for whatever they needed for at least a week, potentially a lot more depending on how efficient the solar aspect was.

Satisfied, she climbed the stairs back into the kitchen and started rifling through cabinets. She found boxes of stale cereal, several gallons of water and a case of soda. Annoyed with the lack of food, she jerked open what she thought was a coat closet and stopped, staring in shock.

A pantry. Cans of fruit and vegetables lined the top shelves. There were cans of stew and soup and pasta. Jars on the bottom shelf held flour, sugar, coffee grounds and tea bags. There were several boxes of pasta and jars of sauce. Tuna, canned chicken, something called Spam, and bags of powdered milk rounded out the contents.

Elated, Zeke fished through the cabinets for a big pot and filled it with cold water from the sink. She used a match to ignite the pilot on the gas stove and placed the pot on the burner to heat. That done, she poked her head out and saw Dev chopping wood next to the house. Satisfied he was safe, she ascended the steps to see if she could find clothing for them.

She entered the master bedroom first. It was done in blues and browns with a thick quilt rumpled on the bed and blue sheets underneath. She wrinkled her nose and kicked a stray pair of boxers on the floor to a corner.

The drawers yielded plenty of clothes that Dev could make use of. She selected a pair of sweatpants, a gray thermal shirt, and thick socks for him before entering the bathroom.

Immediately uncomfortable, she looked at Braxton and Griffin's things. There were still tubes of deodorant left on the counter, a lipstick left open, a silk slip thrown in the corner. Towels hung on the shower rod and a blow dryer was still plugged in. A nearly empty box of condoms sat next to the sink.

They'd had a life here, as short as it'd been. They'd brushed their teeth next to one another, maybe arguing over who was hogging the sink. They'd showered, made love, made a home with the little time they had had there. Seeing the remnants of it and knowing how the story ended tore at Zeke's heartstrings.

She felt that even more keenly as she moved into the bedroom that had obviously been Griffin's. Seeing her clothes hanging in the closet, a book lying on the nightstand, her handwriting on a grocery list tossed carelessly onto one of the dressers. Everything told a story of a woman Zeke had never met but without whom she would not exist.

"We were happy here for the weeks before we left."

Zeke whirled, drawing her weapon and leveling it at the blonde standing behind her. She narrowed her eyes and backed up, giving herself some space. "Who the hell are you and what are you doing here?"

"Occasionally Gabriel likes to call me out of Heaven and asks me to come down here and help with things." The woman smiled. "I'm Griffin, Zeke. It's nice to meet you."

"Griffin is dead. Dead people don't stand in bedrooms and talk to you. Who are you and how do you know who I am?"

Griffin chuckled. "I do from time to time. As I said, Gabriel sometimes asks me to be involved. How long has it been since the third task?"

"Almost thirty years." Zeke lowered the barrel of the gun slightly. "Why are you here?"

"You're having a rough time dealing with the death of your parents and with figuring out your place in this mess. Gabriel thought I might be of some help." Griffin sat on the bed and crossed her legs. "I had to do this once before when Braxton was struggling with my death."

Zeke lowered the gun another notch. "There's a lot of death going around."

"And much more yet to come. I'd like to offer you some comfort if you're interested in hearing it."

"There's no comfort for a woman who shot her own father."

Griffin's eyes flashed with a mixture of anger and understanding. "By the very nature of my existing, both mine died, and my grandparents. Hundreds of deaths lie firmly on my shoulders. That doesn't make it my fault, any more than what you did is yours." She looked around the room, a sad smile on her face. "Braxton taught me what love is in this house. Perhaps you'll let Dev do the same for you."

"I know what love is. I had it from my parents. I have it from the rest of my family."

"It's not that kind of love I mean. You either will or you won't, and there's nothing I can do about it either way. Your parents are in Heaven. I've seen them. They're together, and they're happy. They have no idea what's going on with you, no concept of time, and no awareness you're not there. You'll be together again once your time is done, but mourning for those who have left isn't for the dead, it's for the living. If you need more time to grieve and to mourn, then take it, but don't continually beat yourself up for what happened. There was no other choice, and your parents don't blame you. They aren't angry, and they aren't sad."

Zeke closed her eyes for a moment. "I'm handling it, really. I had a rough go for a little while, but I'm managing it now. Being here, with the memories you must have, it just made me think about things. Made me wonder who you are and think about the whole damn thing."

"Wondering and thinking is fine." Griffin stood and looked in the closet. "I never even wore most of these. Braxton's sister, Sam, bought them for me and put them in here to make sure I had clothes. I didn't, other than the ones on my back. Feel free to take whatever fits you. God knows I won't be needing them anymore." She laughed, humor lighting her eyes when Zeke fumbled for a response. "Don't be so serious. I've had thirty some odd years to get used to being dead." She folded her arms. "Let's get to it since I don't have very long before they're going to yank me back in. You're not doing this for nothing. I know you're tired of the killing. We all are, but every step you take is taking you toward where you need to go. Trust the path, and trust the people around you. Don't miss out on something good in your personal life, either. I know that's secondary and Gabe would be pretty pissed at me for telling you this since to him the mission is all that matters, but Dev's a good guy and he's good for you. Don't make him pay for what someone else did."

"I don't need love advice from a dead woman." Zeke sighed when she realized how harsh her words sounded. "I didn't mean it."

"Yes, you did, and it's okay. I'm a dead woman, but I also know a bit about what you're going through. I enjoyed my time in this place. No one will find you here. Take some time and do the same. Gage will find the sword, and when he does, it will be time for you to move quickly. Don't waste the time you have to enjoy your lives. That's just as important as all the other stuff."

"It seems almost like a waste to send you down here to talk about my personal life."

"That's only a small part of it. Your feelings about the whole mission moving forward could affect the outcome, and that's what scares Gabriel. It's important you understand there will be an end to this. You will help bring it about, and there will be time to rest once your part is done. Stay the course. That's the take away from all of this."

Zeke opened her mouth to speak, but Griffin was gone before she could. She heard the door slam and then Dev's voice.

"Zeke! Downstairs, now!"

Worried, Zeke lifted her gun and raced down the stairs. She dashed through the living room and into the kitchen, skidding to a stop as she saw Dev.

His face was pale and his hands were covered in blood. His shirt was damp with sweat and his jeans were soaked through with the thick red liquid. Zeke dropped her weapon on the counter and rushed to him.

"What happened? What did you do?"

His face pale and pinched, Dev shook his head. "I haven't chopped wood since I was a kid. I wasn't paying attention and caught myself in the thigh. It feels bad."

"Take your pants off." Calmer since she knew he wasn't actively dying, Zeke grabbed a rag and wet it in the faucet. "Is there anything in there?"

"Don't think so. Hurts like a mother fucker, though." He peeled off his jeans and stood in his boxers. The gash in his thigh was deep and jagged and the meat of his leg was red and raw against his paler skin. "Damn. I think it hurts worse now that I can see it."

"It always does." She wiped the blood away. "It looks reasonably clean. This is going to hurt."

She laid her hands against his thigh and concentrated on the wound, glancing up briefly when he grunted and squeezed his eyes shut in meager defense against the pain of healing. Slowly, she worked the muscle, knitting it back together and forming new skin, pink and thin, to cover the wound. She sat back on her haunches and studied her work, satisfied with the job.

"How's it feel?"

"Weird. I've never been healed before." He touched the faint scar gently. "Thanks. I'd have been in a world of hurt on my own with that."

"Good thing you have a Healer with you then." She stood and smiled at him. "If we're really lucky, we should have some hot water by now. The generator is hooked into big batteries. There are solar panels somewhere."

"Out back next to the wood pile. I cleared them off. They look like they're in pretty good shape." He limped to the sink and washed his hands, smiling when the water turned lukewarm. "It's getting there. I'm going to brave the cold and rinse off." He looked at the boiling water. "I'm assuming you found something to cook in that water?"

"Pasta. I figured spaghetti sounded pretty good."

"Sounds amazing. How long until we eat?"

Zeke dumped a box of noodles into the water. "Fifteen minutes. You have time to slough off some of that dirt. I'll take a shower after dinner. I'm just dirty. You're sticky and bloody."

"There's more than one bathroom, and plenty of room in both showers." Dev reached out and grabbed her hand. "Come up with me. Noodles don't need help cooking."

She shrugged and followed him up the stairs into the master bath. Dev turned on the water and stripped off the last of his clothing, stepping under the heating spray. Zeke followed suit and joined him, wiggling her way in between him and the water so she could get wet.

Quickly, they both washed hair and body. Dirt, blood, and grime ran down the drain until the water flowed clear. Worried about the noodles overcooking, Zeke hopped out before Dev was done and snagged a towel, wrapping it around herself and dashing down the hall to get clothes from Griffin's closet.

As she left the room, she caught sight of herself in the mirror, the lines and curves of her face that looked so much like the women who had come before her. Ignoring the pang of grief and guilt at the thought of her mother, she loped downstairs to drain the noodles.

Five minutes later, she had glasses of wine poured and plates of pasta with jarred sauce on the table. Dev entered the room wearing sweatpants and a t-shirt and sniffed the air appreciatively.

"I don't remember the last time I ate something not out of a can."

"Since we left California." She nodded to the bottle. "There's a whole room in the basement filled with wine. We could stay drunk for a month on what's down there."

Dev ignored the wine and dug into the food. After a minute of chewing, he swallowed and cleared his throat. "This is great." He reached out and patted her hand. "You're being quiet."

"I saw Griffin upstairs while you were outside. I was thinking about her and what her life was like while they were here, and then she was just there behind me. Gabriel sent her to talk to me about not giving up."

Very deliberately, Dev placed his fork on the table. "Griffin is dead."

"I know. I told her that a couple times, but she didn't disappear. I'm not crazy."

"I don't think you're crazy. We live in a fucked up world. I suppose it's not outside the realm of possibility Gabriel can hail dead people back from Heaven to do tasks. He's hands off enough to want to use them as pawns." He sighed deeply. "Do you want to talk about it?"

"There's not much to talk about. They're worried I won't do my part because of how I'm handling Mom and Dad."

"I think you're handling things fine, and we're going to get through it together." Dev rubbed his thumb across her knuckles. "Try not to let it bother you. As long as we do what we have to do, we'll be fine. It doesn't matter what they think. I know you'll handle it and so do you, and as long as you know you can do this, that's all that matters."

CHAPTER NINETEEN

March 10th, 2060 – Colorado

ZEKE WAS yanked from sleep by Dev's voice. She blinked against the bright light streaming through the window and sat up, clawing her hair out of her face. Glancing at her watch, she scowled and swore.

"Dammit, Dev, it's only seven a.m. Why the hell are you waking me up?"

Laughter tickled up the stairs. "We have company. Deacon and Amaya are here."

Torn between excitement and terror over why they had come, Zeke sprang from bed and dashed from the room, barely pausing to tie her hair away from her face. She ran down the stairs and slid several feet when her socked feet hit the wood floors. She waved her arms wildly to regain her balance and rushed at Amaya, flinging her arms around the other woman and hugging her tightly.

"Don't tell me why you're here for a minute. Just let me enjoy seeing you for a full sixty seconds before you break the bad news."

Amaya laughed and wrapped her arms around Zeke, returning the embrace. "Well, rest easy. We're here with good news, not bad."

Zeke closed her eyes and took a deep breath. "In that case, Dev will make breakfast and we can all have some coffee." She glanced at the melting snow on the floor. "Did you guys hike in?"

"Carys and Elisa told me where they dropped you two off, and I flashed us in to that spot and we came on foot the rest of the way." Deacon bent to hug Zeke. "We didn't want to risk your cover."

Dev shuddered. "A hundred fucking miles in the snow. We spent two nights crammed into one sleeping bag trying to stay warm."

Amaya laughed. "When he says by foot, what he really means is he used those wonderful wings both you men are gifted with, and we cut the trip down to a few hours."

Dev scowled. "I wish I could have done that. Deacon's are for function, mine mostly for show. Anything more than an hour and I'm tapped out." He led the others into the kitchen. "There's not a lot to choose from, but I can manage some pancakes well enough. No milk though, so you'll have to live with coffee or water."

Zeke poured mugs of coffee and placed a bowl of sugar on the table. "The house is pretty well stocked with dry goods, so we have enough food and water, but if it's not in a can, we don't have it. The exception is flour, sugar, stuff like that, but no meat, no dairy."

Amaya shrugged. "We're as used to it as you are. Michael spoils us with fresh food, but we've all spent enough time in places like this that we know how it is."

Zeke sat down next to Amaya. "How's Finley and the baby?"

Amaya's face lit up at the mention of her older sister. "She's great. I got to see them for a weekend last month with Mom and Dad. The baby is a boy. She named him Alexander—Xander for short. Eden is still with them. Mom and Dad aren't anymore. It's too dangerous, and Finley's husband doesn't want the danger there."

Zeke scowled. "Braxton and Alaria would never do anything to put any of them in danger. If the husband doesn't know that, he shouldn't be the husband for much longer."

Amaya shook her head. "Chris is a good guy—he's just protective. He's a Warrior who trained under my dad, so he knows the score and doesn't want to take chances while they're more immobile." She glanced over when Deacon cleared his throat. "Don't start. We're not in a hurry. There's no reason we can't talk for a while."

Deacon sighed deeply. "We found the sword."

Zeke turned to look at him. "Where?"

Amaya closed her eyes. "You aren't going to like it."

Zeke waved the concern away. "I was never going to like it. The damn thing is being guarded by Cambion or demons. Of course I'm not going to like it. Where is it?"

Deacon answered. "New Orleans."

Dev stiffened at the stove and turned to face the other three. "Are you sure?"

Deacon nodded. "Positive. Gage and Dad both confirmed it."

Zeke leaned back in her chair and swore softly. "You warned me I wasn't going to like it. New Orleans is suicide. The whole fucking city is monster central. There's no way to get in and out without being found. Even my power won't work with the Devils and their Cambion offspring, and that place is crawling with both."

Amaya smiled grimly. "There are ways. There are some allies there we're getting in touch with, and we'll get you in there." She looked at Deacon. "I know Deacon doesn't agree with me on this, but I've discussed it with Mom and Dad, and we're all on the same page." She leaned back and folded her arms. "Have you ever heard the story about when my parents went to Hades?"

Dev shook his head. "No. Well, I know they went there during the final task, but I don't think I ever heard anything specific."

Deacon narrowed his eyes. "While they were there, they met a Devil named Rhadathamus. He had been trapped there when Beelzebub closed off Hades centuries earlier. He helped Alaria and Braxton get across the different sections so they could get to Beelzebub."

Zeke nodded. "Right, I remember this. He's not a very strong one, but he's a straight shooter. What about him?"

Amaya grinned. "After they got out, he disappeared. He helped them out but wasn't invested enough to dedicate to their side. He just wanted to be on his own and not a part of the fight. Anyway, he ended up settling in the French Quarter. He's still there. In fact, he's one of the biggest neutrals left. He runs a brothel, stays out of the fight, and just keeps living his own life. Mom was able to get in touch with him, and it took some convincing, but he's willing to help us get into the city and keep us safe while we're there."

Zeke shook her head. "Oh, no. You two aren't going. No way. The whole fucking point of this is to keep the two of you safe until the end. I'll go, Dev will come with me, and we'll be fine. If we need help, I'll call in Lux and Zane." She crossed her arms and glared at Amaya. "It's not worth the risk of you being found. You're the key to everything, Maya. You're the only one who matters, and Deacon is the only other possible way to get things done, and even that is speculative because he doesn't have the human side you do."

Dev cleared his throat. "I agree with Zeke. Lux and Zane have their part, the two of you have yours, and we have ours. This isn't about the three of you women, or the six of us doing things together. This is very much individual. We can't do it together because being together makes everything riskier."

Amaya sighed. "That's what Deacon keeps saying, but I hate being in this position. We're sitting home with Michael training and doing nothing while the rest of you are out here risking your lives. It's not right. We're no better than you are. We can be of use. We can help."

Zeke reached across the table and wrapped her hands around Amaya's. "Sweetie, nothing about this is right or fair. And you are better than us. You're the one person God picked to stop Lucifer. We would all die to keep you alive. Just like Griffin was the Chosen, you're the only hope for survival. As long as you're alive, we're still in the fight." She squeezed Amaya's hands tightly. "I know it sucks, but we have to keep you safe. That means not parading you through New Orleans."

Amaya deflated. "I just want to do something other than sit at home and knit. I hate feeling like I'm warm and safe while the people I love the most are in the most danger."

Deacon rubbed her shoulder. "Neither of us like it, but it's the hand we've been dealt, and we're dealing with it." He leaned back. "But back to the topic. Rhad isn't getting involved in the fight. He's agreed to make sure you can get in safely and not get caught, and Alaria and Braxton seem confident he's not going to rat you out, but it's far from a safe plan."

"Nothing about this is safe." Dev chuckled and rose to refill his coffee cup. He picked up a spoon and scooped sugar into the cup, stirring absent-mindedly as he considered the situation. "When is it you need us to leave?"

Deacon answered, "We're waiting to get the official date from Rhad, but I think you've got close to a week. Amaya and I are going to leave from here and start putting together the stuff you'll need. Lux and Aradia are working on a list of witchcraft supplies you can make use of, and Gage is figuring out the weapons. The two of you need to stay here, stay out of sight, and we'll keep you up to date on everything that's going on with moving to New Orleans. Once you move in there, all communication has to come through Rhad, which is the part that makes me really nervous. I hate trusting this whole thing to a Devil."

Amaya scowled. "My mother was a Devil. Just because someone made a mistake several million years ago doesn't mean you can hold it against them indefinitely."

Deacon stared at Amaya in amusement. "My mother is a Devil, too, love, and she's an evil bitch to boot. I love your mother. She helped raise me, and I would trust her with my life. That does not mean I am going to have blind faith in a Devil I've never met and who has never done anything to make any of us believe he is on our side."

Zeke held up her hand. "Whoa. I get it, the two of you don't agree, but it doesn't sound like we have much of a choice, so this is the way it's going to be for the moment." She looked between them. "Are the two of you staying for a while or are you dashing off?"

Amaya looked at Zeke sadly. "I so wish we could stay, but we can't. We have a few hours, but not much longer. It's too risky. If you want to come back to Michael's, you could wait for word there."

Dev shook his head. "No. That puts you all at risk. For better or worse, this is the way it is. Zeke and I are being hunted. There's no way we would put you at risk by coming back there before it's time for the two of you to do your thing."

Deacon stood and began clearing plates. "Honestly, the sooner we get back, the better off we'll be. The wards up around this place made it impossible to get a message through, we couldn't take the risk of just flashing into the yard, and neither of you have a sat phone, so someone had to come and tell you what was going on." He glared at Zeke and Dev. "Seriously, if you hadn't needed Carys and Elisa to get you over the Atlantic, we wouldn't even know whether or not you were alive after the attack in Scotland."

Dev sighed. "That might have been for the best, truthfully. The less contact we have with one another the safer we all are. It's the rule we've lived by our whole lives, and we need to continue that way." He looked to Deacon. "It's harder for you and me a bit, I think, since we're used to living at Michael's and being together as a team, but right now, we have to do the same as the girls have."

Amaya smiled sadly. "We do what we need to do." She nodded at Deacon when he laid his hand on her shoulder. "Okay." Please call me if you need me. I'd love to stay, and I know it would be safe for a few hours, but Deacon's right. It's safer if we go." She reached into her pocket and withdrew a satellite phone. "Call if you need something."

Dev took the phone and tucked it into one of the kitchen drawers. "We'll be fine. You two be careful going back and let us know as soon as you have some more information on how we're going about getting the sword."

Deacon nodded and reached for Amaya's hand to tug her in the direction of the door. "We will. Stay safe."

Zeke zipped up her coat and wrapped a scarf around her neck before shoving her hands into gloves. The boots she wore were tight. She'd discovered her feet were a half size bigger than Griffin's had been, making the boots a little uncomfortable.

Stretching her toes in an effort to give herself a little more room, she opened the door and stepped out into the cold. Snow landed on her head and shoulders on its way to the ground, and she scowled at it. March and still snowing.

The axe they'd used to chop wood leaned against the side of the house, and she picked it up on her way to the woodpile. A large log splitter stood covered with tarps several yards away. Zeke looked at it longingly. Having the splitter working would have cut the time they spent chopping wood by at least three-quarters. Dev had spent almost an entire day trying to get it running and hadn't been able to. Thirty years in the elements had been too much for the piece of equipment.

Dev was the one who normally chopped the wood, but he'd fallen asleep on the couch an hour earlier. Zeke wasn't sure he'd even been to bed before Amaya and Deacon had arrived. In the three hours since they'd departed, Zeke had pouted about not getting to spend time with her friend, and Dev had read part of a book and fallen asleep.

Feeling only slightly guilty about half a day with no training, she picked up a chunk of wood and placed it on the stump used for splitting. After his accident with the blade, Dev had taken to a sledge hammer and wedge to cut wood, but Zeke still preferred the axe. She folded her fingers around the handle and swung in one smooth motion, driving the blade into the wood and splitting it into two pieces.

Stooping to pick them up, she tossed them toward the house to make it easier to carry them in once she was done. Repeating the process, she grabbed another chunk to chop.

Zeke was so engrossed in her work that she didn't hear the slight snap as twigs broke in the woods. It felt good to work physically.

Training was a controlled environment where both she and Dev carefully monitored their movements to avoid hurting one another. But this, this was work.

She chopped and tossed, picked up and placed, over and over again until her shoulders and back screamed from the exertion of swinging the axe and her chest hurt from the cold air she continually sucked into her lungs. Pleased with herself, she smacked the stump with the edge of the blade to plant it and stood, placing her hands on her hips. She started to stretch, lifting her arms above her head and leaning backward when she caught a glimpse of the wood line. She froze.

Azazel stood at the edge of the woods, bare-chested even in the harsh winter weather. He wore leather pants and boots, with his long hair flowing around his shoulders. On either side of him stood several humans holding guns. Zeke needed only to look at them once to know they were Familiars—humans under the control of a demon or Devil who had no concept of what they were doing. They had no soul, no consciousness, and would do the bidding of the creature in charge of them without a thought.

Zeke put her hands on her hips with a cockiness she didn't feel and stared at the Devil. "I'd ask what you're doing here, but I'm pretty sure I already know the answer."

Azazel grinned, showing straight white teeth. "You're a smart girl. You know I'm here to kill you. I couldn't believe how lucky I was to catch sight of that damn Nephil flying out of here. I knew who he was immediately, and set out to gather some humans to help me get to whomever was left here. Imagine my surprise when I find it's two of the most wanted Nephilim in existence. I was so thrilled. Imagine how happy Beelzebub and Lucifer will be when I bring the two of you chained up and drop you at his feet."

Zeke glanced at the handle of the axe and measured the distance. "You don't really expect me to believe you just happened to see them, do you?"

Azazel smirked. "Crazy as it sounds, that's precisely what happened. See, there's a Hell Gate not too far from here. It's where your mother and Michael burst out all those years ago. We train some Cambion there." He cocked his head to the side. "Didn't you know that? You're in dangerous territory being this close. It's a couple hundred miles, but still."

She counted the Familiars carefully, needing to know precisely what she was up against. Thirteen of them. Doable. She listened hard, hoping Dev was awake in the house but sensing nothing.

"I'm not going willingly."

Azazel grinned. "I'd be bored if you did." He looked from side to side. "I suppose it's not a big deal if you end up dead. Lucifer will be happy you're no longer a threat."

"I'm a threat as long as I'm breathing."

The Devil lifted one eyebrow. "Then let's see what we can do about remedying that, shall we?"

Zeke lunged for the axe as the Familiars began firing. She whirled, the blade flashing as she darted behind the wood pile to avoid the onslaught of bullets. Tossing out one hand, she used her limited telekinesis to send the spray of projectiles hurtling back into the crowd. Four of the Familiars dropped to the ground.

Ignoring the pang at human lives ending, she braced herself for the onslaught of Familiars. They came at her in a mass of flailing limbs and unseeing eyes. The axe was unwieldy in her hands as she slashed and hacked at the horde. She felt the unmistakable burn and sting as a bullet slammed into her thigh and gritted her teeth against the pain.

Blood slickened her grip on the handle, and she gasped for breath. Dev burst out the side door, sword in hand and went straight for Azazel. The two men clashed, the sound of colliding metal filling the yard as their swords struck one another. Zeke pressed her gloved hand to her thigh, hissing as blood poured from between her fingers. She gingerly felt the other side, closing her eyes in one moment of relief as she located the exit wound.

Dev was handling Azazel. Zeke snuck one look over the wood pile and saw the men fighting viciously. She had to trust him to handle it. There were still six Familiars left with guns, and she had to deal with them.

All she had was a fucking axe. Which would have been more than enough had the Familiars been unarmed. But they had assault rifles, which meant they had the advantage. If she didn't deal with them soon, they would endanger Dev's life as well.

Gritting her teeth and holding her breath, she darted out from behind the wood and sprinted across the yard to the bodies of the four Familiars she'd killed with their own bullets. She stooped as she ran, snatching up one of the rifles. Without stopping, she dashed behind the house and into the field, trying to get some distance from Dev and Azazel. Anything she could do to lower the odds he got shot was worth it.

After a hundred yards, she slid to a stop, noticing off-handedly that she was on ice. Not knowing whether the ice was a puddle or a pond, she turned and faced the Familiars racing after her. Taking a breath, she lifted the weapon and, brought the butt to her shoulder and leveled the barrel.

She fired seven times and watched four of the six drop. The other two were firing rapidly, their bullets whizzing by her. She took one brief moment to appreciate that even possession couldn't turn an average human into a good shot.

Zeke winced as one of the bullets grazed her arm, slicing through her coat and flesh. She glanced sideways to check the damage before firing again. Her bullet struck home, hitting one of the remaining two in the chest and driving it to the ground.

The last one lowered the barrel on his gun and fired rapidly at the ground. Zeke realized what he was doing one heartbeat too late. She whirled to run, her boots finding little traction on the ice. Before she could get away, the ice below her feet exploded as bullets hit it, and she dropped through and into the frigid water beneath.

CHAPTER TWENTY

DEV DROVE his sword up, slicing through Azazel's chest and crunching through bone. He chanted a spell to keep the Devil from vacating his body, watching with grim satisfaction as the black and red lights flashed in the eyes of a quickly dying host.

He scored his wrist on the blade, forcing Nephil blood into Azazel's mouth. He didn't have the ability to truly kill the Devil, but he could send the essence of him back to Hell.

When the body went limp and the light in the eyes went out, Dev dropped it and looked around for Zeke. He turned in a circle, searching for her, and the blood in his veins turned to ice.

The last Familiar stood near the edge of a hole in some ice. There was no sign of Zeke. His heart in his throat, Dev raced toward the bank, swinging his sword once to kill the last Familiar. Without a second thought, he charged into the water, breaking ice with his hands and body in a desperate search for Zeke.

Finding nothing, he took a deep breath and ducked his head under, looking for any sign of her. The water made his vision blurry, but he was able to make out her form, clawing desperately at a patch of ice, unable to get through or figure out which way to go.

Choking on water and terror, Dev surfaced and hacked at the ice with his sword. He struck it with the handle over and over clearing a path to where Zeke had been. When her body bobbed to the surface, unmoving and face down, fear unlike he had ever before experienced rose in his chest.

He grabbed Zeke in his arms and swam to the bank as quickly as he could. He laid her on the ground, shaking her shoulders in an attempt to wake her up. When she didn't move, he tore at her clothes, stripping her from the waist up.

Her skin was tinged blue and water seeped out of her mouth, telling him that she had sucked in a lungful. He pressed his ear to her chest, nearly sobbing from relieve when he heard her heart beat. It was weak, but it meant there was hope.

Struggling to remember what to do, Dev gathered Zeke in his arms, running toward the house, his only thought getting her warm. When she gagged and water gushed from between her lips, he stopped long enough to shift her, allowing the liquid to drain out.

Again moving, he kicked the door open and strode into the house, moving directly toward the fireplace. He deposited Zeke on the couch began undressing her, pulling off wet boots and socks, followed by her jeans and panties. He wrapped her in the afghan from the back of the couch and rose to start a fire, swearing when he saw the basket was empty.

Torn between getting more wood and staying with Zeke, he raced up the stairs, ducking into one of the bedrooms and ripping the bed clothes from the bed. Returning to the living room, he tucked the blanket and sheets around her, then grabbed the basket.

He raced outside with the basket and gathered up the wood that she'd been chopping before the attack. He slammed the door shut on his way back into the house and turned the deadbolt before working on building a fire. Once the wood had caught and a fire was crackling in the hearth, he ran upstairs to grab more blankets, bringing every one he could find to the living room.

Zeke lay on the couch, her whole body shaking as she shivered. Dev stripped his own clothes off before picking Zeke up and holding her close, wrapping blankets around them both. He sat on the floor in front of the couch to get closer to the flames, praying furiously that she would wake up.

It took nearly twenty minutes before Dev's body stopped shaking and heat began seeping into him again. He held Zeke flush against himself, lending her what body heat he had, scooting as close to the fire as he dared. She stirred several times, opening her eyes for a moment or two, then drifting back into unconsciousness. Exhausted from the battle and his own swim in icy water, Dev felt his eyelids grow heavy. Adjusting Zeke against his chest, he leaned back against the couch and closed his eyes, allowing himself to drift off, lulled by her breathing.

It was Zeke moving that woke him two hours later. Sitting up, she blinked rapidly, trying to make sense of what had happened and where she was. Her voice cracking, she spoke.

"What happened to Azazel?"

Dev sat up, groggy from sleep and grateful to see her awake and speaking. "I sent him back to Hell."

"We need to get out of here. It's not safe anymore. They found us."

"We'll leave soon enough. You couldn't walk out of here right now, babe. We're safe for the moment." He stroked his hand over her hair. "How did they find us?"

"The Hell Gate. He said he was there and saw Deacon fly out."

"Did he tell anyone else we're here?"

"I don't know. I don't think so." She leaned her head on his shoulder. "What happened?"

"You went through the ice on that pond out back. I barely got to you in time. Another minute and you'd have been dead."

"You saved me."

Dev rested his cheek on her head. "I always will." He pressed a kiss to her hair. "You scared me, Zeke."

"Scared myself, too." She shook her head. "Stupid fucking Familiar almost took me out. I'd have been the laughingstock of Heaven with that shit."

He rubbed her arms briskly. "You're hurt."

Zeke looked at the cut on her arm with mild surprise. "I'd forgotten about that. I got shot, too. In the thigh." She shifted the blanket to look at the round hole in her leg. "I can fix them both."

She concentrated on using her Healing abilities, knitting the skin closed and reforming the muscles. Within two minutes, both wounds were closed. She collapsed against Dev's chest, exhausted from the act of healing herself.

Dev held her gently, rubbing her arms in his hands. "You need to eat. Are you okay to stay here for a minute while I get you some food and something to drink?"

Zeke nodded. "I'm fine. I'm freezing, but I'll be okay for a few minutes."

Dev slipped out from behind her and padded to the kitchen, unashamed with his nakedness. He peered out the windows and reached out with his sensing ability, searching for any sign of danger. Feeling nothing, he poured two glasses of whiskey and warmed up bowls of soup.

Zeke drained the glass in one gulp, enjoying the burn as the alcohol slid down her throat, warming her up from the inside. They ate soup in silence, Zeke's hands still trembling from the cold. Dev took the bowls back to the kitchen once they were empty, again checked to make sure the house was secure, and knelt in front of Zeke, unwinding the blanket from her legs.

"I need to get the blood flowing into your legs and feet better than it is. They're still ice-cold." He rubbed her foot between both of his hands, warming her skin and massaging her flesh.

"I don't know if that hurts of feels good."

Dev laughed. "Probably both." He worked his way up her calves, one and then the other. "How are you feeling?"

"I still feel chilly, but much better than I did." She smiled softly. "You're taking good care of me. I appreciate it."

Dev ran his hands up her thighs, rubbing her muscles with his fingers, kneading the tension and chill out of her body. Zeke leaned back against the couch and closed her eyes, enjoying the feel of his hands on her body.

"Does it make me a horrible person that you're really turning me on right now?"

Dev chuckled and lifted one of her legs, pressing a kiss to her ankle. "There's nothing horrible about you." He rubbed his cheek on her calf. "You're always so soft and smooth."

"I don't like being hairy." She tugged the blanket down to expose her breasts, her nipples already tightly beaded, her skin glowing in the firelight. "I want you."

Dev looked up to meet her gaze. "You're weak from healing yourself. I don't want to hurt you."

Zeke shook her head. "I'm a little sore and tired, but I've got enough energy for this. I want to."

He skimmed his fingers up her leg to the juncture of her thighs, parting her and pressing his thumb to her. Zeke jumped and wiggled, pressing her hips up and out, inviting him in. He stroked his thumb back and forth, giving her stimulation.

Zeke met his gaze with her own and lifted her hands, laying them over her own breasts. She rubbed her nipples between her fingers, rolling the tender beads in them and scraping her nails over the tips.

Dev groaned deeply. "This is not what I intended to do. I had only the best of intentions. I was going to warm you up and let you sleep until morning."

Zeke laughed and pressed herself against his hand. "Change of plans. You can warm me up from the inside." She reached for his hand and brought it to her breast. "Fuck me hard to take the edge off, then we'll do it soft and slow."

Dev looked down at her with desire in his eyes. "I love you, Zeke."

Instead of being scared or angry, Zeke smiled. "I know. I love you, too." She rose to her knees and wrapped her arms around his neck. "I tried not to, but I can't help it." She pressed a kiss to his mouth. "You saved my life today. You've showed me that we can be together and be better than we were apart."

"I hate that it took almost dying to make you see that, but I'm glad you did." He dipped his head to taste her skin.

Zeke's head rolled to the side to give Dev better access to her neck. He gently turned her body until her back was against his chest. He wrapped his arms around her, pressing her hard against him. She moaned softly at the feel of his body touching every inch of hers. Slowly, he spread his palms on her stomach, running them over her skin and up her body until he covered each breast with one hand. Her head lolled back onto his shoulder and she reached around to grab his hips for balance. Dev nipped her shoulder lightly, soothing the slight sting with a lap of his tongue.

Zeke closed her eyes and let herself drift on the sensation of his hands on her body. She felt the steely softness of his erection pressing against her bottom and anchoring herself against him. He rubbed her nipples with his thumbs, tweaking the sensitive peaks until her breath came in panting gasps.

"Spread your legs and lean forward."

A bolt of desire rocketed through Zeke and she eagerly followed his directions, spreading her knees to part her thighs and leaning forward until her breasts were pressed against the couch cushions. He reached between her legs and slid the pad of his thumb over her, rubbing her clit gently until she was hovering on the edge of release. Only when her body was tense with need and her fingers gripped the fabric of the cushions as she reached for climax did he withdraw his hand and plunge into her, anchoring his hips against her and spearing upward, impaling her on his shaft.

Zeke cried out and her body pulsed around him. Her chest

flushed with desire, and she rolled her hips back, rocking against him, desperate to find orgasm. Dev pushed firmly against her, trapping her between his body and the couch as he moved slightly, barely stroking back and forth. He reached around to her front, dipping one hand between her legs and urging her to part them further, opening her completely to him.

Zeke panted and whined when he parted her lips and rubbed her clit again. "I'm going to last about thirty seconds if you keep doing that."

Dev's laugh rumbled against her ear. "That's okay. I'll just ride you through it and straight into the next one. No one says you can only get off just once."

She reached down and yanked his hand away. "I don't want you to make me yet. I want to feel you doing it." She pressed back against him harder. "Dev, please."

Without a word, Dev thrust into her, drawing almost all the way out and stroking back in firmly. Zeke gasped and moaned, her body jumping and tingling from the pleasure of him. Her muscles undulated, clamping on him and releasing until he nearly went cross-eyed. With a growl, he leaned over her and began moving, hard and fast, driving into her over and over again, his penis slick and wet from her body. He gripped her hips in his hands and yanked her back, slamming into her and changing the angle so he rubbed against her clit each time he stroked.

Zeke groaned and fisted her hands in the couch cushion. Her legs trembled and she bit down on her lip to keep from crying out as pleasure speared through her with each stroke of his body. She felt orgasm building, the hot claws of it rising up in her body until every inch of her tingled and vibrated with want.

"Do it. Come for me." Dev's voice was low and raw as he pumped into her. "What do you need, baby?"

His voice barely cut through the fog of climax filling Zeke's head. She mumbled something unintelligible and thrust against him, meeting him pump for pump. With a mangled cry, she jerked twice and toppled over the edge and into climax, her body pulsing around him.

Dev groaned when he felt her release and drove up into the wet heat, seating himself deeply as he let his own orgasm overtake him.

Zeke wiggled slightly to relieve some of the pressure on her chest from Dev's weight pressing her into the couch. When he didn't budge, she wiggled harder.

"It's hard to breathe with you pinning me to a large piece of furniture."

Dev laughed and forced his nearly limp arms to lift him up. He withdrew from her and reached down to pull off the used condom, freezing when he realized he wasn't wearing one.

"Well, fuck."

Zeke looked over her shoulder as she forced herself up onto the couch. "You okay?"

He looked sheepish. "I am for the moment, but you might kill me in just a second."

She narrowed her eyes suspiciously. "What did you do?"

"It's what I didn't do that's the problem." He looked pointedly at his penis. She followed his gaze, looking confused. It took a minute, but realization dawned in her eyes and she paled.

"Well, fuck."

He couldn't help but laugh. "My sentiments exactly. I forgot. I don't even know if we have any or if there are any here that are any good."

Zeke rubbed her palms on her thighs. "Well, there's nothing to be done about it now. I didn't think about it, either, and it's just as much my responsibility as it is yours. There's a half box of condoms upstairs, but they're thirty years old and I have no clue if they're any better at all than using nothing." She sighed deeply. "If you knocked me up I'll cut your dick off."

"How's the timing?"

Zeke did some mental calculations. "Shitty."

Dev felt the first icy tendrils of fear in his chest. "Whatever happens, I'm here for you."

She sighed. "There's no sense in worrying about it now. The damage is done, and we'll either be stocking up on diapers or we won't. We could try to find a pharmacy for the morning after pill, but those are hard to come by, very expensive, and I don't know if we want to be that out in public."

"It's worth a try. How long do we have?"

"I don't know. A couple days? I've never had to take it before." She ran her hands through her hair and yanked. "Dammit, we do not need a baby right now." She glanced at Dev and smiled at the look on his face. "You look like I just shot your puppy."

He heaved himself up onto the couch next to her and snagged one of the blankets from the floor. "I feel bad. I wasn't thinking. I don't know why it slipped my mind. I've been using the damn things since I was practicing putting them on when I was fourteen years old and desperate to find out what a woman looked like naked."

Zeke rested her head against his shoulder. "We'll manage. The odds are in our favor, biologically speaking, and it'll be weeks before we know anything. We can't worry about it for weeks. We'll give ourselves ulcers. Go get the box from upstairs and we'll see if they're usable. If not, well, I guess it's no penis-in-vagina sex for a while."

Dev laughed. "The fact that you didn't say no sex at all for a while makes me deliriously happy." He rose and stretched. "I am sorry, Zeke. I'd never put you in a tough spot on purpose."

Zeke swatted his ass. "I know that. I was the one practically jumping you on the floor. It's just as much my fault as yours. Now go get the damn box so we know if we can do it again."

Dev loped up the stairs and into their bedroom. He rifled through the drawers in the bathroom then picked up the box on the sink, peering into it. There were twelve foil wrappers in the bottom. He tore one open to inspect, looking for cracks or tears in the latex. Finding none, he tucked it carefully back in the wrapper, knowing he would have to use it soon or throw it out, and hoping Zeke was open to the former.

Curious, he opened the medicine cabinet and grinned when he found an unopened box. Tucking it under his arm, he checked the closet, every drawer in the bedroom and the other bathroom.

"Well, the box on the sink still looks good, there was an unopened box in the medicine cabinet, and I found four in the nightstand drawer in the second bedroom. I think we're good for a while." He grinned at her as he dropped the haul onto the coffee table. "I opened one up to check it, and it appears to be functional."

"That's good." She took the wrapper he held out and ran her fingers over the thin latex. "There's only one way to really know for sure, though."

Dev lifted one eyebrow. "And what way is that?"

She reached out and ran her hands over his penis, smiling when it began to harden and lengthen. "Try it out."

Dev took the condom and laid it on the couch, tucked safely inside the wrapper. "I was hoping you'd say that." He slid onto the couch with her, fitting their bodies together and leaning down to capture her mouth in a kiss. "Let's do some product testing."

CHAPTER TWENTY-ONE

March 18th, 2060 – Arkansas

"AT LEAST it's warmer here." Zeke hefted her backpack out of the car Dev had hotwired before leaving Colorado and slung it across her shoulders.

"It is warmer. Rhad said to hang out here for a few days until he's ready for us."

She looked over her shoulder at Dev. "I know. I was there." She glanced at her watch. "It's Friday now, and we should be good to go on Wednesday, so five days." She looked up at the apartment building. "This is going to be an interesting stay."

Dev looked around the street, taking in the burned out cars and the debris littering the pavement. In the building they'd been directed to, most of the windows were broken out and one wall was crumbling.

"It's not the Ritz, that's for damn sure."

"It's not supposed to be. We just need to lay low, keep out of sight and hope no one finds us."

Both jumped when they heard a loud crack and a tall, slim man with a bright red ponytail appeared. Zeke drew her gun and leveled it at the man, her hands steady on the trigger.

"Who are you?"

"Relax, love. I'm Rhad. Nice to meet the both of you." Rhad

extended a hand to Dev and scowled when the man didn't take it immediately. "Oh come on, it's not like I have some sort of 'hey, I'm a good guy' card to show you. If I wanted to hurt you, I wouldn't be alone, and I certainly wouldn't be unarmed."

Dev hesitantly shook the Devil's hand. "We weren't expecting you."

"I never know when I can get away, and I wanted to make sure you were somewhere safe where I could meet you whenever I could." He glanced at the apartment building. "I think you'll find it more comfortable inside than it appears from out here." He flicked his wrist and smiled when the locks clicked open. "It's not fancy, but it's comfortable, and there's running water."

Zeke lowered the gun and gestured to Rhad. "You go in first."

Rhad sighed and looked at Dev with a forlorn expression. "She's a suspicious one, isn't she, love?"

"She's a smart one." Dev nodded toward the door. "You heard her."

Shrugging, Rhad sauntered through the door and into the first apartment on the lowest level. It was sparsely furnished, with a couch, dinette, and one chair in the living room. The kitchen had a refrigerator and a stove, and there was one bedroom to the rear of the unit with nothing other than a bed. Zeke looked around, noting that everything was clean and in one piece, and nodded.

"This'll do just fine. Is there water? Or food?"

Rhad nodded toward the kitchen. "There's electric and water both, with a stocked fridge and some pots and pans in the cabinet. It's not a lot, but it'll be enough to get you by for a few days. I'm working on getting you set up inside the city, but getting what I need in order to protect you has proven to be difficult. There's a lot going on right now and a lot of upheaval over everything with your group. We don't have a lot of time, since there's talk of moving the sword again. Lucifer knows you're after it, he knows Lux and Zane are after Beelzebub, and he's well aware that if the four of you succeed then it's only a matter of time before Amaya and Deacon come after him."

Dev perched in one of the chairs and stared at Rhad "How long until they'll decide whether or not to move the sword?"

Rhad sighed deeply and dropped down next to Dev. "I don't know. I wish I did. Talking of moving it at all puts me in a hell of a spot. Honestly, if I hadn't already promised Alaria I'd help, I'd back out. If they decide to move it, I won't know where it's going. I can object to the removal, and maybe buy a few days, but that will raise suspicion if it's stolen in that period of time. It would put Lucifer's cronies on my trail, which is not where I want them to be. I never intended to pick a side in all of this. I enjoy having my city and living here, and I don't want to do anything to jeopardize that. On the flip side, I promised Alaria, and there are very few people I fear more than her. I'm also not a Devil who often backs out of a promise, so you can see my conundrum."

Zeke bit her tongue to keep from smiling. "Let's just try to be in and out before it becomes an issue. Do you know where the sword is right now?"

"I do, but I'm not going to tell you." Rhad glared at her. "The last thing any of us needs is the two of you coming in like avenging Nephilim and burning my city to the ground. I'll help you, but we play by my rules. I'm going to bring you into the city, set you up somewhere safe, and get you the schematics of where it is. Then, we'll develop a plan to get the sword and get out of the city, hopefully with no one being aware of what's happened. I'm not in charge of the sword or its protection, and I'm not even supposed to know what's going on at all."

"We're not idiots, and we're not going to jump the gun on this. We want to get in and get out with as little carnage as possible, but we need as much information as we can get to ensure we can do our job." Dev crossed one leg over the other and folded his hands on his thigh. "I think you can understand that."

"I do, and even better, I respect it. I know it's a hard thing for the two of you to trust a Devil. You weren't even thought of back when Alaria was one, and you've had nothing but bad experiences with Devils. Not all of us are as evil as you've seen. There are plenty out there doing what I'm doing and just trying to stay alive and off the radar in this world we live in." Rhad raked his hands through his hair. "I'm not going to do anything to betray either of you or to risk your lives. Alaria and Braxton got me out of Hades when they didn't have to, and they never came after me. I need the two of you to trust me."

Zeke looked at Dev and nodded slightly. He shifted his gaze back to Rhad. "How long do you need before you can bring us into the city?"

"It'll be close to a week. I'm sneaking Aradia in tomorrow to put up some protections, but after that I'll have to change the security patrols, put up some fronts for who's staying there and figure out how to hide the fact that you're Nephilim. I know you have a shield, and that'll help, so there may be a way to magnify it so Devils and higher level Cambion won't be able to detect you, but I'll figure it out one way or the other."

Zeke crossed her arms. "Is this place secure?"

"Enough. It's far enough outside New Orleans that it's not patrolled. I'll try to keep people away from here the best I can, but I can't swear to you there won't be any stragglers. If there are, dispose of them as quickly and as quietly as you can. I'd recommend you hide first and hope you aren't found, but if you're detected, you'll have to kill everything that's here. Whatever you do, don't let anyone get out of here alive. If there's even a whiff of someone trying to come in, the sword will be moved before we know what's happened."

Dev nodded. "Okay. We'll play ball for a few days. We'll stay inside when we can, keep quiet and not draw attention to ourselves. But if you haven't come back for us in a week, one of us is coming in to see you."

Rhad's eyes darkened. "Doing that would ensure all three of us die before this task of yours is over. I don't want that. I'm sure you don't want it, either, so do us all a favor and keep your panties untwisted until I get this figured out. I'll check in every couple of days."

Before either Zeke or Dev could open their mouths, Rhad was gone. Zeke shook her head in disgust and glared at the chair where he'd been. "I hate when they do that. Even more, I hate that they can go wherever they want and I'm limited to a city block."

Dev gestured to their surroundings. "What the hell are we supposed to do for a week in this place?"

Zeke shrugged. "I think we need to start out by checking it out and clearing all the other buildings around here. It's not unlikely that there are some creepy crawlies hiding somewhere inside the town. After, I think we need to cast some protection spells. Nothing big or it'll alert people flashing in, but just enough so we can get a feel for if someone or something arrives. That way we know what's coming before whatever it is knows we're here."

Dev nodded and heaved himself to his feet. "It wouldn't be a bad idea to load up on as many supplies and ammo as we can. We've got no way of knowing what we're going to face after we have that sword or how long we're going to have to hide out. Two cars full of gas and loaded with supplies and weapons would be a nice safety blanket to have."

She looked out the window and studied the smattering of buildings still standing. "I see some shops that look like they might not be completely gutted. Let's give it a try." She picked up her vest and strapped it across her chest. "I think we go in packing though. There's no telling what we might find."

Dev tossed her two clips for her rifle. "I'm with you there." He picked up his own vest, fastening it tightly before bending to rifle through the bags they'd carried in. "Let's get the car unloaded so we have it to bring back anything we find."

Zeke held up her hand, gesturing to Dev to halt. Slowly, she crouched at the door to the sporting goods store they had decided to start with. She fished her lock pick kit from a pocket on her vest and inserted it carefully into the lock. Dev pressed his shoulder to the brick door frame, his hands folded around the butt of his pistol, which was carefully aimed at the door.

They heard the click of the pins and bolts turning at the same time. Zeke jumped back, allowing Dev to take point, and they went through the door together, Zeke shining a flashlight around the interior of the store.

There was dried blood on the walls. It stained the floor and covered the windows so very little light got in. Dev pulled out his own light and clicked it on as they moved throughout the store methodically, checking for signs of life before they even looked at the contents of the shop. Zeke checked behind the counter, kicked open the door to the office and lowered her gun.

"Dev."

Dev quickly moved to stand beside her, taking in the scene on the other side of the door. A Devil's trap had been drawn in the room, and the doors and windows were lined with salt and gunpowder in an effort to keep out whatever had been trying to get in. On the floor were five bodies—two adults and three children. The body of what Zeke assumed was the father had a gun still clenched in one hand, and the mother had wrapped herself protectively around her children.

"I wish I could say I've never seen anything like this before." Dev ran his hand over his face. "It was death or be possessed. He chose to spare them being tortured and murdered or turned into Familiars."

Zeke rubbed the bridge of her nose. "We have to stop it, Dev.

People can't live like this. It's not right." She crouched and studied the bodies. "I feel like we should bury them or something."

He shook his head and squatted next to her. "Just leave them. They're not in there anymore, and they chose to die together. Let's not disrupt them." He stood and pulled her up. "Let's see if there's anything in here we can make use of."

"Try not to disturb them at least."

Quickly, they moved through the store, checking every drawer and cabinet for anything useful. Ultimately, they came up with a large buck knife, two boxes of shotgun shells, a scope for one of their rifles, and a case of MREs.

Loading their haul into the car, Zeke locked the door behind them, marking the glass with spray paint. She looked around, scanning the rooftops before walking back to the car then sliding into the passenger seat next to Dev, who was fiddling with the controls as he waited for her.

"We have a guest."

Judging that the threat wasn't serious by the tone of her voice, Dev didn't even look up. "That was fast."

"I don't think it has anything to do with us or with Rhad. We knew the odds of this place being completely empty were slim. There's almost always a straggler or two. Not a vamp because it's out in the sunlight, and I don't think it's a human. Can you get a feel for it?"

Dev reached out with his ability, searching for whatever Zeke had seen. "Feels like a Cambion. Reasonably powerful. It's a woman, if that makes a difference. I don't feel any others, so I think it's safe to say she's alone. How do you want to play it?"

"Well, I think we need to kill her."

"That goes without saying." He chuckled and exited the car, heading toward the next building. "If we race after her, she'll run and we might never catch up. We need to be smart here, especially since she's not attacking us."

Zeke lowered her sunglasses to shield her eyes from the bright light and so that whoever was in the town didn't see her scanning the rooftops. "She's armed. I see a short sword and a rifle, so we need to get in off the street before she thinks she can get two shots off. Let's go into the next shop, see what she does, and make a plan."

"Sounds good to me. The pawn shop is just across the street."

"Goody."

It took only thirty seconds for them to cross the street and for Zeke to pop the deadbolt. Once inside, Dev shut and locked the door, and Zeke swept the inside for inhabitants. Finding none, she jerked her chin toward the office at the back with no windows.

"If it's just one, I can handle her. We need to draw her attention to us for a few minutes. I'm thinking I go out the back, climb up one of the fire escapes and head toward her from up top. She's just on the next roof over, and if she's busy watching you, then I might be able to sneak up on her. Let's wait a couple minutes, then you go out with a box of stuff to the car. Yell back telling me to hurry up or something and then have a conversation. I figure you can go back in and come out once, maybe twice before she starts to get suspicious. Once I've got her pinned on the roof, you can flash up."

"Works for me." He grinned at her. "Don't do anything stupid."

"I won't."

Zeke tucked her pistol into its holster and slung her rifle over her shoulder. She slipped through the store to the back door, slowly turning the lock and easing the door open, sighing in relief when it didn't squeak as she opened it. Lithely, she climbed onto the dumpster in the alley then caught the lower rung of the fire escape and lifted herself onto it.

She heard Dev slam the front door and drop a box into the trunk. After several seconds, she heard his voice. "Come on, Zeke. There's nothing in there we can use. It's been picked over." There was a pause as she climbed. "I don't care if you found more guns. Without ammo they're useless. We can only fire one at a time."

Ten seconds later, the door opened and closed as Dev went back inside. Zeke continued to climb, hugging tightly to the building as she wiggled her way up. After thirty seconds, she reached the top step with her head and hooked her leg around the ledge, pulling herself up and rolling onto her stomach in one motion.

Lying completely still, she listened to more of the fake conversation between Dev and no one and did a military crawl to the ledge. The woman was standing at the edge nearest the street, her back to Zeke and her gun lifted to her shoulder. Knowing she had very little time, Zeke judged the distance between the buildings with her eyes and gritted her teeth.

She climbed to her feet and backed up several yards to give herself a running start. Taking off, she launched herself off the roof and through the air, landing on the neighboring roof in a crouch, immediately drawing her weapon and leveling it before standing up.

The woman whirled as soon as she heard the impact of Zeke landing, her rifle anchored to her shoulder. Her hair was red instead of white, telling Zeke immediately that the woman was not a Cambion. She met the eyes of her adversary and felt a punch to her gut. Dev's eyes.

"Denise?"

The woman's eyes flickered. "How do you know my name?"

Zeke briefly considered whether to lower her weapon then decided Dev's sister was no threat and brought the barrel down several inches. "I know your brother. It's Dev down there. Didn't you recognize him? He thinks you're dead!"

Denise lowered her gun slightly. "That's what I wanted him to think." She flexed her finger on the trigger.

Zeke saw the motion a split second too late and dove to the side. She wasn't fast enough, and the bullet slammed into her gut, just above her hip and slightly to the right. She brought her gun up, firing, but Denise was on her feet and fast, dodging the shots and drawing her sword in one motion. Zeke scrambled to her feet and ripped her knife from its sheath, preparing for battle.

CHAPTER TWENTY-TWO

DEV HEARD the gunshot and prepared to flash himself to the rooftop when a snap sounded behind him. Whirling, he froze, anger swelling in his chest as he saw who was standing behind him.

"Mason."

The Cambion smiled. "Dev. It's been a long time. What, a year now?"

Dev clenched his fist and conjured a sword. "You son of a bitch. I'm going to rip you apart with my bare hands."

Mason clucked his tongue. "You're welcome to try. Meanwhile, you're darling sister is up there slaughtering your girlfriend."

"Denise is dead. I watched you kill her."

"You saw what I wanted you to see. We had a very powerful Devil with us there that night, one that projected a vision for you to see. Denise is very much alive and up on the roof. I believe she just shot the other Nephil you're here with."

Anger and confusion mixed together, rising in Dev's chest and rolling through him. "She would never have gone with you willingly."

"To the contrary, the whole thing was her idea. Denise swore her loyalty to Lucifer months before we raided Michael's nonplace. She planned the whole thing. She wanted you dead."

"I don't believe you."

"Well, then, let's wait down here until she's done killing your girlfriend, and we'll ask her ourselves." Mason laughed. "That's your choice. See your sister and get your answers or save your girlfriend. If you can get through me, that is. Seems to me you'll end up dead before the end of this little meeting here."

Dev heard the sounds of battle on the roof and knew Zeke was alive and fighting. He turned his full attention to Mason. "How did you find us? Have you been following us?"

"Actually, no. Believe it or not, we were camped here waiting for word to go into New Orleans and get the sword. Lucifer was considering moving it, and we're the transport this time. We were in Europe fighting Nephilim, so when we heard we might be needed, we headed here. We're supposed to get word on it within a couple weeks."

Dev tested the weight of his sword in his hand and measured the distance between himself and Mason. "What is it with people about to die wanting to talk my damn ear off?"

"You're the one about to die. I know your weaknesses. We trained together for years. I know everything about you. All of Hell is looking for you. I'm going to take your head to Lucifer." He shrugged. "Besides, the longer we stand here chatting, the longer Denise has to finish off that bitch of yours." He grinned salaciously. "When we're done here, covered in the blood of our enemies, I'm going to take your precious baby sister back to our spot and fuck her until she's screaming for mercy. Then I'm going to do it again."

With a strangled roar, Dev lowered his shoulder and charged Mason, driving down with his sword. Mason twirled to the side, and Dev's sword collided with the pavement, sending a shock of pain up his arm. He steadied himself, turned, and continued his assault. Mason drew his own weapon and their blades clashed, sending sparks flying.

Dev barely noticed when Mason's sword scored across his back, slicing through his vest and into skin. He didn't react when the tip of the blade caught his thigh and ripped through muscle, opening a large gash. When his own blade found flesh and slashed through Mason's bicep, and a jolt of satisfaction and vengeance rocketed through him.

The two men battled, their blades clashing over and over again. Both had blood slickened hands, and both were sporting deep wounds. Sweat poured from Dev's forehead, dripping into his eyes and stinging as he fought. With a grunt, he managed to bring

Mason in close, using the handle of his sword to bash him in the nose.

Mason's sword hit the ground with a clatter, and Dev threw his aside, content to pound on the other man with his fists. He tackled Mason around the waist and drove him to the ground, pummeling his face and stomach with punches. The sound of breaking bone and crushing cartilage gave Dev great satisfaction.

Mason struggled, kicking and punching, trying to get Dev off of him. Dev barely felt the blows being landed. Red swarmed his vision field, and he continued to pound, striking over and over again. Finally, he wrapped his hands around Mason's neck and squeezed, watching hiseyes bug out of his head.

Mason clawed at Dev, digging furrows in his hands and arms as he tried to free himself from Dev's grasp. Blood vessels began bursting in Mason's eyes, tinging them with blood. More blood leaked from the corner of his mouth as he bit down on his own tongue inadvertently.

After another tense minute, Mason went limp as life seeped out of him and his eyes went flat and dead. Dev continued squeezing for a full thirty seconds longer before he managed to convince his fingers to release. He collapsed onto the ground, his chest heaving as he caught his breath and his fingers cramped and stiff from squeezing so hard for so long.

His gaze cleared, and he stared at Mason for a long moment before climbing to his feet. He was petty enough to kick the body once before flashing to the roof to help Zeke.

"Do you really think you can kill me with a hunting knife and a pistol?" Denise taunted Zeke as she stalked toward the other woman.

Zeke pressed one hand against her wound, the other wrapped around the handle of the knife. "I think I can kill you with my own bare hands if I need to. You're a Nephil. My powers work on you."

She sent out a wave of power, knocking Denise back several steps. She took the opportunity to kick the other woman's rifle off the edge of the roof, sending it clattering to the ground below. Denise sent her own bolt of energy back at Zeke, who leaped to the side to avoid it.

"Why are you pretending to be dead? Don't you care what this has done to your brother?"

Denise laughed and took a step back. "No, I don't care. I hate that self-righteous bastard. Always acting like he was taking care of me. All he ever wanted was to be a martyr. 'Here, Denise, you eat.' 'Here, Denise, take the blanket. I don't need it.' And then he'd lord it over my head, reminding me constantly of how I needed him for every little thing." Denise laughed bitterly. "When I met Mason, I met someone who saw me as an ally, as an equal, and who didn't view me as a little girl who needed saving."

Zeke narrowed her eyes. "You think so little of your brother? That he sacrificed for you for his own glory? You don't know him at all."

"You just fuck him. Don't pretend you know who he is. How long have you know him? A few months at best? You certainly weren't around when I was there. He'll get tired of your pussy soon enough and move along to the next. It's what he does."

Slowly moving her gaze around the roof, Zeke began to work out a plan. She moved incrementally toward the middle of the roof, positioning Denise closer to the wall as they circled one another.

"Why not just leave? You were involved in the attack, weren't you?"

Denise smiled. "You're a smart girl. Yes, I was involved. It was the only option. If I had just left, Dev wouldn't have ever given up looking. I couldn't take that risk. I faked my death. It was surprisingly easy. Didn't take much effort at all." She shifted her grip on her sword. "I had honestly hoped that I'd never see him again, but then the two of you showed up in our town while we were waiting to hear about the word. As soon as I saw you come in, I knew we would have to take you out. We were getting ready to move in when Rhad showed up. For a minute or two, I really thought I wouldn't have to do anything, but then he left, and you were still alive. Lucifer is going to be very interested in knowing Rhad has betrayed him."

"In order for Lucifer to find out, you would have to leave here alive, and that's not about to happen."

"You would really kill your boyfriend's twin sister? I may have hurt him, but I'm still his blood. He'll never forgive you if you kill me."

Zeke shrugged. "If you're right, I'm just a warm pussy anyway. What do I care if he's mad at me for doing what's necessary?" She looked at Denise sharply. "In that regard, I think we're a lot alike. We always do what's necessary, no matter the cost."

Denise laughed. "Well, you're right about that much, I'll give you credit there." She hefted her sword. "Let's do this. One of us isn't making it out of here."

Zeke nodded. "Oh, I know."

Digging her heels in, Zeke took off, running full bore toward Denise. She tackled the other woman, wrapping her arms around her waist and driving her backward, tipping them both off the edge of the roof.

Zeke clamped down on the urge to flash, using her powers to keep Denise from doing the same. They hit a car below with a crash of metal and glass. Zeke screamed from the impact as jagged metal cut through her skin in several places. She wrenched the sword from Denise's hand and threw it aside. With one smooth motion, she drove downward with her knife, stabbing into Denise's chest and cutting straight through her heart.

In pain, relieved, and torn, Zeke rolled off of the wreckage of the car and fell to the ground, hitting hard and staring up at the sky. Moments later, Dev's face appeared in her field of vision.

She blinked several times, trying to force her vision to clear. Dev squatted down next to her, taking in her wounds. He grabbed her arms and heaved her to her feet, wrapping his arm around her waist.

"I need to get you back to the apartment. You're hurt pretty badly."

"I'm sorry, Dev. So damn sorry."

Dev shook his head. "She was going to kill you. I was coming up onto the roof and heard the tail end of the conversation. She wouldn't have hesitated." He blinked back tears laced with pain and hurt. "That wasn't my sister."

"It still hurts, and I'm still sorry." Zeke winced and pressed her hand harder into her stomach. "Not to worry you, but she shot me."

Dev's head snapped around. "She shot you? Where?"

She moved her hand and showed him the blood pouring out of her gut. "It's not good. The bullet is still in there."

"Fuck." He stooped and lifted her in his arms. "Let's get home, and I'll see what can be done."

"I'm likely going to pass out soon." Zeke laid her head against his chest. "You need to get the bullet out and stop the bleeding the best you can. My mother told me a story once about when she was hurt badly and her body took over healing while she was unconscious. If we're lucky, my Healer abilities will do what they need to. If not, do you know how to do a blood transfusion?"

"I know how." Dev strode purposefully down the street, his

heart pounding in his chest. "You're going to be okay, baby. I'm not going to let anything happen to you."

"It's not good. There's a chance I won't wake up. If that happens, I need you to know I meant it when I told you I loved you." She blinked back tears and fought off a wave of dizziness. "If we make it through this, I'll make sure we have everything we want. We'll have a baby. Hell, we'll have as many as we want. We'll get married. We'll manage to have it all, no matter what the world looks like."

"Don't talk like that. When you wake up and I remind you that you promised marriage and babies, you'll be mortified."

"Probably."

Dev chuckled softly as he climbed the stairs to the apartment building. "I told you I'll always take care of you. I'll take care of you this time, too."

Zeke's vision swarmed with black dots, and she fought to stay conscious. "I don't want to die."

Fear rose up in Dev's chest, wrapping its icy tendrils around his heart as she went limp in his arms.

Dev had always hated the feel of blood. It was just slightly thicker than water and sticky when it started to dry. The color was odd, too, almost black when it was in a pool, red in a smear, and brown when it dried.

He knew unequivocally when he stripped off Zeke's clothes to take stock of her injuries that seeing her blood was worse than any other. The harsh red against the cool alabaster of her skin tied his stomach in knots. He took a deep breath and snagged the bag with their medical supplies from the floor. Thanking God they had taken everything they'd been able to find at the cabin, he dumped the contents onto the floor and rifled through it.

Looking at the forceps and clamps with apprehension, he picked up a bottle of rubbing alcohol and one of betadine. Gritting his teeth, he poured the alcohol into her stomach to kill any germs.

The blood mixed with the alcohol and sloshed onto the floor, forming a pink puddle. Ignoring the urge to gag, Dev pulled on a pair of gloves and gingerly inserted his finger into the wound, searching for the bullet. His fingers brushed the metal of the edge of the round and he sent up a quick prayer that it was intact. The bullet had entered just above her hipbone, and he didn't feel any damage to any organs. Scowling when it occurred to him he wouldn't know what it would feel like had there been internal damage, he chose to believe everything was fine inside her body.

Knowing there was no way to be sure of her chances and what damage there was without sophisticated medical equipment, he used his other hand to insert the forceps and grip the bullet, pulling it out. Once the projectile was on the floor, cast aside as he withdrew the forceps, he unscrewed the cap on a bottle of styptic powder and dumped half of it onto the hole.

The only thing to do was wait and see if the powder was enough to slow or stop the bleeding. If it was, he was reasonably certain there was no internal bleeding. If it wasn't, he would have to jeopardize their safety by calling for help.

When no blood continued to bubble out and spill onto Zeke's skin, Dev let all the air in his lungs whoosh out. He waited two more minutes then used a wet cloth to wipe away the goopy powder, exposing the wound underneath. He flushed it out again, holding his breath until he was sure it wasn't going to begin gushing again.

Even more than he hated blood, he hated stitching someone up. Skin was rubbery and tough when one tried to work the needle through. Knowing it was necessary despite his dread, he picked up the suture kit and began preparing to stitch Zeke's side.

Dev worked through each step, stitching up the wound, cleaning and bandaging all the other little nicks and cuts, then dressing Zeke in sweats, a sweater and thick socks before tucking her into the bed under a blanket. That done, he stripped himself, washed off the blood and grime, and spent five minutes studying the gash in his thigh.

It needed stitching. He knew that beyond any doubt. The slash was deep and wide, spanning his entire thigh and cutting through the dermis into muscle tissue. The problem, as he saw it, was that he didn't have anything stronger than spray on lidocaine and aspirin, and he also knew beyond any doubt the pain from stitching himself would be intense.

Procrastinating on the inevitable, he took several minutes to slather ointment on his own nicks and cuts then returned to staring at his thigh, which was still bleeding sluggishly. Annoyed with his own reluctance, he folded up his belt and held it in his teeth, picked up the needle, and jammed it into his leg.

CHAPTER TWENTY-THREE

March 20th, 2060 – Arkansas

ZEKE WAS surprised when she opened her eyes. She blinked rapidly, forcing herself up onto her elbows and looking around. The sky was dark outside, though she wasn't sure if it was morning or night. Dev was nowhere within sight.

She started to sit up and yelped at the bolt of pain in her side. Yanking up her shirt, she gingerly pulled the bandage away and stared at the line of blue stitches against her pale skin. Moving slowly, she managed to get to her feet, pressing a hand to her forehead when a wave of dizziness rolled over her. Knowing she needed to eat, she nudged open the door to the bathroom to check for Dev then limped into the kitchen.

She opened a can of tomato soup and drank it straight from the container. Not nearly satisfied, she rifled for a pan and dumped a family-sized can of ravioli into it before opening a bottle of soda and chugging half of it in one gulp.

The sound of the door at the bottom of the stairs opening trickled up to her, and she hobbled across the floor, snagging a pistol and holding it tightly against herself, pressing her back to the wall as she waited to see what, or who, was coming up.

Dev came around the corner carrying a box, and Zeke rushed toward him, limping heavily. He dropped the box as soon as he saw her, enveloping her in a hug, both of them ignoring the pain that rocketed through their bodies from their just barely healing injuries.

Dev grabbed her face in his hands, raining kisses over her forehead and cheeks. "I was starting to be afraid you wouldn't ever wake up. You were unconscious for two days."

Zeke blinked back tears. "I was surprised when I did. I thought for sure I was dead. How did you fix the bullet wound?"

"It didn't hit any organs. It's a fucking miracle, but I'll take it. I gave you blood twice, but I didn't know if we're the same type or if I was making things worse." He buried his head in her neck. "Dammit, Zeke, don't you ever do this to me again."

"I can't make any promises, but I'll try my level best." She looked up at him with sadness in her eyes. "It wasn't a big deal when my mom was here. She could heal me in no time. Now that she's gone, what I can do for myself is limited and takes a lot out of me." She stepped back to the stove and turned the heat off. "I can probably fix you, though. That way at least one of us would be in fighting shape in case there's anything or anyone else in this place."

"There's not. I spent the day combing through and disposing of the bodies from the fight. I didn't want anything here to draw attention to us. I also loaded up a car and left it in a garage a few miles up in case we have to make an escape and can't take the one we have."

"If I don't get us patched up, then we won't be ready to go with Rhad when he comes. I'm barely moving, and you're not doing too much better."

Dev wrinkled his nose. "I'm fine. Sore and I have a few stitches, but there's nothing that won't be fine in a few days."

"It's what's going to happen between now and then that makes me nervous." Zeke filled two bowls with ravioli and handed him one. "Once I eat, you're going to let me heal you. It won't take too much out of me, and you'll be way better off than you already are." She picked up forks and hobbled to the table. "If something were to happen right now, I wouldn't even be able to get down the stairs with this hole in my gut, and you're in no shape to carry me. We'd both be dead. At least if I can heal you, you'll be able to manage things better. I'll still be dead weight, but at least you'll be at full strength."

Dev sat across from her. "You're never dead weight. We'll get through everything together. Rhad can wait, or he can go fuck himself if he doesn't want to. He should have known he had Cambion camping out here."

Zeke chewed her first bite slowly as she thought about what she wanted to say. "How are you handling what happened? I can't even imagine how hard it must have been finding out about Denise."

Dev glared at her, his eyes nearly black with anger and grief. "She betrayed everything we are. We were born to fight for God, and instead she joined with Lucifer. I don't even know who that person was. She wasn't the sister I grew up with. The Denise I knew was sweet and a little too soft for this life. She let her heart lead, and I thought that got her killed. The Denise out there was hard and mean. It wasn't the same person."

She reached across the table and folded her hand over his. "I think you should continue to separate the memories that way. Let her be dead last year. No one needs to know about what happened and no one needs to know she was still alive. We're the only ones who were here."

"The Cambion obviously know she was alive. Lucifer has to know. It'll get out somehow that she didn't die, but I'm in no hurry for Michael and Deacon to know about it, let alone Elisa and Carys." Dev shook his head and speared a piece of pasta. "There's nothing good to come of talking about what happened."

"I'd take it away from you if I could. When my parents died, you were the one and only thing pulled me through that first night. Without you there, I'd have sat on the floor and let them find me and kill me. I wish there was something I could do to bring you through this because in a lot of ways, what you're going through now is worse than what happened to me."

Dev smiled sadly. "We'll get through it together. That's all we can do." He squeezed her fingers and picked up another bite of pasta.

"I think they hurt worse coming out than they did going in."

Zeke chuckled and continued using the small scissors she held to cut the stitches in Dev's leg. "That's because it's not even really started to heal yet, which, believe it or not, is good because it's easier for me to do it when it's still somewhat fresh." She pulled out small pieces of thread and dropped them on the floor. "How many wounds are there?"

"The thigh is by far the worst. I put a couple stitches in my arm, but I was doing it one-handed, so they're not very neat, but they did the job." He rolled his shoulders. "There's a decent slash across my back. I managed to get the bleeding stopped with a towel, but I can't do anything about it because of where it is."

"I'll take care of that too, don't worry." She finished cutting the sutures and leaned back, out of breath from even that small amount of movement. "I need to work up the energy to heal my stomach. It'll take at least a week for me to be useful at all with it the way that it is, and we don't have the time. Even if I can't finish it off and I just end up jumpstarting the process, I'll be better off than I am now."

Dev pulled his shirt over his head and dropped it onto the floor, leaving him clad in only a pair of boxers. "You'll do what you can, and we'll deal with what's left. I guarantee you if I'm good to go, nothing is going to happen to you. I wouldn't let it."

Zeke pressed one hand to each side of the gash in Dev's thigh and closed her eyes, letting the warmth of healing wash over her. Dev gritted his teeth when his skin stretched and went back together, wincing at the pain of her healing him. Sweat beaded on Zeke's forehead, and her breathing became labored as she struggled to do something that had always been as easy as being.

After several tense minutes, the gash on his thigh was little more than a pink scar and the pain that had been constant since Mason's sword had sliced through his flesh abated. Zeke leaned back against the chair, pressing her hand to her stomach and blinking rapidly.

"That's good enough. I can run with that healed. I don't need you to do the rest."

Zeke shook her head. "No, I'll do the rest. Turn around."

"You're tired and hurt."

"And I won't be any more of either of those things after I do this. Turn around."

Reluctantly, Dev turned to allow her to reach the long slash on his back. The edges of his skin had started to dry as it died and his whole back felt tight from the open wound. It was red and swollen, with the beginnings of infection already set in. Carefully, Zeke laid her hands on his skin and went to work, taking the time to clean out every trace of infection before she brought the edges together and sewed the muscle shut, sealing it with new sinew and skin.

When his arm was healed as well, Zeke leaned her head back and closed her eyes, waiting for the dizziness and nausea to pass. "I'll sleep for a couple hours, eat something else, and then I'll be ready to try to heal myself. Even the brain drain from that will only last a day or two."

"Why does it take so much more for you to heal yourself than other people?"

"I don't know for sure. My mom always thought it's because those of us with gifts like this are supposed to use them to help other people, not to help ourselves. From a practical standpoint, when I heal someone, I use their own energy and their own body to spur the healing. It takes a very small amount of my energy to do it. When it's me, I'm using already depleted stores to try and fix something that's wrong. I can do it, but I end up twice as drained as I was when I started."

"I'd like to say it's probably just the second, but knowing God and how He views things sometimes, I imagine it has something to do with the first, too." Dev leaned down and pulled on his shirt, stretching his arms above his head and grinning when he felt no pain. "You do a damn good job at that, babe."

"I should hope so. If Michael hadn't interfered with my conception, I'd have just been a Healer. I'm more comfortable with those abilities than my Nephil ones." She laughed softly. "He's the only thing even resembling a parent that I have left now."

"That's not true. Aradia and Gage look at you like a daughter and so do Braxton and Alaria."

She sighed deeply and heaved herself to her feet. "I know. I'm just still feeling sorry for myself a little bit. I'll be fine. I'm hurting and I'm tired and I'm hungry."

"We can fix two of the three." Dev walked to the kitchen. "Do you want some more soup? There's some beef stew or chicken and rice. On the sweeter side, there's a can of cherry pie filling, two cans of oranges, and some chocolate pudding."

"Is there flour and sugar?"

Dev rifled in the pantry. "Yes, and yes."

"What about shortening?"

More rifling. "Bingo."

"I can make a cherry pie."

Dev's head snapped up, and he goggled at her. "Real pie? Like with a crust and everything?"

"Like with a crust and everything."

He pressed his hand to his heart. "I will worship the ground you walk on for the rest of eternity for a cherry pie."

Zeke grinned despite her pain. "Help me to the table."

Chapter Twenty-Four

March 28th, 2060 – Arkansas

Zeke ground her teeth together and forced herself to keep moving. She swung her whole body around and lashed out with her elbow, striking a blow before dropping her shoulder and rolling away, coming up on her feet and managing to jump just in time to avoid a sweeping leg aimed at knocking her down. Clenching her fists, she brought them up to protect her face, jabbing twice in rapid succession as she pivoted her upper body to avoid blows.

Dev was covered in sweat, and his lip was bleeding from one of the shots she landed as they sparred. He caught her fist as she punched, using her momentum to jerk her forward and tucking her under his arm and dropping to his knees in order to lay her flat on the ground. She swore as her face hit the mat and struggled for ten seconds before going limp.

"Give. God dammit."

Dev released her immediately and stood, extending a hand to help her up. "You're doing great. I'd say you're very nearly back to normal."

"You call normal getting beaten four out of six times?"

"When I'm a half-foot taller than you and seventy pounds heavier, yeah, I do call that normal. Besides, you're barely healed."

Zeke lifted her shirt to inspect the puckered scar from her

gunshot wound. "I'm getting there. Rhad should be coming any day now to get us. It's been a week."

"I told you I would, didn't I?" Rhad crossed his legs as he appeared in the folding chair near the thick rubber mat Dev and Zeke had been fighting on.

Dev grabbed a towel and draped it across his shoulders, staring blandly at him with no visible reaction to Rhad's sudden presence. "It's about damn time you came."

Rhad lifted his eyebrows. "From the look of her belly, I'd say I came not a day too soon. What happened?"

Zeke held up her hand to stop Dev's undoubtedly sarcastic response. "There were two Cambion set up here. We got into a bit of a scuffle. Neither survived."

Rhad sat up straighter. "Who were they? Why were they here? Are you sure there were just two?"

"They said they'd been placed here in case the sword had to be moved and expected to get word on it within a couple weeks. That was a week ago, but there's been no movement here. We found their radios and have been monitoring them, but nothing's come through." She shrugged. "I'm no expert in Cambion communication, but it seems that unless there was someone close, they'd be using the radios."

"They would." Rhad nodded. "Good, so we know the order hasn't come out. I spoke to Beelzebub briefly a couple of days ago, and they seem to be reasonably happy with the way things are going right now. He's not happy two of his biological children have suddenly been killed, especially since they were very well hidden several hundred miles apart, but I don't think the two of you are going to want to tell me what's going on with that, are you?" When they both stared at him stonily, he laughed. "I didn't think so. And I probably don't want to know, if the truth is told. It behooves us both to know only what is necessary and not a bit more so I'll grudgingly thank you for not assuaging my curiosity." He sighed and stood up. "Okay, well, I'm ready for you whenever you're ready. How much time do you need?"

Zeke rubbed her hands on her thighs. "I could use a shower if there's time, and we'll need a little while to gather some things up."

"Take your time. I'll wait." Rhad gestured for them to precede him back inside the apartment. "I've got you set up with an apartment in the French Quarter. That's where most of the witches live, so the magic Aradia has woven to protect you both won't raise eyebrows. It also has the benefit of being very near to where I live, which will offer you a little protection. I took the liberty of making sure you both have appropriate clothing. This will be a nice change for you both. There's electric, hot water, a fully stocked fridge, including dairy and meat, so you should find all the comforts of fifty years ago and then some."

Dev blinked. "It's only been a month and a half since we were in LA. We had all of that there."

Rhad lifted his brows. "Well, if you don't want it, I can certainly arrange for you to sleep in a barn and eat potted meat."

Zeke laughed. "That won't be necessary. We're grateful for what you're doing." She rifled through her bag and removed clothing. "I'm going to go wash up. Dev, would you start packing?"

Dev waved her off. "Don't worry, I've got it."

Rhad waited to speak until he heard the water running in the bathroom. "Is she healthy?"

"Mostly. She's good enough that we don't need more time."

"Are you certain?"

Dev looked up from packing ammo. "Are you asking because you're concerned or because you don't want to risk your ass?"

"Both. If my ass gets hung out to dry, odds are yours is in the sling right next to me. Like it or not, we're in this together, love, and we're going to have to trust one another to get through this. I know you don't know me, and I know you don't have a single reason to trust me, but Alaria does, and that should mean something to you."

"Braxton trusting you means more to me, to be honest. Alaria spent several million years as a Devil. Braxton's only ever been a Warrior."

"I don't care which one of them you trust more. They both trust me enough to send you here, and Aradia trusts me enough to come here to help shield the two of you. I could have killed the three of you any time for the past week. Notice you're still alive. I keep my promises. I always have, and I always will. I just need to know both you and Zeke are healthy enough to do what you're going to have to do. If you're not, I can give you a few more days."

"We're good to go. A few more days and we're both going to go stir crazy."

Rhad tapped his fingers against his chin. "Okay. Let's get this show on the road then. Take only what you can carry. I don't think anything will happen, but you need to be able to make a speedy retreat if something does. You can always come back here for the rest of it, and the car you're using will be moved to just outside the city. We'll drive it down, and then I'll take you both in from there. Once you're there, there will be some rules. There are Cambion in New Orleans, and there are demons and Devils. I have all the baddies roaming my streets."

Dev lifted his eyebrows in mock surprise. "You're kidding! I'd never have guessed."

"Sarcasm isn't needed." Rhad glared at him. "If you'll be so kind as to let me finish, what I was starting to say is that Aradia is waiting to cast a very inventive glamour spell on the two of you. She's been working on it for the last week. It will shield your true identities to anyone who doesn't already know you. For example, you'll look exactly the same to me, but to a random passerby, you will look as if you are Cambion. That will explain your abilities, and with all the other beings around, it will be extremely difficult for anyone without your exact abilities to tell the difference between a Cambion and a Nephilim, especially when you have the white hair and blue eyes of the Cambion."

"It's hard for me to tell the difference sometimes, especially if I'm at a distance. With Zeke's ability to hide her abilities, plus the glamour spell, it should work."

"I'm risking my ass on it working, so it had damn well better. If the two of you get caught, I get caught, and I'm not about to risk that. Mind you, if Lilith or Beelzebub show up, you're likely fucked, but they don't come around often. Abalam pops in from time to time, but he's just been wandering since Abaddon was killed. Three fucking decades and he's still moping around."

Zeke came out of the bathroom, dressed in jeans and a long sleeved t-shirt. She rubbed her hair with a towel and toed on her tennis shoes one at a time before addressing either of the men. "Shower's yours. As far as Abalam, I wouldn't count him out of things. He may be grieving his buddy, but he's still very dangerous, and he's wily. He isn't going to just disappear from things. If he's still around, there's a reason. From the things my parents told me about their run-ins with him from before, he was responsible for a lot of death, and he's likely got a bone to pick with Gage and Michael for killing Abaddon. Dad was there, too, but he's dead now, so there's nothing Abalam can punish them for. He might not be a danger to us right now, but Lux and Zane need to watch for him and so do Amaya and Deacon, especially."

Rhad shrugged. "Not my concern. My concern is the two of you and the sword." He looked between them. "Let me make one thing very clear. Even being in charge of the city where the sword resided, even though I'm not part of the security on it, is enough to get me executed if Lucifer is in a bad mood. Depending on how things go down, you may need to make room for a third in the getaway car."

Zeke grinned. "We're not going to let them kill you. Alaria and Braxton both say we can trust you, and even Michael grudgingly admitted you can be counted on to keep a promise. I know this is dangerous for you, so we'll do whatever we have to do."

Dev grabbed clothes and disappeared into the bathroom. "Let's not borrow trouble yet."

Zeke shoved her clothes into a backpack and began breaking down all of their weapons to more easily pack. "What're the rules with carrying a weapon?"

"Most people do. There are skirmishes pretty often with humans and Cambion, so it's not unlikely you might need to protect yourself. We're one of the most peaceful cities out there, but that isn't saying too much these days." Rhad rolled his eyes and cracked his knuckles. "It's like everyone decided we were going back to the Dark Ages when the world ended. Bullets are a finite resource, so everyone is using swords and axes again."

"It's not too hard to find ammo yet. At least it hasn't ever been for us."

"You're not a human trying to get from one place to another without being eaten by something." He looked sad for a brief moment. "It's hard to look back and remember how things used to be before this started. Even when I was trapped in Hades, I could watch Earth through the pool. I always enjoyed seeing what humans were doing. Now, they're just struggling to survive. There are a select few who have managed to keep their lifestyles by swearing allegiance to Lucifer, but anyone who worships God is an endangered species."

Zeke lifted her eyebrows. "You don't worship God. Why does this bother you?"

Rhad waved one of his hands carelessly. "I wasn't a very powerful Angel and have even less power as a Devil. I wanted the freedom to do whatever I wanted. I liked to play. I enjoyed being a God in the Underworld, and I enjoyed people. Heaven was too stuffy. I'm a free spirit, and no one appreciated that. So I ended up with Lucifer, and I didn't regret it, even after the Fall. At least not until I got stuck in the Underworld. Once I got stuck there, then I really regretted it." He laughed and stood, stretching his hands over his head. "My point being that I was never blood thirsty. I don't particularly enjoy pain, unless of course it's in the context of sex, and then it can be enjoyable." He wiggled his eyebrows at her.

Zeke laughed in spite of herself. "There's a part of me that really wants to like you."

Rhad grinned. "I'm a likeable guy. I'm a simple guy. I want good booze, a warm bed, yummy food, and a great lover. I think everyone else should have those things, too, so when I got the New Orleans post after everything went to shit, I decided it would be a safe place for everyone. Humans and Nephilim can't roam the entire city freely, but the Quarter, and my places, are safe for whomever wants it. Lucifer might not like it, and I'm damned positive the rest of the Cambion and the Devils don't, but they've left me alone for the most part."

She crossed the room to the pantry and began boxing up the canned food. "I got the impression from Amaya that you just run a brothel there. How much sway do you actually have?"

"A bit. The short explanation is that the most powerful Devils run things. I'm not one of them. Fortunately for all of us, I'm good with people, love to fuck, and have produced a veritable shit ton of Cambion for cannon fodder." He wagged his finger when Zeke looked horrified. "Don't start with me, young lady. We don't feel things like you humans do. I've never met even one of them, and if I hadn't done it, Lucifer would likely have questioned my loyalty, so don't presume to judge me for my potency."

Zeke held up her hands. "I wouldn't dare."

"Good. Now, to get back to the topic at hand, I like sex."

"That was the topic at hand?"

Rhad laughed. "Yes. Because I enjoy it so much and with great regularity and with a wide variety of partners, I decided it would be fun to ensure others have access to low-cost, healthy pleasure providers. Ergo, I opened a series of brothels in New Orleans, centering in the Quarter, and this started back before things got like they are now. By the time things got really bad for those of the human persuasion, I was well established. I employ quite a few humans, and I wanted to keep them safe, so I reached an agreement early on with the Cambion. Over a few years, I opened a few more places, took on more people, and added a hotel, which I turned into a safe house. Now, it's almost an unspoken rule that nothing funky goes on in one of my places, and there's normally peace inside the

Quarter."

"What about with the sword? How close are you going to be able to get us?" Dev spoke from the bathroom door. He snagged his boots in one hand and sat at the table to pull them on. "Don't get me wrong. I think it's great you have a neutral zone, but our goal is to get that sword."

"Understood. Listen, love, things are informal in New Orleans. There are some higher ranking Cambion there, but they mostly live outside the Quarter and are busy with the rich human population they farm for hosts and incubators. When things need to be kept safe, they come to me because no one knows the city better. I had the place where it's at built when I learned it was coming, along with four other dummy sites, and I was there when they placed the damn thing in the vault." Rhad looked between them. "Are you ready to go now?"

Zeke shouldered her backpack and picked up a box. "Let's get this show on the road."

CHAPTER TWENTY-FIVE

April 3rd, 2060 – The French Quarter, New Orleans

"RHAD SENT a note that we should come down to his place tonight. He's going to give us the schematics for the museum where the sword is. With any luck, we'll go get it tomorrow night and be out of here."

Zeke looked up from the book she was reading when Dev spoke. "Okay. Which place is he at?"

Dev studied the small map scribbled on the back of the note. "One of the brothels a few blocks down. That one seems to be his favorite." He shook his head and chuckled. "There's also a line about looking pretty and having some fun tonight."

Zeke lifted her eyebrows. "I'm not sure why he thinks we would want to come play in a whore house, but I suppose I appreciate the sentiment." She laid the book on the side table and stood. "I don't like dressing up."

Dev snagged her around the waist and drew her close against him. "Maybe you put on something trashy, and I can pretend to pick you up. Then we sneak back here and have wild, dirty sex, and afterward, we can take a dip in the hot tub Rhad thought we just had to have for some reason, and then do the whole wild and dirty sex thing again."

She laughed and wriggled from his grasp. "As fun as that sounds

I don't think I want to pretend to be a prostitute."

Ever hopeful, he wiggled his eyebrows. "I'll play the hooker if you want."

"Again, as delightful as that sounds, I think I'll pass." Zeke brushed a kiss over his mouth. "I'll go get changed and gussy myself up a bit."

"Zeke."

Zeke turned her head and looked back. "Hmm?"

"I haven't brought up what you said when you were hurt yet, but you need to know that when this is all said and done, I will be bringing it up."

She briefly considered pretending not to know what he was talking about. Deciding against it, she nodded slightly. "I wouldn't expect anything else." Without another word, she continued up the stairs and into the bathroom, flipping on the light and jumping when she saw Griffin perched on the bathtub, her legs crossed and looking pristine in all white. "Holy fuck, you scared me! What are you doing here?"

Griffin smiled. "My role here is two-fold. It's not safe for any Angel to come in here because they would be detected. My soul is human, so Gabriel and Michael decided I was uniquely suited to come talk to you since you already know who I am." She sighed deeply. "It's too much to ask to be able to just relax once you're dead these days, apparently. They keep dragging me out of Heaven to come down here and work. They don't care at all that my part in this ended thirty years ago."

Zeke held up one hand. "I don't think they sent you here to complain. What's going on?"

"The death of Denise and Mason, whoever the hell the two of them are, is now suspected and a squad has been dispatched to come here and remove the sword. They're two days away, so you'll need to move quickly. From what I've seen, it's being led by Lilith, and there are six very powerful Cambion with her, including Alexi."

"We're planning to go in tomorrow night to get it. That's all that we can do. Rhad is giving us the plans for the museum tonight. It took him a little longer than he thought to get them. Unless, of course, he's playing us and is really on their side."

Griffin shook her head. "No. Rhad, as far as I've been made aware, is true to his word, and I don't believe he would betray Alaria and Braxton after they freed him from Hades."

Zeke leaned against the sink and folded her arms. "How come

you never just pop in when Dev's around?"

"It's not comfortable for me to exist on this plane. My body is long ago rotted and my soul belongs in Heaven. In order for me to function on Earth, I have to find someone with whom I have a connection. It was easy with Braxton since he was my husband and easy with Alaria because she was so involved in the Choosing. With you, there's a blood tie since you're my great-granddaughter. I have no connection to Dev. At least not yet."

Zeke straightened. "What's that supposed to mean?"

Griffin looked at her sternly. "You know precisely what it's about, and don't you even pretend otherwise. He may be a bit in the dark about the functioning and timings of women's bodies, but you're not, and neither am I."

Stubborn, Zeke shook her head. "I have no idea what you're talking about."

"Since the topic now is the second reason I was sent down, we'll continue on with it. You're well aware of when your parents and Lux's parents were approached by Michael about hosting Nephilim. Since then, there have been many thousands born, as there have been of Cambion. Now that the first generations of the two hybrids are adult, there has been the emergence of the second generation. The oldest are around ten, I believe. They are more powerful than even their parents and have seemed to be taking the strongest abilities from each parent. That has encouraged Angels and Devils to mate with Cambion and Nephilim in an attempt to see if they can create beings as powerful as Angels and Devils. This makes it even more important to succeed in killing Lucifer and banishing the Devils. With this new development, it is only a matter of time before humanity is gone. Humans will be of no more use than livestock. They'll be hosts for demons and turned in to Familiars, but there will be no need for them even to host the Cambion and Nephilim."

"That's all very tragic, but I'm not sure what it has to do with me."

Griffin sighed and stood up, placing her hands on her hips. "I don't appreciate you playing so dumb. Tell yourself what you'd like, but we both know what's going on here. I understand you're scared and that you don't know what to do, but I expected you to face this the same way you have everything else. Head on." She looked at her granddaughter pointedly. "At the very least, I would have thought you'd have told Dev by now."

"There's nothing to tell him!" Zeke raked her hands through her hair and paced the bathroom. "There's nothing good to come of this."

Griffin softened. "Ezekiel, my love, there's all the good in the world to come of this." She reached out and skimmed her fingers over Zeke's cheek. "Listen to me. I never got to know your grandfather, or your mother. I know you only a little. But I have been where you are standing now. I have gone through this fight. I know how you feel and how scary it is, but you are not alone. Your parents watch over you, the others are there for you, Dev is solid and strong and loves you. I know the world sucks, but you are blessed to be surrounded with strength, and love, and support. If you tell no one else, tell Dev. A man has a right to know he's going to be a father." Closing her eyes, Griffin continued. "Do you know much about me?"

Confused by the abrupt change in topic, Zeke shook her head. "Not a lot. The basics of the Choosing."

"When I was a teenager, I had a child. Without that child, you would not be standing in front of me as your mother never would have existed. Do you know how that child came to be?"

"No. Mom never told me."

"I was raped as one of the events Alaria got to wipe out my humanity." Griffin smiled softly. "Amazing to think that not so very long ago, the woman who now loves you as her daughter was a Devil as evil as any had ever been. She tricked a boy into allowing possession and used him to violate me. Having a baby out of that was one of the worst, and best, experiences in my life. When I birthed your grandfather, I couldn't even look at him. I didn't want to. I never believed that things happen for a reason until I found out about the Choosing. Now, I look back and think about the reason for my attack, the reason for my baby to be born." She reached out and took Zeke's hand, holding it tightly. "You might not be able to see it now, but there is a reason for all of this. One day, you will look down into the face of your child and know why it happened. It's one of my deepest sorrows that I never got to have more children—that I never raised one. I envy you that chance even knowing what you'll face. There is beauty to be found in even these circumstances if you'll let yourself see it."

Dev bent over to tie the laces on the dress shoes Rhad had paired with the suit he wore. Feeling ridiculous in the clothes, he scowled at the tie and tossed it toward the closet in a half-hearted show of rebellion. Slipping on the jacket, he ran a hand through his hair and descended the stairs to wait for Zeke to appear out of the bathroom in the best way possible. With a scotch.

He poured the drink slowly, relishing the sound of the alcohol sloshing in the glass. Inhaling the scent before sipping, he held the liquid in his mouth, swirling it before swallowing and closing his eyes as the liquor burned its way down his throat. Good booze was a rarity and he always took the time to properly appreciate a good drink when he got one. He heard steps on the stairs and turned, smiling as Zeke made her way down them, dressed in a short, black leather skirt with fishnet stockings showcasing her legs, and a green corset that hugged her body tightly, showing off her curves. Her hair, almost black, was swept off her shoulders and pinned messily to her head, several tendrils falling loose to frame her face and skim over her throat and shoulders, drawing attention to her creamy skin.

"Screw going to see Rhad. I'm going to keep you here and enjoy that outfit."

Zeke didn't answer. She stepped off the last stair and crossed the room, reaching out and handing Dev the box in her hand. He looked down blankly, blinking rapidly when he saw that she had handed him a box of condoms. He grinned widely.

"Nice to know you had the same thoughts."

"That's not what they're for."

Confused, Dev looked again to make sure it was, in fact, a box filled with condoms in his hand. Finding that he was right, he looked at her quizzically. "I'm not aware of another use for condoms aside from sex."

Zeke closed her eyes and took a deep breath. "Throw them away."

Deflated, he scowled. "The whole damn box went bad? What happened? The ones we've been using have been fine."

"We don't need them anymore."

Dev turned the box over in his hand, trying to make sense of what Zeke was saying. Confused, he placed the box on the end table and looked at her. "Did you find some birth control pills or something? Or is this your way of telling me you've decided we shouldn't be together anymore?"

"This is my way of telling you I'm pregnant."

Dev froze, his eyes darting back and forth across her face,

searching for some hint that she was playing a joke. Finding none, he ran one hand over his face and continued to stare at her, his mind racing. "I think this whole thing will go better if you just tell me how you want me to feel,because I don't want to have a response here and piss you off."

Zeke couldn't help the smile that pulled at the sides of her mouth. "And here I was hoping to gauge how I feel off of how you reacted to the news."

Concerned, Dev took a step forward. "Are you mad?"

She shook her head. "I'm not mad. I don't know how I feel. Scared, mostly, I think. There's a little bit of regret tinged in there, and a little bit of something that feels kinda like excitement, but I'm mostly just scared."

"Your parents managed to do it. So did Lux's and Amaya's. Braxton and Alaria had two more kids of their own and raised Finley on top of it. It obviously can be done."

"I'm a soldier. I fight. It's what I was born to do. It's what I've done my whole life. I don't know how to be anything other than this."

Dev sat down on the arm of the couch. "Do you intend to stay pregnant?"

Zeke dropped down next to him. "Yes." She shrugged. "I could find someone who could end it if I wanted, but I don't want to. The fact that I'm scared and not angry or upset about actually being pregnant tells me I don't want to get rid of it." She folded her hands in her lap and tapped her fingers together anxiously. "I didn't want to tell you yet."

"How long have you known?"

"Just a few days. My period was due last week and I'm like clockwork. I found an old test under the sink upstairs and peed on the stick. I got two lines, which the instructions tell me means it's positive."

"Don't those things have expiration dates?"

"Griffin popped in upstairs when I went to change and confirmed it. She was pushing me to tell you. I was going to wait until after everything so we weren't both distracted, but she's right. You have a right to know."

Dev laid his hand on her shoulder. "I'm here for you. Through everything. No matter what happens, I'm here, and I'm not going anywhere."

"I know that." She laid her head against his side. "You're one of the good ones. I've known that since the day we met. I know you wanted this, but I don't want to bring a child into this world."

"Then let's change it for the better. If we destroy the sword, and the link to Beelzebub, then Amaya can go for Lucifer. Just destroying the sword might help turn the tide for us. We might be living in a demon-free world by the time the baby is born."

Zeke closed her eyes for a moment. "It would be nice, but I'm not holding my breath on it. No, we're likely going to have to raise our child in the same world we grew up in. There's nothing good about it, but we'll love it, and we'll protect it, and someday, he or she will be sitting exactly where we are, having the same discussion and trying to make the world better for their children."

Dev stroked his hand over her hair. "Michael once told me that we fight a fight that will never be won but must always be fought and that we have to keep living a real life because living and loving and not letting this world define us is a victory over Lucifer every day."

"I know, and I agree with him. We've said before that fighting can't be all we do or they've won already. We have to keep marching forward. I just never thought I'd bring a child into a world where we struggle to live. I want better than that."

He extended his hand. "Well, let's take the first step. Let's go get the fucking sword and make this world better." He squeezed her fingers when she placed her hand in his. "And when we're done, we'll come back here and I'll make love to you until you're limp." He pulled her up and led her toward the door, tucking her arm in his. "As soon as we're done with the sword, I think we should get married."

Zeke shook her head and sighed, a small smile ghosting across her mouth. "Of course you do."

CHAPTER TWENTY-SIX

RHAD WAS sitting on what appeared to be a throne when Dev and Zeke entered the brothel. There was a busty redhead sitting with her legs across his lap, and an even bustier blonde giving him a shoulder massage. He waved them in when he caught sight of them, signaling to a waitress who, aside from an apron, was naked.

"Welcome, welcome. Rhona, would you please get my guests something to drink?" He turned to them. "What'll it be? Wine? Bourbon?"

Dev cocked his eyebrow at the surroundings and glanced at the waitress. "Scotch if you have it. On ice."

"Coming right up." The waitress turned to Zeke. "For you, ma'am?"

"Just water. Thanks."

Rhad looked curious but said nothing. "Ladies, could you excuse us? I have some business to attend to with these two lovely people." He swatted the blonde on the ass as she crossed in front of him. "I'll come find you both later."

Zeke laughed and dropped into one of the chairs in the room. "Sounds like you have a fun night planned."

"I have to get my jollies when and where I can, love. You never know when Lucifer will take it all away, and I intend to enjoy as much as I can before he does." He sprang out of his chair and went to the desk across the room. "I'm sorry things have taken so long, but I just got the plans last night." He spread out a schematic across the table. "The sword is here." He pointed to an area. "It's inside a vault. There are four coded locks to get into it, and some wards, so you'll need to get past all of that. I have the codes, but they're changed every forty-eight hours, so you'll have to go in by six a.m. the morning after next. There are fourteen roving guards, all demons. They work in shifts, and the change is at two a.m. That would be the easiest time for you to get in is during the shift."

"Are there cameras?" Dev leaned over Zeke's shoulder to get a better look.

"There are. There's a bank of cameras in the old security office. For the most part, everything that was in the museum, still is. I took over here soon enough after stuff starting falling in that there wasn't a lot of damage done to the infrastructure. Everything is in basically the same spot as it is on the map here. The sword is in the vault where they used to keep very valuable pieces of art, and we had it converted to make it more secure. There is electric to the building, so all of the cameras are in working condition."

Zeke studied the paper with a critical eye. "Basically, we have to beat demons and technology here, which isn't going to be easy." She whistled softly. "We're going to have to go in separate. One for the sword, and the other for the cameras. What's the outside access look like?"

"There are the main double doors, which are secured with a chain and padlock." He paused when the waitress came back in with drinks. He snagged the bottle of scotch off the tray and placed it on the table. "That'll be all. Thank you, love." Once the waitress had gone, he turned back to Zeke and Dev. "I don't recommend that entrance. In the back is an emergency exit, there's a door on the east and west walls, and there's roof access. That will bring you in the closest to the vault, but it's small. I don't know if you could fit through it, Dev."

"What about air shaft access?"

"Nothing a human can fit through on the outside. Once you come in through the roof, there is a shaft up there you could probably squeeze into if you needed to, but again, I don't recommend it for Dev, and it'd even be tight for you." Rhad sipped his scotch and swirled the liquid around his glass. "I'll leave the ins and outs to the two of you since it's safest for all of us if I don't know the details of your plan. Do you have any questions for me before I hand over the papers and get back to my lovely ladies?"

Zeke studied the map closely. "Do you know the routes security takes?"

Rhad shook his head. "I wish I did, but I don't."

Dev gestured to an area on the map. "This looks like it's been blocked off."

"It has. There was some damage to that section of the building about twenty years ago. Instead of repairing it when it wasn't being used for anything, I just had it sealed off."

"Sealed off with what?"

"Brick and wood. Nothing fancy. Enough to make sure transients weren't getting in there. It's not impenetrable if that's what you're getting at."

Dev grinned. "I'm not getting at anything." He rolled up the schematics and folded them into a neat square, tucking it into his pocket. "I think that's all we need."

Zeke nodded. "I've got everything I need to go on." She looked at Rhad solemnly. "You might want to have all the demons and Cambion you can otherwise engaged somewhere away from the museum tomorrow night. If all goes well, we'll be gone within thirty-six hours."

Rhad drained his glass. "I hope you won't be offended if I tell you I hope you get out of here and that I never see either of you again." He grinned at them both. "Don't get me wrong, I think you're both great, but having you here makes it much more difficult to enjoy myself."

"Believe me, we haven't had a great time, either." Dev placed his hand on Zeke's shoulders. "We'll let you get back to the leggy blonde and the busty redhead."

Rhad went back to his throne and draped himself across it. "Bless you both. I'll have fun enough for all of us." He waited until Dev reached for the door. "By the way, congratulations on the wee one."

Zeke whirled. "How?"

"How did I know? You asked for water, and Dev's staring at your belly like it's going to rear up and bite him. It doesn't take a genius." Rhad shrugged. "Don't worry. I'm not going to tell anyone." He smiled. "Treasure the opportunity. The one thing you Nephilim get right is how you care for the children of this war."

Dev opened the door. "You're all right, Rhad. You're all right."

To keep up appearances, Zeke and Dev remained in the brothel for close to two hours after leaving Rhad's chambers. They flirted with some of the other patrons and staff, Dev had several drinks at the bar, and they both turned down multiple offers from paying customers. After the third time she'd had to discourage a client from helping himself to a handful of ass, Zeke decided it was time to leave.

Going in search of Dev, she found him pinned to the wall with two women pressed against him. One had her hands under his shirt and the other was reaching for his zipper as Dev batted their hands away, trying to escape without drawing attention. Surprised when she felt desire at seeing him covered in other women rather than the anger she had expected, she strode purposefully across the room, winding her way through the throng of people.

"Sorry, girls. This one's mine. I already paid a premium for him." Zeke's voice was calmer than she'd anticipated and Dev's gaze shot up to hers when he recognized her voice.

Catching on quickly, he nodded. "That's what I've been trying to tell them." Grinning at the other women, he shrugged. "She's a demanding one. I don't think there's enough of me to go around tonight."

Zeke grabbed Dev's hand and yanked him toward her, brazenly dragging her hand across the fly of his slacks and rubbing his crotch. "It's time to go. I paid for the whole night."

As soon as they were out on the street, Dev grabbed Zeke and pulled her flush against him, enjoying the contrast between the cool night air and her hot skin.

"Looks like I get to play the prostitute after all." He brushed a kiss over her lips. "Since you paid for the whole night, why don't you tell me how you want to spend it?"

Zeke looked up at him through her eyelashes, surprised by how turned on she was by the exchange. Deciding to go with it, she lifted one shoulder in what she hoped was a careless shrug. "We'll start with hot, hard, and fast and see how much bang I can get for my buck."

Dev grabbed her hand and started dragging her down the street. "Let's get home, then."

The minute they were through the entry, Zeke slammed the door shut and pinned Dev to it, clamping her mouth on his. Her fingers, nimble and quick, worked the buttons on his shirt loose from their holes, and she pressed her hips against his. Dev's hands streaked down her back, sliding over her bottom and lifting her until she wrapped her legs around his waist.

He switched their positions, pressing her back against the wall and tangling both of his hands in her hair. He dragged her head back, savaging her throat with his tongue and teeth. She groaned gutturally and dug her nails into his biceps, arching her back to anchor herself against him. Dev fumbled with the laces on her corset, trying to untie them. His fingers tangled in the cords and, frustrated, he ripped them out, sending scraps of fabric floating to the floor.

Zeke shifted in his arms, wriggling lose and stepping down. She slid his open shirt off his shoulders and deftly unbuckled his belt, yanking the strip of leather from the belt loops. His pants and boxers fell to the floor, and she ran her hands down his chest, scratching her nails over his stomach and wrapping her fingers around his erection.

Taking one step back, she slid the straps to her corset down her arms, baring herself from the waist up. Her eyes never leaving his, she lowered herself to her knees and folded her mouth around his steely hardness.

Dev's eyes crossed, and his hips jumped as his dick was enveloped in wet heat. He twisted his hands in her hair, guiding her head in toward his body, her mouth sliding over him. She ran her tongue from base to tip, swirling it around and sucking lightly. Using her teeth, she lightly nipped at the sensitive skin on the underside of his penis, wrapping one hand around the base and lavishing attention on the shaft and tip. Dev groaned and closed his eyes, gripping the door knob in one hand and the entry table with the other.

She licked and sucked until Dev's knees grew weak and blood rushed into his penis. He jerked his hips up and tugged sharply on her hair. Zeke looked up, her eyes hot and hungry and smiled as she released him, licking one last time from end to end, never breaking eye contact with him.

Rising to her feet, she slowly lowered the zipper to her skirt and wiggled it over her hips, sliding it down her legs and tossing the garment carelessly over her shoulder. Cocking an eyebrow, she slipped her fingers beneath the waistband of her stockings and peeled them off, revealing skin an inch at a time.

Dev raked his eyes over her, taking in every inch. He slid his gaze over her face, down the slim column of her neck, over her breasts, lingering on her dusky nipples. When she blushed from his scrutiny, he continued his journey downward, enjoying the view of her creamy pale skin and lush curves. Her warrior's body was striking, and he drank her in, taking in the muscles and planes years of battle and training had carved.

Dev dipped his head and nipped at her neck, catching one of the tendons in his teeth and scraping gently. "If I could paint, I would paint you just like this. A warrior goddess with a set of hips that makes a man's eyes cross." He lowered his hands to span her stomach. "Not to be overly sentimental or to embarrass myself, but there's a very primal part of me that cannot wait to see you grow with our baby. I know the timing sucks, and I know neither of us were prepared for this right now, but the human in me is having a very elemental response."

Zeke lifted her arms and twined them around his neck. "If there's one thing I've learned, it's that we're just pawns in God's chess game. Everything happens for a reason and at the time He wants it to. We're having a baby because we're meant to have one right now. There's a part of me that dreads what it means for our future, and a part of me that's excited about it." She grinned when he slipped his arms around her and grasped her ass. "Is this about celebrating new life?"

Dev grinned. "Maybe a little." He stepped away slightly and bent to stroke his tongue over one of her nipples. "Mostly it's because I want you." He sucked the protruding point into his mouth and swirled his tongue around it, humming in satisfaction when her knees went weak and she clasped at his shoulders.

Zeke's eyes drifted closed, and she grinned when he lifted her and placed her on the hall table. He lifted her breasts in his hands, rubbing the fleshy globes and stroking his thumbs over her nipples, one still wet from his mouth. She groaned when he gently tugged her nipples and gasped when he pinched slightly, the small bite of pain melting into the pleasure of his touch.

He slowly lowered his head and licked each of her nipples, drawing in the taste of her and enjoying the texture of her skin against his tongue. He blew on them, causing chill bumps to rise on her flesh and then pulled one into his mouth, caressing the nub with his lips and tongue before nipping sharply with his teeth. Zeke's hands tightened on his shoulders, and she slid her hips forward on the table, pressing herself against him.

"No more foreplay. I want you inside of me."

Dev glanced up at her breathless plea and lifted one eyebrow.

"And here I was going to pay you back for earlier."

Zeke shook her head. "Don't get me wrong, you are fucking brilliant with your tongue, but I want to feel you now. I don't want to wait any longer."

His smile was sexy and wicked, and he ran his hands up her thighs. "Wrap your legs around me and hold on tight."

Curious, she did as she was told and cinched her legs around Dev's waist, looping her arms around his shoulders as he lifted her. He spread his thighs slightly and locked his arms under her bottom, hefting her up slightly and bending his knees to get the right angle. Slowly, he probed the entrance to her body with the tip of his penis and sank into her slowly, spearing up into her, rocking his hips and thrusting gently until he was firmly seated inside of her.

Zeke gasped and closed her eyes, her hips jerking against his and her body desperate for friction. Slowly, he pressed her back against the wall to support her weight and slid out and back in, his dick gleaming from the moisture produced by her body. She was hot and wet and tight as a fist around him. He rapidly stroked into her several times, enjoying the slick heat offered by her body.

Zeke dug her nails into Dev's shoulders, pressing down with her palms to give herself some leverage to increase the speed of his thrusts. He pounded into her, hard and fast, taking pleasure from her as fast as he gave it. Their breath came in shallow gasps and their bodies were both covered in a thin sheen of sweat. Both strained and reached for orgasm, solely focused on their own release.

Zeke felt herself rocketing up the crest of orgasm and grasped it, clenching herself around Dev and jerking her hips to change the angle, giving herself the friction she needed. His fingers dug into her ass, and he pressed his face into her neck, trying to stave off his orgasm until she found hers. Slamming into her harder, he ground her head against the wall, forcing himself into her as deep as he could go.

Her legs came loose from around his waist, and he gripped her thighs, holding them open and supporting her weight with his forearms and the wall. She glanced down and stared, mesmerized by the sight of his wet cock working its way in and out of her body as he thrust his hips.

As her orgasm built, Zeke's head fell back, jutting her chest toward him, her nipples hard and rosy, her chest flushed with desire. Her whole body tensed, and she gripped his shoulders harder, the words tumbling from her lips both begging him to stop and give her more in equal measures.

Dev gritted his teeth and continued to stroke into her, his whole body aching with the need to come. "I'm not going to last much longer, baby. You feel too good."

Zeke gasped and struggled to form words. "Almost there. God, it feels too good for you to stop."

Dev pressed his body against hers, burying himself deeply and driving his hips into hers. Zeke sank her teeth into her bottom lip and her nails bit into Dev's back, drawing blood as she clutched him. With a ragged cry, she plummeted over the edge of release and into orgasm, pleasure rocketing through her body and spearing into her until every inch of her hummed and throbbed with the sensation. She clenched around him, her muscles twitching and gripping him tightly. Dev drove up into her one final time as his own climax swept him away, his hips pumping against hers as he came.

It was several moments before either of them could move. Dev regained his footing first and stepped back, carefully placing her feet on the floor and bracing his arms on the wall for balance. Zeke leaned heavily against the table, her hands pressed to the top to keep herself steady.

Zeke attempted speech first. "That was amazing."

Dev grinned. "I concur." He looked around. "It seems like we have sex in odd places just as often as in a bed."

"I like it. Spontaneity and all." She pushed off the table and reached out to touch his shoulder. "I made you bleed."

Dev looked at the nail marks in his skin. "I enjoyed it. They'll heal." He gathered up their clothes. "Do you want to head up to bed?"

She shook her head. "No. We need to stay up as long as we can and sleep through the day some so we're sharp for tomorrow night. The last thing we need is for one of us to be tired and unable to focus."

"Okay, well, I'm going to go put on some clothes, and then we'll go over the plans Rhad gave us and work on a finalized course of action." He swatted her butt as she walked up the stairs. "After that, maybe we can try out the bed up here for a change. I'll even let you be on top."

Zeke chuckled. "Let me? There's no letting me to it. I'll be on top if I want to. Besides, it isn't like you don't prefer I be on top."

"I never said I don't." He drew her in for a kiss. "One more night and we're finished, baby. We've almost done it."

"One more night and we're free of this." She tugged on pants and faced him, echoing the sentiment. "Let's just hope we survive it."

CHAPTER TWENTY-SEVEN

April 4th, 2060, The French Quarter, New Orleans

THERE WAS a lot of thought that went into getting ready to stage a burglary. Everything had to be perfect. Clothing was important, since getting snagged could slow them down, which could lead to being captured or killed. Zeke was well aware of that as she selected snug black fatigues and a tight black tank with a long-sleeved shirt overtop. She took care to check each pocket on her vest before putting it on to make sure she had everything.

In one pocket she carried a small penlight, in another her lock pick kit. One had a knife, yet another a multi-tool, and one the scope for her rifle. On her utility belt, she had a large blade, a small hatchet, several extra clips of ammo, two stakes, and a Maglite. Her holster strapped a pistol to each thigh along with one extra clip for each. On her back, she carried a small pack with a sawed-off shotgun, two bottles of Holy water, salt, gunpowder, the map of the museum, and more bullets, including wooden ones for vampires and silver ones for werewolves.

Her rifle was her preferred weapon. Much like her mother, Zeke was an excellent marksman and was confident picking off threats with the sniper rifle. She carried the weapon over her shoulder and her silencer in one pocket on her pants.

Dev was loaded similarly, with a couple exceptions. Where she carried a hatchet, he liked a machete. He also carried rope and a small toolkit. His preferred weapon had always been a sword. Dev favored getting up close and personal with his enemies instead of shooting from a distance. There was something much more satisfying about drawing an adversary in close and hacking at it with a sword than there was pulling a trigger. Luckily, his powers didn't force him to choose which to carry. He carried a gun and could conjure a sword.

They readied themselves together, making sure everything was properly loaded and accessible. Dev chose similar clothing in a pair of black army pants, a tank and a thin sweater. Instead of thigh holsters, he wore one across his shoulders and chest with a machete on one side and a pistol on the other.

"I'm not even nervous about this," Zeke spoke softly, her hands over her head as she plaited her hair into a braid to hold it back from her face.

"In one sense, we've been preparing for this our whole lives." Dev strapped his utility belt across his hips. "Let's go over things again. Once we get to the museum, we'll split up. I'll plant the charges on the side where the damage was done. The guards should think it's a collapse and check on it. Once they detonate you'll drop in through the roof and I'll get in through the main entrance and go directly to the security room. From there I'll be able to guide you in and keep an eye on any stray guards. After you have the sword, we'll go out the back exit and head immediately toward the car we packed."

"It's simple, with only a million ways everything could go to hell in a handbasket."

He grinned. "Just the way we like our plans." He bent to lace his boots. "Are you ready?"

"As ready as I'll ever be. Did you make sure there's nothing we're leaving behind that could be used by the Cambion?"

"I did a sweep before I came up." He slung his pack over his shoulder. "Let's get this show on the road."

Even New Orleans was relatively quiet at one-thirty in the morning. There were very few people on the street, and those who were mostly appeared to be sex workers not employed by Rhad and some demons patrolling. Both Zeke and Dev knew there were vampires lurking in the shadows waiting to prey on whoever got close enough first.

Zeke amped up her shield to cover them both as they moved through the alleys and weaved around buildings, going out of their way to avoid being seen. At one-forty-five they arrived at the museum. Dev set the charges on the repaired side, turned on the timer, and they stood across the street to look at it.

"We've got ten minutes until the shift change. There aren't any cameras along the walls, and only one on the roof. You'll have about two minutes to get in there once the change starts. I'm going to climb up the side of the building and get ready to drop down from the roof as soon as you give me the word."

Dev nodded and looked at his watch. "Don't worry about it. We've got this. We'll be fine." He stooped to open his pack and withdrew the small device Rhad had given them before leaving the brothel the night before. "If Rhad's right, when I use this, it will jam the signal to the cameras for about sixty seconds. That'll give me enough time to get in. I'm going to wait until two to push it and hope the guards coming in the back entrance will distract the ones leaving so they don't notice me at all."

Zeke laughed. "I know the plan." She loped across the street. "Worry about your own ass, not mine."

Dev watched as she hugged the side of the building and jumped up to grab hold of the access ladder leading to the roof access. He kept his gun anchored to his shoulder, and his head swiveled from side to side as he made sure no one spotted Zeke as she climbed. Quickly, she slithered over the edge and disappeared.

Looking at his watch again, he squatted down and waited until two a.m. Exactly as the clock turned, he pushed the button on the electronic jammer and waited until he saw the light on the camera turn from green to red.

Knowing he didn't have much time, Dev jogged up the steps and stooped to pick the lock. The padlock was easily disposed of and the handle lock little more than a joke. Sliding through the doors as quietly as possible, he reached between them to lock the padlock and pulled the doors shut as the light turned back to green.

There were cameras all through the interior. He was in the blind spot between the exterior camera and the first interior one and had to remain there until the charges detonated. He checked the dial on his watch again and mentally counted down the seconds.

Four minutes after he'd slipped in the doors, the building shook as the charges detonated. He heard shouting and scrambling upstairs and waited thirty seconds before dashing out from the shadows and running straight for the security office.

Up the stairs, down the corridor, into the first room on the left.

He weaved his way between old sculptures and tapped the code into the panel by the door in the corner. It beeped twice, and he heard a quiet click as the door opened.

The room was empty. A bank of screens against one wall showed twenty-four angles throughout the museum on a rotating basis so no one room or area went more than twenty seconds without being displayed. He could see the guards congregating at the piles of fallen debris and tapped that screen to turn on the volume.

"Looks like the whole damn thing collapsed."

"I've been telling everyone this place is a death trap with all those repairs." A demon sighed and shook his head. "More fucking work for us to patch these walls up tomorrow. Should we notify Rhad? Or the Cambion?"

One of the others shook his head. "Nothing to be done about it tonight. There're some old tarps inside. Let's hang them up, and that'll be good enough until morning."

Dev watched as the guards tacked up tarps. He reached out and found Zeke with his mind and slipped inside.

"Guards took the bait and are at the detonation site. I'm in the security room. Now would be a good time to come in through the roof."

"I've got it open and am dropping into the rafters now."

Dev watched as Zeke's feet appeared on the screen, followed by the rest of her as she shimmied down the rafters and dropped to the floor, landing in a crouch and glancing around to make sure her surroundings were clear.

"They're starting to come back in now. That didn't take as long as I'd hoped. Turn around and head down the stairs to the left. Once you're down there, I want you to slip behind the steps and hunker down for a minute. They're coming back my way, and I need to deal with the guards coming into this room before I can guide you in."

"Got it."

Dev watched the monitors closely, following the progress of the guards as they split up and three headed toward him. He placed his rifle on the floor and drew his knife, knowing he needed to dispense with the guards as quietly as possible. He stood to the side of the door, knife in hand and his heart pounding in his chest.

The door opened slowly and the first guard came in. Without hesitation, Dev grabbed him from behind and dragged the blade of the knife across his throat, cutting deep and dropping the body in one smooth motion.

The other two came in fast, trying to draw weapons. Dev grabbed the second and slammed his head into the wall, disorienting him enough For Dev to move on to the third. He dodged one punch, took a second to the nose and kicked out, striking the demon in the stomach and driving him back several steps.

The second was back up, and Dev struck out, driving his knife into the chest of the demon. He fell, clutching his chest and trying to vacate his body. Dev chanted under his breath, using an exorcism said backward to hold the demons inside their hosts. The third managed to catch him with an elbow to the throat, and Dev coughed before continuing the chant. He slashed with the knife, missed, then kicked out, sweeping the demon's feet out from under him. Without hesitation, Dev dropped to the floor, plunging the knife into the chest of the final demon.

That done, he took the time to pile the bodies in one corner and dump salt in their mouths to keep the essence of the demons from seeping out before dropping into the chair and turning back to the monitors.

"Three down."

Zeke's voice was light and full of humor. "That was fast."

"I'm that good. You ready to rock and roll?"

"Let's go. Direct me."

Dev looked at the screens. "There's a clear path for you right now to the stairs leading to the basement. You'll slip out and take a left into the main room of the museum. There's no one in there now, but there are two guards heading that direction, what looks like about thirty seconds apart. Once you're through the atrium, there's a door at the back and a stairwell."

"Got it."

Zeke slipped out from behind the stairs and jogged down the corridor and into the atrium. She slowed for a moment to admire the beauty of the artwork hanging on the walls, taking it in with one look, then dipped her head and continued to jog across the floor, her footfalls barely audible on the marble floors.

"Incoming. One demon coming from the right hand entrance. You don't have enough time to get across."

"I thought you said I had time?"

"I thought you did. It's just one. You can handle it."

"I know I can. I just don't want to draw attention to myself."

"Then kill him quietly."

Zeke drew the silencer from her pocket and screwed it onto the barrel of her rifle. She lifted the weapon to her shoulder and peered down the sight, waiting until the demon guard opened the door and entered before pulling the trigger.

The noise of her ejecting the shell and loading a round into the chamber was louder than the shot had been, and the demon crumpled to the floor with a perfect, round hole in the center of his forehead.

"Nice shot. Another coming at you from the door you came through."

Zeke turned and slipped behind a pillar to wait, aiming as the guard came through the doors. His light fell upon the first guard she had killed, and he had time to make one grab for his gun before her finger tightened on the trigger and a bullet slammed into his skull.

"Hide the bodies."

"I'm not an idiot."

She slung her rifle over her shoulder and grabbed one of the two by the feet, dragging him to a closet and stuffing him inside, pausing long enough to pour salt in his mouth. The second followed the first, and she wiped blood from her palms onto the thighs of her pants.

"Did you remember to salt all the guards you killed?"

"No one got out on me. I know as well as you do what to do to the bodies."

"No needy to get snappy, cowboy. I'm the one with the license to grump."

"Get down the stairs before you have to fight off more guards. Five are dead, but there are still nine in the building."

Zeke shook her head in annoyance and headed for the stairs, taking them two at a time down to the basement. "Anything in front of me?"

"There's one guard at the door to the vault. There's no good way to pick him off. You'll have to take him on without the benefit of surprise."

"Just one?"

"Just one."

Zeke drew her buck knife and opened the door into the basement slowly. She crept through the dark, using a penlight to illuminate her path. She clicked it off when she caught sight of the vault and the guard sitting in a chair flipping through an old magazine.

Thinking through her options, she pulled one of the stakes from her utility belt and hurled it across the room, grinning triumphantly when it hit something metal on the other end and made a loud noise. The guard jumped up and shined his flashlight in the direction of the noise.

Zeke took the opportunity to dash from behind the wall and charge the guard from behind. She launched herself onto his back and wrapped one arm around his forehead, drawing her other hand across his throat with the blade.

Blood bloomed on pale skin, a thick liquid that bubbled out of the long, jagged gash and ran down the demon's chest, soaking into his shirt. He struggled for several seconds then went limp and sagged to the floor. Zeke stumbled, hopped off his back, and winced when she nicked herself with the tip of the knife.

"Nice job. Get the body stashed and get in the vault. Six down, eight left."

Zeke dragged the body behind some stacks of boxes, filled its mouth with salt and then returned to the door, tapping in the code on the keypad. The light flashed green, and she yanked open the door and entered the vault, taking her bag off her shoulder as she did so.

The sword was inside a safe, which used a different code. She tapped it in and pulled open the door.

"For something so powerful, it looks like an ordinary piece of metal."

"Well, grab it and get out."

She reached out and grabbed the handle, yelping when the sword burned her hand. "Dammit! What the fuck, Dev?"

"I have no idea. What happened?"

"Damn thing burned me." She looked down at the angry, blistered skin on her palm. "Is that supposed to happen?"

"I have no idea. Find something to wrap it up in and let's get going."

Zeke glanced around the room and grabbed a piece of canvas wrapped around a painting. She tossed the fabric over the sword and shoved it into her bag, taking care to settle the point away from her body.

"Okay, get me back to the roof."

"Everything is clear right now. Go back the way you came."

Zeke nodded and hefted her bag, darting out of the room and heading back through the basement and up the stairs. "Where are the guards?"

"Well, two are coming to me, but nothing looks headed your way. I see two in the main entry where I need to go out and two in the east wing. The other two are staying where we detonated the charges."

"I could pick them all off. The two at the entrance would be easy."

"There's no need to take the risk."

"You'll be running blind once you come out of there with six, maybe eight, guards here and no me to help. You can lead me around, I'll pick them off and then we both go out the front. The odds are that none of them will even see me coming."

"I don't like it. That's not the plan we made."

"Plans are supposed to be altered to fit the circumstances. Just take me to the two at the entrance."

Dev sighed and peered at the monitor. "Go back across the atrium and instead of going upstairs, go to the right and down the hall. It'll take you right there. Once you're done, wait for me before you go anywhere. I have to take care of the two coming at me."

"Gotcha."

He picked up his pistol and swiveled to face the door, hearing footsteps coming across the room. The keypad beeped as the code was input, and the door swung open, revealing two guards, one of whom was carrying a bag.

"Hey, Joe..."

Whatever the rest of the sentence was going to be, Dev ended it with two gunshots, one to the head and one to the chest. The second guard barely had time to react before Dev pulled the trigger twice more and dropped him.

Dev dragged both bodies into the room and placed them next to the other three, using the last of the salt in his pack on them. "You okay, Zeke?"

"Two more down. What's that bring us to, ten?"

"Yup. I have to say, I really like being able to see exactly where the enemies are and where they're going."

"If only it was that easy all the time. Where to next?"

"I think we head out. Everyone on the monitor is stationary. Unlock the front door and I'll meet you there in sixty seconds."

Dev checked the monitors one final time before leaving the

security room and backtracking down the hall and stairs to meet Zeke in the entrance. Together they exited the museum and locked the door behind them.

"Let's get to the car and get out of here."

Before Zeke could respond, a door slammed from across the street, and they both turned to look at the Cambion approaching them. Zeke immediately recognized his handsome, chiseled face.

"Alexi."

Alexi smiled and waved his hand, signaling the other Cambion who were with him to exit their cars. Zeke counted nine, including Alexi.

"Did you really think it was going to be that easy? That you would just waltz in there, kill a few demons, steal our sword and waltz out?"

Zeke shrugged. "Yeah, kinda." She reached for the hatchet on her belt. "Looks like we were wrong."

CHAPTER TWENTY-EIGHT

ALEXI HELD up his hand to stop the Cambion with him from charging the two Nephilim. "I'll give you credit. You managed to get into New Orleans, one of the biggest demonic holdings in the world, break into our museum and get our sword without being caught." He tapped his index finger against his lips. "How do you explain being able to do that?"

Dev shrugged. "We're that good. What does it matter? You're here to kill us. We're determined to get out of here. Let's get this fucking thing over with and see who's left standing at the end."

"Do you really think you can defeat us? I brought eight of my best warriors, and you're in a city crawling with those who worship Lucifer. As soon as we start making noise, you'll be swarmed with demons and Cambion. You don't have a prayer of escaping here alive."

Zeke glanced at Dev and broke into a run, tackling him and flashing at the same time, transporting them as far away as she could manage and knowing when she did it that she only bought them seconds. The Cambion would follow the flash signature and be on them almost instantly.

She managed a block and a half—the outer limits of her ability. As soon as they landed, Dev propelled them forward again, giving them another three blocks. Within a second, he shook her off and stripped off his vest and shirt, forcing his wings from his body. He held out a hand to Zeke and dragged her close, pinning his vest between them. By the time the Cambion appeared on the street, they were high above it.

Bullets streaked through the sky as the Cambion fired at them. Dev continued higher and higher still until they were out of range.

"We won't have long once we get back to the town we were in. We're not going to get out of here without fighting them. We're going to have to hack our way out."

Dev nodded sharply. "I've come to that realization myself. Good thinking to get us out of the city, though. Once we're back there, we have some advantage in that we know the area and we can split up. We're not going to be able to stay together. We have to split them up, isolate them, and take them one at a time." He looked down at her. "Or we run. I can fly until we drop out of the sky, and we run."

Zeke shook her head. "I'm sick of running. Let's take these fuckers out. If we can kill Alexi, that's one less Lux and Zane have to go for, and it's too good an opportunity to pass up. Eight is a relatively small squad for him to come with, so I think we have a decent shot if we can keep from getting pinned down."

"When we land, you hide the sword as well as you can. Somewhere they'll never find it. Then you get as far away from the place as possible. I'll keep them away from you. How many times can you flash in a row?"

"A few if they're short. From building to building I could do maybe ten or twelve."

"I'm better than that, so I'll try to keep them confused and after me. If we both bounce around some, it'll be hard for them to figure out which signature belongs to each of us and where we're at."

"I need to get someplace high and well-protected. If I can get to where I can snipe, we'll have a better chance." Zeke looked around, making sure they were still safe.

"Then find where you want as soon as the sword is hidden." Dev flapped his wings and angled down. "Cambion can't fly, so I figure we've got fifteen to twenty minutes to get ready. If they're here, they'll know where we were by now, so this'll be the first place they check. We'll load up on weapons at the car then split."

Zeke nodded. "I'm ready."

Dev landed, and they were both moving before he even managed to retract his wings. Zeke wrenched open the car door and popped open the trunk, revealing the stash of weapons they'd placed there. Both pulled out Kevlar vests to replace the utility vests and exchanged stakes and Holy water for more bullets. Zeke pulled on gloves and looped her utility belt around her shoulder and under her arm to allow her to strap a leather belt with a sheathed short sword around her waist.

Dev selected more bullets and stuffed grenades into his vest. Slamming the trunk, they exchanged one long look at one another before running in separate directions.

Zeke stayed off the main street and crept through the shadows. She knew exactly where she wanted to put the sword. One place she hoped the Cambion would never find it.

She made one detour to the hardware store and emerged with a can of spray paint. Knowing time was ticking down, she sprinted to the other end of the town, ducking in a side door to the single church. Debris littered the stairwell, and she jumped over what she could, trying to leave it undisturbed in a meager effort to disguise her tracks.

The sanctuary was mostly undamaged. Several pews had been broken by falling ceiling tiles, and the altar was in two pieces, but the stone floor was intact and the entry looked undamaged. Sighing in relief, she jogged down the aisle and into the large entryway.

Whichever denomination had built the church had certainly liked their grandiosity. Zeke took a second to ponder that as she studied the statues in the entry. In one corner was a sculpture of the Virgin Mary and the baby Jesus, and across from it was a metal and stone statue of an Angel—she assumed it was Michael—wielding a sword.

Very carefully, she removed the sword from the statue and set it aside to take with her. She shook the can of paint and sprayed Lucifer's sword until it was completely covered in gray paint. Satisfied, she jammed the handle into the statue's hand. Not wanting to waste time, she picked up the fake blade and ran back out the way she had come.

She disposed of the sword in a dumpster two blocks over and began assessing the town for the best vantage point. Deciding the tower of the town hall would work best, she forced her way into the building and climbed up, leaving her sniper rifle and ammo where it would be relatively safe until she needed it. First, though, they had to lay their flash trail to sufficiently confuse the Cambion.

Dev was already hard at work, popping up one place only to run ten yards and disappear again. Zeke had barely done three flashes when she felt the unmistakable sensation of Cambion appearing.

Drawing her hatchet, she wrapped her hand around the handle just below the head and pressed herself tight against the wall of the building nearest to her. She crept forward slowly, craning her neck to get a view of what was going on in the main street.

The Cambion were well armed with pistols and swords. She didn't see any rifles and gritted her teeth in grim satisfaction over that. There wouldn't be a competing sharpshooter. Alexi turned to face his men, his skin and hair luminescent in the thick black of night.

"Find them. The first to bring me one will receive a great reward. Don't let either of them out of here alive. Their transportation abilities must be nearly exhausted, and they are merely two against nine. Be aware for more Nephilim transporting in. They are cowards and will undoubtedly be calling for help." He glanced around. "Spread out and find them."

Perfect. Nine against two was only deadly if it was all at once. Nine made them cocky, and Zeke was confident she and Dev were more than a match for any of the Cambion one on one. Spreading them out would ensure they all died.

The Cambion separated, going eight different directions while Alexi remained in the center of town, opening himself up. Zeke glanced over her shoulder to make sure she was clear and began the dangerous journey to the tower of Town Hall.

Dev watched from the shadows as a Cambion made its way toward him. He gripped the handle of his sword tightly, and his whole body tensed as he waited for the perfect opportunity to spring. A gun would have allowed him some distance, but the sound of the shot would also bring attention, and the last thing he wanted was to be surrounded.

The Cambion walking down the street was short and stocky. Dev knew before he made a move that it would be a brutal fight if he let the other man get in close. Not wanting to spend precious time and energy battling with every Cambion he saw, Dev tucked his sword back into its sheath and withdrew a slim knife.

The blade was short and sharp, with the handle weighing slightly less than the blade to allow it to spin right when being thrown. Tipping the weight slightly to the blade ensured the knife always wanted to land blade first.

Carefully aiming and waiting until the opportune time, Dev drew back his arm and released the knife on the upswing, propelling it forward and striking the Cambion in the throat.

Perfect shot.

Blood erupted from his throat and the man gripped the handle with both hands, ripping it from his throat. Tearing the blade loose only made the bleeding worse, and it poured down his chest in a waterfall of red. He hit his knees and fell to the ground, hands trapped underneath him. It took only seconds for rivulets of blood to run out from underneath the body and trail down the street.

Knowing he needed to move fast and far, Dev flashed to the top of a nearby building to get a better view of the whole town. He saw Zeke duck into the town hall and a Cambion enter after her ten seconds later, though he wasn't completely sure it was because he had seen her or just because it was the next building on his list to search.

Whatever the reason, Zeke was going to have to handle herself. The building was too far for him to flash to without drawing attention and it was too dangerous for them to be together while they were being hunted. Their odds were much better separate.

Ignoring the pang at leaving Zeke to fend for herself, he jogged to the other side of the roof and climbed down, swinging in through an open window.

Zeke entered the tower and went straight to her rifle. She assembled it efficiently, snapping the silencer and scope into place and balancing it on the windowsill. Pressing her eye to the scope, she prepared for her first shot when she heard footsteps coming up the stairs.

Moving as fast as she could, she dropped the rifle on the floor and grabbed her hatchet, holding it tight to her body. She pressed herself against the wall next to the door and waited until the Cambion burst into the room. With a yell, she launched herself onto his back, hacking with her blade, sinking the head of the hatchet deep into his arm.

The Cambion was half a foot taller than her and nearly twice as large. He shook her off easily, sending her flying into the wall. She groaned as her head struck brick and scowled at the thick line of blood left behind.

Rolling her shoulders and gripping her weapon even tighter, she charged again, swinging low and slashing into the Cambion's thigh. He roared in pain and picked her up, holding her over his head and slinging her at the window. Glass scraped at her hands and stomach as she scrambled not to go through, and she managed to duck fast enough to miss the first swing.

She pivoted on one foot and punched out, cramming her fist into his nose. Blood spurted and bone crunched; satisfied, Zeke kicked out, propelling him back several steps. She'd lost her hatchet in the struggle, so she drew her knife and clutched it in one hand, crouching and readying herself for another onslaught.

They clashed violently, limbs colliding over and over, both determined not to let the other get the upper hand. Zeke was smaller and wily, though each time he landed a blow was excruciating. She threw her elbow back and slammed it into his throat, whirling around and following it with a jab to the gut and swiping with her knife. She cut into his chest and watched as blood stained his shirt.

She heard a scramble below and knew Dev was fighting another one. Scared the noise from the street would attract more Cambion, she charged forward and slashed violently, slicing into whatever she could reach. She barely felt the hits he landed on her and whirled to avoid a kick, arching up with her knife and ramming it through one of his cheeks and up into his head.

She watched grimly as the life seeped from his eyes and his body collapsed to the floor. She grasped the handle of the knife in both hands and wrenched it free, wiping the blood from it on the Cambion's shirt. Not taking time to check herself over, she ran for the rifle, hefting it and balancing it on the windowsill.

Dev was fighting off three Cambion, and she saw two more running down the street. Zeke took a deep breath to calm herself and leveled the sight, taking into consideration the angle and distance of the shot, the movement of her target, and the interference of the wind and humidity. She adjusted the barrel slightly and pulled the trigger. A red dot appeared on the forehead of one of the Cambion, and he collapsed to the ground.

Another breath, another shot, another Cambion dead. She leaned forward to get a better angle on the three Dev was fighting and smiled slightly when she saw it was down to two. That meant at least four were dead, maybe more if Dev had killed more than one. She found her shot, pulled the trigger, and swore when the bullet hit dirt.

Working the slide, she ejected the spent casing and loaded another into the barrel. Pulling the trigger faster than she should have, her second shot nicked the Cambion's arm but didn't find home. Cursing hotly under her breath, she fired again, smiling when she watched the Cambion's head explode. Taking down one of the two he had been fighting cleared the way for Dev to run his sword through the third.

Zeke had almost turned away from the window when she saw a flash of light glint off metal. She peered down and saw Dev land on his knees, a knife protruding from his chest.

"No!"

Her scream exploded from her lips before she knew it was coming and she flashed before she realized what she was doing, only to find she couldn't hold the transport and fell the last ten feet.

The fall broke something in her arm, and she struggled to get to her feet, knowing as she hobbled and tried to run that there were Cambion running toward them with shouts of victory. There were two, plus Alexi. Too many for her to handle with a broken arm and no Dev.

She hit the ground on her knees next to him and grabbed him with both hands, pouring everything she had into him. She was concentrating on Dev so intensely that she barely felt the bullet slam into her shoulder. A second ripped through her thigh. Blood mixed with dirt to form a brownish red paste.

Dev writhed on the ground, hurt and dying. She managed to grip the handle of the knife and yank it out as she healed him. Even as she worked on his wound, she knew she was dying. A third bullet slammed into her back, and she threw her head back and screamed as the pain sliced through her. She fell, hitting the ground, her vision blurry and tinged with red. She dragged herself over to Dev, draping herself over him and giving him every drop of life she had left.

Satisfied he was alive but knowing neither of them would be for long, Zeke fell onto her back and stared up at the sky, grief filling her eyes with tears as she thought about the child dying with her and Dev dying beside her. Softly, she managed to whisper.

"I'm sorry, Michael. We failed."

Zeke closed her eyes as the Cambion surrounded her, and she heard Alexi's voice.

"Nice try, Nephil. Where's the sword?"

She faintly heard a crack and then a familiar voice. "You'll never find it, you fucking bastard."

Lux and Zane charged into the fray, Lux skidding to her knees and muttering under her breath, spinning magic to keep Zeke from bleeding to death. Zane's sword flashed, and he hacked through the Cambion, beheading one before they realized what was happening. Alexi flashed out, and the final Cambion tried to follow, but Zane grabbed him with his bare hands, gripping tight and holding until the Cambion fell to the ground, his eyes flat and dead.

"Zane, I need your help!" Lux desperately tried to heal Zeke. "I got the bullets out, but I don't have enough healing magic. I can't fix it."

Zeke grabbed Lux's wrist and spat out a mouthful of blood, trying to speak but finding she couldn't.

Zane stooped. "I can't. You know I can't touch them. If I touch her, I'll kill her."

Lux grabbed Zane's wrists over his sleeves. "Trust me. I can funnel you. Trust me to touch you. Death and life are opposite sides of the same coin. If you can bring death, you can give life. It's hard, and it'll drain you because it's not what you're supposed to do, but you can do it. She's dead anyway. You can't hurt her."

Zane looked at Zeke and closed his eyes for a moment before glancing back at Dev, unconscious but alive. "Dev would never forgive me if I don't at least try. What do you need me to do?"

"Give me your hand. I need to touch your skin." She glared at him when he hesitated. "Do it. You're not going to hurt me. I promise."

Lux seized Zane's hand in hers and gasped as she felt the wave of death flowing from his skin. She focused it, forcing it through the prism of the citrine hanging around her neck to cleanse it. When the light came through the other side white, she forced it into Zeke's body, watching in awe as the wounds healed and her blood stopped flowing. New skin formed, turned pink then white, and then the scar faded.

Lux released Zane's hand and sat down hard, her whole body humming from the power that flowed out of him. He stuffed his hands into his gloves and sat next to her, observing the two unconscious Nephilim, his breathing fast and hard as he tried to catch his breath, reeling from the output of power. After several deep gulps of air, he managed to reach out and toy with the chain around Lux's neck.

"Your citrine broke."

Lux looked down at the stone that had turned black and cracked into two pieces. "I can get another one. It worked. I was able to cleanse your power and use it to help her."

"Thank God it didn't end with you dead, too." He leaned back on his arms. "We need to get them conscious and get the sword. It won't be long before Alexi comes back with reinforcements. I can't believe we got that fucking close to him and didn't get him."

"We will. We'll kill him."

Dev coughed and sat up, grabbing his chest. When all he found was blood and a scar, he looked around in a panic, his eyes finally settling on Lux and Zane.

"What the hell are you two doing here? What happened? Zeke?" He looked at her prone form. "Oh my God, is she okay? The baby?"

Lux seized his hands and held them tightly. "She's fine. Michael heard her call out and sent us. We got here just in time. Zane and I fixed her. I think the baby is fine, but it's too early to tell. I can sense the heartbeat, and it seems strong, but we won't be sure for a few weeks. She's early on yet. If I had to guess, less than four weeks. The heartbeat just started a day or two ago, so there's still a lot that could go wrong."

Zane held out a hand and helped Dev climb to his feet. "We need to get that sword. Where is it?"

"Zeke hid it. I don't know where."

Lux glared at him. "And what if I'd been a minute later and she'd died? We wouldn't have a clue where to look."

"It's a moot point because she's fine, but the next time, I'll remember to ask her. We were a little preoccupied." Dev ran his hands over his face. "Is there a way to wake her up?"

Lux leaned over and pressed one finger to Zeke's forehead, whispering softly. Zeke jerked in her sleep and came to, clawing and gasping. She clutched her chest and grabbed at her shoulder and thigh, surprised to be alive. She looked around at Lux and Zane and threw herself into Lux's arms.

"How are you here?"

"Michael sent us. You should have called for help earlier."

"I thought we could handle it. We weren't expecting them. We weren't ready."

Zane cleared his throat. "No offense, but we need to get that damn sword and get out of here. Where did you put it?"

"In the church. There's a sculpture of an Angel in the front. I spray painted the sword and put it in his hand." She blinked when the other three stared at her. "What?"

Zane laughed. "That's fucking brilliant." He shook his head. "I'll go get it and meet you back here in five minutes to flash out."

EPILOGUE

ZEKE TOOK a deep drink of tea and looked around the table at Dev, Deacon, Amaya, and Michael. "What do we need to do with the sword?"

Michael smiled grimly. "It's been destroyed. I ground it to dust and scattered it over the seven seas. The first step has been taken to unlink Lucifer from his sword. Lux and Zane are closing in on two of the progeny of Beelzebub, and I expect them to eliminate them in the next few days. I had to call them away to aid you, but they're back now."

"I'm sorry it went that way. I thought we had it handled, and then it all went to shit." Dev ran his hands through his hair and glanced around the table. "I guess we should've run."

"Yes, you should have." Michael laid his hand on Dev's shoulder. "Or you should have called for me sooner. You nearly died." He looked at Zeke fondly. "I'm proud of you. I know your parents would have been, too. Both of you." He stood and cleared his coffee cup. "I'm going to attend to a few things that need attending. Amaya, you and Deacon will go with Gage and Aradia in two days to continue your training. Aradia swears to me she can teach you both some magic to help you with Lucifer."

Amaya nodded. "We're ready, but I still think we should be able to go help Lux and Zane. Or if you won't let us, send Zeke and Dev. They're all healed up now."

Michael shook his head. "No. Ezekiel needs to rest here until she delivers. With what has happened, she is in much more danger than ever before, as are you, Dev. It's safest for everyone if you both stay here."

Zeke looked down at her stomach. "That's eight months. I'm not staying here with my feet up for seven fucking months."

Dev lifted one eyebrow. "Yes, you are, and I'm staying with you. We'll help run things from here.. There's plenty of work to be done without interfering with Lux and Zane. We're not going to be bored, especially with having to plan for a baby."

Amaya wrinkled her nose. "What planning? They need diapers and a place to sleep. That's it. Maybe some clothes."

Zeke chuckled. "Spoken like a true big sister." She rested her hands on her stomach. "I'm just glad it's over with. I hate turning it over to Lux and Zane, but if anyone can handle it, it's them. I mean, for Christ's sake, Zane can kill someone by touching them. It doesn't get more badass than that."

Deacon sighed deeply. "You'd think so, but I've known him for a long, long time. I can tell you for certain it causes more problems than it solves." He stood and carried his mug to the sink. "I can only hope he ends up figuring out how to trust himself and control the power. If he doesn't, he isn't just deadly to our enemies, he could be deadly to Lux."

About the Author

Sirena N. Robinson is an author who lives and works in the foothills of the Appalachian Mountains. When she is not helping her characters defeat unspeakable evil, she spends her days working as a drug and alcohol counselor and as a court-appointed attorney in the local Juvenile Court. A firm believer in wearing many hats, she spends many weekend traveling the country with her husband, daughter and Bengal cats attending cat shows. On off weekends, she can be found with the rest of her family at a hunt-test or field trial helping shuttle dogs or holding down the fort at home, caring for the menagerie of dogs and cats living in her house.

Sirena writes in several genres, focusing primarily on novels with paranormal or supernatural elements. She has several other novels in various stages of planning, including a futuristic crime series. She writes both because she loves it and because she has no choice and is a self-proclaimed slave to her characters. She considers herself incredibly lucky to be the one chosen to tell their incredible stories. Keep in touch with Sirena via her blog at sirenanrobinson.blogspot.com or through her publisher Supposed Crimes, at supposedcrimes.com.

www.ingramcontent.com/pod-product-compliance
Lightning Source LLC
Chambersburg PA
CBHW070625170726
48291CB00003B/876